Echoes of Mercy

Kim Vogel Sawyer

A NOVEL

DOUBLEDAY LARGE PRINT HOME LIBRARY EDITION

WATERBROOK
PRESS

This Large Print Edition, prepared especially for Doubleday Large Print Home Library, contains the complete, unabridged text of the original Publisher's Edition.

ECHOES OF MERCY Published by Waterbrook Press
12265 Oracle Boulevard, Suite 200
Colorado Springs, Colorado 80921

All Scripture quotations are taken from the King James Version.

The characters and events in this book are fictional, and any resemblance to actual persons or events is coincidental.

Published in the United States by WaterBrook Multnomah, an imprint of the Crown Publishing Group, a division of Random House LLC, New York, a Penguin Random House Company.

Waterbrook and its deer colophon are registered trademarks of Random House LLC.
ISBN 978-1-61129-273-2
Printed in the United States of America

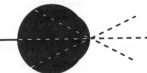

**This Large Print Book carries the
Seal of Approval of N.A.V.H.**

For Bev and Bonnie,
who help pray me through

Come unto me,
all ye that labour and are heavy laden,
and I will give you rest.

—Matthew 11:28

Chapter 1

**Late September 1904—
Lincoln, Nebraska
Caroline**

Caroline Lang slapped the thick packet of meticulously handwritten notes onto the center of Noble's leather desk blotter and then flopped into the nearest chair. The spindled legs slid on the glossy oak floor, raising a high-pitched complaint. Instead of apologizing for the scratches her carelessness had surely created—Noble was the most persnickety perfectionist she'd ever known—she said, "There you are. A completed report on accommodations for the sugar beet harvesters. I earned my week's leave with that one." She grimaced at her purple-stained fingertips. "If I never see another beet, it will be too soon."

Noble had the gall to chuckle. "Oh, now, Caroline, you didn't like beets before I sent you to Omaha. You've always said they stink when they're cooking."

"They do." She nodded emphatically, causing several escaping tendrils from her simple bun to bounce on her shoulders. "And they don't have to be cooked to stink. You ought to smell them when they're just sitting in a bin in the sun." Wearily she pushed to her feet. "I intend to spend my week of leave sleeping. You know where to find me if you have any questions about the report, but I'm sure you'll find it concise. I was trained by the best, after all." She aimed a fond grin at her friend and mentor.

Noble set the leather-bound packet aside without peeking in it. "You know I trust you, Caroline."

His simple comment warmed her, and she gave him another smile as she turned toward the door.

"And since I trust you..."

Something in his tone stilled her hand, which hovered midway to the polished brass doorknob. She glanced over her shoulder and caught him stroking his beard, his familiar sign of worry. She returned to the chair, seating herself carefully this time. "What is it?" Fear struck, making her mouth go dry. "Has something happened to Annamarie?" She prayed Noble's sweet, frail wife hadn't met with harm while she'd been away on an assignment. She loved Annamarie almost as much as Noble did.

"Annamarie is fine."

Relief slumped Caroline's shoulders. "Oh, thank heaven..."

"But, unfortunately, I lost an investigator." Noble's face pinched into creases of sorrow. "A fine man—Harmon Bratcher. He leaves behind a wife and two sons."

"Oh no..." As an investigator for the Labor Commission, Caroline knew they could meet danger. Sometimes entering workplaces to openly explore, other times posing as workers to observe the business practices on the sly, their presence was rarely welcomed and occasionally threatened. Even the required travel held various hazards. Each time she set out, Noble prayed over her for her safety. She depended on him and Annamarie praying her through the investigations. So far she'd always come back unscathed. Tired, yes, but unscathed. Her heart ached for poor Mr. Bratcher, for his family, and for Noble, who felt accountable for his agents.

Caroline rounded the desk and bent down to wrap her arms around Noble's shoulders and press her cheek to his. His thick white beard tickled her jaw, but she didn't pull away. He needed the comfort, and she needed to offer it.

He patted her wrists in a silent thank-you. "It has been difficult, I confess. I considered him a good friend."

Although Caroline couldn't claim Bratcher as a friend, she'd met him and admired his strong stance on changing the laws concerning the age of workers in the United States. The coalition to end child labor had lost a strong proponent with his untimely passing. She shifted to perch on the edge of Noble's desk, leaving one hand on his broad shoulder in a gesture of comfort. "What happened?"

"According to the ruling from law enforcement officials, he broke his neck when he fell into an elevator shaft."

Such a horrific way to end one's life. But mixed with the horror, she experienced a niggle of wariness. "You don't believe the ruling, do you?"

Noble pinned her with a steady look. "I suppose it could be true. Accidents happen, especially in factories. But the week before he fell, I received a telegram from Harmon saying he intended to sneak into the factory on Sunday—the only day no workers were on duty— to retrieve questionable bookkeeping records he'd glimpsed the week before. But he died before he could submit any other information. There were no documents on his body. So I can only surmise he fell into the shaft before he laid claim to the records, or—"

"Or someone took them from him," she

finished.

Noble nodded somberly. He caught her hand. "Caroline, I know you just returned from an investigation. You're tired and have rightfully earned your week of rest. But there's an opening at the factory where Harmon died."

Caroline stiffened, anticipating his next request.

"The opening is for a toter, a job generally given to women." His fingers tightened on her hand. "You're my only female agent. Would you go to Sinclair, apply for the position, and use it to look into Harmon's death? I'd need to send you out on this evening's train."

The entire journey home she'd anticipated a lengthy soak in a hot bath followed by days of lying on her comfortable feather mattress in a state of languor. The thought of departing that evening without even a few hours of rest made her want to groan. But how could she deny Noble when he'd done so much for her?

Noble went on. "Of course, we can't

make investigating Harmon's death your official reason for being there. We'd be overstepping our bounds with the local authorities. So, as far as the commission is concerned, you'd be there to finish Harmon's report on the factory's safety features...or the lack thereof. Harmon sent several messages about his findings. He was especially concerned about the number of underage workers at the factory, but he died before submitting a full report."

Caroline gave a start, her pulse speeding into a gallop. "Underage workers?"

Noble's lips formed a grim line. "According to Harmon, this factory seems to have a disproportionate number of child workers."

Her tiredness melted in light of this new information. The opportunity to further her personal battle to end child labor and to put Noble's worries to rest concerning Bratcher's death proved too tempting to resist. "I'll go."

The relief in Noble's face compensated for the loss of her hot bath and days of lazy recuperation. "Bless you, Caroline. There's no one else I would trust with this mission."

His confidence in her both touched and terrified her. After all, one investigator had already died in the factory. **Go with me, dear Lord.** She drew in a deep breath and vowed, "I won't let you down, Noble. I promise."

Chapter 2

Sinclair, Kansas
Caroline

If he didn't choose her, she might stamp her foot and wail. The overnight train trip from Lincoln to Sinclair and then her frantic dash from the train station to Dinsmore's World-Famous Chocolates Factory had left her wilted, exhausted, and more than a little grouchy. Weariness momentarily sagged her shoulders, but Caroline resolutely straightened her spine and held her chin high while the hiring agent walked slowly along the line of six hopeful women, scraping each of them from head to toe with an unsmiling gaze.

His boot heels thudded against the

polished wood floor of the stuffy office, carrying over the muffled clanks and wheezes seeping into the room from the factory below. Each resounding thump was a nail pounding into the lid of a coffin. He would bury the hopes of five of the women who'd answered the advertisement for a new toter.

The man came to a halt before the timid-looking girl on Caroline's right. His charcoal pinstriped suit and crimson silk ascot beneath his goatee gave him a dapper appearance, but his furrowed brow and piercing eyes ruined the effect. He'd introduced himself as Gordon Hightower, and befitting his name, he seemed to peer down his nose at all of them. The man was as intimidating as an army sergeant making an inspection.

The poor girl in front of him squirmed, pressing her chin to one hunched shoulder and grinding the toe of her worn brown shoe against the floor. Sympathy twined through Caroline's heart for the girl, who was surely no more than fourteen years of age. For one brief moment Caroline found herself hoping the girl would be chosen. Judging by her tattered frock, scuffed shoes, and filthy knuckles, she needed the job. But Caroline pushed aside the fleeting thought with steely determination. She must be the single new hire invited inside that factory. How else would she uncover the details of Harmon Bratcher's death?

Quick as a lightning strike, Hightower thrust his hand forward and grabbed the girl's upper arm. A startled yelp emerged from her, and her eyes flew wide open. Caroline nearly intervened—he had no right to terrorize the poor child so—but fear of being sent out the door held her silent.

Hightower gave the girl's arm several quick squeezes, and then he released her, his lips pursed in disgust. "You haven't got enough meat on your bones to tote a broom, let alone carry trays of confections." His derisive tone snapped out like a lash, and the girl cringed beneath the words. "We asked for a toter.

Qualifications are strong arms and able legs. Didn't you read the notice?"

Up and down the line, the women flicked glances at the others' forearms. The one on the far end clenched her fists. Caroline stared at the firm muscles displayed beneath the taut fabric of the woman's faded blue sleeves. If strong arms were a qualifier, the hiring agent would certainly choose that woman over all the others. Caroline's determination to be an employee of Dinsmore's factory wavered.

The girl released a helpless whimper. "I...I dunno how to read, sir."

Caroline closed her eyes, a familiar frustration filling her breast. What had kept this child from attending school? Other jobs? A mother who needed extra hands at home to help with younger siblings? No matter the reason, the girl's inability to read or cipher destined her to a life of poverty.

"I can't use you." The man flipped his wrist, the dismissive gesture showing no hint of empathy.

Tears welled in the child's wide blue

eyes. "But I gotta get hired on, sir. Already been turned away at three other places. My pa he said he'd beat me senseless if I didn't get this job."

Hightower folded his arms over his chest and scowled at the girl. "You can't be a toter. Toting takes strength. You haven't got strength."

"But I do!" The girl clasped her hands beneath her chin, her expression pleading. "I'm stronger'n I look. Honest, I am. Can'tcha just gimme a chance?"

The agent leaned in, his nose mere inches from the cowering child. "Those trays hold up to fifteen pounds each. Toters haul three trays at a time. You drop one load, and a good five dollars' worth of candy is wasted. That's too much to risk." He caught her arm again and gave her a little push toward the door. "Now get. Tell your pa to pay better attention to the qualifications next time he sends you out."

With sobs heaving her skinny shoulders, the girl scuttled out the door, but the sound of her distress drifted from the hallway and flayed Caroline's soul. She gazed at the open doorway, sending up a silent prayer for the girl. A tiny seed of hope wiggled its way into her heart. If the girl couldn't secure a job, maybe her parents would send her to school instead. She'd learn to read, to write, and to figure sums. Then in a few years when she was full grown, she could find a decent job. Not all parents were as heartless as her own. This girl might have a chance to—

"You!"

The barked command ended Caroline's musings. She jerked upright, blinking several times. Hightower stood before her, his frown fierce. She licked her dry lips. "Yes, sir?"

"How old are you?"

Caroline hesitated. She knew what she was supposed to say, and she knew the man would accept it. Her round face and smooth skin gave the appearance of someone much younger than her true age of twenty-seven. The Labor Commission had given her stern instructions to carve five or six years from her age when asked. The fabrication helped hide her real identity. Even so, lies didn't slip easily from her tongue. She lifted her chin in a flirtatious manner and tiptoed around the question. "Does it matter?"

"It might."

She offered a coy shrug. "The qualifications didn't include a specific age." He grunted—a very ungentlemanly sound that contrasted with his refined attire. He cleared his throat and moved down the line, snapping out questions and summarily sending the next three hopefuls out the door by turn.

With the final slam of the door, Caroline and the thick-armed woman remained as the only contenders for the single position as toter. Caroline quickly examined her competition, noting the woman eyed her with equal interest. Dislike gleamed in the woman's beady gaze. Clearly, she intended to secure the position no matter the cost. But Caroline's need was too great for her to concede defeat. She might be tired, rumpled, and less muscular than the other woman, but she would win.

With God's help, she amended, she would win. Noble expected it. And the future of Kansas children depended on it.

Hightower strode behind a massive, clean-topped desk that filled the center of the room. He frowned at the pair of women. "Come over here."

In unison they moved to the opposite side of the desk and stood side by side. Caroline's belly churned. She linked her hands and let them fall loosely against the front of her wrinkled skirt, hoping the casual pose would hide her inward nervousness. How she hated this part of the process. No matter how many times she vied for positions, it never got easier. When she shared her reservations with her supervisor, Noble always chided her, reminding her that being chosen fulfilled the commission's purpose.

But it also meant someone else must lose.

She glanced again at the other woman, who glared at Caroline like an angry bull. Beneath the bluster Caroline glimpsed a desperation that pierced her as deeply as the young girl's wails of despair had. Lines fanned from the corners of the woman's eyes. Gray hairs lay among her dark tresses, which she'd slicked back from her face into a severe bun. The thickened waist and sagging jowl spoke of years. Forty? Forty-five? Caroline couldn't be sure, yet she knew the woman was old enough to have a family. Did she need this income to support several children?

Once again her stomach clenched as remorse smote her. She fought the ugly emotion, reciting Noble's gentle admonition in her mind. **"You're there to do good, Caroline. Set aside the guilties, and remember you're the only one who can do the real job."** The "guilties," as Noble called them, didn't completely dissolve, but she calmed. Yes, she was here to do good. Good for Noble, for the Labor Commission, and for the current generation of Kansas youngsters and the generations to come. She would focus on those people rather than the needy individual standing beside her.

Hightower had opened a drawer and

removed two sheets of paper and a pair of stubby pencils. He slid the items across the desk. "Answer the questions. I'm going to prepare a test, and I'll be back in a few minutes." His wide strides carried him across the room and out the door.

The other woman poked her tongue out the corner of her mouth, snatched up her pencil, and began scrawling words onto the waiting lines.

Caroline lifted the page and glanced at it. Name, hours available to work, expected wage... She'd answered the questions more than a dozen times before on previous missions and knew the appropriate responses. Even so, she hesitated. Somehow putting lies down in black lead on cream paper made them more glaring.

The other woman gave Caroline a conniving look. "You need me to..."

Pride swelled. She'd never set foot in a schoolhouse, but thanks to Annamarie, she could read and write as well as anyone who'd attended several years of school. "I can do it."

The woman heaved a mighty sigh. "Fine." She bent back over her page.

Despite the grim situation, a grin twitched at Caroline's cheek. What might the woman have written for her if given the chance? It would be amusing to see, but she had a job to do. Placing the page on the desk again, by rote she filled in the lines with her carefully invented information, tweaking the facts just enough to mask reality but not so much it would raise suspicion.

Just as she finished, the door opened, and Hightower breezed back in. A sugary scent accompanied him, almost heady in its sweetness. Saliva pooled beneath Caroline's tongue, and her belly twisted in desire to taste the treats being manufactured on the lower levels. Chocolate smelled so much better than beets.

He plucked the sheets of paper from the desk and held them out. "So we have Carrie Lang and Agatha Brewer. Correct?"

Caroline nodded, and the older woman blared, "Mrs. Agatha Brewer, that's right."

"I see neither of you has factory experience," he went on, his gaze bouncing from one page to the other, "although Mrs. Brewer has worked in a bakery and a hotel laundry."

Her round face flushed pink. "That's right. Ten years at both places. I ain't afraid of hard work."

Caroline's hopes lifted. If Mrs. Brewer had more experience, she'd demand a higher wage. Caroline, with her supposed inexperience, would require much less, giving her an advantage. Factory owners always filled the unskilled positions—and toting required no skill whatsoever—with lower-wage employees first. A bitter taste attacked her tongue as she considered how some filled their floors with children, who worked the same hours for less than half the compensation of an adult.

"I see you're both available to work ten hours Monday through Saturday." Since he seemed to be talking to himself, Caroline stayed quiet, but Mrs. Brewer inserted, "Mm-hm. Mm-hm." He muttered a couple more comments, too low for Caroline to discern, and then he frowned at Mrs. Brewer. "Am I reading this correctly? You'll accept the starting wage of four dollars a week?"

"That's right."

Caroline drew back in surprise. With twenty years of work experience, why wouldn't Mrs. Brewer demand a better wage?

The hiring agent pinned Mrs. Brewer with a steady glare. "You could make more than that as a hotel laundress. The Claiborne Hotel in Wichita gives its laundresses five dollars and four bits a week."

Mrs. Brewer's pink jowls quivered as she seemed to chew the inside of her cheek. Some of her bravado faded. For a moment Caroline thought she saw tears in the woman's eyes. But then she straightened her rounded shoulders and peered at the agent through squinted eyes. "Qualifications didn't say a person had to ask for wages to match her experience." She sucked in a breath and held it, her pink cheeks reddening as the seconds ticked by.

The man shook his head and tapped his thigh with Mrs. Brewer's paper. "All right, then. It's your choice."

The breath wheezed from the woman's lungs, bending her forward slightly. Her relief was so evident Caroline came close to offering a few comforting pats on her sloping shoulder. Obviously Mrs. Brewer needed a job badly enough to grasp whatever crumbs were offered. Caroline tried to swallow the unpleasant taste filling her mouth. Fighting for the position became more difficult by the minute.

Smacking the pages onto the desk, Hightower pointed his chin toward the door. "Come with me to the landing now for a...test. When that's finished, I'll tell you who'll be the newest toter at Dinsmore's World-Famous Chocolates Factory."

Caroline followed Mrs. Brewer and the agent to the L-shaped landing for the factory's loft. A rich, sugary aroma rose from the lower floors, reminding Caroline she hadn't eaten any breakfast. Her stomach rolled with desire as Hightower led them to a table at the far end of the landing. Early-morning sun slanted through a square window, highlighting the top of two stacks of dented, tarnished trays filled with brown mounds—walnut-sized chocolates, each adorned with a swirl and a dusting of finely chopped nuts. They looked wonderful and smelled even better. Her knees quaked as hunger struck hard.

"Only the top tray has candy," the agent explained, gesturing to the stacks. "The bottom two have rocks. This way, if you drop them, there won't be as much waste, but the weight is comparable to trays filled with chocolates."

Mrs. Brewer angled one eyebrow. "How much weight did you say was on there?"

"Forty to forty-five pounds."

The woman grimaced.

He scowled. "Is that a problem, Mrs. Brewer? Because this is what a toter does. She totes trays from the candy-making center to the packaging center."

Mrs. Brewer shook her head.

"All right, then. I'll give each of you a

stack, and at the count of three, I want you to head to the other end of the landing, turn, come back, and put the trays on the table again. Then pick them up and repeat the process two more times. Do you understand?"

Mrs. Brewer smoothed her palms down the front of her skirt. "Yep." Her voice held little confidence.

The aroma of the chocolate was making her dizzy, but Caroline nodded. "I understand."

The man handed Carrie the first stack. She curled her fingers around the lip of the bottom tray and held tight. A tiny, involuntary grunt left her lips, but she managed to balance the trays against her rib cage. She watched as Mrs. Brewer took her stack of trays from Hightower. Perspiration broke out across the woman's upper lip, and her face paled. Caroline started to ask if she was all right, but the agent whipped out a timepiece from his pocket, held it aloft, and announced, "Go!"

Chapter 3

Oliver

Oliver Dinsmore topped the stairs and closed the heavy door behind him, muffling the noise of the machinery below. His ears continued to buzz as he stepped into the center of the long upstairs landing. Two women—one older with rivulets of sweat pouring down her red face, and one with her lips set in a grim, determined line—trudged toward him. He shifted the newsboy-style cap higher on his forehead to get a better look. Each woman carried a stack of three trays bearing chocolates. Dinsmore's World-Famous Chocolate Coated Vanilla Creams from the looks of them. He nearly snorted in self-derision. Had he really recalled the entire title of the confection? Father would be so pleased.

He pressed his back to the wall as the women passed him, giving them as much room as possible. At the end of the landing, as if choreographed, they made the turn in unison. But then the older one jolted as if stung on the rump by a hornet, and she stumbled. One chocolate rolled to the edge of the top tray. The woman gasped and tipped the trays the opposite direction. Oliver started to call out a warning, but before the words could escape, a good half-dozen candies and twice as many rocks—**rocks?**—spilled over the edge and clattered against the wide-planked floor.

The second woman had managed the corner without mishap and continued on, but at the racket she stopped and looked back. Sympathetic dismay replaced the determination he'd seen earlier on her face. Oliver found it a strange reaction. Shouldn't she gloat? She'd just won some sort of ridiculous competition.

Gordon Hightower, the factory's manager and self-assigned hiring agent, stormed toward the older woman, who stared in utter despair at the scattered rocks and candy at her feet. He waved his hands around. "Mrs. Brewer, what were you doing? Clumsy, clumsy! A toter must first and foremost exercise care. You didn't manage to go thirty paces without spilling."

Oliver frowned. Hightower didn't need to berate the woman so. Mother managed a dozen servants in their home and never once raised her voice or resorted to ridicule. And their home ran with precision. Hightower tended to abuse his position of power—something Oliver intended to rectify when he controlled the factory reins.

Tears streamed down the woman's round, red cheeks, and her body quivered. If someone didn't help her, the entire load would hit the floor. He darted out and took the trays. The unexpected weight stole his breath as well as the defensive comment poised on his tongue.

"Yelling at her isn't going to help." The

younger woman spoke up. Indignation colored her tone and expression. "I'm sure she's just nervous. Why not let her have another go?"

Oliver shook his head, uncertain he'd heard correctly. Was she championing her competition? Surely she understood only one would be chosen.

Hightower snorted. "Another go might result in even more lost chocolates."

"And it might prove her capable of handling the task," the bold woman countered.

Oliver hid a smile. She had a full, dimpled face wreathed by springy reddish-brown curls, which had escaped her lopsided mobcap. Her blue flowered dress was so rumpled it appeared she'd slept in it the night before. The messy hair and disheveled clothing gave her an almost childish appearance. But how bravely she faced Hightower. Amusement as well as admiration swelled within his chest. She was a corker! And since she'd spoken up, he could stay silent, which was probably wise, considering he'd "hired on" less than two months ago and couldn't risk being given the ax. Not just yet.

Shifting her trays a bit higher, she fixed Hightower with a steady look. "But you won't know unless you offer her the chance."

Hightower rolled his gaze to the ceiling and huffed out a mighty breath. "Miss Lang, you—"

"Thank you, miss, for speakin' up for me, but there's no need for another chance." Mrs. Brewer hung her head. Her shoulders drooped, and one strand of gray-threaded hair flopped across her tear-stained cheek. "I...I got a bad back. That's why I left the laundry. Couldn't plunge them sheets up and down anymore. Since toting didn't necessarily mean bending, I was hoping I could do it. My arms, they're plenty strong. But my back..."

Oliver knew he should pay attention to Mrs. Brewer, who had sadly bared her soul to Hightower, but he couldn't stop staring at Miss Lang. She'd come in looking for a job. Now that Mrs. Brewer had confessed she couldn't handle it, the job was hers by simple elimination. She should be smiling, celebrating, or at the very least looking relieved. Instead, she appeared regretful. But why? She'd done nothing wrong except possess a back strong enough to support a stack of trays.

Still balancing her load, Miss Lang approached Mrs. Brewer. "I'm sorry about your back, ma'am. But as willing as you are to work, you ought to be able to find employment somewhere. I will pray for you."

Oliver shook his head in wonder. A corker... Miss Lang was indeed a corker.

Mrs. Brewer sniffled. "Thank you, miss. I'll take them prayers. Still got three youngsters at home and no man to earn for us."

Regret deepened to sorrow in Miss Lang's gold-flecked brown eyes. "How old are your children, Mrs. Brewer?"

"The boys are fourteen and eleven, and my littlest one—my only girl—is ten."

Hightower plunged his hands into his pockets and gave the woman a speculative look. "Your boys are plenty old enough to work. Maybe we could use one of them on the floor."

Miss Lang released an indignant gasp. "Oh, but—"

"No, sir, not my boys." Mrs. Brewer straightened, swiping the moisture from her full cheeks with chapped palms. "I've made it clear to every one of my youngsters, from Tad down to Bessie, they're to take all the schooling they got coming to 'em. None of my youngsters'll be working a full-time job until they got a twelfth-grade graduation certificate in hand. And that's that!"

Miss Lang beamed. "Good for you, Mrs. Brewer!" If her hands weren't occupied holding the trays, Oliver wagered she'd embrace the other woman. Tears appeared in her eyes—apparently tears of happiness.

Hightower harrumphed. "If you change your mind, the floor spots open regularly. Feel free to send your boys over. I'll remember the name Brewer and give them first dibs."

Mrs. Brewer flicked her hands across

the bodice of her dress as if removing any vestige of the factory from her well-worn frock. "Your memory'll need to hold that name for a good long while, sir. Four years at the least." Shifting to face Miss Lang, she touched the younger woman's hand. "Thank you for your kindness. I wish you well in this job." She headed for the stairs without so much as a glance at Hightower.

He let out a soft snort and turned to Miss Lang. "You've proved you can handle the weight of the trays. Now walk them to the table and set them down. If you can do it without dumping anything, the job is yours."

Her head held high, Miss Lang moved with grace to the table under the window at the far end of the landing. A few rocks jiggled, causing a gentle rattle, but none rolled free when she lowered the trays to the table. Oliver marveled at how easy she made it appear. His arms ached with the weight of the trays he held. She clasped her hands behind her back and sent Hightower a saucy grin. "So? Am I hired?"

The man drew back with a start, and Oliver nearly bit his tongue in half stifling a chortle. Her sass might not go over well with Hightower, but Oliver liked it. He liked it a lot. So refreshing compared to the staid, prissy women Father and Mother had pushed at him over the past few years. He could get attached to this one. With a niggle of remorse, he reined in the thought. His parents expected him to marry within his station. He might be seen as a mere worker by the other employees at the factory, but he knew better. When he'd completed his purpose here, he'd return to his home. To rule, as his father put it, the Dinsmore dynasty. Becoming attracted to a toter, no matter how appealing he found her, must be avoided.

Caroline

Caroline held her breath. Had she pushed her cheekiness too far? When she was overly tired or overly aggravated—and right now she was both—she tended to cover her true feelings with a display of intrepid spunk. As a child she'd used gumption to defend herself against unfairness and heartache. As an adult she found the habit refused to die even though the Bible she strived to follow advised a humble spirit. Tomorrow, after a night's sleep and a long prayer for Mrs. Brewer's family, she'd practice humility. She hoped she'd be back so the hiring agent could witness it.

"You're hired," the man snapped.

Caroline released her breath, nearly collapsing from relief. No matter how supportive Noble had always been, he wouldn't be pleased if she failed on this mission. She dipped her head in a gesture of appreciation. "Thank you, sir."

"You'll start tomorrow morning at six o'clock sharp."

"Yes, sir."

Hightower spun to face the young man who'd saved Mrs. Brewer from dropping her trays. Caroline admired his willingness to offer assistance, and although he hadn't said a word, she'd been aware of his watchful gaze. While he and the hiring agent engaged in a low-toned exchange, she took the opportunity to give him a covert appraisal.

Dressed in a pair of dark trousers, gray suspenders, and a rolled-sleeves checked shirt, he appeared to be a factory worker. But his hair looked clean, combed, and recently trimmed around his ears. No whiskers dotted his cheeks or chin. Although he sported a brown tweed newsboy cap—typical factory worker topping—it sat on his thick blond waves at a precise rather than a careless angle, denoting a sense of pride. Despite the weight of the trays in his arms, he held himself erect, his posture that of the gentry.

Puzzling... She tucked his image away in the back of her mind. She'd reflect on it later when she didn't feel so fuzzy. Suddenly he turned, his gaze meeting hers, and grinned. How disconcerting to be caught staring. She whisked her attention to the trays beside her and, drawing once more on brashness, pinched a chocolate from the top tray and popped it into her mouth.

Creamy chocolate melted on her tongue, releasing the flavor of the rich vanilla center. She pressed her palms to her stomach and closed her eyes, relishing the delectable taste and smooth texture. No doubt part of her pleasure was the lack of food in her belly, but even an incredible hunger couldn't completely account for her intense reaction to the candy. No wonder these creams were world-famous. A bit of heaven now dissolved in her mouth.

Hightower folded his arms over his chest, his eyebrows rising. "Miss Lang, I assure you, your employment will be short lived if you sample from every tray you're asked to carry."

The man standing beside the agent released a brief, low chuckle. Humor glittered in his eyes. The teasing expression softened his appearance, and something within Caroline seemed to melt as readily as the chocolate had on her tongue.

Oh my, she **was** overly tired.

Her cheeks blazing, she stepped away from the table. "I apologize, sir. It won't become a habit."

"Good." The agent turned back to the other man. "Moore, put those trays on the table. Then give Miss Lang a copy of the factory informational pamphlet, help her complete a timecard, and show her where to punch in." He gave Caroline a halfhearted nod. "Welcome to the Dinsmore family, Miss Lang." He returned to his office, leaving her and the man named Moore standing at opposite ends of the landing.

Caroline stared at him while he stared at her. She'd never been so thoroughly unsettled by a man, and she had no desire to spend another minute in his presence. Yet she wouldn't know the clock-in protocol if she didn't accompany him as Mr. Hightower had instructed. Even so, she remained in place as if rooted, uncertain how to proceed.

In a wide-legged gait, he moved to the

table and thumped the trays onto its scarred surface hard enough to make the rocks bounce. He glanced at the chocolates on the trays and then at the closed door behind which Mr. Hightower had disappeared. With a boyish grin, he tugged a handkerchief from his pocket and unfolded it across his wide, smooth palm. Still silent, he filled the center of the handkerchief with chocolates from the two available trays, seemingly choosing the ones with the most minced nutmeats on top.

Caroline watched the growing mound as a nervous giggle built in the back of her throat. If Mr. Hightower stepped out and caught them pilfering candy, they'd both be let go before her employ even started. Yet she did nothing to stop him.

When the handkerchief held all it could, he deftly tied the corners together, creating a lumpy pouch. Supporting the package with both palms, he held it out to her like an offering.

Caroline took a step back. "I couldn't."

His eyes—a pale green heavily flecked

with gold—twinkled. "They'll get tossed. Right good waste, if you ask me. Someone oughta eat 'em." He used workman's slang but spoke in a cultured tone that didn't match the rough phrasing. "Why not be that someone?"

Oh, how she wanted those chocolates. The delightful flavor of the one she'd eaten still lingered in her mouth, enticing her to partake of more. She caught handfuls of her skirt in both fists and spoke decisively, trying to convince herself as much as him of the wrong. "It's stealing."

He tipped his head and examined her over the knot of white cotton. "Suppose you'd come across these in the garbage bin an' you could see they were good chocolates, not mucked up by trash an' such. Would you eat 'em then?"

Embarrassment heated Caroline's face. As a child she'd often chosen her supper from slop bins behind hotels and restaurants. Although it pained her pride to respond truthfully, she nodded.

"Well, then, think o' what I told you.

These'll get dumped. An' when they do, it's likely they'll get ruined by other garbage, an' then they'll just be wasted." He bounced the packet, releasing a sweet scent from the loosely woven cloth. "Why not save 'em from being wasted?"

Caroline's resolve faltered. "Y-you're sure? I don't want to get you in trouble."

He released a low chuckle. "No worries, miss."

She sent a long look at the remaining chocolates in the tray. Although he'd filled the handkerchief, he'd barely made a dent in the total supply. All those others would be thrown away, and she could put the ones he'd salvaged to good use. She sighed. "All right."

A smile broke across his face. He pressed the packet into her hands. "Now, let's go get you a timecard."

"First..." She swallowed her remaining pride. "Can I take those that dropped on the floor, too?"

His brow pinched. "Those'll be dusty, miss."

Dusty, yes, but not nearly as tainted

as some things she'd eaten in the past. And less likely to be missed. "I can brush them off."

He examined her for a moment through slitted lids. Then he shrugged. "Well, all right, if you want 'em. You got someplace to put 'em?"

She held open the wide pocket sewn into the seam of her skirt.

His grin returned, his teeth a slash of white in his tanned face. "I hafta tell you, miss, you're a corker. A real corker. C'mon, let's get your pocket filled, an' then I gotta get back to work."

Chapter 4

Gordon

Gordon pressed his ear to the door and listened. Had they gone? He detected no mutter of voices. No scuffing of feet on the floor. He cracked open the door and peeked at the landing. Empty save the table and trays.

A satisfied grin tugged at his cheeks. He darted to the table and removed the top tray from both stacks. Then he quickly redistributed the rocks evenly among the remaining four. Not that he would be questioned. Every worker in this factory knew he held the power to hire and fire. But he still didn't want whichever underling—in all likelihood the newest janitor,

Ollie Moore—who cleaned up his mess to discover the inequity between the stacks.

When he finished, he slid the top trays back in place. He started to turn away, then paused, putting his finger in the spot where Miss Lang had removed a vanilla cream. He closed his eyes, recalling the expression of delight that broke across her face when she ate the candy. She had a few more years on her than he normally preferred, but, oh, she was a comely one—full cheeked, bright eyed, and curvy in all the right places. She also possessed more than a smidgen of sass. He sniggered. She'd be fun to chase around the melting pots.

He'd chosen her the moment he'd spotted her among the line of hopeful hires. But he'd known better than to be too obvious. He'd scared off one or two in the past by being overzealous—some girls were like timid mice. And he had to answer to the bossman concerning his hires. Eventually he'd have to explain why he chose someone with no factory experience over one with a lengthy work record. So he'd hatched a scheme to make sure the old, fat one would fail.

Cold sweat broke out across his back as he recalled Moore taking the stack of trays from Mrs. Brewer. At the time Gordon had nearly crawled out of his skin in alarm, certain he'd be found out. But the fool hadn't even noticed it was a good ten pounds heavier than the average stack. And when the woman had confessed she wasn't up to the job, she took all the responsibility on herself. It couldn't have worked out better.

He helped himself to one of the vanilla creams, congratulating himself for his cleverness. As he tossed it into his mouth, he considered the shame of having to throw away full trays of chocolate. So many candies wasted. But wait... He scowled. He'd snagged those trays right from the sorting table. The candies had been lined up in neat rows and columns, ten by eight. Now even the candies on Miss Lang's tray had shifted. Could they have moved that much during their journey as they were carried up and down the landing? Curiosity mounting, he did a quick count, then let out a startled huff. Nearly a dozen were missing from her tray!

He turned toward the stairs, and his gaze fell on the spot where Mrs. Brewer had tipped her load. Rocks still lay scattered, but the chocolates were gone. A picture formed in his head. Yes, Miss Lang had certainly enjoyed that candy—so much so she'd helped herself to even more.

Throwing back his head, he let loose a torrent of delighted laughter. He hurried into his office and scrawled a note to himself detailing the missing chocolates and their resale value. He tucked the note into a tiny hidden cubby beneath one of the drawers, and as he slid the drawer closed, a grin grew on his face. He would enjoy extracting payment for those vanilla creams.

Caroline

Caroline swung the little packet of chocolates as she made her way toward the train station. She'd stashed her bag in a locker since there'd not been time to deposit her few belongings in her new abode before dashing to the factory. She yawned, not even bothering to cover her mouth. Oh, to go directly to her room and sleep the day away. She never slept well on a rocking train. But the emotional upheaval of the past hour had exhausted her even more than the lack of sleep. Tiredness made her bones ache, but she couldn't leave her bag past noon without paying an additional nickel. She wouldn't squander money, no matter how small an amount. Even so, she could hardly wait to get to her room and collapse.

As was his custom, Noble had arranged her lodgings. She'd reside in a small room in a boarding hotel for women near the factory. Perhaps securing the room in advance was foolhardy considering she'd had no assurance she'd be hired, but Noble had insisted. His deep, husky voice rang in her memory. **"It won't matter if you don't get hired as a toter. Other spots will open up. You just keep going in until they finally take you. In**

the meantime you'll be close enough to nose around, ask questions, gather information. You won't waste the room."

She smiled, fondness for the man chasing away a bit of her weariness. He had more confidence in her than she had in herself, but that made her all the more determined not to disappoint him. He'd be pleased she'd been hired.

She retrieved her bag, then plopped it onto a bench and unbuckled it so she could put the chocolates inside. She'd give the handkerchief a good wash in her basin this evening and tomorrow return it to Ollie, as he'd insisted she call him. If all the workers at Dinsmore's were as friendly as Ollie Moore, she'd have no trouble settling in. She gave a start. Why was she thinking of settling in? Had she forgotten her purpose so quickly?

Noble always lectured her not to get too comfortable. Comfort could lead to carelessness. Carelessness could jeopardize the investigation. This particular mission would take extra focus since it had a twofold purpose—completing Harmon

Bratcher's investigation of the workers' safety and satisfying Noble's concerns about the agent's death. And of course she also wanted to further her personal agenda of convincing the factory managers to hire adults for all positions rather than employing children. She gave the valise's straps a good yank, reminding herself to be careful.

Bag in hand again, she headed for the boarding hotel. She sucked in a big breath of cool, coal-scented air. How good to have the hiring process finished. She still felt bad, though, for those who were turned away. Was that poor girl Mr. Hightower had sent out the door being beaten right now by her father for failing to secure the toter's position? She envisioned the girl—young, thin, shabby braids pinned across her head from one ear to the other. The hairstyle was probably intended to add years to her appearance, but instead she'd seemed bedraggled. Just thinking of her made Caroline's heart hurt. She wished she knew the girl's name so she could find her, offer her some assistance.

She reached the corner, paused to allow two wagons to pass, then trotted to the opposite side of the street. As she stepped onto the boardwalk, the screened door to the general goods store banged open, and the very girl who'd stood next to her in Mr. Hightower's office came flying out. An angry, apron-wearing man followed closely on her heels. Instinctively, Caroline dropped her bag and caught the girl by her sleeve. The girl jerked free, but her sudden movement ripped the faded fabric. She came to a stop and gasped, staring at the spot where her skinny, filthy arm peeked through.

"Gotcha!" The man collared the girl and shook her hard. "You no-good thief! I'm gonna give you what for. I'll teach you to steal from my store!" He raised his hand high.

The girl drew up both arms to shield herself as his wide palm swung toward her cheek. Before his hand connected with her face, Caroline grabbed his elbow with both hands. He grunted and tugged, his red face reflecting fury.

"You will not strike that child!" She held tight, indignation giving her more strength than she knew she had. "Shame on you, attacking someone so much smaller and weaker!"

"Well, somebody's gotta teach her!" The man wrenched his arm free and took a step back, releasing the girl's neck. Instead of running, she hunched forward and sobbed into her hands. The man gave her a disgusted look. "Comes into my store, sticks her dirty hands in my cracker barrel, then starts eating right there next to the barrel! When I ask for money, she says she hasn't got any. That makes her a thief in my book."

In Caroline's book it made the girl desperately hungry. "How many crackers did she eat?"

"Three—maybe four."

Caroline withdrew her little money purse from her pocket and snapped it open. "I'll pay for them."

"Fine." He held out his beefy palm. "That'll be two bits."

Caroline cocked one eyebrow. Did he take her for a fool? "Twenty-five cents for a few crackers?"

"Who knows how many I'll hafta throw away? She touched half the barrel with her grimy hands." He bounced his hand. "Two bits or I take her to the sheriff."

Caroline ground her teeth. She didn't have enough energy to argue with the stubborn coot. She removed a twenty-five-cent piece from her purse and placed it on the man's palm. "There you are. Paid in full."

"Humph." He shot the girl another murderous glare. "You stay outta my shop, young lady, you hear?" Clenching Caroline's coin in his fist, he stormed back inside without waiting for a response.

As soon as he'd slammed the door behind him, Caroline caught the girl's wrists and pulled them away from her face. Everything within her wanted to offer sympathy, but the shopkeeper had been right about one thing. Someone had to teach this girl that stealing was wrong. So she swallowed any words of comfort and assumed her sternest voice. "Stop crying."

"I-I can't."

"Yes, you can, and you will."

With a few shuddering gulps, the sobs ceased. The girl stared at Caroline with wide, tear-wet eyes. A hint of belligerence glittered behind the sheen of moisture. "You gonna call the sheriff on me?"

Caroline released one of the girl's wrists, snatched up her bag with her free hand, then pulled the girl into the alley, away from curious onlookers. "No. I don't think the sheriff much cares about a few crackers."

A smile trembled on the corners of the girl's lips.

"But God does."

The smile disappeared.

"And you should be more concerned about pleasing Him than anyone else. Haven't you ever read the Bible?" As soon as the question left her mouth, she realized her error. The girl couldn't read. She'd said as much in Mr. Hightower's office.

The girl folded her arms tightly over her

skinny chest and looked away. "You're makin' fun of me."

"No, I'm not." Caroline gentled her voice. "Look at me." She waited, but the girl kept her gaze aimed to the side. "Look at me, please."

Very slowly the girl shifted her head until she looked directly into Caroline's eyes. Caroline glimpsed her own reflection in the girl's large pupils. She saw a reflection of herself in the girl's hopeless state. What would have become of Caroline if Noble hadn't stepped in, taught her, aimed her in a better direction? This girl needed a Noble in her life. But Noble wasn't here.

Caroline sighed. "What's your name?"

"Letta. Letta Holcomb."

"Well, Letta, there's a very important book called the Bible. God gave us the book to help us know the right way to live. One of the things He says in His book is that we shouldn't steal. Stealing is wrong."

The girl raised her dirt-smudged chin. "What does it matter if you take somethin' from rich folks? They got more'n they need anyway." She flapped one hand toward the general goods shop. "That man in there? He's got shelves full o' stuff. All I wanted was a couple o' crackers. He could've let me have 'em."

"Maybe he would have, if you'd asked." Caroline stifled a yawn. My, she was tired. But she had to get through to this girl. "Taking something that doesn't belong to you is wrong no matter what it is or how rich the person is who owns it. Stealing is wrong."

"So if I asked you right now to gimme the money in your purse, you'd give it to me?"

Caroline gaped at the girl. "No!"

Letta pursed her lips. "That's what the man would've said, too. So I hadta take them crackers if I wanted some." She huffed. "My brothers've snagged crackers plenty o' times without gettin' caught. Guess I'm just not as good at bein' sneaky. I'll hafta be more careful next time."

The girl's aspirations were sorely lacking. Caroline swallowed a frustrated growl. "Letta, you're going to get your-self in trouble taking things that don't belong to you. You cannot steal. Next time I might not be around to pay for what you nabbed. Next time the sheriff might be called, and you could end up being locked away. Is that what you want?"

The defiance faded. Defeat sagged the girl's spine. "Probably be better than goin' home."

Caroline could no longer resist offering sympathy. "Is it that bad?"

The girl nodded. "I wanna go home, get some breakfast." She clutched her stomach. "But soon as I do, Pa'll take the strap to me 'cause I didn't get that job. He says gatherin' rags ain't enough to earn my keep. I gotta bring in more. An' if I can't pay in money, I'll pay with my hide. Dinsmore's was my last hope."

Caroline didn't know how to respond. Her parents hadn't loved her or they wouldn't have sold her, but they'd never struck her. Letta's father was far worse than her own. She fiddled with the well-filled little purse in her pocket. "Did he expect you to bring money home today?"

"No. Just the promise of it. But without a job I don't got no promise to give." Letta cringed, folding into herself. "But he'll keep his promise. I can count on that."

How could she send this girl home to a furious man bent on beating her? Noble had sent her to the Dinsmore factory to investigate a death, but in her heart she'd come to this town to help children. She'd be the worst kind of hypocrite if she simply walked away from Letta. Her fuzzy brain tried to think... **Think...** She gasped. "Letta! I have an idea!"

Chapter 5

Caroline

As Caroline raised her hand to knock on the unpainted door of Letta's home, she prayed the warped, rotting porch boards would support her weight long enough to have a talk with the girl's father. She stood as still as possible, but even so, moans and creaks rose from beneath her feet.

Letta stood so close, her warm, rapid breaths stirred the fine hairs on the back of Caroline's neck. The child crossed her arms over her middle and hugged herself, trembling from scruffy braids to scuffed toes. The girl's obvious nervousness did nothing to offer Caroline confidence that Mr. Holcomb would approve her scheme. But she still had to try. So she tapped. Waited. No response.

Letta whispered, "Pa sleeps days since he works nights at the train yard. Might hafta bang a little harder if you wanna rouse him."

Caroline considered this new piece of information. "Maybe I should speak to your mother instead."

The girl squirmed. "Don't rightly know where Ma is. She, uh, kinda took off about a year ago. We ain't seen hide nor hair of her since. Pa's been specially irascible since she left."

A sleepy man would be grouchy and less likely to be reasonable. Perhaps she should visit this evening after both she and Mr. Holcomb had enjoyed a good rest. She started to ask Letta when would be a better time to speak to the man, but Letta reached past her and gave the door three solid thumps with her fist. Then she darted behind Caroline.

"Who's out there?" The raspy voice came from somewhere deep inside the house.

Caroline leaned close to the door and hollered back. "My name is Carrie Lang, Mr. Holcomb. I'd like to speak to you, please."

Feet pounded on the floor inside the house, and the door wrenched open. Mr. Holcomb glowered from the other side of the doorjamb. Suspenders dangled at his knees, and the open neck of his long johns exposed a thick thatch of graying, coarse hair. "Whatever you're sellin', I ain't buyin'."

Caroline forced herself to look directly into his whisker-dotted face. "I'm not selling a thing, Mr. Holcomb. I'm here to purchase something from you."

He snorted. "Whaddaya think I got worth sellin'?"

Caroline gathered the remainder of her spunk and stated boldly, "Letta's time."

His bushy eyebrows descended into a sharp V. "Letta?" He looked left and right. "Where is that girl?"

Letta eased from her hiding spot behind Caroline. "I'm here, Pa."

Caroline ceased to exist as the father

and daughter launched into a rapid exchange.

"You get that job like I told you?"

"N-no, Pa."

"Why not?"

"Man said toters hafta have strength. Said I didn't have enough."

"An' you just let him say it? Didn't do nothin' to prove him wrong?"

"He wouldn't let me, Pa! Honest! He just told me to git on home an' tell you to pay better attention to the qua...qualifications next time."

Fury emanated from the man. Letta scuttled behind Caroline once more, and Caroline took advantage of the momentary lapse in the conversation to speak her piece. "Mr. Holcomb, if you'll allow me one minute of your time, I'll tell you how Letta can earn four dollars a week."

The man's attention shifted from his daughter to Caroline so quickly he nearly staggered. "Four dollars?" He barked out the amount, surprise lighting his face. But then he scowled. "You ain't got nothin' shady in mind, do ya? Burbank next-door might let his girls work the brothels durin' the night, but no daughter o' mine's gonna—"

Caroline raised both palms, staving off his words. "I assure you, sir, my idea is far from shady." Clasping her hands in a prayerful position, she hurried on. "Letta tells me she hasn't had the opportunity to attend school. I believe receiving an education would be very beneficial to her, so I am offering to pay her four dollars a week to go to school and do the lessons."

He cocked his head, disbelief breaking across his grizzled face. "Where you gonna get four dollars a week to give her?"

The Labor Commission paid her so she had no need for the money from the factory. But why tell him so? "Never mind that. Just know I'll pay Letta four dollars a week to attend school." She aimed one finger at the man. "But she'll have to prove to me she's learning. I'll want to see her assignments each week, complete with markings from the teacher, and I will quiz her on the lessons. She'll earn that money."

The man scratched his head, his lips forming a sly smirk. "If she goes, my boys'll probably think they can wile away their days sittin' at a desk instead of goin' out rat catchin' an' tin collectin'. That means losin' their eight bits a week."

A dollar was a small price to pay if the boys could attend school, too, but Caroline wouldn't be manipulated into a bartering match. "Letta can share her lessons with her brothers. She'll be their teacher." A fanciful idea flooded Caroline's mind. In spite of her weary state, she smiled. "Maybe she'll grow up to teach a whole class full of youngsters someday. Wouldn't that be a fine thing?"

Letta beamed at Caroline, then turned her eager face in her father's direction.

The man snorted again. "Can't imagine any kin o' mine bein' smart enough to be a teacher."

The girl wilted.

Caroline's parents would have said the same thing about her, but look at what she'd become, all because Noble had taught her to lean into God's strength. She placed her arm around Letta's thin shoulders, silently vowing to give this child the same encouragement she'd received from Noble. "You can't know what Letta could achieve unless she's given an opportunity to show you. So, Mr. Holcomb, will you accept my offer? Four dollars a week..." She dangled the carrot, watching his face for signs of softening.

He scratched his cheek, his dirty nails rasping over the coarse whiskers. Finally he blew out a breath and shook his head. "All right. She can go."

Caroline held back a happy squeal.

"Leastways 'til somethin' better comes along," he added on a sour note. "Now lemme sleep." He slammed the door in Caroline's face, leaving her alone on the porch with an ecstatic girl.

Letta grabbed Caroline's hands, dancing in place. The floorboards moaned in protest. "You did it, Miss Lang! I never would've thought he'd say yes, but you did it!"

Caroline squeezed the girl's hands and offered a bright smile, but then she forced a serious look. "Remember what I told your father about you proving to me you're learning before I will give you the money. You have to earn those four dollars, Letta, by paying attention and finishing your lessons. Do you understand?"

She nodded, her smile bright. "I understand. An' I'll do it, miss. You'll see."

Caroline steered the girl off the creaky porch. "Come with me now so you'll know where I live. I'll expect you to come by every day when I get off work so I can look at your assignment."

Letta scurried along beside Caroline, wringing her hands. "If I have trouble, will you help me some? Reckon school'll be plenty hard, an' I'm a little scared about how it's gonna go."

"I'll help you," Caroline said, hoping she could keep the promise. She might be in Sinclair for months or maybe only for weeks. So many things depended on how quickly she uncovered the cause of poor Harmon Bratcher's demise. For a moment she questioned the wisdom of getting Letta's hopes so high. She caught Letta's hand and forced her to stop. "But, Letta, I want you to remember something very important. Your best help in every part of life comes from God. If you ask Him to help you, He will. Every time."

"God will help me," Letta recited with a solemn nod, her eyes round. "Yes'm. I'll remember you said so."

"Good." Caroline set her feet in motion, but instead of turning toward the boarding hotel, she aimed herself to town. She had a purchase to make—something to offer as a reward to Letta for starting school. If the girl was going to learn to lean on God's strength, she'd need to study God's very own book. Caroline hoped the general merchandise store carried Bibles.

Oliver

Oliver tinkered with the hinges on the entry door to the factory floor. **Tap, tap, tap** on the pin with a ball-peen hammer.

Push, pull, push, pull on the door while staring at the brass plate. Scowl. Shake his head. **Tap, tap, tap** again. Did he look convincing? His first week he'd felt every bit an inept clod each time he retrieved a tool from his belt, uncertain whether he should use one intended to pound, pinch, or poke. Who could have known that assuming the role of janitor would prove so taxing? But his education hadn't prepared him for menial labor.

Workers filed past. Men in overalls or trousers and chambray shirts, tin lunch-pails in hand and caps tugged low over sleepy eyes. Women with aprons covering their dresses and ruffled mobcaps framing their faces. Children with drooping eyes and dragging heels. In turn, they paused to jam their cards into the punch slot just inside the door and then slip them into the little holder marked with their names. Most acknowledged him with a wave or smile, the occasional "Morning, Ollie" from the fellows and "Good morning, Mr. Moore" from the youngsters and the ladies. He responded to each in kind, calling the names of those he could recall and substituting "sir," "miss," and "kiddo" for those he couldn't.

He continued to mess with those hinges as if fixing them was the most important task on his list of duties. But it was as much a ruse as his carefully chosen working-man's attire. The hinges were fine. Didn't even squeak. But what other excuse could he use to loiter near the time clock until Miss Carrie Lang arrived? In three more minutes the shift bell would clang, and he'd have to leave this post whether he wanted to or not. He hoped she arrived on time. Hightower wouldn't hesitate to deliver a tongue-lashing in front of the other workers if she dared punch in even a few seconds past six o'clock.

Oliver dropped to one knee and shifted his attention to the locking mechanism. The first thing he intended to do after Dinsmore's World-Famous Chocolates Factory transferred into his hands was to sit down with Hightower and have a long talk about leading without lording. Father had always been satisfied with

Hightower's service, but over the past weeks Oliver had decided the factory manager had a lot to learn.

Three more workers hustled past—two men and a lad of perhaps twelve years. Oliver stifled a groan of frustration. Where was Miss Lang? She'd seemed so eager to get started when he'd given her a quick tour of the factory floor yesterday. He was delighted to add her to the Dinsmore "family," as Father preferred to call their employees. Her concern about being accused of stealing chocolates hinted at her honesty. Her attentiveness as he explained the time clock, the lunch procedure, and the break schedule showed a true interest in doing things right. He had no doubt she'd be a diligent worker.

He inserted the tip of the screwdriver into the slot of one screwhead on the latch plate, loosened it, then retightened it while he kept one eye on the back alley, hoping to see Miss Lang approach. The tool slipped from his hand, bounced twice, and rolled against the doorjamb. Releasing a disgruntled huff, he snatched it up. Worry nibbled around the edges of his mind. Had she decided not to work here after all? He glanced at the time clock. If she arrived even one minute past six, she'd be written up as a late arrival. She was almost out of time. His hands began to sweat.

Settling back on one heel, he pondered why he cared so much. He hardly knew her, and she was only one of nearly two hundred workers. Yet something about her had touched him. He mulled over the scene in the upstairs landing yesterday—the pair of women carrying trays in a competition to win the privilege of performing the task in exchange for roughly sixty-six cents a day—and he uncovered the reason. Her tender heart. It had hurt her, genuinely hurt her, to see the other woman lose.

The patter of running feet on hard-packed earth reached his ears. He leaped up, the tools in his belt clanking together, and stepped aside as Miss Lang dashed past, dark curls bouncing on her apple cheeks. Card in hand, she whammed it into the machine and pressed the lever. Oliver peeked over her shoulder as she pulled the card free. Black, smudged numbers proclaimed 6:00 a.m. on the top of the card. She'd made it! He slipped the screwdriver into the leather pouch and stepped up beside her.

She swept a small hand across her brow, pushing one springy coil aside. It dangled beguilingly along her temple. "I feared I'd be late."

He followed her as she moved to the card rack and slipped hers into place. He waited for her to offer an excuse— an alarm that failed to ring, a trolley car blocking her pathway—but she offered none. He continued to trail her, doublestepping to keep up, as she turned and headed for the candy-making center.

A dimple flashed in her cheek as she sent a quick grin in his direction. "I hoped I would see you."

Father would berate him if he knew how much her statement pleased him. "Oh?"

"I wanted to return your handkerchief." She whisked it from the pocket of her swirling skirt and held it out to him. "I laundered it last night. Well, I washed it in my sink with a little lye soap. I didn't have an iron, so it's rather rumpled. But no chocolate stains, see?"

He held it to the light and pretended to examine it, but truthfully he was admiring the tawny freckles scattered across the bridge of her nose. "I see." He tucked the handkerchief into his pocket. "I trust that you—" He nearly slapped his forehead. Her sweet, mellifluous voice, devoid of the common slang of the other workers, encouraged him to drop his guard and speak like the educated man he was. But he didn't dare. He rubbed the end of his nose, pretending to fight off a sneeze, then said, "So...didja enjoy those chocolates?"

She laughed, a delicate trickle of merriment that broadened his smile. "I didn't eat a one. I gave the pocketful to some children who were playing in the street and the handkerchief's contents to a girl named Letta to share with her brothers."

Another example of her tender heart. "That was right kind of you, Carrie."

She shrugged and didn't reply. When they reached the candy-making area, stacks of trays, no doubt filled by the previous shift's workers, waited for transport. "It looks like I'd better get to work. Thank you again for sharing the vanilla creams. The children were delighted to receive them."

He should leave, but he wasn't ready to go. He searched for a reason to continue talking with her, and he realized she hadn't carried in a dinner bucket. "You didn't bring your lunch."

An odd smile quirked her lips. Her shoulders rose in a tiny shrug—the right one slightly higher than the left. "I suppose one day without lunch won't hurt me." She lifted the top three trays from the nearest stack and turned.

He found himself blocking her pathway. "Join me."

Her eyebrows shot up.

He shrugged, imitating her gesture by raising his right shoulder nearly to his earlobe. "I have plenty, and I'd like to share. Meet me in the break room at eleven." He held his breath. Would she see him as too forward? He sweetened the invitation. "Ham and cheese sandwiches, deviled eggs, and strawberry tarts. With cream."

"Oh my..."

He hid a grin. She still hadn't agreed, but he needed to let her get to work before Hightower spotted them chatting. He inched backward, allowing her to ease past. He called to her as she walked away, "Eleven o'clock. I'll be waiting."

A single bob of her mobcap sent his pulse stuttering into happy hiccups. He spun, a grin stretching his cheeks, and came face to face with Gordon Hightower. The man's scowl chased away Oliver's elation.

"Moore, I'd like a word with you."

Chapter 6

Gordon

Gordon watched Carrie Lang's dangling apron ties bounce against the full gathers of her skirt as she scurried away. She didn't flout her figure the way some women did, exaggerating the swing of her hips. But her natural sway was enticing enough.

The sound of someone clearing his throat pulled Gordon's focus from Miss Lang's delightful curves. Ollie Moore stood staring at him, his lips set in a near scowl and his narrowed eyes seeming to look beneath Gordon's exterior to the thoughts roiling in his brain. Gordon adjusted the lapels of his jacket, lifting his chin in a manner used to cow the lesser workers. Moore didn't flinch.

"You wanted to speak with me?" Moore spoke genially, but his eyes continued to glint like steel.

Gordon gritted his teeth. How he'd love to remove Ollie Moore from the employment books. Every other worker in this factory kowtowed to him. But this one—this one wore arrogance like a shield. He'd disliked Moore the moment he'd entered Gordon's office, his hat in his hand but his shoulders set bold and square as if his being hired was a right rather than a privilege. Gordon had wanted to refuse to hire the man, but the owner, Fulton Dinsmore, had specifically recommended Moore—his first time to intrude upon Gordon's hiring process. Consequently, he didn't dare ax Moore. But he could make the worker's life so difficult he chose to find another place to work. Then old man Dinsmore couldn't hold Gordon accountable.

"One of the overnight workers came in drunk and lost his supper in the melting room. Go mop up the mess." He paused, waiting for the man to blanch. He didn't. Gordon swallowed a curse. "When you're done there, grease the conveyor belt cogs."

Moore angled his head to the side. "I greased those cogs yesterday." He glanced down at his tan britches as if the grease smudges on his thighs were a badge.

Gordon pasted on his fiercest scowl. "Their infernal squeak gives me a headache. Do it again, and this time do it right." He barked the command, puffing out his chest with as much pomposity as he could gather. "Then mop the candy-making floor and scrub the sorting tables. I walked through there this morning and found caramel stuck everywhere." An exaggeration. He'd found a tiny smudge of caramel on the leg of one table.

A slight frown marred Moore's brow— the first hint that Gordon might be break-ing through his seemingly impenetrable control. "The night-shift janitor scrubs the tables because they're never empty during the day."

"They are during the sorters' lunch break."

Moore's frown deepened. "My lunch break's the same time as the sorters'."

Gordon came close to chortling. He'd finally managed to ruffle the man's feathers. "Take your lunch at a different time. Cleaning those tables is more important than filling your stomach." Folding his arms across his chest, Gordon offered a sardonic smirk. "Unless, of course, you'd rather arrange your own schedule...at some other factory."

"I'll get it done." Moore turned and headed for the janitor closet.

Gordon watched him go, then shifted his gaze to the bustling factory floor. He smiled. None of the workers dawdled at their duties or huddled in groups to gossip. Even the youngest children scurried to and fro, intent on their tasks. A few of them glanced in his direction, as if seeking approval, but he offered none. No one had ever thrown him as much as a breadcrumb when he was a boy. Why should they have more than he'd been given?

Satisfied all was well, he turned toward the wooden stairway leading to his loft office. As much as he liked his office with its observation window looking out over the main work floor, he abhorred climbing those stairs. It was always hot in the factory, thanks to the constantly bubbling vats of chocolate and steam-powered generators, so mounting the stairs—eighteen of them in all—made him sweat. He hated sweating. If he desired exercise, he'd take a meandering walk through the park at dusk with a lovely girl clinging to his elbow.

Until two weeks ago he'd used the company elevator rather than the stairs. He neared the elevator and veered clear of it without conscious thought. An image filled his mind—Bratcher's crumpled form at the bottom of the shaft. Gordon shivered even as perspiration broke out across his forehead. The man had been a nuisance, pestering Gordon to change the factory's entry age for workers from ten years to sixteen. On more than one occasion, Gordon had wished Bratcher would shut up and go away. But he hadn't wished him dead.

Gordon set aside thoughts of Bratcher. He was dead and gone, his aspirations to change the entry age of workers buried with him. And now there was another undesirable commanding his focus. He'd make a list of unpalatable chores for Ollie Moore to complete, and by the end of the week, surely the arrogant worker would choose to go elsewhere. Gordon was certain Moore wouldn't be clumsy enough to plunge down an elevator shaft.

Caroline

Caroline entered the room set aside for the workers to eat their lunches. A pair of trestle tables with benches ran the length of the floor. Chattering women and children crowded around one table, their higher-pitched voices nearly masking the low-toned mumbles of the men, who lounged around the other.

The arrangement would have surprised her had she not been given a list of company rules by Ollie Moore yesterday. "No fraternization between the sexes" held the number two position with "No late arrivals" above it. On her first day she'd already come close to breaking rule number one, and she'd worried all morning about her intention to break rule number two by sharing Ollie's lunch. But it appeared her concerns were for naught. Ollie wasn't in the room.

Disappointment at his absence created an ache in her middle. Or perhaps only hunger nibbled at her. She'd munched an apple purchased from a street cart on her way to the factory, but she'd given her little box lunch of crackers, cheese, and tinned sardines to a beggar. She didn't regret the decision. The ragged man had accepted the simple food with tears in his wrinkled eyes, stinging her heart. If she hadn't already taken a bite of the apple, she'd have handed it over, too. Ollie's offer had seemed a reward for unselfishly sharing with someone in need, but now it appeared she'd go without lunch after all. She supposed it served her right for knowingly going against Mr. Hightower's rules.

She squared her shoulders. Silly to fuss over a missed meal. She'd gone without hundreds of lunches in her lifetime. She would survive one more. Moving to the table of women, she located a gap and wriggled her way in. Once she sat, she couldn't help releasing a soft sigh. How wonderful to be off her feet for a few minutes. She ached from her shoulders to her toes from carrying her load of trays back and forth, back and forth. She'd stopped counting at seventy-two trips. Such a chore. She closed her eyes, savoring the moments of relaxation. Noble owed her two weeks of leave for taking on this particular job.

Thoughts of Noble jarred her, reminding her of the reason she was in Dinsmore's World-Famous Chocolates Factory. She had a mystery to unravel. Sitting upright, she leaned her elbows on the table and flashed a smile at the thin-faced woman seated across from her. "Hello. I'm Carrie. I'm new."

The woman nodded. The ruffle of her mobcap fluttered. "Thought so. I'm Mildred." She indicated those seated on her right and left. "This here's Helena, and this is Stella. We're all sorters." A hint of pride entered Mildred's tone as she stated her position. "Sittin' over there next to you is Evangeline and Daisy. They're mixers."

Caroline's nostrils filled with the sweet, fruity essence emanating from the two beside her. "You must have been mixing something with raspberry this morning."

Daisy said, "The filling for raspberry creams."

Caroline inhaled deeply, drawing in an aroma so rich it flavored her tongue. "It smells delightful."

"It does 'til you've smelled it every day of every week for more than a year." Daisy crinkled her nose in distaste, but teasing winked in her eyes. "Before I started working here, I welcomed a box of sweets from a fella. These days I prefer hair ribbons or flowers."

The other women laughed, and Caroline joined them even though a little part of her heart ached. Never in her twenty-seven years had she received any kind of gift from a fellow. Except from Noble, and he didn't count.

Caroline turned her attention to Daisy. "You've worked here an entire year?"

Daisy picked up her sandwich—corned beef on rye bread, if Caroline wasn't mistaken—and took a bite. "Uh-huh. Hope to stay until me and Robby get married."

"You're getting married?" Caroline heard the shock in her voice, but she couldn't squelch it. The girl looked so young—maybe seventeen. Much too young to be someone's wife, in Caroline's opinion.

Stella rolled her eyes and groaned. "Oh, don't ask her about Robby. We'll never hear the end of it."

Daisy giggled. "You'd brag, too, if you had a handsome fella like Robby courting you." She hunched her shoulders and fluttered her lashes at Caroline. "Robby's a crater here at Dinsmore's, but he works nights. Keeps us from frattruh-nizin'.'" She giggled again, and the others snickered behind their hands.

Caroline sent a curious glance across the women's faces. "What's funny?"

Mildred removed a pickle from the tin box in front of her. "We shouldn't laugh at Mr. Hightower's rules. He is the boss around here, after all. But it's hard not to, considering..." She turned to look toward the door. Seemingly assured all was safe, she leaned toward Caroline. "He's the biggest breaker of rule number two. You'll need to watch yourself, Carrie. You're real pretty, and you've got a nice figure. That man loves to sneak up on the buxom girls and pinch their bottoms. He's cornered a couple of them and stolen kisses, too."

Indignation roared through Caroline. "He does no such thing!"

All five women nodded emphatically, their expressions serious. Stella said, "Oh, he does. And nobody can stop him, 'cause if you complain, you lose your job."

Caroline's fingers itched to record the women's statements in the little notebook she carried in her pocket. Noble would be interested in what they'd said. But she'd have to wait until she was alone. She needed these ladies to trust her, and making notes in their presence would surely arouse suspicion. "I'll be careful," she said. "Is there anything else I should know? Any other"—she chose her next word carefully, not wanting to frighten them into silence—"dangers?"

Evangeline said, "What do you mean?"

Feigning nonchalance, Caroline shrugged. "Work-related hazards of which I should be aware."

Evangeline shook her head. "Nah. The men they handle the most dangerous jobs—stoking the coal, keeping the boilers going, loading the filled crates on flats for the railroad... Our jobs are easy."

Caroline could have argued about her job being easy. Why didn't Mr. Hightower give men the task of toting? They seemed better suited to lifting and carrying the heavy trays. And the women hadn't mentioned the incident involving the elevator. She pondered asking a direct question about Harmon Bratcher's death but feared sounding too nosy on her first day. A good investigator knew when to push and when to back away. For now she'd back away. At least about Bratcher.

She shifted the focus in a personal direction. "What do the children do?"

Helena wiped a smear of jam from her mouth with a checked napkin and then pushed the stained cloth into the bottom of her empty tin. "Whatever they can. Line up empty chocolate boxes for the sorters, put paper wrappers on trays, scrub down the machinery, sweep under the tables, cart out the trash. There's always something for them to do."

Caroline had witnessed children in other factories performing dangerous tasks. She blew out a small breath, relieved the jobs here wouldn't cause injury even if working did steal their opportunity for education. But injury was possible, because one man had died. She started to ask how long each of the women had worked at the Dinsmore factory, but a shrill whistle sounded. Lunch break was over.

The workers unfolded themselves from the benches and shuffled toward the door, depositing their empty buckets and boxes with a series of clanks and thuds on a table on their way out. Caroline fell in with those leaving while another group filed in. In the middle of the line entering the lunchroom, Ollie lifted his hand and caught Caroline's attention. He mouthed, "Step aside."

She hesitated, her feet slowing. The woman behind her bumped into her shoulder, pushing her out of the line.

Ollie leaped to her side and touched her elbow. "Do you still want that sandwich?" His pale eyes, lined with lashes far too thick to belong on such a rugged, handsome face, offered a silent apology.

Her stomach rumbled. She wanted the sandwich. But even more she wanted to know where he'd been. She hadn't taken him to be the kind to make a promise and then break it. But there wasn't time for either the sandwich or an explanation. "I have to get busy." She moved sideways, inching toward her work area.

"I'll save one for you," he called after her. "We can meet at shift's end."

Oh, the temptation. And not because she wanted the sandwich. Ollie's attention stirred something to life within her. Had she ever relished the overtures of a man before? If only she weren't on an assignment... But she wasn't here to be wooed. Besides, Letta would be waiting to share about her first day at school. Caroline wouldn't abandon the girl. "I can't. I have a commitment."

She turned her back on him and scurried off as if a coyote nipped at her heels. Ollie Moore could easily become a distraction. She'd need to keep her distance. Forcing her tired arms to lift yet another stack of trays, she replayed the disappointment clouding his face as she'd refused his offer. For the remainder of the afternoon, the image danced in her memory, pricking her with regret. As much as she always found her position as an investigator fulfilling, on this day responsibility was a greater burden to bear than the filled trays she carried.

Chapter 7

Caroline

"Thank you again, miss... I mean, Carrie." Letta's shy grin split her face. "I'll be here tomorrow, just like I promised. You can count on it!"

Caroline watched Letta move up the sidewalk, her steps so light she almost seemed to float. Her one day as a school-girl seemed to have carved years from her countenance. At the beginning of their hour together, the girl had confided she felt awkward sitting among the first-year students, all much smaller and younger than she was, but when Caroline asked if she wanted to quit, her eyes had opened wide. "Oh, no, miss!" she'd exclaimed. "School's a marvelous place! I want to stay until I've learned all my head can hold!" She'd then gone on to tell Caroline every detail of her day, from the opening recitation of a prayer to the teacher's distribution of homework. Letta proudly held out her personal assignment—to write the first twelve letters of the alphabet on paper the teacher had given her and draw a picture representing the sound each letter made. Of course, she'd also requested Caroline's assistance, and Caroline couldn't refuse.

Now as Letta headed home to prepare an evening meal for herself and her bro-thers—"And show 'em the letters so they can learn 'em, too," she'd confided—Caroline's stomach twinged. The susten-ance of the morning's apple had long since abandoned her. She'd locate the nearest café, partake of the biggest meal on the menu, and then use the telephone in the boarding hotel's lobby to call Noble and give her first day's report. She hoped she would be able to inject as much enthusiasm into her recitation as Letta had with hers.

Two blocks up the street Caroline detected the aromas of fresh-baked bread, roasting meat, and cinnamon—a nearly intoxicating combination. She forced her tired feet to hurry and came upon a small white building with a recessed doorway and the name Durham's Café painted in square blue letters on a board above the porch. She cupped her hands beside her face and peeked through a slit in the green-checked curtains hanging behind the plate-glass window. An L-shaped counter with tall stools provided seating. All but one were already filled, assuring Caroline of the café's popularity.

With her stomach twisting in hunger, she entered and crossed to the lone available stool, situated between a middle-aged man in a dark suit and a younger man in stained dungarees and a striped shirt with the sleeves rolled above his elbows. She stifled a groan as she climbed onto the stool, the muscles in her legs and back resisting the movements. Not until Caroline had settled herself at the counter did she notice no other female filled a seat. And every male—those on her right and those on her left—gazed in her direction. Forks froze midair above enameled tin plates. All conversation ceased. Faces registered either humor or confusion. Eyebrows rose or descended.

Caroline glanced nervously up and down the row of faces. Had she inadvertently entered a male-only establishment? Such places existed in larger cities. She pressed her palms to the worn but clean counter, prepared to dash out. Before she could move, however, a round-faced woman with a starched, ruffled apron covering her ample front bustled from a door on the far right, balancing three plates in her hands. "All right, Reggie," she announced in a bright, warbling voice, "got your stew, biscuits, an' pie. Tom, your pie's—"

Her gaze found Caroline, and she stopped so suddenly one fluffy biscuit scooted off the edge of the plate and hit the floor with a burst of crumbs. The woman's mouth dropped open in surprise, then curved into a smile of welcome.

"Well, I'll be... Hello there, honey. What's your name?"

Caroline flicked another uncertain glance across the gathering of men. "I... My name is Caro—Carrie Lang."

The woman bustled to the counter, her gray skirts flapping above the toes of her battered brown boots, and plopped the plates down with a whack. "I'll getcha another biscuit in a minute, Reg." Wiping her hands on her apron, she edged to the opposite side of the counter and then stretched her hands toward Caroline. "I'm Kesia. Kesia Durham."

Caroline gripped the warm, leathery palms. Despite her feelings of discomfiture, she couldn't help but smile. The woman radiated friendliness. "Hello, Miss Kesia."

Kesia aimed a stern frown at the young man on Caroline's left. "Where're your manners, Patrick?" She turned the frown on the older man on Caroline's right. "You, too, Willis. All you fellas, quit gawkin' at the poor girl an' eat your supper. You act as though you ain't never seen a female before."

The younger man, Patrick, shoved his fork into the pile of greens on his plate. "Well, Kesia, I ain't. Leastwise not such a purty one in here."

Caroline cringed. Lowering her voice to a whisper, she addressed Kesia. "Is this a...gentlemen-only eatery? If so, I—"

Kesia's laughter rolled, her face crinkling merrily. With her white mobcap, plump, rosy cheeks, and ruffly apron, she reminded Caroline of a drawing she'd seen of Mrs. Claus. "Oh, honey, forgive me, but such a question..." She wiped her eyes, still chuckling. "No, no. I tend to cater to a mostly male crowd, but that's just 'cause females generally have their own kitchens an' fix their own dinners. We ain't used to seein' naught but men resting their elbows on my servin' counter." She reached out and gave Caroline's cheek a gentle pat. "But your pretty face is a welcome sight, especially when you take a gander at this sorry lot o' fellas."

The men grinned, none seeming to take

offense.

"But enough jawin'." Kesia plunked one fist on a beefy hip. "You must be hungry, hmm? Tonight I'm servin' stew an' biscuits, beans an' ham with collard greens, or pot roast with mashed turnips, carrots, an' peas. Which o' those tickles your fancy, honey?"

They all sounded wonderful. But considering her empty stomach, Caroline chose the biggest meal, just as she'd intended. "The pot roast, please." She spotted no price board, but whatever the cost, she'd pay it. She was famished, but even more, Kesia had already earned a place of affection in her heart.

"Comin' right up." Kesia spun and headed for the doorway, calling over her shoulder, "Tom, I ain't forgot your pie. I'll bring it after I bring Miss Carrie's dinner. Ladies first!"

To Caroline's relief the men turned their attention to their plates. The low buzz of voices resumed, and by the time Kesia returned with Caroline's overflowing plate and Tom's pie, she'd set aside her discomfort and was able to take up her fork without a moment's hesitation. Just before cutting into her beef, she remembered she hadn't offered grace. She set the fork back on the counter.

Kesia stopped, Tom's large wedge of cherry pie in hand, and looked at Caroline. "Somethin' wrong, honey?"

Once again Caroline found herself being scrutinized. Heat flooded her face, but she shook her head and answered. "No, ma'am. It all looks delicious. I just need to bless it first."

One of the men guffawed. "Good thinking. Otherwise you might get indigestion."

Kesia waved her hand at the man, scowling. "Hush that. I won't have you pokin' fun at somebody who's got the sense to thank the Good Lord for her blessings, big an' small. All o' you, stop your eatin'." She waited until every last man followed her order. Then she folded her hands and bobbed her chin at Caroline. "Go ahead. Say your prayer."

Caroline stared at the woman. Aloud? In front of everyone? She'd never prayed before an audience. The men fidgeted, waiting for their opportunity to continue eating. Swallowing a nervous titter, Caroline folded her hands and closed her eyes. She hoped everyone else closed their eyes, too. By now her face must be as bold red as the cherries in Tom's pie.

"Dear Lord, thank You for this food." The aroma rising from the plate nearly turned her stomach inside out with eagerness. She amended, "For this **marvelous** food. Please bless the hands that prepared it, and may it give me strength to do Your service. Amen."

A mumble of voices echoed, "Amen," and the men dove back into their plates.

Kesia leaned on the counter and beamed at Caroline. "So what brings you to Durham's, honey? Like I said, I don't get too many gals in here. Hope you don't mind if I bend your ear a bit."

Caroline grinned. "Not if you don't mind me eating while we talk." She took her first bite of tender beef. "Oh...," she moaned around the mouthful. "This is divine."

"Bay leaf an' garlic, baked slow in a low-burnin' oven," Kesia stated matter-of-factly. "You live around here? Haven't seen you before."

Between bites Caroline shared her carefully crafted script of information. The food stuck in her throat occasionally as guilt overtook her. She hated fibbing to this dear, friendly woman. At least some of what she'd shared was truthful—she was an orphan, she had been accepted as an employee at Dinsmore's factory, and she did reside at the Sherwood Boarding Hotel.

Patrons finished their meals and left, dropping money in a little bucket hanging from a nail at the end of the counter before heading out the door with calls of farewell to both Kesia and Caroline. New men sauntered in to fill the vacated stools. Kesia ran back and forth, serving meals, but she always returned to Caroline and to their conversation as if no interruption had occurred.

Caroline ate every bite of the food on her plate and used a biscuit, shyly offered by the man named Reggie, to mop up the remnants of gravy. The moment she finished, Kesia whisked her plate away and replaced it with a bowl containing a slice of cinnamon-laden peach pie nearly hidden by a fluffy mound of whipped cream. Caroline clutched her stomach and moaned. "Oh, Miss Kesia, I'm so full I'm ready to pop. I can't possibly eat this, too."

The woman offered a teasing wink. "Well, then sit there a bit an' let your dinner settle. Let some room for that pie open up."

Caroline didn't think her stomach worked that way, but she sensed Kesia's pleasure in visiting with a female customer. After the woman had been so kind, Caroline wouldn't abandon her to the male throng. She propped her chin in her hands. "All right."

Kesia grinned and poured her a cup of coffee, then bustled to the kitchen to prepare a plate for the latest arrival, an elderly man with an overgrown mustache and a thick gray beard hiding the bottom half of his face. Caroline tried not to stare, but she couldn't help but wonder how the man would manage to eat. When his food arrived, he solved the problem by clutch-ing the long mustache hairs in his fist and holding them aloft while shoveling beans into his toothless mouth. No one else seemed taken aback by his behavior, apparently accustomed to his odd means of feeding himself. Caroline followed their example and aimed her focus elsewhere.

Kesia leaned on the counter, flashing a weary smile at Caroline. "So you've hired on at the chocolate factory, huh? Lots of folks in this neighborhood make their livin' at Dinsmore's factory. Do you like it?"

Caroline took a sip of the coffee. "I just started, but, yes, I think I'll like it. The people are friendly, much like you." Kesia fussed with the lacy edge of her cap and blushed at the compliment. Caroline continued. "I'm only a toter, but I hope to become a packager." Packagers rode the elevator to the lowest level, where the chocolates were boxed for shipping. If she was going to learn more about

Bratcher's untimely death, she needed access to the elevator.

"It's good to have ambitions," Kesia mused. "Kinda surprised, though, that a pretty young girl like you ain't aimin' her sights for a man instead of a job."

Kesia couldn't know Caroline held no desire to tie herself to a man who would demand she see to his needs and cater to his wants until he'd drained the life from her. And Kesia wouldn't know, because Caroline never talked about her real past. Only the manufactured one created by Noble. She forced a smile. "Oh, maybe someday, but for now I'm enjoying my independence."

Kesia chortled, shaking her head. She smoothed the ruffles climbing across one round shoulder. "Independence is nice, I suppose, but so is marriage. I've had both, you know. Spent twenty-two years with my Isaac, an' I'd say a good twenty o' them was happy." She laughed, and Caroline joined her. Then she sighed. "Been **independent** now for comin' up on ten years, an' most o' them's been good, too. Life's what you make of it, I suppose."

Caroline pondered the woman's statement. To her thinking, life was more trying to make something of what one had been given, but she wouldn't argue. She started to ask how Isaac had died, but the door behind her opened, and another customer entered.

Kesia straightened, sending a bright smile in the direction of the newcomer. "Here you are! I was startin' to think you'd found yourself another place to eat your supper."

A chuckle rumbled. Caroline jolted. She'd heard that low-pitched sound before. Tingles crept up her arms as recognition bloomed. She slowly turned as Ollie Moore strode up to the counter, his cap crushed in one broad palm.

"Ollie," Kesia said, "this here is Carr—"

"Carrie Lang." Ollie slid onto the vacated stool next to her, his unusual eyes pinned on her face. "How splendid..." He ducked his head briefly, grimacing, then met her gaze again. "It's sure good to see you."

Chapter 8

Oliver

Oliver could scarcely believe his good fortune. He'd wanted time with Carrie, and here she sat like a queen on her throne in Kesia's little café. A dot of gravy smudged the corner of her mouth, drawing his attention. But he shouldn't stare at her lips. It might give him ideas. Even though Hightower was nowhere around to chastise them for "fraternizing," Kesia might not appreciate his kissing one of her customers.

He rested one elbow on the counter and offered a bright smile. "So you've stumbled upon Miss Kesia's place, huh? Lucky you. I've eaten nearly every meal here since I started workin' at the factory coming up on two months now. She's the best cook in town."

Kesia flapped her hands at him, her twinkling eyes shining with a fondness he reciprocated a dozen times over. "Now how could'ja know there's no better cook if you've only been eatin' here?"

Oliver had eaten at the finest restaurants in Wichita, Kansas City, even France. But he didn't dare say so. He gave a cavalier shrug. "Some things a man just knows. An' I have to say, I envy the man who snags you for his bride."

The older woman tittered, her rosy face growing rosier. "Well, you're a flatterer for sure, but I know how you like my biscuits. Lemme get you half a dozen along with a bowl o' venison stew."

"That sounds perfect, Kesia. Thank you." He waited until she bustled off and then nodded toward the bowl of pie resting undisturbed in front of Carrie. "If you've got any qualms about trusting Miss Kesia's cooking, set 'em aside. Your mouth'll surely thank you for letting it taste her peach pie."

Carrie wrinkled her nose prettily. "I've already indulged in her delectable pot roast and vegetables, so I'm aware of her culinary skills." She scooped up an acorn-sized blob of whipped cream with her finger and poked it into her mouth. When she licked her lips clean, she captured the little spot of gravy as well. "I'm not reluctant to trust her pie. I'm just too well sated at the moment to risk adding more to my stomach."

Oliver blinked. He'd struggled to maintain his workman's style speech in front of this woman, and suddenly he understood why. She spoke like someone with breeding, inviting him to do the same. He blurted, "You're educated."

She drew back, her eyes widening in alarm. "Wh-what?"

Father always fussed about Oliver consorting with the underprivileged. **"They'll likely pursue you to gain access to your wealth. A man with money must always be diligent against gold diggers."** He'd heard the warning so many times it rang through his memory without invitation. But if she came from a background similar to his, he could set aside his reluctance to get to know her better.

He leaned forward slightly, lowering his voice to keep their conversation private from the others still enjoying one of Miss Kesia's homemade dinners. "Where did you study?" His heart beat with hope. "Abroad?"

Her face paled. "You're mistaken. I'm not educated."

He frowned. "You must be. The way you speak, the words you choose." She shook her head with great emphasis. The coiling strands of hair trailing down her neck slapped against her shoulders, and one delightful corkscrew curl slipped loose from its moorings to frame her cheek. "I read a lot, that's all. I'm particularly fond of English literature. Have you ever read Bunyan's **Pilgrim's Progress**? It's one of my favorites." Her hand trembling slightly, she lifted her fork and pressed the tines through the pie's flaky crust. She took a bite, swallowed, then sent a quavery grin at him. "You were right—this is scrumptious."

Oliver watched, puzzled, as she shifted her focus to the pastry. She meant to turn the conversational tide. But why? Did she fear he'd tell Hightower she possessed education that qualified her beyond the position of a mere toter? A hopeful thought entered his mind. If he divulged his background of affluence, might she repay him in kind with an honest answer?

He opened his mouth, prepared to spill his secret, but he caught himself and clamped his jaws shut. He couldn't tell her. Not yet. Not until he'd examined every aspect of factory work. When he became its manager, he wanted a plan in place to ascertain his workers were content on the job. Happy employees were hardworking employees—that was Father's motto. And what better way to learn what was needed than to move among the workers, becoming one of them? But if he told even one person the entire truth, word might spread through the factory, and then the workers would keep their distance from him the way they did with Hightower. They'd never trust him with their concerns.

"Here you go, Ollie." Kesia slid a plate of biscuits and a large bowl of stew in front of him. Steam rose from the bowl, creating little beads of condensation on the peach fuzz above her upper lip. "Sorry it took me so long. That scroungy cat showed up at my back door again, yowling loud enough to scare the moon out of the sky. So I tossed it some scraps to shut it up."

Oliver hid a smile. Kesia's disgruntled tone didn't fool him. She liked that old yellow-and-white-striped tabby. And Carrie's actions—pretending to bury herself in a piece of pie—didn't fool him, either. Anyone could see she was only chopping it into pieces rather than eating it.

Kesia must have noticed Carrie's destruction, too, because she frowned at the bowl. "Here now, you're makin' a mess of that pie. If you ain't hungry, just leave it."

Carrie's cheeks glowed pink. She put down her fork. "I'm sorry, Miss Kesia. I hate to waste it, but your good pot roast dinner filled me quite adequately."

Kesia's smile returned. "No worries. It won't go to waste. I'll feed it to the cat."

A bemused grin twitched at the corners of Carrie's mouth. "The cat eats peach pie?"

"The cat eats anything I throw at it." She rolled her eyes, feigning great disgust. "I'm just sure as sure it's expectin'. Won't be long, an' I'll be runnin' over with kittens. An' then what'll I do?"

Oliver, his gaze on the turn of Carrie's delicate jaw, said, "You'll give them peach pie, too, because you can't resist feeding any hungry creature that comes along." He nudged Carrie lightly with his elbow. "You're new here, so you probably don't realize Kesia doesn't ask for money in exchange for the food she serves."

Carrie turned a startled look at Kesia. "You don't? But then how—"

"Now that ain't quite all the way true, Ollie. Don't be makin' me out to be some saint." Kesia, her lips set in a scowl, snatched a rag from her apron pocket and set to scrubbing the spot where the filling from Carrie's pie had splashed over the edge of her bowl.

Oliver chuckled. Kesia was the closest thing to a saint he'd ever met. He clarified, "She doesn't ask a set amount for the food she serves. She lets every person put whatever he can afford into the bucket as payment. And if some can't afford anything at all, well"—he shrugged—"she feeds 'em anyway."

Tears swam in Carrie's eyes, deepening her irises to a rich, dark chocolate. "That's so kind of you, Miss Kesia."

Kesia grunted, but her cheeks wore bright red banners. "Oh, listen to his ballyhoo. He's just finaglin' for another packet o' ham an' cheese sandwiches— that's what he's doin'." She shook the rag free of crumbs and jammed it back into her pocket. "If you're wantin' more sandwiches for tomorrow's lunch, Ollie, just say so. No need to carry on like a carpetbagger."

He and Carrie exchanged a grin, and awareness of their silent communication filled his chest. He forced his attention back to Kesia. "I do need a box lunch for tomorrow." He gave Carrie a questioning look. "And Miss Carrie might need one, too. Am I right?"

Carrie sighed, scrunching her face into an embarrassed grimace. "He's right, Miss Kesia. I...I don't cook."

Oliver's curiosity rose another notch. The only women he'd encountered who didn't cook were women of wealth, who had staff to see to meals.

"You don't cook?" Kesia's graying eyebrows flew high. "But—" She covered her mouth with two fingers. Sympathy softened her expression. "Oh. You were orphaned. I s'pose you didn't have a mama to teach you, then." She patted Carrie's hand. "Well, don't you worry. I'll fix you up with a real nice lunch. Ollie here favors my smoked-ham-and-white-cheese sandwiches. Make the cheese myself with milk from a nanny goat. That sound all right to you?"

Carrie smiled, but Oliver noted that it wavered. "Your ham-and-cheese sandwiches would suit me just fine."

"I'll go put 'em together for you right now. Yours, too, Ollie. An' I'll throw in a piece or two of the gingerbread left over from this morning's breakfast." Kesia scurried through the kitchen doorway.

Oliver contemplated Kesia's comment about Carrie being an orphan. Might it be, following her parents' demise, someone robbed her of her inheritance? If so, her work at the factory would make sense. He rested his elbow on the counter, leaned in, and asked softly, "Miss Carrie, about you losing your parents... Did—"

Carrie slid from the stool. "I'll be sure to reimburse Miss Kesia well for the dinner." She must have had more bites of the pie than he'd realized, because cinnamon and peaches wafted on her warm breath. She hurried to the bucket, her skirts swirling, and retrieved a little purse from her pocket. She scowled into the purse's belly. His heart tripped. How much could she afford to pay, considering the small amount a toter earned at the factory?

He angled his gaze to his plate to allow

her privacy. A solid **clunk** sounded. Oliver gave a start. Unless she'd tossed it into the bucket with force to feign a large contribution—and he couldn't imagine her doing such a thing—she had dropped a heavy coin. He waited until she'd slipped out the door. Then he briefly abandoned his supper to peek into the bucket. On top of the scattered pennies, nickels, and dimes, a silver dollar glinted up at him.

Oliver stared in amazement at the coin, envisioning the woman who'd paid twice what he'd ever deposited into Kesia's bucket for a meal. She must be rich. And educated. Yet she worked as a toter in his father's chocolate factory.

Kesia stepped from the kitchen, holding a package wrapped in paper and tied with twine. She searched the café, her wrinkled face pursed in confusion. "Where'd Carrie go? I got her sandwiches an' gingerbread here."

Oliver said, "I'll take it to her, Kesia. We work the same shift at the factory."

"That sounds fine." Kesia plopped the packet into Oliver's waiting hands. "She's a right nice young lady. An' the way she set into her supper, I'm thinkin' she doesn't eat proper." Her wattle jiggled as she lifted her chin high. "But if she comes here again, I'm gonna offer to teach her how to cook a thing or two so she can see to her own needs. Ain't right bein' her age an' not able to fend for herself around a cookstove." She turned and headed back to her kitchen.

His feet moving slowly, Oliver returned to his stool and sat. Questions cluttered his mind, questions he felt certain Carrie would avoid answering. But he wanted to know. Because if she was all he suspected her of being, he'd take her home and introduce her to his parents as soon as he could end his charade.

Caroline

Caroline reached the boarding hotel, closed herself in the little cubby containing the hotel's lone telephone, and called Noble. As wonderful as it was to hear his familiar voice—a voice that had calmed her nightmares, patiently delivered lessons, and encouraged her to seek God's way above all others—she kept the call short. Partly because she had little of a professional nature to share other than she'd been hired. But mostly because Noble knew her well. His investigative skills combined with his deep affection for her would surely detect her confusion concerning Ollie Moore. And she wasn't ready to talk about the strange attraction she felt toward Ollie. Not even with her beloved mentor.

"Keep your journal, as I know you will," Noble said, his deep voice more fatherly than authoritative as it crackled through the line, "and call again Saturday evening. Maybe by then you'll have uncovered some tidbit that will help us learn what happened to Harmon."

A quick resolution was always the commission's preference. But Caroline realized a quick resolution meant moving on to the next job. For the first time in the nearly seven years she had posed as a factory worker to explore firsthand the working conditions, she had no burning passion to finish and move on. What odd hold did this place...or its people...have on her?

"Rest well tonight, Caroline." Noble's kind blessing warmed her heart.

She hugged the telephone earpiece tight against her head. Although an illusive something held her here, she missed Noble and his sweet wife—the best people she'd ever known. "Thank you, Noble. Greet Annamarie for me, and tell her I've found a wonderful little café where I can take my meals."

A laugh came from the other end of the line. "She still intends to make a decent cook of you someday. But I'll tell her. Good-bye."

"Good-bye." Caroline placed the earpiece in its cradle and climbed the stairs to her third-floor, one-room apartment, her leg muscles protesting the entire way. She always requested the least ostentatious accommodations, claiming it cut costs, but Noble knew the truth. Why put her in a full-size apartment with a kitchen that wouldn't be used? She was a terrible cook. But not even Noble knew the reason why she resisted time in a kitchen.

She pushed the memories aside and moved to the little desk in the corner, determined to focus on her purpose for being in Sinclair. She opened her journal and recorded the day's feeble findings and her expenses. As she wrote "Dinner at Durham's Café, $1," she gasped. She'd asked Kesia to make her a lunch, but then, trying to escape Ollie Moore and his question, she'd left without waiting for it.

Recalling the look of elation on Ollie's face—and it had been elation, not surprise—when he'd accused her of being educated, she closed her eyes and swallowed a mournful moan. His esteem for her had gone up, and she'd gloried in it. But then she'd instinctively told him the truth. She was not educated. At least not in the way he'd inferred. But she was smart enough to know she'd piqued his curiosity, and that could be a problem.

Setting the commission journal aside, she lifted a second one from the desk drawer—her personal journal, which no one except God ever saw. She flipped to a fresh page, dipped her pen, and wrote in her neat, slanting script. **Dear God, I find myself drawn to Ollie Moore. I hardly know him, so these feelings make no sense, but they're real. And I can't let them continue. The more we're together, the more I'll be forced to lie to him, and I don't want to lie to him. So keep us apart, please.**

She paused, her heart pounding. Miss Kesia's comment about setting her sights on marriage had left her unsettled. She'd never wanted to be beholden to a man, and she'd never met a man who stirred her affections enough to consider breaking her lifelong resolve. Until now. If God honored her request, might she be abandoning a relationship with the only man who possessed the ability to touch her heart? Such an opportunity shouldn't be squandered. But what other choice did she have? She was here under false pretenses. No man, especially a man as caring and open as Ollie Moore, deserved to be duped.

Placing her pen against the page, she added, **I mean it, God. I want us kept as far apart as possible.** But even as she blew on the ink to dry it, she realized another lie had just been released.

Chapter 9

Caroline

Caroline, her leg muscles aching from yesterday's long day on her feet, trotted awkwardly toward the loading table as the shift buzzer blared in her ears. The other two toters, Edith and Tessy—middle-aged women who'd worked together for almost a year and had exhibited no desire to draw Caroline into their tightly woven friendship—were already at the tables, reaching for trays. The night shift always left trays filled and waiting so the morning arrivals could immediately begin toting.

The pair exchanged snide looks as Caroline puffed to a halt next to the table. The taller one, Edith, sniffed. "We've already carted a full load each." Perspiration glistened on Tessy's lined forehead. Her chin doubled as she lowered her head and glared at Caroline through thick eyebrows. "You came late yesterday, too."

Yesterday the beggar had slowed her. Today she'd overslept after tossing and turning far into the night. Caroline lifted a stack and offered an apologetic grimace. "I'm sorry. I—"

"Carrie!"

At the intruding male voice, Edith and Tessy pursed their lips and ambled off, trays in their arms. Caroline inwardly groaned. Hadn't she spent half the night begging God to separate her from this man? And here he came, pursuing her first thing. She ignored the shout and shuffled after Edith and Tessy.

Ollie fell into step beside her. "Carrie, I brought the sandwiches Kesia made for you."

She should have known he would volunteer to play delivery boy for the affable Kesia. **God, weren't You**

listening at all last night? Aware of the disapproving glances being sent her way by the other toters, she ignored Ollie, placed the trays on the transport cart, and then limped toward the loading tables, where more trays waited.

Ollie shoved the paper-wrapped packet at her. "Here. Take this to the lunchroom before you carry another load of candy."

Her hands closed around the lumpy brown packet, and she stopped in surprise. "It's cold!" She cradled the package against her middle. Although it was early fall, the vats of boiling chocolate and assorted fillings kept the factory as warm as the steamiest August day. "How can it be cold when it's so hot in here?"

He grinned. "I have an icebox in my apartment. Keeps things nice and cool."

She lifted the packet to her cheek. "Oh, it feels delightful."

A low chuckle rolled from his chest. "Go put it in one of the lunchroom iceboxes. You can hug it again on your break."

What was she doing? She must look like a ninny! She pushed it back at him. "I can't take this. I left before paying for it."

He held his palms up, rejecting the packet. "No worries. I dropped two dimes in the bucket for you."

Carrie tucked the little bundle in the bend of her elbow and dug her coin purse from her pocket. "Then let me—"

"No need." His wide, friendly grin set her heart flopping in her chest like a banked trout. "Twenty cents was a small price to pay to put Kesia's mind at ease." He tipped forward, assuming a conspiratorial air. "She's worried you don't eat right. Says she hopes to teach you to cook so you can fend for yourself better."

Embarrassment washed away on a flood of discomfort. She took a backward step, and the packet of sandwiches fell to the floor. She started to bend down and retrieve it, but a catch in her back jolted her upright once more. Ollie bent over with ease and scooped it up, then extended it toward her. She clutched her little coin purse two-handed, her pulse scampering in frantic beats. The sweet smile in his eyes held her captive.

He held the packet out to her. "Here you are."

"No."

"You have to eat. Take it."

Remembering the delicious meal she'd consumed yesterday evening, her stomach pinched at the thought of rejecting Kesia's sandwiches. She would accept them on one condition. "Not unless you let me pay for them."

"I don't want your money."

"I cannot allow you to pay for my lunch."

"It was only twenty cents!"

"Which is a significant portion of your pay as a janitor."

He shook his head, a wry grin playing on the corners of his lips. "You're a very stubborn woman, Miss Lang." His lunge for the sandwiches had dislodged his cap, so it settled low on his forehead, giving him a rakish appearance. Oh, but he was irresistible. And he shouldn't call her stubborn when he so thoroughly exemplified the word. A lesser man would have thrown up his hands in frustration and stormed away, but there he stood, trying to convince her to take those sandwiches so she wouldn't miss her lunch.

She swallowed a nervous giggle. "I know."

"Very well." He shifted the packet to one hand and held his cupped palm to her. "Twenty cents, please."

She removed two slim dimes from her purse and placed them in his hand. His fingers closed around the coins, brushing her flesh with his fingertips. She jerked back as if stung. "Th-thank you."

One of the sorters with whom Caroline had sat at yesterday's lunch break—Stella, as Caroline recalled—bustled by. She sent a stormy glare in their direction, reminding Caroline she'd spent too much time arguing over the sandwiches instead of working.

She snatched the packet from his hands. "I need to get back to work." She moved to the long table as quickly as her stiff muscles would allow, placed the wrapped sandwiches underneath it, then lifted a stack of trays.

Ollie traipsed along beside her as she headed for the carts. "Tell you what... Since I have an icebox at my apartment and the cheese on those sandwiches should be kept cool—Kesia said so—I'll store your lunch at my place every night and bring it in the morning for you."

Caroline knew she should say no. Deliberately meet Ollie every morning?

How would she manage to stay focused on her investigation if she started each day gazing into his green-gold eyes? She blew out a huff of aggravation and said, "All right."

His grin lit the room. Walking backward, he gave a wave. "Great! Bye now, Carrie."

Caroline plopped the trays onto the cart. Chocolates jiggled, losing a few of their nutmeat sprinkles.

Tessy, who'd just placed her stack of trays on the opposite side of the cart, gasped. "Be careful! If their tops aren't completely covered, the sorters'll set them aside. Too much waste, an' it comes out of our pay!"

"I'm sorry," Caroline said as the two

women shuffled toward the loading tables side by side. "I'll be more careful from now on."

"See that you are," the woman snapped, her dark eyes flashing fire.

Over the course of the next two weeks, Caroline often thought about her promise to be careful. She exercised great care in lifting, carrying, and lowering trays, despite her perpetually aching muscles. None of the chocolates suffered damage due to careless handling. She only wished she could say the same about her heart.

No matter what time she entered Durham's Café for her supper—early if Letta didn't have a great deal of home-work, later if she did—Ollie was sure to amble in only a few minutes behind her. She began to suspect he hid around the corner, watching for her arrival. She considered taking her meals elsewhere, but she couldn't bear to abandon Kesia, and she truly enjoyed visiting with her at the end of the day. So she didn't argue when Kesia gave Ollie two lunches each evening, even though she knew she'd have to meet him in the morning to retrieve one. Those brief minutes each morning were torture as her prayer for God to keep her away from Ollie went unanswered.

At least she was able to begin gathering information for Noble. At lunch—the only time employees had an opportunity to visit without fear of reprimand—she asked dozens of questions. By maintaining a casual air even when the answers stirred anger or frustration, she drew out the other workers' concerns and complaints. She began purchasing bags of licorice whips, which she distributed to the youngest workers, and with the candor of children, they eagerly responded to her queries while munching on the treats.

But no matter whom she asked—child or adult—about the investigator who'd fallen down the elevator shaft, no one would say more than "That was a dreadful accident." Caroline had learned to read beneath answers. If people blinked too rapidly, refused to meet her gaze, or fidgeted while answering a question, she presumed they were hiding something. She'd observed none of those suspicious gestures from any of the people who'd spoken about Harmon Bratcher, and she began to wonder if Noble's concerns were baseless. Perhaps Bratcher's death was, just as the workers claimed, a dreadful accident.

She said as much to Noble when she made her Saturday night call, and his sigh of disappointment carried clearly through the line.

"Caroline, I wouldn't have sent you to Sinclair if there weren't sound reasons for suspecting something more sinister. You know how vocal Harmon had been about changing the entry age for workers. That kind of talk always stirs up trouble in factories, especially ones with a high number of child laborers. I looked over the notes he sent during his time at Dinsmore's. More than thirty percent of the workers are ages ten to sixteen."

Caroline had counted the number of children on the floor during her hours but hadn't realized the percentage was so high. She ached anew at children spending their tender years toiling. "But in the two weeks I've been here, I haven't uncovered one inkling of evidence that his fall down the shaft wasn't accidental."

"Because you're going by hearsay." Noble's fatherly tone turned stiffly professional. "Caroline, you've been trained better than that. Asking questions is only part of an investigation. What else have you done to determine the likelihood of an accident?"

To Caroline's chagrin, she couldn't offer a reply. Because she'd done nothing. She stood ramrod straight in the little cubby with the receiver to her ear, fully expecting a well-deserved lecture. Instead, she heard Noble's soft intake of breath, a sign he was thinking.

"Perhaps you're on the wrong shift. According to the notes Harmon sent, he spent the majority of his time overseeing the night shift. It's possible you simply need to connect with the right people to determine whether or not the death was the result of faulty equipment or something much less innocent. Find out if there's a night-shift opening, and take it if there is."

"What if there isn't a suitable opening?"

"You may have to stay put until one becomes available."

Caroline's emotions seesawed between elation and angst. Oh, to enjoy more time with Letta, Kesia, and—she sucked in a breath, unable to deny it—Ollie. But more time meant greater expense for the commission and more toiling under Hightower's supervision. Something about the man set her teeth on edge. She pushed aside thoughts of Hightower and focused on Noble's voice crackling through the lines.

"Of course, if you manage to unearth evidence that precludes the necessity of lengthening your stay, we'll bring you back at once. But we need facts. And make sure you gather lots of notes about the working conditions as well, to complete Harmon's assignment."

"Yes, Noble."

"Caroline,"—his tone changed again,

losing its impersonal edge and becoming paternal—"Annamarie and I miss you around here. We'll be happy to see this issue solved so you can come home."

Caroline melted into the wooden chair pressed against the wall. "I miss you, too, Noble." For the hundredth time she pondered the twist of fate that had allowed her parents to birth seven children—none of whom received half the care and attention Kesia offered an alley cat—while Noble and Annamarie were barren. When Noble had carried her, racked with fever and so weak from lack of nourishment she couldn't even walk, from her roach-infested cellar room to his home where Annamarie nursed her back to health, she'd finally been given a glimpse of what it meant to be loved. She owed this couple her very life.

And look how she repaid them—doing a slipshod investigation and spending her hours mooning over a factory worker instead of focusing on her job. She gripped the receiver with both hands and spoke firmly into the mouthpiece. "I'll finish

Harmon's report. I'll learn as much as I can about the elevator and how it works, and I'll talk to people who worked with him. If something is awry at the Dinsmore factory, I'll find it."

Chapter 10

Gordon

Gordon rested his palms on the ledge of his private observation window and peered down at the work floor. A satisfied sigh heaved from his lungs. Yesterday afternoon's lecture about dawdling seemed to have had its desired effect. The workers resembled ants scurrying over a mound of sugar cubes this morning—busy, busy, busy. When Mr. Fulton Dinsmore made his monthly appearance at the end of the week, he'd find nothing amiss. Not while Gordon was in charge.

He returned to his desk and slid into the tall, polished chair. Rocking gently, he glanced at the assignment roster laid out on the center of the desk. Every position filled. He hoped Dinsmore wouldn't toss the name of another potential worker in Gordon's direction. He still wasn't sure why Dinsmore had been so set on instilling that   arrogant Ollie Moore at the factory. His pulse skittered at an uncomfortable thought. Might Dinsmore have placed Moore as an informant, to observe and report on Gordon's leadership skills?

Gordon got up and stalked the length of the office and back again, chewing on the inside of his cheek. It was common in some of the larger factories, but Gordon had never suspected Dinsmore of the tactic. Mainly because, with the exception of Moore, he'd left the hiring to Gordon.

Of course, Gordon bribed a handful of workers to share any possible breaches of conduct. And why not? He couldn't be everywhere, so those additional eyes ensured he could give comprehensive reports to Dinsmore when asked. The information he'd received from Stella, one of his favorite tattlers, rolled in the back of his mind. His pacing came to a halt. Apparently his newest toter, Carrie Lang, had begun receiving packets from Ollie Moore on the morning of her second day of employment. Additionally, she'd spent much of her lunch break asking questions—general questions about the factory's operation and more specific questions about jobs assigned to the youngest workers. Gordon scowled. Did he have yet another crusader like Bratcher in his ranks?

Dinsmore always praised Gordon for his ability to turn a tidy profit in the factory. He rewarded Gordon well for his efforts, too, with a year-end bonus equal to one percent of all monies earned above expenses. Bratcher's insistence on hiring able men to fill the positions currently filled by children meant shelling out higher wages. No man would be satisfied with a mere two dollars a week, but children snatched those coins from his hand along with a bag of imperfect chocolates every Saturday and dashed off content. The more children he employed, the more profit he'd show. Any fool could see the wisdom in hiring youngsters.

That pesky investigator's plunge down the elevator shaft had ended his crusade, and although Gordon wouldn't celebrate the man's death—the entire situation had been ghastly—neither would he mourn it. When Bratcher died, his crusading fire had died with him. Peace had settled once more on Hightower's world. And he didn't want someone else—not even the attractive young woman Carrie Lang—stirring those embers to life again.

Perhaps a private conference with Miss Lang was in order. A smile twitched his lips. Yes. He'd enjoy a few moments alone with the newest hire. Perhaps her questions were mere curiosity, although her connection to Moore increased Gordon's suspicions. Whether her queries were innocent or intentional, some carefully worded warnings should be enough to silence them. And if she chose to ignore his warnings, he'd just let her go. Problem solved.

Caroline

"Hey! Carrie!"

At the shrill call Caroline balanced the trays bearing Chocolate-Covered Caramel-Nut Squares against her hips and paused in her trek toward the loading carts. One of the factory's message bearers, a freckle-faced ten-year-old named Otis, bounded to her side. Caroline, although weary, offered a smile in an attempt to erase the furrows marching across the boy's forehead. No child should look so serious. "What is it, Otis?"

The boy wrung his hands, his gaze flicking toward the observation window high above them. "S'posed to tell you Mr. Hightower wants to see you."

"All right. Let me deposit these trays, and I'll—"

"No, miss. He says now." Otis shuffled back and forth on dirty bare feet. "An' he says to consider your meetin' with him as your lunch break."

Despite her desire to put Otis at ease, she couldn't stop her own frown from forming. All morning she'd anticipated the plum pudding and rich sausage bread she'd purchased from Kesia. Of all the lunches she'd enjoyed from Kesia's kitchen during her time in Sinclair, the sausage bread was her favorite. If Mr. Hightower robbed her of her entire lunch break, she'd be none too happy. But she wouldn't launch her frustration on the little messenger.

Forcing a smile, she gave a nod. "Very well, Otis. Tell him I'm coming."

The other two toters sent Caroline scathing looks and muttered to each other when she lowered her trays to the loading table and moved away. She hoped Otis would tell them she had no choice but to abandon her post. She caught her skirt between her fingers and mounted the stairs, her thoughts rushing ahead to the meeting. What could Mr. Hightower want with her? Might he be advancing her to the position of packager?

According to the other workers, Hightower rarely advanced people until they'd been employed for three months.

She'd only been at Dinsmore's a little more than two weeks, but she'd worked hard to gain Hightower's approval, just as Noble had instructed. Perhaps her efforts would soon be rewarded. Oh, how she hoped so. She'd already assured Noble the factory had some of the safest work practices she'd seen, although she did feel a few jobs given to women and children should be performed by men. Even so, considering other factories she'd investigated, she had few complaints about Dinsmore's operation. Now if she could fully investigate the elevator, either uncovering a malfunction or finding proof that Bratcher's plunge could not have been accidental, then she could complete her private report and move on.

She paused on the top step, contemplating all that leaving Sinclair would entail. Abandoning Letta, who daily blossomed as the world of learning opened before her; leaving Kesia, who in a very short time had become a dear friend; and losing contact with Ollie, whose pale-green eyes and endearing grin haunted her dreams even as she strove to keep her distance from him. Closing this assignment would cause her much loss, yet it would please Noble. And pleasing Noble should take priority over everything else. It **should**—but did it? She refused to contemplate the answer.

Setting her feet in motion, she scurried across the landing to the doorway leading to Mr. Hightower's office. The door stood open, presumably in readiness for her entrance, but she paused and tapped on the doorframe.

The man sat at his desk, leaning back in his massive wooden chair and cupping his chin with one hand. He didn't even glance in her direction, but at her knock he said, "Come in, Miss Lang, and close the door behind you."

Apprehension caused Caroline's scalp to prickle. Being in the factory manager's office with the door closed held no appeal, yet she shouldn't disregard his instruction. Not if she was to be trusted with a more responsible position. She clicked the latch into place and then crossed to his desk.

"You wanted to speak with me?"

"Yes." Very slowly he turned, the chair springs releasing a low **ting** with the movement. His gaze seemed fixed on the door behind her rather than on her face. "Apparently there is some confusion concerning your duties here at Dinsmore's."

Caroline crinkled her brow. "Sir?"

With a jerk of his head, he pinned her with a fierce glare. "Confusion, Miss Lang. You are apparently confused."

A cheeky retort formed on the tip of her tongue, but she sent up a quick prayer for control and managed to swallow the comment. "I'm sorry, sir. About what am I confused?"

He eased to his feet, his palms on the desk top as if poised to leap over it. "You are here to work. To carry filled trays from one area of the factory to another. You are not here to interrogate other employees or to make sheep's eyes at certain employees of the opposite gender or even to make suggestions for improving this factory's operation."

Caroline's thoughts raced. She'd been careless. Noble had instructed her about proceeding with caution, never arousing suspicion, but somehow she'd failed. Apparently her infatuation with Ollie Moore, despite her best efforts to curb it, had affected her performance as an investigator. Humiliation brought a rush of heat to her cheeks. She cared not a whit about being berated by Hightower, but realization that she'd failed Noble pierced her deeply. She lowered her head.

"The questions will stop, Miss Lang." Mr. Hightower rounded the desk, barking out one word with every step. "The flirtation will stop, Miss Lang. The suggestion that children should not be allowed on the factory floor will stop, Miss Lang."

He stood directly before her, his presence commanding her to meet his gaze. Slowly she raised her face and looked into his angry, glittering eyes. And as he attempted to skewer her with his fury, she found herself racing backward through time to another angry boss, another set of unyielding commands. The remembered fear and helplessness of those moments washed over her, causing her knees to tremble. She'd only been a child. She'd had no defense against the one who owned her every waking minute. But she wasn't a child any longer, and whether he realized it or not, Mr. Gordon Hightower was not her real supervisor.

Indignation filled her, followed by a rush of strength only her years of serving with Noble could have developed. Setting her shoulders square, she drew in a breath of fortification. "Mr. Hightower, I assure you I have never indulged in unnecessary conversation while on duty." She deliberately used a firm yet reasonable tone lest she be accused of disrespect. "Any questions I've asked other employees have been during our lunch break—the normal give-and-take between co-workers. As for flirtation, you are mistaken. I am here to work"—he needn't be apprised of the true nature of her work—"and nothing more. So it seems, sir, the confusion lies somewhere other than with me. Now if you'll excuse me, I have trays awaiting transport." She turned to leave.

"I'm not finished with you yet!"

The roar, coming from directly behind her left ear, made her jump. She froze in place. He stomped around her, stopping between her and the door. "There is still the issue of your suggestions for improvement."

Caroline set her lips in a tight line. She couldn't deny his third accusation. She had mentioned her concerns about youngsters being given responsibilities beyond their years and the possible ramifications should they fail in their tasks. There were many truths she was forced to withhold, given her purpose for entering the factory, but she wouldn't deny her feelings about children working long hours rather than attending school.

"It was never my intent to insult you or Mr. Dinsmore." Caroline's mouth felt dry in the face of Mr. Hightower's intimidation. She swallowed and continued, drawing on the bravado that had carried her through many difficult assignments. "But surely you can see—"

"What I see, Miss Lang, is an employee who lacks the proper recognition of her place." Mr. Hightower leaned close, his hot breath smacking her in the face. "If your suggestions are wanted or needed, they will be requested. Until then, you will remember your only purpose here is to carry trays of chocolate."

"But—"

His eyes narrowed, becoming slits of malevolence. "Miss Lang, on the day you were assigned the position as toter, did you take from this factory a goodly portion of Vanilla Creams?"

Instantly an image of Ollie gallantly offering the handkerchief bundle on his open palms filled her memory. A smile threatened, and she ducked her head before Mr. Hightower witnessed it. "Yes, sir. I confess I did carry away several of the candies from the trays used to prove my ability as a toter."

He cleared his throat—a raw, guttural sound. "Do you realize that you've just confessed to stealing?"

Caroline recalled Ollie's reasoning that the candies would be thrown away anyway. She also recalled telling Letta it was never right to take something that didn't belong to her. Empty of any defense, she met his gaze and stood in silent acceptance of his statement.

"Rule number five for employees of this factory is 'No removal of goods without express permission from the management.' I do not recall granting you permission to help yourself to the creams." A knowing look crept across his face. "As a matter of fact, I believe I told you clearly that making a habit of helping yourself to the candy would result in your instant dismissal."

Cold chills broke out across Caroline's frame. Would he let her go? She hadn't finished her investigation. She couldn't lose this job and go back to Noble in defeat. She clasped her hands behind her back to control the trembling. "Mr. Hightower, it only happened the one time. It won't happen again."

"I can make sure it doesn't by removing you from the employment roster."

So she'd lost before she'd even begun. Defeated, she offered a miserable nod and hung her head.

"But I don't believe that's necessary."

She shot her gaze upward, uncertain she'd heard correctly. "You aren't releasing me?"

He pushed his jacket aside to slip his hand into his pocket. He raised his other hand and twisted his finger through the coil of hair dangling along her throat. "Not this time."

Something in his expression frightened her even more than the prospect of being fired. Mildred's warning about Mr. Hightower cornering the girls to steal a kiss rose from her memory. Her stomach roiled. She wanted to step away, but he continued to hold the strand of hair, trapping her in place. Besides, retreating would take her deeper into his office and farther from the door. She wouldn't create a greater distance between herself and the exit.

Lord, protect me...

As quickly as he'd caught hold of her hair, he let go, giving the coil a stinging yank as he drew his hand downward. Caroline's legs nearly gave way with the intense rush of relief. He stalked to his desk, leaving her quivering in indignation near the door.

"But the incident is on my report. Should you choose to disregard any more of the factory's rules, I will have no choice but to send you packing." He spun to face her. "Do I make myself clear, Miss Lang?"

She forced a reply through clenched teeth. "Yes, sir."

"Very well, then. Go. And no lollygagging in the lunchroom."

Caroline gave a quick nod and threw the door open. She dashed onto the landing, peeking over her shoulder to be certain he wasn't pursuing her, and she collided with a solid chest. The air whooshed from her lungs, and a pair of hands caught her arms, holding her upright. She'd barreled into Ollie Moore.

Chapter 11

Oliver

Oliver held Carrie's arms tightly. She trembled beneath his hands. Alarm bells rang in the back of his mind. Although he'd never witnessed it, he'd heard rumors about Hightower making advances on some of the factory girls. Rage rose, and he leaned close to Carrie's face and rasped, "Did he touch you?"

She shook her head and wriggled free of his grasp. Stepping a few feet away from him, she wrapped her arms across her stomach and shuddered.

Oliver frowned. She was lying. But why protect Hightower? Had the man threatened her into silence? He took a step toward her, his hand extended in entreaty. "Carrie—"

"Moore!" Hightower's harsh bark stopped Oliver in his tracks. "Get in here."

Oliver resented the man's dictatorial attitude, but he had little choice except to obey if he hoped to continue as a worker. He offered Carrie an apologetic look, then turned and strode into Hightower's office. "What do you need?" Despite his efforts to be respectful, his words held a note of challenge.

"I had to release two craters this morning—lazy bums were caught sleeping **again**. Post this notice about openings on the job board." Hightower thrust a paper at Oliver.

Oliver picked up the square of paper and read it. He tapped it with his finger. "You haven't indicated which shift."

Hightower yanked it back and scrawled the words night shift below the request.

Oliver tipped forward, his gaze on the page. "Qualifications?"

The man huffed. He added, **Must be able to wield a hammer.**

"Any age restrictions?"

Another mighty huff exploded.

Oliver gritted his teeth. Hightower's penchant for expelling blasts of air grated on his nerves. Such a denigrating sound, meant to intimidate. Hightower whisked the paper across the desk. "It's hardly a skilled position, Moore. Any fool can bring a hammer down on a tack. No doubt even a woman could do it." He flopped into his chair and yanked a drawer open, his attention shifting to the drawer's contents. "Just post the notice. I'll sort through the contenders for likely candidates."

"All right. Two openings for night-shift craters. Anything else?"

"No."

Oliver turned to leave, eager to find Carrie and ascertain she was all right. "Moore!"

Oliver paused in the doorway but didn't turn around.

"Fulton Dinsmore, the factory owner, intends to visit later this week. He's requested a personal meeting with you." A thread of jealousy seemed to wind through Hightower's statement.

Oliver swallowed a snort of amusement, envisioning Hightower clenching his fists in frustration. "Oh?"

"Yes." The word snapped out. "You will behave appropriately in his presence."

Oliver always behaved appropriately in his father's presence. Since he had nothing to say concerning Hightower's demand, he offered no response.

Hightower blasted another aggravated breath. "You may go."

Oliver darted for the stairway. He rounded the bend and came upon Carrie, who stood just inside the door at the top of the stairway, her back pressed to the wall, and her pale face aimed toward him. "Carrie..."

"I want to be a crater."

He jolted. Whatever he'd expected her to say, it wasn't that.

"It's a night position, correct?"

Oliver nodded, unable to locate his voice. This woman always managed to surprise him.

"Then I wish to apply. Do you think I

have a chance of being hired?"

He stared at her. Her colorless face and stiff posture indicated a lingering fear from her time in Hightower's office, yet she spoke with strength. No timid hothouse flower, this one. How he admired her. He forced a casual tone. "It'll be up to Hightower, of course, but he gave no specific qualifications other than being able to swing a hammer." If she had the strength to carry the heavy trays of chocolate, she certainly had the strength to pound tacks through wood.

She pursed her lips into a cynical moue. "Yes. I heard his remark that even a woman could do it." With a glib shrug, she pushed off from the wall and opened the door. The factory noises assaulted them, and as she began moving down the stairs, she raised her voice to be heard over the wheeze and rattle of machinery. "So he'd be open to my application?"

Oliver trailed alongside her, his gaze locked on her profile. Her rosy lips were set in a determined line that contrasted with the soft curve of her round cheek.

She was hardly a petite woman—full figured although far from plump. The top of her head reached the underside of his nose, and he stood an inch above six feet. Despite her stature and strong nature, he still desired to protect her. He'd never met a woman who inspired so many conflicting emotions.

He pushed past his musings to answer her question as they moved across the busy floor to the loading tables. "I don't see why not. But I'm curious why you'd want it. Craters earn less than toters, and the night shift is the least desirable of the three shifts."

"I have my reasons." A little pigtailed girl carrying a bag of sugar staggered into their path, and Carrie stopped abruptly to avoid running the child down. She stared after the girl for a moment and then spun on him. "Besides, if I take it, some hapless child will be spared the task of hammering tacks into boards when he should be sleeping."

Her adamancy sent him backward a step. He raised his eyebrows and peered at her, unblinking.

"Are you aware, Ollie, that this factory hires a greater percentage of child workers than any other factory in the state of Kansas?"

Of course he was aware. He and Father had discussed the situation at length, and he was proud of their inclusion of younger workers.

Her eyes blazed as passion ignited her features. "One-third of the workers here are under the age of sixteen. One-third!" Throwing her hands outward, she glowered at him. "Boys who should be sitting in a schoolhouse, dipping some little girl's braid into the inkwell, are instead stacking crates or pushing a broom. Girls who should be making sheep's eyes at the boys are wrapping chocolates with gold foil or sprinkling nuts on the tops of candies. Sprinkling nuts, for heaven's sake!"

Defensiveness tiptoed through Oliver's center, and he found his voice. "Making sheep's eyes at some boy on the opposite side of the schoolroom is more important than earning a wage?"

She narrowed her eyes. "Don't be facetious."

"I'm not. You said girls should be making sheep's eyes instead of working." He slipped his hand into his pocket and leaned his weight on one hip, assuming a casual position that belied the tightness in his chest. "Working gives them a means of providing for themselves or helping their families. Working teaches them a skill they can use well into adulthood. Working—"

"Working steals everything that is precious!" Carrie's voice rose, and several workers paused to look in their direction. Oblivious to the curious gazes, she continued her emotional tirade. "The hours they spend on the factory floor rob them of the opportunity for an education. When they leave the factory, they're so tired they don't want to play. Their lives become a drudgery of work, sleep, work, sleep, and one day they awaken in a grown-up, exhausted body, wondering why they feel so much older than their years." She gestured to the bustling floor at large, her trembling hands pointing toward one work station and then another. "What kind of future does this promise to them, Ollie? Tell me that."

Her impassioned plea moved him. He wouldn't deny a rush of feeling. But did he agree with her? No. His father provided a service to the families of Sinclair by allowing children to earn a wage and learn a craft. Many of the youngsters pushing a broom today would be the ones tomorrow creating new flavors of candies or traveling to distant places to sell Dinsmore's chocolates in new market-places. Their lives would be enriched by the opportunities offered at the factory.

He said staunchly, "A bright one."

Her face crumpled. The depth of disappointment reflected in her deep brown eyes pierced him. But he believed what he'd said, and he wouldn't change it. These children's lives would be better because he and his father were willing to teach them a skill. Remove children from the roster of workers? He had no intention of doing so.

Caroline

Caroline battled the desire to cry. Why did Ollie's words hurt so much? **"A bright one,"** he'd said, completely sure of himself and yet so wrong. Why couldn't he see the harm done to these little ones forced to labor away the most tender years of their lives? Memories from her childhood rose up to haunt her—memories of such tiredness her very bones ached, of hunger that was never satisfied, of stinging blows across her shoulders from the master's rod when she made a mistake. Painful, bitter memories. She wanted so much more for the children of this community. And, admittedly, she wanted Ollie to want more for the children, too.

Defeated, she spoke stiffly. "Please inform Mr. Hightower of my interest in the position as crater."

"Carrie, I—"

She ignored him and scurried to her work station. Over the remainder of the day, Ollie repeatedly moved into her line of vision, his expression pleading. But each time she steadfastly pretended he wasn't there. She had a job to do, and he'd already stolen too much of her focus. Now that he'd made clear his position on child workers, he'd given her the impetus she needed to turn her attention fully to the job Noble had sent her to do.

When she clocked out at the end of her shift, she headed for the job board to see if the third-shift crater positions had been posted. To her surprise, Letta waited in the rectangle of shade cast by the board. The girl's eyes were red rimmed, and rivulets carved by tears decorated her thin, dirty cheeks. Concern immediately rose in Caroline's breast. She hurried to the distraught child.

"Letta, what is it? What's wrong?"

"It's my pa, Miss Carrie. He's terrible sick. Burning up with fever an' hurtin' bad in his gut. I stayed home with him today an' took care of him, but he needs doctorin'. **Real** doctorin'. But he..." Letta gulped, fresh tears raining down her face. "He says we don't got money for a doctor.

I don't know what to do." The girl began
to wail.

Caroline took the girl's hand. "Now
don't worry. I'm sure he—"

"Carrie?" Ollie stepped up beside her,
his gaze sweeping from Letta to Caroline.
"What's the trouble?"

Caroline gave Letta's hand a little tug,
guiding her toward the road. "Nothing
over which you need concern yourself."

Letta called in a wobbly voice, "My pa's
real sick."

Ollie caught up to them. "Should I
summon the factory's physician?"
Caroline sent a startled frown in Ollie's
direction. His kindness touched her, but
something about his query raised
questions in the back of her mind. How
many factory workers used the word
summon?

Letta turned hopeful eyes on Caroline.
"Oh, please, Miss Carrie. Can he fetch
the doc? I'd feel so much better if a real
doctor looked at Pa." Her brow puckered.
"But would he come? That doc's for
factory workers, an' Pa...Pa don't work at

the factory."

Ollie touched Letta's shoulder. "Don't worry. I'll bring him." As if suspecting her desire to flee, he pinned Caroline with a stern gaze. "Wait here. I'll be right back."

Letta shifted from foot to foot, gnawing her thumbnail to the quick, while factory workers filed past. Caroline considered ignoring Ollie's demand and hurrying off to Letta's house without him, but concern about the seriousness of the father's illness held her in place. If the factory doctor was willing to offer his services, she should allow him to do so for Letta's sake.

Only a few minutes had ticked by when Ollie came trotting toward them. A man in a brown three-piece suit, with a gold watch chain looped from vest pocket to pocket, followed close behind him.

Ollie gestured toward the man. "This is Doctor Ernst. He said he'd come with us."

Us? When had Ollie become a party to the errand? Caroline opened her mouth to protest.

"But we must hurry." The doctor patted

the bulging pocket holding his watch. "I'm on call and shouldn't be away from my post for more than an hour."

Arguing would only waste precious minutes needed for Letta's father. Caroline gave a nod. "This way."

Letta set a quick pace. The men followed closely, their thudding footsteps loud. Caroline sensed Ollie's gaze on the back of her head, but she kept her eyes aimed ahead. When they reached Letta's house, the girl darted across the bare yard to the sagging porch. Without a backward glance, she flung open the door and ran inside. Caroline and the two men entered the dark house behind her.

A foul stench greeted them. Caroline covered her nose with her hand and ducked aside. Very little sunlight penetrated the pair of dust-coated windows, and no lantern lit the space. But she made out the dark shape of an open doorway on the right beyond a spattering of sad, worn furniture. Labored breathing could be heard from the opening. The doctor pushed past Caroline and disappeared into the room.

Ollie strode after the doctor. Before he stepped through the doorway, he glanced back at Caroline. "Aren't you coming?"

The odor—the combination of something rotting and body excrement— made her dizzy. Unwelcome memories crowded to the forefront of her mind. How could a mere scent, no matter how unpleasant, conjure such sharp images? She shook her head. "I'll wait outside."

"Letta might need you."

Ollie's reminder stirred Caroline's sympathy, but she wouldn't enter that room. She couldn't face the ugly reminders of her past. "Tell her where I am." She dashed out the door before guilt drove her across the threshold of Mr. Holcomb's bedroom.

Chapter 12

Caroline

Wild crying came from the house—Letta, obviously in great distress. Caroline spun from her perch on the edge of the porch and looked toward the open doorway. Should she go to the girl? She pressed her palms to the porch boards with the intention of pushing herself upright, but her fingers curled around the splintery ends and held tight. She could not enter that house with its foul essence of her childhood nightmares. Hanging her head, she sent up a silent petition for the Lord to offer Letta the comfort she could not.

The patter of feet captured Caroline's attention. Two boys in tattered clothing galloped toward the house. Their red hair and freckled faces identified them as Letta's younger brothers. She jumped up and waylaid them at the edge of the yard.

"Who are you?" the smaller of the pair asked, squinting up at Caroline.

"I'm Letta's friend Carrie Lang."

"You the one makin' Letta go to school?"

Although Caroline wasn't forcing Letta to attend school, she nodded anyway. "That's right."

The boys exchanged a disgusted look. The older one grimaced. The smaller one—apparently the self-appointed spokesman—crossed his arms over his chest and stated, "That Letta, she's got real bossy since she started goin' to school. Makes us sit an' write our letters every night. I don't much like it."

Caroline clasped her hands. "Oh, but learning is a wonderful thing. You should thank Letta for teaching you." She offered a smile but received only scowls in reply. She sighed. "What are your names?"

"I'm Lesley," the younger one said. He poked his thumb at his brother. "This here is Lank."

Lank swung a bulging burlap sack gently to and fro in his clenched fist, making its contents clank.

Lesley beamed. "Did real good today with our tin collectin'. Pa oughta be happy. Gonna go show him. C'mon, Lank."

The pair started to push past her, but Caroline stopped them with her extended hand. "Wait, boys. You can't go in yet."

Two dirty faces glared up at her. "Why not?" Lesley asked.

"Because a doctor is in there with your pa, and he needs it to be quiet." Lesley stamped his bare foot against the ground. "But it's gettin' on to suppertime. Didn't have us no lunch 'cept for some jerked beef Lank snitched from a cart. I'm wantin' to eat."

Caroline nibbled her lip. The doctor had said he wouldn't stay long, but if Mr. Holcomb was desperately ill—and Letta's wails seemed to indicate he fared poorly— it might be quite a while before she could allow the boys to go inside. She reached into her pocket and removed the little notepad and pencil she always carried.

"I tell you what we'll do. I'll leave a note here for Mr. Moore so he can tell Letta where to find you. You can leave your bag of tin by the porch, and I'll take the two of you to a little café for supper." Kesia would welcome these dirty boys as exuberantly as she had the scraggly alley cat.

Lesley's fine red eyebrows shot high. "A café? Really an' truly? Ain't never ate in a café before." Then the child's bright countenance faded. "But we don't got money to be buyin' supper in a café."

Lank gave a scowling nod. He collared his brother and pushed him toward the porch.

Once more Caroline stepped into their pathway. Hands on her hips, she pinned them with a stern frown. "You are not going into that house until the doctor says it is safe. Your father could have any number of illnesses— measles, diphtheria, scarlet fever..." She searched for more examples. "The mange."

The boys' eyes grew round. Lesley nudged his brother with his elbow. "Saw a dog with the mange once, Lank. It was purely awful."

Caroline nodded. "That's right. And you could get it, too, from being in there with him." She shrugged, stepping aside. "But if you'd rather catch the mange than go get some supper with me, then—"

Lank tossed the bag toward the porch. It hit the foundation and rolled with a clatter.

"We'll go with you," Lesley said. "I'm not wantin' the mange."

Caroline hid a smile. "Very well." She quickly wrote a note informing Ollie she'd taken the boys to the Durham Café and instructing him to bring Letta there. She slipped the note under the door and hurried back to Lesley and Lank. Pressing her palms to their backs, she ushered them toward town.

Caroline rested her chin in her hand and watched Kesia fuss over the boys. Although they barely glanced at her— their focus was on their plates of roasted wild turkey, cornbread dressing, and golden cooked carrots—the older woman showed no resentment for their lack of appreciation. She refilled their glasses with milk, spooned more gravy over their dressing, and tucked napkins more securely under their chins, all the while smiling, as if catering to a pair of dirty urchins gave her great pleasure.

The men seated at the counter kept a wide berth from the boys, however. Caroline couldn't blame them. Lank and Lesley probably hadn't bathed in a month. Letta wouldn't think to make them, and no boy their age would give himself a bath. But as soon as they'd finished eating, Caroline intended to fill the elongated tub at the end of the hallway for their use. They would complain, no doubt, but she'd win. This pair of red-headed scamps would go home clean if she had to wrestle them into the water.

Kesia removed the boys' empty plates and returned with wedges of buttermilk pie dusted with nutmeg. Lesley licked his lips and jabbed his fork through the creamy filling. At the first bite he closed his eyes and murmured, "Mmm."

Kesia grinned, her eyes sparkling. "You like it?"

"I sure do." Lesley forked up another huge bite. "Best pie I ever ate." Lank dug into his pie, too, but he remained silent. Caroline had quickly discovered Lank allowed Lesley to do most of the talking. Whether the older boy was shy or distrustful, she hadn't determined. But she suspected, given time, Kesia would win him over. The woman surely possessed the kindest heart in Kansas.

The boys finished their pie, and Caroline dropped several coins into the bucket to pay for their meals. She headed toward the pair to inform them where they were going next as Kesia delivered a large chunk of moist-looking cake to one of the other diners, and Lesley leaned over the counter to keep sight of the speckled plate.

Kesia caught him gawking and laughed. "You wantin' some of my good apple-walnut cake, Lesley?"

Lesley bounced on his stool. "Uh-huh!"

Kesia turned to Lank. "What about you?"

Lank merely shrugged, his head low.

Kesia patted Lank's shoulder. "I'll getcha some. You just sit tight." She headed for the kitchen.

Caroline eased back onto the stool, chuckling to herself. She hoped she had enough money in her purse to pay for all the food these two could consume. They acted as if they hadn't eaten in years. But she wouldn't deny them, no matter how much they wanted to eat. She'd never wish hunger on a child. Not even a silent, unappreciative one like Lank.

Just as Kesia set the cake plates in front of the boys, the door opened, and Ollie came in. His serious expression raised a swell of apprehension. Caroline told the boys, "Stay here and eat your cake. I'll be right back." She hurried across the floor to meet Ollie. "Where's Letta?"

"At the hospital with her pa. She wouldn't leave."

Caroline's heart leaped. "You had to take him to the hospital? It's that bad?"

Ollie nodded grimly. "Doc Ernst says his appendix burst. He might not make it." His gaze shifted to the red-headed pair hunched over their cake plates. "Not sure what to do with those two. They can't go back to an empty house by themselves. Letta said they don't have any kin here in town—their closest relation is an aunt who lives near Baldwin City." He scratched his head, setting his cap askew. "They haven't seen her for a couple of years at least, according to Letta, but I suppose we could wire the woman and then put the boys on a train."

A knot of sympathy tightened Caroline's throat, nearly strangling her. She wrung her hands. "Do they even know this aunt? What if they don't want to go?"

Ollie shrugged. "Somebody has to take care of them, Carrie. They aren't old enough to be on their own."

Tears pricked behind Caroline's eyes. She gazed at the boys, who leaned their elbows on the counter and visited quietly with Kesia. The amiable woman had already extracted a great deal of information from Lesley, including their ages. At eight and ten, they were far too young to be left unattended. But she couldn't bear the thought of shipping them to a virtual stranger, who might not even want them.

"Or I suppose we could..."

Ollie's musings caught Caroline's attention. She looked at him, eager to hear what he might suggest.

Uncertainty pinched his brow. "They're kind of small, but I wonder if Hightower might find a place for them at the factory."

Put them to work? Why, it was no better solution than sending them on a train to an unfamiliar city. "No! Absolutely not!"

Ollie closed his eyes for a moment, drawing in a breath as if gathering his patience. Then he fixed her with a pleading look. "Carrie, I know how you feel about kids working, but at least at the factory they'd be off the streets. And they'd have supervision. I would keep an eye on them."

She glared at him. "No."

"There's a room in the basement with some cots—the doctor uses it as a sick bay. They could bunk down there at night. I get all my meals here with Kesia, and they could eat with me."

Caroline gritted her teeth. **"No."**

"It'd only be until their father gets better and can take care of them again." He released a wry **humph**. "Not that he's done such a fine job of it up 'til now, letting them run wild all day. A cot in the basement and regular meals would probably seem like paradise to those two."

"Not paradise," Caroline snapped. "Prison."

Angry furrows formed on Ollie's brow. "That's taking it a bit far, don't you think? The kids who work at the factory have the choice of working or not. No one forces them to work. And they're paid for their labor."

"Not enough to compensate for what they sacrifice." Caroline hissed the words. She waved a hand toward Lesley and Lank. "I won't argue about your providing them meals from Kesia"—But how could a factory janitor afford to feed the two boys in addition to himself?—"or arranging for them to sleep in the doctor's sick bay. However, they will **not** spend their days working. They will attend school, just like their sister, under the supervision of a teacher."

"And who'll send them off to school? Who'll help them with their homework?"

Caroline lifted her chin. "I will."

"How?"

The simple question left her reeling. How would she manage such a feat while filling a full-time factory job and continuing her investigation? If only she had no need to masquerade as a worker. She could perform her investigation while the children were in school or at night while they slept. Then an idea struck, and she grinned, triumphant. "If I work third shift as a crater, I'll be free during the day to see to the boys' and Letta's needs. As you suggested, they can sleep in the doctor's infirmary at night while I'm working."

He shook his head slowly. "It's commendable that you want to take care of these kids, Carrie, but when will you sleep?"

"While they're in school. Don't you see? It's a perfect situation for the boys."

A small hand tugged at Caroline's skirt. Lesley peered up at her, his face scrunched into a worried frown. "You talkin' about Lank an' me?"

Ollie crouched down and put his hand on Lesley's small shoulder. "That's right. We were talking about how your pa has to stay in the hospital for a while."

"He gots the mange?"

Ollie drew back, and Caroline stifled a chuckle at his startled look. She touched Lesley's oily hair. "No, but he is sick. He's **very** sick." She swallowed. If he died, what would become of these children? She wouldn't be in Sinclair forever. Who would care for them when she went on to her next assignment?

Tears swam in Lesley's blue eyes. "But I didn't get to tell him we found lotsa tin today. Can I go to the hospital an' tell him?"

"Not tonight," Ollie said, his voice kind. "Tonight you'll—"

"Tonight you'll come home with me," Caroline inserted. "And tomorrow you and Lank will go to school, just like Letta." She sent Ollie a firm look, daring him to contradict her.

He sighed and pushed to his feet, keeping his hand on Lesley's shoulder. "That's right, Lesley. You'll go to school."

Caroline smiled, the victory won.

Lank shot off the stool and stomped over. The thus-far silent boy aimed his scowl toward Ollie and growled, "Ain't guh-guh-guh-goin' to school. An' yuh-yuh-you cuh-cuh-can't make me."

Chapter 13

Oliver

Oliver held his guffaws in until he'd placed two blocks' distance between himself and Carrie's boarding hotel. Then he allowed the laughter to roll. What a sight, watching her take charge of those two freckle-faced urchins, who fought like tigers to avoid being dunked in a tub of water. But she'd won. By gum, she'd won. And he wagered a spit-shined Lank and Lesley would be sitting behind a school desk by the end of the week. What a corker she was.

His amusement died, however, as he approached the hospital. He'd promised Carrie he would check on Letta and Mr. Holcomb before turning in. How he'd managed to tangle himself in these children's lives, he didn't know. Father and Mother had often requested his assistance in putting together boxes for the poor at Christmastime, and he'd delivered his fair share of meals to shut-ins as part of his parents' philanthropic endeavors, but he'd always performed the deeds out of obligation rather than from a real desire to serve. Now that he'd met the Holcomb children—had seen not only their need but Carrie's deep concern for them—he couldn't turn back. He'd do whatever he could to help.

When he entered the hospital, he found Letta hunkered on a long, padded bench pressed against the wall just inside the doors. Her red-splotched face and watery eyes stirred his sympathy. Such a huge burden this young girl carried. His childhood had been idyllic—parties, travel, the best schooling, his every need met promptly, and most of his wants provided as well. Some things in life were far from fair. But at least he could ease a few of Letta's worries by assuring her

Lank and Lesley were being cared for while their father recuperated. He refused to consider what would happen to the children if Mr. Holcomb didn't recover. He hitched the legs of his britches and sat beside the girl.

She cast a doleful look in his direction. "Nurse chased me outta Pa's room. Said I was in the way." Fresh tears pooled in the girl's eyes. "I oughta go home, see to Lank an' Lesley, but I'm scared to leave. Just in case Pa needs me."

If Carrie were here, she'd place her arm around Letta's shoulders and offer comfort. But for him to do such a thing would be highly improper. And uncomfortable. Instead, Oliver offered the girl a warm, encouraging smile. "Don't concern yourself about your brothers. They're spending the night with Carrie." He was gratified by her weak sigh of relief. He added, "There's room for you, too, if you don't mind sleeping on the floor."

The girl shook her head. "Nah. If the boys're fine, I'll just stay here." She patted the seat. "It's as soft as my pallet at home. An' this way I'm close if somethin' hap-happens with Pa." Her chin trembled, and she blinked rapidly, but she held the tears at bay.

"You're a brave girl, Letta," Oliver said. He meant it, too. No wonder Carrie liked Letta so much. They were a lot alike.

"I don't feel brave." Letta leaned her head against the wall, and her eyes slid shut. "I'm worryin' about how we're gonna pay the bills for the hospital. I reckon it'll cost dear, 'specially since Pa's gonna have that operation. Some man pestered me about givin' him money before they'll try to fix his belly. Pa's got my goin'-to-school dollars hid someplace, but—"

Oliver frowned. "Going-to-school dollars?"

Letta nodded, a brief smile lighting her thin face. "Uh-huh. Miss Carrie gives her factory wages over to Pa so he'll let me go to school. Otherwise he'd set me to workin'." The smile fell. "But I ain't sure where he tucked 'em away. He don't tell me nothin'. Not since Ma cleared out his money jar an' took off like she done."

Oliver shook his head, certain he'd misunderstood. "Carrie gives her wages to your father? She pays him, what—a dollar?"

"No, sir. She gives him what I'd earn if I was a toter."

Oliver stared in disbelief at the child. "She gives him the entire amount?"

"She sure does." Letta sat up and aimed a look of wonderment at Oliver. "Me goin' to school was awful important to her. Never met anybody so set on book learnin'."

The information sat like a boulder in Oliver's stomach. How could Carrie afford to give away every penny she earned? She'd denied being educated, and he suspected she'd deny being affluent if he asked. But how else could she afford to offer her earnings to Letta? He recalled the silver dollar in Kesia's payment bucket, and the boulder of uncertainty grew.

Letta released a sigh. "But I promised the man I'd search the place an' bring him somethin' soon as I could." She stared blankly at the opposite wall as if drifting away somewhere. "'Course, that means I gotta go to the house instead o' stayin' here..."

Oliver set aside his musings about Carrie for the moment. He couldn't fix the greater burdens of Letta's life, but he could ease one portion. He said, "I'll talk to the financial administrator. You stay here where you'll be close to your father."

A crooked smile appeared on her face, offering a thank-you. After several long seconds of silence, she turned her head and gazed steadily into Oliver's eyes. "Mr. Moore, do you think Pa's gonna die?"

Without conscious thought he placed his hand gently over Letta's where it lay fisted against the rumpled skirt of her dress. Offering the comfort felt good. Better than he would have imagined. "Letta, your father is very, very ill. Many people who've suffered a burst appendix die from the infection."

The girl sucked in her lower lip and nodded—a slow, jerky bob of her head.

"But not all of them die. Some of them get better. And that's what we'll hope for."

"An' pray for?"

Letta's simple question set Oliver back. Pray? He believed there was a God in heaven. He knew what it meant to pray. From his earliest memories he'd attended church with his parents at least three times a year and had listened to prayers uttered by the minister from the pulpit. Father offered a blessing over meals when guests visited their home. But had he ever engaged in a deliberate conversation with God?

He cleared his throat. "Well, yes, Letta. Of course we'll...pray."

A huge sigh lifted Letta's skinny shoulders. "Miss Carrie says God's always listening an' that He answers when we pray. I figure if lots of us are askin' Him to make Pa well, then He'll be more likely to say yes." Tears flooded her eyes again, and one spilled downward past her quavery smile. "Thank you, Mr. Moore."

Oliver nodded, but inwardly he quaked. Had he just agreed to do something for which he was not equipped?

Gordon

Gordon sat at his desk and glanced at his observation window. All morning long the sounds rising from the factory floor spoke of busyness, of industriousness, of organized chaos—a familiar melody he always found comforting. Although there was no cause for concern, he contemplated putting on his suit coat—his dictatorial armor—and peeking out to assure himself his expectations were being met. Instead, he forced his attention back to the checklist laid out on his desk top. Such a lengthy list to accomplish in preparation for Fulton Dinsmore's upcoming visit. And most of it he had to do himself.

He growled under his breath, rolled his shirt sleeves to his elbows, and tapped the tip of his pencil against one line, frowning. Ordinarily he enjoyed delegating. Watching the workers hustle to follow his commands gave him a sense of power even if he was just the manager and not the owner. But for the boss's visits, he couldn't delegate. **Wouldn't** delegate. He couldn't risk any mistakes. Too much was at stake.

A brisk tap at the door interrupted his focus. Now what? He barked, "Come in." His irritation melted, however, when Miss Carrie Lang stepped into his office. A welcome diversion. He rose, setting his checklist aside. "Ah, Miss Lang." He allowed his gaze to sweep from the top of her white mobcap to the toes of her brown boots peeping from the hem of her full dark-blue skirt. Such a fetching figure she presented. It took all the strength he possessed to stay on his side of the desk. "What brings you to my office on your lunch break?"

A second person stepped through the doorway, sweeping his hat from his head as he entered. Gordon's smile of welcome turned into a frown of displeasure. What was Moore doing here?

Miss Lang gestured toward Moore. "We needed to speak with you about the third-shift crating position, as well as ask an important favor."

Gordon flicked a glance across both faces. Serious. Determined. Not a hint of hesitation to be found. Their apparent ease in his presence—no humble bowing of heads, no nervous wringing of hands—rankled. He started to order them out of his office. He had his own work to do. But letting them state their purpose and then denying their request would put them in their rightful place.

He banged one fist on his desk top. "Well, get on with it, then. I don't have all day."

Moore nodded to Miss Lang as if giving her permission to speak first. She clasped her hands primly behind her back and lifted her chin, facing Gordon with a confidence he found both admirable and irritating. "I'd like to apply for one of the crating positions. If possible, I would like to start tonight."

Gordon gawked at her. "Tonight?" He rounded the desk and leaned on its corner, folding his arms over his brocade vest. "Even if I gave you the position, you wouldn't be able to start tonight. You'd need some sleep."

"I would leave now, sleep this afternoon, and come back at ten this evening."

My, but she had nerve! Gordon snorted. "So you'd be irresponsible enough to leave your post midshift for the sole purpose of taking a nap?" He injected as much sarcasm as possible into his voice, but the woman didn't cringe.

She sent a brief look in Moore's direction, the corners of her mouth twitching into a secretive smile. "Actually, Mr. Moore is willing to take over the task of toting trays until you're able to hire another toter."

Gordon's chest went hot, disbelief mingling with disgust. How dare the two of them realign his roster without consulting him? "Mr. Moore has his own duties. Duties, I might add, he frequently bumbles. Considering his lack of skills, he's lucky I let him keep his position as janitor. Given his ineptitude with a mop and scrub brush, why should I trust him to carry trays of confections?" He wanted to peek at that insufferable Moore and witness how his arrows of insult had pierced the man, but he determinedly kept his focus on the woman.

Miss Lang said, "Mr. Moore is stronger than the women, so he could tote four or five trays at a time, as opposed to our three. Therefore he would accomplish the same amount of work in less time. Then he'd still have hours available to see to his other duties."

Gordon raised one brow. "You seem to have it all worked out to your satisfaction." He shifted his gaze to Moore. "I suppose you're in full agreement with this arrangement, Moore?"

The man shoved his cap into the pocket of his britches and ran his hand through his hair. If Gordon's gibes had bothered him, he gave no evidence of it. "I told Carr—Miss Lang—I was willing to step in and help. Getting the third-shift position is important to her."

Gordon glared at Miss Lang, who responded with a calm he couldn't comprehend. "Why?"

Standing tall and confidently before

him, she spoke evenly. "I've recently taken on the responsibility of caring for three children whose father is very ill and is in the hospital. Working nights would allow me to see them off to school, sleep while they're away, then feed them supper before coming to work."

Moore moved a little closer to Miss Lang as if forming a united front. "Miss Lang's new responsibility leads us to the favor we want to ask."

The use of the word we rang like an alarm in Gordon's mind. Apprehensive yet curious, he stiffly waved a hand in invitation.

"The children are young—too young to be left alone in an apartment all night. There are several cots in the lower level room set aside for a sick bay. But as you know, it's hardly ever used for that purpose. Miss Lang and I hoped you might—"

Gordon leaped up. "No, no, no."

For the first time Miss Lang's shoulders wilted. She held out her hands in entreaty. "But—"

"No." He leaned toward her, nearly touching his nose to hers, and spoke through clenched teeth. "I will not have some ragtag street urchins taking up residence in my—" He caught himself and quickly amended, "in this factory."

Defensiveness flashed in the woman's eyes. "They are not ragtag street urchins. They are well-behaved children facing a difficult situation with their only parent unable to provide them care. Where is your Christian compassion, Mr. Hightower?"

He settled back on his desk, continuing to fix Miss Lang with his fierce glare. "I'm a businessman, Miss Lang, not a preacher or even a social do-gooder. I needn't concern myself about extending compassion to the downtrodden." Who'd ever extended compassion to him? Even Fulton Dinsmore, his supposed benefactor, hadn't pulled him from that orphanage to make him a son but to put him to work in his factory. He'd vowed way back then to be the one in charge someday, and he hadn't won his position of leadership by being compassionate. "My only job is to make sure this factory runs smoothly, which it cannot do if there are unsupervised children spending hours beneath its roof."

"They wouldn't be unsupervised."

Gordon narrowed his gaze. "Are you defying me, Miss Lang?"

She closed her eyes and sucked in a long, slow breath. Then she turned a penitent look upon him. "No. I'm trying to explain. If I'm here at night, they would be under my supervision."

Wasn't she something? He couldn't stop a snide laugh from exploding. "How can you do your job and supervise children? One would take precedence over the other, and either way the factory's productivity would suffer." He pushed off from his desk and strode to his chair. "The answer is no. Now, if there's nothing else—"

Ollie stepped to Gordon's desk and rested his fingertips on the beveled edge. "Mr. Hightower."

Although the worker spoke calmly and

maintained a bland expression, Gordon found himself bracing for a storm. Moore's unperturbed exterior seemed to hide a roiling undercurrent. Gordon's legs went weak, and he dropped into his desk chair. Safely behind the barrier of his solid walnut desk, he gathered the courage to send Moore a sneer. "What?"

"I respectfully ask that you grant Miss Lang's request to be moved to a third-shift crater and that the cots in the sick bay be made available to Letta, Lank, and Lesley Holcomb until their father is released from the hospital and is able to care for them again." The man's lips quirked into a cunning smile. "The charitable act could garner approval from city leaders. You might even receive a commendation for extending such generosity and solicitude toward the underprivileged. The subsequent publicity could be quite beneficial to the factory, encouraging people to purchase even greater quantities of Dinsmore's World-Famous Chocolates in support and appreciation of your benevolence."

Gordon opened his mouth to order the arrogant man out of his office, but the sound of applause came from the hallway. Both Moore and Lang turned toward the sound, their backs blocking Gordon's view. Then a man's voice—a deep, familiar voice that caused Gordon to break out in a cold sweat—boomed, "Hear, hear! Spoken like a true philanthropist. Mr. Hightower, I support this young man's request and commend him for making the suggestion."

Rising shakily to his feet, Gordon squeaked out, "Mr. Dinsmore, sir. Y-you're early."

Chapter 14

Caroline

Caroline stepped aside and surreptitiously examined Mr. Fulton Dinsmore, owner of Dinsmore's World-Famous Chocolates Factory. His well-tailored suit, silk cravat, and dapper top hat, which he held in the crook of his arm, communicated effectively the financial success of his endeavors. Endeavors that were built upon the backs of underpaid, overworked children. She wanted to resent him, but a teasing twinkle in his deep-set eyes and the pleasant upturning of his lips beneath a neatly trimmed, graying mustache chased away any indignation. Something about the man appealed to her.

Dinsmore strode into the room and gave

Ollie's hand several emphatic pumps. "Mr. Moore, how delightful to discover my recommendation of your employ has resulted in your taking an active interest in the furtherance of the company."

"Yes. Yes." Mr. Hightower pulled his sleeves down to his wrists and shrugged into his suit coat as he rounded the desk. "You were quite correct in bringing this young man to my attention. And of course I'll approve his...magnanimous request." He released a laugh that fell short of true joviality and gave Ollie a few stiff pats on the shoulder. His face wore a tight smile, and his eyes glittered with suppressed fury.

Dinsmore's smile bounced from one man to the other. "I knew from the moment I laid eyes on Mr. Moore that he'd be an asset to the company." A low chuckle rolled from the man's throat. Tucking his thumbs into the little pockets on his vest, he beamed at Ollie. "So good to see you settling in, making suggestions, taking an active interest in the betterment of Dinsmore's. Well done."

Ollie bowed his head. "Thank you, sir."

Hightower rubbed his palms together and emitted a nervous titter. "Well, then, Mr. Moore and Miss Lang, since I must now give Mr. Dinsmore my full attention, the two of you should..." He nodded his head toward the door, his lips pinching into a grim line.

"Oh, of course." Fulton Dinsmore waved a hand flamboyantly toward the hallway. "Don't allow me to keep you from your assigned tasks, Mr. Moore and...Miss Lang, did he say?"

For the first time the factory owner seemed to acknowledge her presence. She bobbed into a curtsy beneath his steady gaze, offering a meek nod. "Yes, sir."

"Miss Lang, thank you not only for your dedication to Dinsmore's but to the children you've befriended. I find your commitments quite commendable, young woman."

He sounded sincere. Caroline thanked him with a smile and inched toward the door. Ollie turned as if to follow her.

Dinsmore pointed at him. "Mr. Moore, I should like a conference with you at the end of your shift."

Ollie planted both feet and stood erect, reminding Caroline of a soldier on parade. "Yes, sir. I shall be certain to make myself available."

As she listened to the pair of tall men engage in their brief, well-mannered exchange, awareness blossomed in Caroline's mind.

"Four o'clock?"

"Yes, sir."

"Very well." Dinsmore offered a warm smile, removing any semblance of pomposity. "Four o'clock in the, er, janitor's office." Now humor glittered in the man's eyes.

Ollie seemed to swallow a smile. "My 'office' will be just fine, sir. I'll turn a couple of buckets upside down so we can sit while we converse." With a final nod in Mr. Dinsmore's direction, he hurried out the door, ushering Carrie with him. He pulled the door shut behind them and aimed her for the stairway. "Now that

Hightower has agreed to change your shift, you're free to clock out. The boys will be back from school in less than four hours, so you won't have a great deal of time to sleep, but—"

Caroline dug in her heels and took hold of his sleeve, forcing him to stop, too. She searched his face, questions crashing through her mind like stormy waves upon a shore. "Ollie Moore, who **are** you?"

Oliver

Oliver blinked twice. He knew what she wanted to know and why she'd asked. Once again he'd slipped into his educated speech. Hightower hadn't seemed to notice—the man was too self-focused to truly listen to anyone—but Carrie with her sharp attention to detail didn't miss a thing. He wished he could snatch back his well-executed admonitions. But if he'd kept silent, Father wouldn't have spoken in support, and Carrie would have been denied the opportunity to take care of Lank and Lesley. So which was preferable—to hold his tongue or to speak?

Pretending ignorance, he stepped away from her. "What'cha mean?"

She frowned up at him, keeping pace as he walked down the stairs. "You accused me of having an education, and now I accuse you of the same thing. The words you threw at Mr. Hightower... No mere factory worker would know the meaning of **solicitude** and **benevolence**. Yet they spilled from you with ease." They reached the floor, and she stepped into his pathway, prohibiting his passage.

"And don't tell me you simply read a lot." Intensity threaded her voice, which she held at a level loud enough for him to hear over the machines but not so loud as to be overheard by other workers. "Because I'm baffled by more than your speech. You offered to provide meals for Lank and Lesley, indicating your income is adequate to extend beyond your own needs. A janitor enjoys such financial freedom? And then there's the way you carry yourself. With dignity. Superiority. I've rarely seen such confidence in common laborers."

He hadn't realized how much he'd revealed of his station. Were the other employees also curious about him? No. Her astuteness went beyond that of a typical factory worker.

She tipped her head and pinched her brows, her expression serious. "So who are you, Ollie Moore? What is your purpose here?"

Oliver peered at her adorably freckled face and bit down on the tip of his tongue. If he told her the truth, word would spread. Perhaps she wouldn't share his secret on purpose, but his parentage could slip out by accident. And when the other workers knew, his opportunity to gather the information he needed to become a good, knowledgeable, understanding leader would be lost. He couldn't tell her the truth. Yet he ached at being forced to lie to her.

"Carrie..." He growled the word and balled his hands into fists. "You ask too many questions."

Her eyes widened, and she placed her palms against her bodice. "Ollie! Are you...are you investigating something?"

He carefully processed her query. One could argue he was investigating the inner workings of the factory, seeking the means to improve operations as well as the working conditions for the employees. He gave a tentative nod.

Delight bloomed across her face. "Are you looking into the Bratcher death?"

Bratcher? Once again she'd surprised him. "That was an accident." Then he scowled, placing his hands on her shoulders. "How do you know about Bratcher's death?" More questions rose from the recesses of his mind. "And how did you know how many child laborers the factory employs? How can you afford to give your wages to Letta and still pay for lodgings and for meals at Kesia's?"

She wriggled beneath his grasp, her face paling.

He held tight. "You've made some con-jectures about me." The word conjectures echoed in his ears. The choice of words would only increase her pondering, but he pushed on. "Now I'd like to know the same things about you. Who are you? What are you doing here?" Bits and pieces of other conversations flitted through his memory, and an unwelcome idea filled his head. He leaned close and rasped a final question. "Are you like Bratcher, a rabble-rouser trying to enforce the same laws as those adopted in the textile industry? Because if you are, I—"

He'd what? Toss her out the door? He held no authority to do so. Nor did he truly want to, but if she was involved in the movement to end child labor, his father's factory—his factory—could suffer. Confused, he left the threat dangling.

She threw her arms outward, dislodging his grip. "I'm no rabble-rouser, but I support those who rally to send children to school rather than to workplaces." Snatching up her skirts, she turned and ran. But she'd gone a few feet when she came to a halt. He watched her back and shoulders heave with several great intakes of breath. Then she spun to face him again.

Her freckles glowed like a spattering of copper pennies flung over snow-covered ground. She tossed her head as if shedding her irritation, and splashes of pink formed on her cheeks. The corners of her full, rosy lips tipped into a polite smile. "Thank you for convincing Mr. Hightower to place me on the third shift. If you wish to provide meals for Lank and Lesley, I will allow you the privilege, and I offer you my gratitude. But, Mr. Moore,"—her gaze narrowed, her eyes shooting darts of warning—"I'll thank you to keep your hands to yourself from now on. Good day."

Before he could form a word, she turned and raced from the factory, leaving him with a bitter taste on his tongue and a fierce ache in his chest.

At the end of his shift, Oliver pushed items against the wall of the supply closet and upended two sturdy buckets in the center of the floor. He commended his father for his choice of meeting locations even though they'd likely bump knees in the small space. But they would have privacy. No one but Oliver entered the supply closet. Their ears would be somewhat protected from the rattle of machinery and the hiss of boilers, but the noise outside the door would prevent others from overhearing, giving them an opportunity to speak freely.

There was so much he wanted to tell Father. But little of it had to do with the factory.

"Forget about her," he ordered under his breath, giving a broom a vicious toss to the far corner. He'd already concluded Carrie was no commoner. She might be a mere factory worker now, but her background was surely as privileged as his own, putting them on an even social level. He cared little about such things anymore. Serving alongside common yet hardworking, honest people had carved away his long-held tenet of separation between the classes. But if Carrie was

caught up in the end-child-labor movement as Bratcher had been, they'd always
be at odds.

Why couldn't she see that all the
youngsters in his father's employ were
paid well for their labor and were protected
from danger? He'd hoped that observing
how smoothly the factory ran would
change her mind about children taking
jobs. But apparently her opinion hadn't
budged an inch. Consequently, no matter
how attractive, how intriguing, how
admirable he found her, her beliefs were
too off-putting for him to pursue her.

He closed his eyes and envisioned her
escaping across the floor. Again and
again he forced himself to recall her
retreating form, willing himself to see her
departure as permanent—as a departure
from his thoughts and affections. But
despite his efforts, at the end of each
reflection, her sweet, fervent face
rushed in to replace the memory of her
disappearing back. Oh, she was
persistent. Even in his thoughts.

He kicked the nearest bucket, sending

it rolling toward the door.

"Oliver?" Father stopped the skidding bucket with his foot. He sent Oliver a puzzled look. "Are you all right?"

Oliver drew in a steadying breath and forced a smile. "I'm fine. Just a little clumsy." He scooped up the bucket and settled it back where he'd had it before and then sank onto its rough bottom.

Father gave the door a yank. The single bulb hanging from twisted wires gave off a harsh glow, highlighting the silver in his father's hair. But he moved like a man half his age as he straddled the bucket and lowered himself to sit. He rested his elbows on his knees, assuming a casual pose that contrasted with his formal attire. Oliver couldn't help but grin. What a pair they must be, Father in his fine double-breasted suit and Oliver in his work dungarees and suspenders.

"How did your meeting with Hightower go?" Oliver asked.

"Very well. The man is extremely organized. The bookkeeping is in order. Invoicing is balanced. Inventory matches what I viewed in the shipping warehouse. I have no complaints."

Oliver grimaced. "I half wish you did have complaints."

Father raised his brows. "Why?"

Removing his cap and placing it over his knee, Oliver admitted, "So I could replace him." He held his breath, waiting for his father to berate him. "You must have sound reasons."

To Oliver's relief, his father seemed interested rather than accusatory. He said, "No solid proof of any wrong-doing, but I've heard rumors about his... impropriety with some of the female workers." Recalling the way he'd grabbed Carrie's shoulders and her warning that he keep his hands to himself, he experienced a wave of regret. Was he any better than Hightower? Abashed, he rushed on. "Many of the workers are afraid of him. He seems to purposely intimidate people."

A thoughtful frown furrowed his father's brow. "I've glimpsed his brusque manner, of course, but credited it to the amount of responsibility he bears. He serves as manager, hiring agent, and bookkeeper, you know."

Oliver knew. It was the one point on which he and Father had disagreed. Oliver wanted to distribute the responsibilities among three employees, creating a checks-and-balances system similar to the one used by the government. But Father was satisfied with Hightower handling all three, claiming he must be doing well because the Sinclair factory had turned a tidy profit each year under the man's leadership, exceeding even the profits made in their Chicago factory. As long as income well exceeded expenses, Father wouldn't release Hightower from his self-appointed position as dictator of Dinsmore's Kansas factory.

"The man is bound to be a bit high-strung, considering his work load," Father continued. "Perhaps people have misinterpreted his intentions."

Oliver shrugged. "Perhaps."

"So tell me what you've learned thus far." He sat up like a chipmunk, pride puffing out his chest. "What plans have you made to improve Dinsmore's World-Famous Chocolates?"

Oliver spent the next twenty minutes sharing ideas for a new line of candies. His father laughed when Oliver mentioned molding chocolate into roses, teddy bears, and farm animals, but when he suggested placing the candies into specially designed tin boxes meant to emulate a vase, a child's toy box, and a barn, his father's laughter turned to a contemplative murmur.

"I like the idea, Oliver." He nodded slowly, his smile growing. "Simple molded chocolate will cost less to manufacture since there won't be any filling, but given the visual appeal, we can still charge the same as for an assortment of truffles or caramels. I can see parents gifting a child with whimsical chocolates or a beau bringing a box of chocolate roses to his sweetheart. In time perhaps we can build the line to include other shapes for specific holidays." He clapped Oliver's shoulder, beaming broadly. "Well done!"

At that moment with pleasure flooding through him, Oliver might have been a schoolboy rather than a twenty-nine-year-old man. A knot formed in his throat, and he cleared it before speaking. "I want to do well, Father. I want Dinsmore's to carry into the next generation."

"That's what I want, too." Father angled his head, a hint of teasing in his expression. "But we can't have you so tied to the factory you neglect to form your own family, or into whose hands will Dinsmore's pass?"

Oliver ducked his head and refused to rise to his father's bait. He wouldn't marry one of the daughters of his parents' social circle just so Father would have a grandchild to carry on the Dinsmore legacy. He wanted to truly love the woman, the way Father loved Mother. And thus far the only woman who had managed to work her way into his heart was a fiery crusader who'd just warned him to keep his hands to himself.

Father's hand descended on Oliver's knee and squeezed. "Son, it seems you have an issue with Hightower's means of management. When I sign the business over to you, you're free to make changes. But don't change things based on your personal feelings about the man."

Grateful to set aside the subject of matrimony, Oliver lifted his head and met his father's gaze.

"Remember, our first priority is to turn a profit. Hightower does that well. Try to learn from him." Father gave Oliver's knee a quick pat and then stood up. "You should know that Hightower has some real concerns about one of his newest hires—the woman you asked to have placed on third shift."

Oliver's heart fired into his throat. "Carrie? Why?"

His lips twitching, Father linked his hands together. "It seems she has been pestering coworkers for information concerning the accident that claimed Harmon Bratcher's life. Since he was specifically inspecting the factory's third rotation, Hightower's concerned her real reason for wanting to join that shift is to stir up trouble."

Oliver could refute Hightower's claim. But if he told Father she needed that shift so she'd be available to Lank and Lesley, he'd have to explain why he knew so much about Carrie Lang. So he phrased a question instead. "Why would she stir up trouble?"

"Hightower believes she knew Bratcher —that she's his relative. If she finds a reason to hold us accountable for his death, she can sue us. Going to court is costly, and it could turn the public against us. Bratcher was well known across the state for his campaigning. If Hightower's suppositions are correct, this woman could create a financial hardship for the factory. Perhaps even force us to close down."

"Carrie wouldn't do that." Oliver spoke firmly, but the moment the words left his mouth, uncertainty fell over him. She'd specifically asked if he was looking into Bratcher's death—had even seemed elated at the idea. Did she have motives of which he was unaware?

Father sent Oliver a sharp look. "I'm not so sure. But I want to discover why she's curious. So I've told Hightower, and now I'm telling you—I want her watched. I want you to watch her."

Oliver's pulse began to gallop. "Sir?"

"Starting tomorrow you'll be on third shift with Carrie Lang."

Chapter 15

Caroline

Kesia slid a packet wrapped in brown paper across the counter toward Caroline. "Here you are. Two cheese sandwiches, some jerked beef, and a nice big apple with nary a wormhole. That oughta keep your Letta goin' 'til lunchtime tomorrow."

Lank and Lesley paused in eating their ham and beans to stare at the lumpy packet. Lank licked his lips, and Lesley turned a disgruntled look on Kesia. "Ain'tcha got nothin' for me an' Lank? How come Letta gets it all?"

Caroline clicked her tongue on her teeth. Apparently no one had taught the boys tact. Or appreciation. In her brief time with them, she'd already been subjected to no less than a dozen stinging opinions about her tiny apartment, her lack of cooking skills, and her insistence on their attending school. Additionally, they'd neglected to thank her for providing them with a place to sleep. She could take their disparagement—she'd been subjected to worse—but she would not allow them to inflict guilt on dear Kesia.

"Lesley, shame on you," Caroline said, frowning at the boy. "Kesia served you a nice, hot supper, and you fuss because your sister will be given the chance to fill her stomach, too? That's a very selfish attitude. Apologize to Miss Kesia."

Lesley gaped at her with round blue eyes. "Huh?"

Caroline raised one eyebrow. "You heard me. Apologize for being greedy." Lesley squirmed in his seat, hunching his shoulders. He muttered, "Sorry, Miss Kesia."

"Now," Caroline continued, letting her firm gaze move from Lesley to Lank, "tell Miss Kesia thank you for your supper."

The boys' faces pursed into matching

grimaces, but Lesley said, "Thank you, Miss Kesia," while Lank muttered something under his breath that Caroline presumed was a word of thanks.

Kesia beamed as brightly as if they'd expressed gratitude without prompting. Reaching across the counter, she gave each boy a pat on the shoulder. "You're as welcome as welcome can be, boys. Finish up them beans an' cornbread, an' I'll bring out a plate o' molasses cookies for your dessert."

The boys bent over their bowls and returned to eating.

Kesia, chuckling, turned to Caroline. "They're quite the rapscallions, aren't they? But they sure liven up the place. Glad you brought 'em in, Carrie. Been too long since young uns sat at my counter."

"I'm glad you don't mind feeding them." Caroline offered a sheepish grin. "They'd have to go hungry if they relied on me for meals."

Kesia shook her finger. "But you wouldn't have to depend on my cookin' if you'd just learn a few recipes for yourself.

When're you gonna let me teach you how to make your way around a cookstove?"

Caroline forced a laugh, hoping Kesia didn't notice the perspiration breaking out across her brow at the thought of working in a kitchen. "Maybe someday, Kesia, when I'm not so busy." But she knew she'd never agree to Kesia's request, no matter how many times she asked. She would never deliberately enter the darkest place of her childhood. She changed the subject before Kesia could argue. "I'm grateful for the lunches you pack for Letta. The poor girl hasn't left the hospital even for a minute in the past two days."

Kesia's wrinkled face pursed in sympathy. "What a dear, standin' by her pa the way she's done. O' course, you carin' for her brothers lets her stay." She dropped her voice to a whisper. "How's her pa doin'?"

Caroline cringed, recalling the man's nearly colorless face on the white starched pillowcase. He'd come through the surgery, but he didn't appear to have much life left in him. "The doctors are hopeful," she said, "but they won't make any promises. He's very weak."

"Well, we'll just keep prayin' an' trustin'." Kesia cleared the dishes left by one of the male patrons and then swept away the crumbs from the counter with a damp rag. Tossing the rag into a basin behind the counter, she smiled at Caroline. "Least he don't have any worries, seein' as how you an' Ollie've taken charge of his kids."

To Caroline's chagrin, at the mention of Ollie's name, her pulse gave a stutter of delight. She inwardly berated herself for the reaction. Taking the third-shift position had done more than give her access to the people who might have witnessed Bratcher's fall—it had removed the possibility of crossing paths with Ollie Moore during the day. She'd told herself only good could come from the arrangement.

Yet all last night while preparing crates for shipping, she'd caught herself glancing up in anticipation at every approaching footfall and then fading in disappointment when the person wasn't Ollie. She'd convinced herself only tiredness created the desire to see Ollie's familiar face. After all, she'd had only a scant three hours of sleep before retrieving the boys from school yesterday afternoon. Today she'd slept a full seven hours. So she wouldn't be looking for Ollie tonight.

She **wouldn't**.

Caroline confided, "Mr. Holcomb won't have to worry about hospital bills, either."

Kesia's fuzzy eyebrows shot high. "Hospital not chargin' him?"

Caroline shrugged, feigning a casual air that belied her deep curiosity. "His bill was paid by an anonymous benefactor. Not even Letta knows who did it. She was crying tears of joy when the boys and I visited her this afternoon. I asked the hospital administrator who'd paid the bill, but he refused to answer—said the person had sworn him to secrecy."

Tears winked in Kesia's eyes. "Aw, such a sweet turn of events. Whoever it was, he's an angel to my way of thinkin'."

Caroline nodded in agreement. She'd

like to thank the person—if she knew who the provider was. Perhaps she could find the time to investigate a second mystery.

Lesley jabbed Caroline on the shoulder with his finger. "I'm all done. So is Lank."

Caroline pretended to inspect their empty bowls. "Good job. You ate every bite." Not that she'd expected anything less. She'd begun to wonder if the boys had tapeworms. How could such small children consume so much food?

"We're wantin' those cookies now."

Folding her arms over her chest, Caroline affected a mild scowl. "If you will ask Miss Kesia politely, I'm sure she'll bring you some cookies."

The two turned pleading faces in Kesia's direction. Lesley said, "Miss Kesia, can—"

"**May**, Lesley."

He scowled and started over. "**May** me an'—"

"Lank and I," Caroline interrupted.

"May Lank an' me, er I, have some cookies?"

"Please," Caroline prompted.

The little boy heaved a persecuted sigh.

"Can— May we **pleeeease** have some cookies?"

Kesia laughed and ruffled the thick hair on Lesley's crown. "Yes, you may. I'll fetch 'em right now. You two put your dirty bowls in my washtub over there, an' I'll be right back."

Caroline watched the boys scoop their bowls, plates, cups, and spoons from the counter, trot to the corner, and deposit their armloads with a clatter. Just as they climbed up on the stools again, Kesia returned with a plate heaped with crumbly molasses cookies. "Don't eat 'em all right now. Save a few for a snack before you go to bed."

The boys nodded and reached for the cookies. While they munched, Kesia tapped her chin with one finger, her expression thoughtful. "I should've put a few cookies in that pack for Letta. Young uns are partial to sweets, an' she deserves somethin' extra for bein' so considerin' of her pa." She gave a decisive nod and headed for the kitchen, calling over her shoulder, "An' don't you put even an extra penny in the bucket for the cookies. Those're my treat." She disappeared from view.

Caroline shook her head, chuckling fondly. Kesia surely had angel wings tucked beneath her calico dress. She returned shortly with a packet of cookies. Caroline instructed Lank to carry the boys' schoolbooks and slates and gave Lesley the task of carrying the food. Kesia accompanied the trio to the door, sending them off with smiles and cheerful farewells. "See you tomorrow!"

"See you tomorrow, Kesia. Thank you." Draping her arms over the boys' shoulders, Caroline aimed them for the hospital.

Lesley squinted up at her, his nose wrinkling. "Ain't we goin' to your place?"

"No. We'll spend the evening with Letta. You two have homework, and Letta can do the lessons, too, so she doesn't fall behind while your father is recuperating." Putting the children to work on lessons would keep them busy, but it would also prevent them from thinking too much about their pa.

"We sleepin' at the factory again tonight?" Lesley asked.

"That's right." Caroline had worried that the boys would be bothered by the factory's noises. Banging hammers, whistling steam, and squeaky cartwheels created a discordant melody that sneaked beneath the door into the infirmary. Yet each time she'd peeked in on them, they were sleeping soundly, seemingly unaware of the cacophony on the other side of the door.

Lank scuffed his toe against the ground and mumbled something. Caroline leaned close and asked him to repeat it, but he shook his head, his lips pinched in a grim line. She turned to Lesley. "What did Lank say?"

Lesley sent a quick look at his brother. "He don't want to go to school no more. Lank...he don't like school."

Caroline squelched a smile. "You've only gone one day. How can you be sure you don't like it?"

Lesley rolled his eyes as if Caroline's statement was too ludicrous to warrant a reply.

Caroline looked at Lank. She wished the boy would talk to her. He whispered to Lesley now and then, but other than his emphatic statement that he would not attend school, he hadn't uttered a word to her or to Kesia or even to Ollie. She'd never met such a quiet boy. Yet intelligence lurked behind his resentful glare. She spoke very gently. "Why don't you like school, Lank?"

The boy set his lips in a firm line and stared ahead as if he hadn't heard her.

Caroline sighed and turned to chatterbox Lesley. "Why doesn't Lank like school?"

Lesley scrunched up his face. "The teacher made us recite things. Made Lank recite things. An' the kids—they all laughed."

"Why did the children laugh? Are the recitations funny?"

Lank snorted.

Lesley shook his head. "Huh-uh. He just can't say 'em without goin'**uh-uh-uh**."

Caroline stopped, drawing the boys to

a halt as well. When Lank had spouted his determination not to attend school, she'd presumed anger had caused him to stumble over his words. But now she understood, and sympathy brought the sting of tears. She leaned down and looked directly into Lank's sullen face. "Is that why you don't talk, Lank? Because you stammer?"

Lank looked to the side, his jaw tightening.

Lesley tugged on Caroline's sleeve. "Pa calls Lank a im...imbecile. Says Ma prob'ly left 'cause she was ashamed to be around a mushmouth." His forehead crinkled. "Miss Carrie, what's a imbecile?"

Caroline ground her teeth, anger rolling through her like an ocean wave. "Something Lank most certainly is **not**." She took Lank by the shoulders and made him turn toward her. "Lank, you do know, don't you, that there's no shame in stammering?"

The look he turned on her spoke of fury but also of a deep, deep hurt. The anguish behind his glare nearly dissolved Caroline into tears. She squeezed his arms, offering comfort with her touch.

"Lank, you're a very smart boy." **Lord, let him believe me. Don't let him go through life carrying a burden of disgrace he doesn't deserve.** "You know the words. That means you're smart. Just because you have trouble saying the words doesn't make you stupid."

His expression didn't change.

She straightened, placing her arm around the boy's stiff shoulders. "Very well, I won't talk to you about it anymore right now." With her other hand on Lesley's back, she aimed them for the hospital again. "But I want you to believe me, Lank. You are very, very smart, and you will find a way to let everyone know just how smart you really are."

They walked in silence the remaining distance, allowing Caroline to plan what she would say to the boys' teacher before school tomorrow. She'd need the woman's assistance to help Lank feel at ease in the classroom and focus on learning. She glanced at Lank's unruly red head and stifled a sigh. Another worry to bear... But at least she could remove her concern about feeding her infatuation with Ollie Moore. Without their day-to-day contact, he was sure to drift from her thoughts.

Thank You, Lord, for separating us. Finally. Despite this added burden, things would be much easier with the factory's janitor no longer stealing her attention.

Chapter 16

Oliver

Oliver hunched in the shadowy area behind a stack of empty crates. The mouth-watering aroma of chocolate mingled with the scent of fresh-sawed wood—an unusual yet somehow pleasant combination. He pinched the brim of the battered suede cap he'd swapped with a man on the street for a nickel and wriggled it until it rested just above his eyebrows and then flipped up the collar of his bulky jacket around his ears. The corduroy fabric brushed his jaw, and he scowled. His whiskers—allowed to grow unchecked to offer another means of masking his face—itched. He poked out his chin and scratched his grizzled cheeks with both hands, nearly sighing with relief. The moment he'd gathered enough information to convince Father that Carrie was no threat, he would razor his face clean of these prickly hairs.

His skin tingling pleasantly from the fierce scratching, he emerged from his hiding spot and snatched the broom from the corner. Head low, he inched across the floor, sending surreptitious glances in Carrie's direction as he attempted to sweep sawdust and discarded tacks into a pile. Who knew the simple act of sweeping was so difficult? The house-keeper at home never scattered particles in all directions when she swept, yet his fumbling swipes often did more chasing than gathering. But maybe it was discomfort more than ineptitude that made the task seem difficult on this night.

His stomach twisted in nervousness. Such a disconcerting task Father had given him—spying on Carrie. For three nights he'd sneaked around corners, listened in on conversations, and observed her every move. Although his clandestine exploits set his teeth on edge—the entire situation made him feel like an interloper in his very own factory—he had to admit, some of Carrie's actions stirred a hint of misgiving.

But instead of making him wary of Carrie, he was finding himself suspicious of Bratcher.

His first night on duty, he'd overheard her quizzing two other employees about Harmon Bratcher. She'd used a glib approach that seemed to fool the young men who moved the full crates to the shipping dock, but he'd perceived an intensity that went beyond mild curiosity. He'd filed away the information she'd gleaned, intending to share it with Father. According to the workers, Bratcher had been found first thing Monday morning, not Monday evening as Hightower had reported. If the workers were correct—and he tended to believe anyone over Hightower—then Bratcher had been in the factory on Sunday. But the factory wasn't open on Sundays. What was he doing in the closed factory? How had he gotten in? Something didn't sound right.

His chin tucked against his shoulder, he pushed the broom over the planked floor behind Carrie and peeked at her from the corner of his eyes. Father would have no complaints about her work ethic. Even while asking questions, she was industrious. Her hammer rose and fell on the round heads of tacks in a steady rhythm. The securing slats lay straight across the cushioning layer of straw, their ends aligned with the crates' top edges.

The other new crater, a boy perhaps seventeen, was sloppy. His placement of the slats left gaps through which bugs could crawl. Some of the narrow strips of wood extended over the edge of the crate, making it difficult to stack the boxes neatly. The boy also wasted time meandering back and forth between the filled crates and the supply of slats, carrying only half enough strips of wood to cover one box.

But not Carrie. She gathered a large number of slats—enough to cover at least a dozen crates before needing to refill her supply. She worked steadily but not rushed, using her time wisely. He still pondered her fascination with Bratcher, yet his admiration exceeded his apprehensions. Whatever compelled her to question Bratcher's untimely demise, she earned every penny of her wages. And Oliver would certainly assure his father of that fact.

He'd also inform Father of some other things he'd observed since arriving on third shift—workers lighting hand-rolled cigarettes in the boiler room, younger workers sleeping for hours between machines when they should be working, two men who'd staggered in half-drunk the past three nights. The night foreman didn't seem concerned about any of these breaches of conduct. In fact, Oliver was certain he'd glimpsed the man removing coins from the pocket of one of the sleeping workers. Father should be informed of such goings-on.

Carrie reached into the little leather pouch dangling from her waist and removed another tack. He watched as she pinched one between her thumb and forefinger, positioned it just so, and then gave it a few gentle taps with the hammer to hold it in place. With it secure she pulled her hand free and raised the hammer high. **Whack! Whack!** Two solid blows drove the tack into the soft wood.

Oliver bent down to pluck unused tacks from the collection of grit on the floor, stifling a chuckle. The other craters sported bandages from accidentally pounding their fingers rather than the tacks. If they'd take a lesson from Carrie, they'd suffer fewer injuries. He should have Hightower instruct the foreman on the proper handling of tools.

His observation of Carrie had revealed more than Father had expected. When he telephoned Father tomorrow morning, he'd be able to report more reasons to commend her than to criticize her, and a rush of satisfaction filled him at the realization. Odd how his feelings tumbled haphazardly where she was concerned. Did he admire her or resent her? Did he want to protect her or protect himself from her?

The break buzzer blared, and everyone put down their tools or set aside their carts and moved in a jostling stream toward the break room. Carrie melded into the center of the throng, and Oliver stayed at the rear, his head low in case she turned around and spotted him. Even with his chin whiskers and low-tugged hat, he was fairly certain she'd recognize him if their eyes met.

At least a part of him hoped she would.

She glanced over her shoulder, and he instinctively dropped into a squat, pretending to fuss with the rawhide string on his right boot. He waited several seconds to make sure she'd turned her gaze forward, and then he pushed upright. He followed the last of the stragglers into the break room and eased his way to the corner, snagging his Kesia-packed lunch tin as he went. Head angled with his profile to the room, he scanned the tables with the corner of his eye. It wouldn't do to sit in her line of vision.

He inspected every corner of the room once and then again. But he spotted no mobcap with spiraling bronze curls escaping the ruffled brim. A frown pulled his brows together. Where was she?

Caroline

Caroline crept along the wide hallway. Her footsteps echoed against the concrete floor, an ominous sound. The hiss and clank of boilers faded behind her as she moved determinedly toward the service elevator. After weeks of waiting she finally had the chance to examine the workings of the elevator. As she eased toward the pine-planked platform suspended by ropes, cables, and gears, she removed the pencil and pad of paper from her pocket. She didn't claim to be an engineer, but she was a fair artist. Noble could share her sketches with someone who possessed engineering skills, and perhaps they could determine whether a severed rope or faulty gear contributed to Bratcher's accident.

She stopped a few feet away from the

elevator, an uneasy chill creeping up her spine. A man had lost his life near this very spot. She felt as though she walked on sacred ground. And suddenly she longed for someone to stand alongside her.

Lord, help me find the truth so Noble's concerns can be put to rest and Harmon Bratcher's family will find peace.

The prayer offered a breath of comfort that settled her skittering pulse. No other workers were near, but she wasn't alone. God was with her. Tiptoeing, she approached the elevator and pushed aside the lattice-style gate. The hinges moaned in protest, and Caroline cringed. Would someone hear? Holding her breath, she froze in place and peered up the hallway. She counted several seconds, cold sweat breaking out across her back. But no one came.

She quietly released her breath and stepped onto the platform. Sturdy one-inch-thick boards, secured snugly with wide iron bands, supported her weight but creaked as the bed swayed from side to side. The motion, although very slight, made her dizzy. She sucked in slow breaths and winged a prayer heavenward, willing her nerves to calm. The tactic worked. **Thank You, Lord.**

Standing as still as possible, she propped the pad of paper against her palm and began a meticulous sketch of the elevator's chain-lift system. Since the elevator was only a platform confined by a shaft rather than a solid box, she could see the ropes that looped from an overhead exposed beam and snaked through iron rings soldered to square side posts. Tongue tucked in the corner of her mouth, she did her best to replicate the workings, but the sawtooth length of iron attached to the wall outside the elevator proved tricky. She paused, squinting at the jagged piece of rust-splotched iron. She touched the tip of her pencil to the page again, determined to draw it as realistically as her limited abilities allowed.

"What are you doing?"

The deep-throated question seemed to come from nowhere. Caroline released a squawk, her entire body jolting in surprise. A black line of lead marred her carefully crafted drawing. As she gazed in dismay at the paper, a man stepped onto the elevator beside her. The bed jerked, and Caroline reached out to grasp something to keep herself upright. To her chagrin, she caught his corduroy sleeve. Lifting her embarrassed gaze from his arm to his eyes—his unusually pale green eyes— she gave another start. Ollie Moore?

"What are you doing here?"

They spoke simultaneously, voicing identical queries, although his voice emerged low, with an undercurrent of suspicion, while hers reflected confusion.

Caroline yanked her hand free of his sleeve and glared into his whiskered face. Whiskers? When had he grown whiskers? "What are you doing here? You don't work night shift."

One side of his lips quirked into a sardonic smirk. "I do now. And as janitor, I have a reason to be in the service hall-way. But craters only ready boxes for shipping. They don't haul them to the loading dock. So what are you doing here?" His gaze dropped to the pad in her hand, and a scowl creased his brow beneath the short brim of a brown suede hat. "What's this?"

Caroline stuffed the pad into her pocket and hurried out of the elevator. "Nothing."

A hand curled around her upper arm, forcing her to face him. "Don't lie to me, Carrie." Anger glittered in his eyes— something new. When combined with the scraggly growth of dark blond whiskers and battered cap, he seemed a stranger.

She wrenched her arm free. "It's just a drawing."

"Of what?" He snapped the simple inquiry.

She longed to escape. How could she have been so careless as to allow him to sneak up on her this way? And how could she answer without lying? She detested this part of her job. No matter how hard she tried, mistruths never rolled glibly from her tongue.

Licking her dry lips, she stammered, "Of the elevator. It...it intrigues me." She'd spoken truthfully. She prayed he wouldn't question the reason for her interest.

"Why?"

Caroline stifled a moan. Wouldn't God answer any of her prayers concerning Ollie Moore? "Because it does!" She affected irritation, hoping to put him off. "And I'm on my break, so I can use the time as I desire. Now, if you'll excuse me, I'd like to—"

The buzzer blared, signaling the end of lunch break.

Caroline shook her head, throwing her hands outward. "Now I don't have time to finish. Thank you very much, Ollie!" She spun and charged up the hallway toward her work station.

Ollie pounded along beside her, his face set in an angry scowl. "Would you slow down for one minute so I can talk to you?"

She lifted her nose and sniffed. "We have nothing to discuss."

He sniffed, too—a teasing sound—and continued to walk alongside her, his stride matching hers. "If you're really curious about the elevator, I could show you the blueprint. The drawing is very detailed."

She came to a halt, spinning to face him. Not even those scraggly whiskers could hide his rugged handsomeness. She made herself focus on business. "You have a blueprint?"

He shrugged. "Sure. There're copies of it in the janitor's closet. The people who installed it left them so whoever worked here could understand the elevator's operation. In case repairs were ever needed."

If she could secure a blueprint to send to Noble, it would be much better than anything she could draw. "I would like to see it. Very much." Despite her effort to rein in her eagerness, her voice bubbled out. She regretted the mistake when Ollie snatched the battered hat from his head and fixed her with a penetrating look.

"I'll show it to you on one condition. Tell me why it's so important to you."

Chapter 17

Oliver

"That's blackmail."

Oliver gave a short laugh. "Don't be dramatic, Carrie."

With a withering glare, she turned and stomped up the hallway, each step an angry outburst.

He fell into step beside her, trying not to grin at her display of ire. The red flush in her apple cheeks couldn't quite cover the freckles. Corkscrew curls escaped her cap and bounced against her slender neck. She pumped her arms, her lips set in a beguiling pout. Sometimes she was entirely too cute.

When they reached the work floor, Carrie returned directly to her station, where crates bearing stamped jewel-toned tins of Dinsmore's World-Famous Creams awaited their cushioning layer of straw and protective lids. Her hammer lay on the edge of one crate, and she yanked it up, then turned to face him, holding the tool the way a brave on the warpath might wield his hatchet.

Oliver instinctively took one step backward.

"You must be the most infuriating man I've ever met, but I'll meet your condition." She spoke through clenched teeth as if the words pained her.

Oliver swallowed a laugh and nodded in acknowledgment.

"However, I cannot talk with you now. I have work to do."

Had he really survived three days of not looking directly into her enchanting face? Perhaps it was only the essence of chocolate in the air, but it seemed sweetness emanated from her. If he kissed her full lips, would she taste as luscious as she appeared? He folded his arms over his chest, glowering at her to hide his yearnings. "How 'bout when our shift ends?"

She lowered the hammer against her leg, the weight of the head pressing her skirt flat. "I can't take the time. I need to wake Lank and Lesley, feed them a cold breakfast—Kesia keeps me supplied with biscuits and cheese—and then visit Letta. She is still staying at the hospital with her father."

Oliver gave himself a mental kick. How could he have forgotten about the children's father. "He...survived?"

She hung her head, a sigh heaving her shoulders. "As of yesterday evening, he was still alive, but things are grim. The doctor fears the infection was too far reaching. They don't offer much hope."

He started to reach for Carrie's hand but stopped short of actually touching her. "I'm sorry. Is there anything I can do?"

She met his gaze. Her eyes held a sheen of unshed tears, heightening the brown of her irises. "You could pray for him and the children."

Oliver recalled his promise to Letta to pray for her father. But he hadn't done so. Guilt smote him, and he inched backward. "Yes. Of course. Well..." He cleared his throat, gesturing weakly toward the mop bucket in the corner. "I'd better go clean the break room. We...we can take a look at that blueprint tomorrow."

"Not tomorrow," she said, a weak smile playing on the corners of her mouth. "It's Sunday. The factory will be closed."

He could let her in on Sunday. He had a key. But he wouldn't tell her so. "Monday, then."

She nodded and returned to securing lids on crates as if he no longer existed.

Oliver retrieved the bucket and mop and ambled toward the break room, his slow gait a contrast to his galloping thoughts. What would happen to the Holcomb children if their father died? Would they go to an orphanage? Would Carrie keep them? Deep inside he wanted to do as Carrie and Letta had asked—he wanted to pray. But how? His studies had given him a broad vocabulary and the ability to use it, but he was even less competent at talking to God than he was at mopping.

Alone in the break room, he plopped the bucket on the floor, wrapped his hands around the mop's smooth hickory handle, and stifled a moan. Images of Letta's and Carrie's faces, both sad and seeking, flashed in his memory. They'd asked him to pray. He'd agreed to pray. So now he must find the means of keeping his promise. He jammed the strings of the mop into the bucket, sloshing water over the edges. It ran like a stream toward his feet and pooled around the sole of his boots. He lifted a foot and shook it, sending droplets in an arc across the floor. Each drop caught the light from the gas lamps and reflected like a miniature rainbow.

He seemed to recall a minister proclaiming the rainbow was a sign of God's promise never to flood the earth again. He smiled as realization struck. Tomorrow was Sunday. Churches would be open. People who regularly attended church, such as Kesia and Carrie, knew how to pray. Tomorrow, instead of sleeping all morning, he would go to church. And he would learn how to pray.

The aching burden lifted. He put the mop to work, a smile on his face. He'd be able to keep his promise after all.

Caroline

Caroline slipped her arm around Letta's shoulders and held tight. Letta slumped on her half of the bench in the hospital administrator's office, her head low and her hands clamped in tight fists in her lap. Although her pale face indicated distress, she made no sound and sat so still Caroline wondered if she even drew air into her lungs.

If only the girl would cry. Rant. Question. Caroline could comfort or assure her, but Letta's silent, emotionless reaction to the news that her father had passed away left Caroline helpless and afraid. Had something within Letta died, too, when her pa left this earth?

The administrator, Mr. Stafford, sat stiffly behind his desk, his expression stoic. "The body is in the hospital morgue. I assume, given the man's lack of affiliation with any of the local churches, you needn't worry about planning a service."

Beneath Caroline's arm Letta shuddered. Caroline gave her a few pats while sending the man on the opposite side of the desk a steely glare. Must he be so cold? "I'm sure his children will be comforted by having at least a short service, Mr. Stafford. They have an aunt in Baldwin City—their father's sister. I'll contact her by telegram and allow her and the children to decide what is appropriate."

The man pursed his lips as if irritated by her interruption. He continued in the same bland tone. "We'll arrange transport to the burial site once you've secured a plot. Please don't dally in making those arrangements, Miss Lang, as we don't have proper...er, storage facilities here."

"Yes, sir, I'll do my best, but I doubt I'll

be able to arrange anything today. It is Sunday, and..." Caroline gulped. Such a dismal way to spend the Lord's day! "I...I'll need to wait for the children's aunt to arrive in Sinclair."

Mr. Stafford rose and peered down his nose at Caroline. "Very well. I'll expect to see you Monday. Early, preferably."

Caroline struggled to her feet, drawing Letta with her. "As I said, I'll do my best." She turned Letta toward the door.

"Miss Lang?"

Caroline looked at the administrator. For the first time his indifference melted a bit. She rewarded the change with a quavery smile. "Yes?"

"Please accept the hospital's condolences on your loss. I assure you, all effort was made to save Mr. Holcomb's life."

Caroline considered asking if the effort had preceded or followed the unknown benefactor's promise to fund the man's stay. But she decided her question would be hurtful to Letta. So she gave a nod and ushered the silent girl out the door. Lank and Lesley waited outside in the hallway, and they dashed to Letta.

Lesley threw his arms around his sister's waist, looking up in disbelief. "One o' the nurses said Pa died an' is gone to heaven. Is it true?"

Letta, her arms dangling at her sides, made no effort to embrace her little brother. She stared unseeingly up the hallway as if in a trance.

Lesley shifted his attention to Caroline. "Is Pa dead, Miss Carrie?"

Caroline propped her hands on her knees and looked directly into Lesley's freckled face. "Yes, Lesley. Your pa is dead."

The little boy's nose crinkled in confusion. "So he ain't comin' home again?"

Could an eight-year-old comprehend the meaning of death? Slowly Caroline shook her head. She brushed Lesley's tousled hair from his eyes. "No, sweetheart. His body died, and his spirit went... away." She looked at Lank, who stood behind Lesley with his arms crossed tightly over his skinny chest, his face set in a scowl. "He won't be able to come home ever again."

"Oh." Lesley stuck out his lips for a moment, as if thinking hard. "Then he won't be callin' Lank a imbecile or takin' the strap to us no more, huh?"

The boy's blithe words pierced Caroline. Had he no pleasant memories of his father? "No. He certainly won't." But neither would he be there to see to the children's needs, provide them with guidance, or watch them grow into adults. Caroline swallowed a lump of sorrow for all the family had lost.

She straightened and held her hands toward the boys. Lesley caught hold, but Lank scooted to the other side of Letta, as far from Caroline's hand as he could go and still be close to his siblings. The boy's behavior stung, but she wouldn't hold his detachment against him any more than she would blame Letta for escaping somewhere inside herself to avoid her emotions. The children might not know the words to express themselves, but she read deep anguish, fear, and confusion on their young faces.

Caroline put her free arm around Letta's shoulders and spoke kindly. "Come. We'll go to the telegrapher's office and send a wire to your aunt so she'll know about your pa. Then we'll visit an undertaker and..." She stopped, reminding herself that most businesses would be closed on Sunday. Except the train station. It operated seven days a week. She could send a telegram from there. Everything else would have to wait until tomorrow.

She escorted the children from the hospital, forcing her weary feet to carry her forward. If only she could fall into her bed and sleep. She'd intended to ask Letta to watch the boys in the lobby at her residence while she caught a short nap. But Letta was in no shape to care for anyone at that moment. There'd be no rest today.

Caroline straightened her droopy shoulders. The children needed her. She could catch up with her sleep tomorrow. Tomorrow... When she intended to retrieve the elevator blueprint from Ollie.

If it showed the possibility of malfunction, then the questions surrounding Bratcher's death might very well be answered. And she'd be called back to Noble's, away from the children. Away from Kesia and Ollie. She'd miss them all equally, she realized.

She glanced at the trio of redheads, and affection nearly strangled her. Although only days old, her relationship with them felt deeply rooted. How could she pass them off to an aunt they barely remembered? She swallowed hard. And how could she not?

Oh, Lord, why did You allow me to involve myself with the Holcomb children when You knew my time here in Sinclair would be short? Why did You bring Kesia and...and Ollie into my life when You knew I'd have to say good-bye to them?

She didn't expect answers. God often allowed things that made no sense to her. Noble and Annamarie had taught her to take one step at a time, trusting God to know what waited around the bend.

But Caroline's natural inclination was to question—it was what made her a good investigator. So she asked, believing that the God who knew everything about her, including her faults, wouldn't be offended by her openness. But even if she didn't expect answers, she wanted them. It seemed unfair to put her in the center of a seemingly unsolvable muddle.

A brisk wind pressed at their backs, and Lank shivered. Lesley crowded close to Caroline, hunching his shoulders. The little boy squinted up at her. "It's awful cold, Miss Carrie. Can we go to Miss Kesia's an' get some cocoa?"

Kesia had treated the children to cocoa one morning for breakfast, and the child hadn't stopped clamoring for it since. Caroline hated to deny him, especially on the day he'd lost his father, but she had to answer honestly. "Miss Kesia's café isn't open today, Lesley. Remember? It's Sunday, and she's always closed on Sundays."

"Oh." The boy seemed to deflate. Then he brightened. "Can't you make us some?

We could go to our house. We got a stove an' kindlin' wood. An' there's canned milk on the shelf. I still got a chocolate bar Mr. Moore gave me. You can stir it into the milk, same way Miss Kesia does. Please, Miss Carrie? Please?"

"Oh, Lesley..."

As they stood on the boardwalk, two sullen faces turned outward and one hopeful face turned upward, a church bell tolled. Caroline looked toward the inviting sound. On the corner a small white clapboard chapel with green shutters framing its arched windows seemed to beckon to her. What better place for her and the children to get out of the wind and find a covering of peace?

"Come, children." She hurried them up the walk toward the chapel, joining several others attired in their go-to-meeting dresses and suits. Although the children wore their regular ragtag clothing and Caroline had dressed in a simple dark-blue muslin frock, no one looked askance at them. Instead, smiles and nods welcomed them. Caroline's heart lifted, eagerness to fellowship with like believers putting a skip in her step despite her extreme tiredness.

She settled on a back pew with Letta and Lank on one side, Lesley on the other. Lesley leaned against her shoulder, seemingly intimidated by the strange surroundings. Caroline offered him an encouraging smile, then turned her attention to the front, where a black-suited minister stepped behind a simple pulpit.

The bell continued to toll until everyone settled into the pews, and then the final note echoed for several seconds, thrilling Caroline with its pure tone. Across the congregation men rested their hats on their knees, and mothers bounced infants on their laps. An organist pressed her fingers to the keys, and all at once the parishioners opened their mouths and poured forth a joyous hymn: "Come, ye thankful people, come..."

Tears stung Caroline's eyes, closing her throat and rendering her unable to add her voice to the others'. But she sang with her heart, glorying in the wonderful promise found in the words of the song. "God, our Maker, doth provide for our wants to be supplied..." She glanced at the children, hoping they were listening. God knew these lost ones wanted to have a home and to be loved, just as she had when she was their age. God had provided for her, and He would provide for them, too.

The realization washed her in an all-consuming peace, and warmth flooded her. She wrapped her arms around the children, placing them into God's keeping with the gesture, while praying for Him to grant all they needed to grow into happy, healthy adults. **Give me all I need, too, Lord. Bestow Your gifts as You see fit.**

As she finished her prayer, she caught a movement from the corner of her eye— someone coming in late. There was a space at the end of their pew if Lank shifted closer to Letta. She tapped his shoulder and motioned for him to move in. He scowled, but he obeyed, and the man who'd entered late, his coat collar high and his hat pulled low, slid into the space Lank had created.

He removed his hat, revealing a head of thick, gold-blond hair. Caroline's pulse skipped a beat. Was it... Then he turned his face and caught her staring. He smiled, his green-gold eyes twinkling.

Caroline zipped her attention forward as another hymn began. Even though she didn't look at Ollie Moore again during the entire service, she was all too aware of his presence on the end of the pew. **Bestow Your gifts**, she'd prayed, and Ollie Moore had plopped himself down within arm's reach. What was God trying to do to her?

Chapter 18

Gordon

Gordon propped his crossed heels on the edge of his desk and linked his hands behind his head. He released a long, contented sigh. How he loved Sundays. Quiet. Solitary. The one day of the week when he could do whatever he pleased without worrying who might see.

Last Sunday had been particularly delightful, thanks to the newest sorter. The silly girl hadn't even blinked in apprehension when he'd instructed her to meet him for private instruction on her new job. Sweet, naive Mandy... His cheeks twitched from the effort of holding back his grin. Now that she understood what he meant by "private instruction," she probably wouldn't ever come again for such a lesson, but it didn't matter. Mandy wasn't the only naive girl in the city, as he well knew.

Dropping his feet to the floor, he pushed off from his chair and strode to the hallway. He paused at the top of the stairs, one ear turned toward the lower level to better catch the silence. Without machines operating, feet running here and there over wood floors, voices calling requests and demands, he felt as though he could hear the factory's solid brick walls sighing in bliss. He added a satisfied sigh of his own, reveling in the marvelous quiet.

Growing up in the Southridge Orphans' Home outside of Chicago, he'd never known what quiet meant. Kids always squabbling for a scrap of food, for a bit of attention. He'd never been one to squabble, though. No need to raise your voice when actions spoke louder than words ever could.

He hadn't been the biggest boy in the orphanage, but he'd learned size didn't matter if you were tough. So he never squabbled. He just puffed himself up like an aggressive alley cat and took what he wanted. And why not? All those benevolence barrels that showed up on the orphanage doorstep, delivered by ladies in black dresses with mouths pursed in sympathy for "the poor little orphan children," never held anything of value.

No, nobody ever gave something of worth. If a person wanted something, he had to take it. He'd learned that early, and he'd never forgotten the lesson. So on Sundays, Gordon gathered as much quiet as he could, only making a noise if he wanted to. Such control silence offered.

On tiptoe he descended three steps. A board squeaked. He frowned. Tomorrow he'd have the new first-shift handyman tighten the joints to remove the annoying sound. Then he continued to the bottom with steps so light and soundless not even a rabbit would have been startled by his progress.

He continued his trek across the floor, placing his feet with such stealth the floorboards didn't register his weight. He'd make a first-class detective if he ever decided to give up managing the factory. But he wasn't ready to leave this post. No other position could offer him more power, greater satisfaction...or more opportunity to abundantly pad his pockets.

A laugh built in his throat, but he swallowed it, determined not to destroy the peacefulness of his surroundings. But it was difficult. Mr. Fulton Dinsmore was an educated man, schooled in England at one of the finest universities. While in Europe, he'd sampled every confection Switzerland, Germany, and Sweden offered and had brought back the key ingredients to create creamier, more flavorful, intensely rich chocolates. Then he'd closed his father's small factory in Chicago and opened this Kansas factory in the center of the country where he could cost-effectively ship his delicacies to every state in the United States as well as the provinces of Canada.

Fulton   Dinsmore   had   put   the

"world-famous" in what had been just Dinsmore's Chocolates. Shrewd, people called him. Some even claimed he was a genius. And he'd placed orphaned Gordon Hightower in a position of leadership.

The laugh bubbled up until he could no longer hold it at bay. Gordon threw back his head and let it roll. The raucous noise bounced from the tin ceiling and back, filling the entire floor with his merriment. He allowed himself a full minute of unsuppressed glee, then abruptly snapped his jaw closed. The echo rang for a few more seconds, slowly fading into silence.

Gordon smiled into the quiet, flicking his gaze here and there, filling the empty corners with images of industrious workers. But instead of tan aprons bearing the logo for Dinsmore's World-Famous Chocolates, in his imagination every worker wore brown—chocolate-colored —aprons with the name HIGHTOWER stitched in bold yellow letters in the center of the bib.

"Hightower's World-Famous Chocolates," Gordon whispered, as if sharing a secret with a friend. The title tasted sweet. And even sweeter would be the money and prestige that came along with it.

Some might call him unappreciative, even felonious, for plotting against the man who'd plucked him from the hungry throng at the orphanage. But he knew better. He remembered the distinguished gentleman placing his hand on Gordon's scrawny shoulder and promising he'd now have a better life.

The thoughts that had filled Gordon's mind—of living in a fine house, eating at a table laden with wondrous foods, sleeping in a big bed with a feather mattress in a room all his own. He'd expected the rich man to make him part of his family. But instead, Dinsmore had deposited him with the manager of the factory and instructed the man to teach Gordon all he needed to know to be a good worker.

A good worker.

Gordon punched the air, nearly throwing himself off balance. He'd learned, all right. He'd learned every despicable task from lowliest trash burner to chocolate mixer to bookkeeper. And after nearly two decades of daily toil, Dinsmore had handed the reins of the factory to him and beamed, "You're my success story, Gordon. I'm proud of you, **son**." Son. Ha! Carefully trained work mule—that's what he'd been. That's what he'd always be until he could claim the factory as his own. And the day was coming.

With a little hop step of happiness, he angled back toward the stairway and his loft office. This time he walked with force, enjoying the thud of his heels bouncing back from the walls. He flopped into his chair, opened the hidden compartment in his desk, and smiled down at the journal containing the past two years' painstakingly recorded transactions.

Another year—perhaps a year and a half—of manipulating the books, of squirreling away assets, of groveling to Fulton Dinsmore, and then he could purchase the factory with the man's own money. Duping Dinsmore would be the culmination of Gordon's fondest dreams.

Caroline

A **tap, tap, tap** intruded upon Caroline's dreams, rousing her from a sound nap. She sat up, trying to determine the source of the noise. On the opposite side of the iron bed, Letta slept, undisturbed. Lank and Lesley lay coiled together like a pair of puppies on a quilt on the floor. Neither so much as twitched an eyelid in response to the tapping. Caroline frowned. Had she imagined it?

It came again—**tap, tap, tap**—and this time she was able to discern the source. Knuckles on a doorframe. Moving as quickly and quietly as possible, she crossed to the door and opened it before the knocking disturbed the children. After their emotional morning they needed rest.

A young boy in a frayed jacket, hat several sizes too big, and shoes with the toes worn through stood in the hallway. When he spotted her, his chest puffed out importantly, and he thrust a folded piece of paper toward her. "Telegram, miss!"

"Shh!"

The boy wilted.

She hadn't intended to crush him. Caroline stepped into the hallway, closing the door with a soft click behind her. She smiled at the crestfallen youth. "I have children sleeping."

"Oh. Sorry, ma'am." He bobbed the telegram at her again. "S'posed to give you this."

Caroline took the telegram and unfolded it. She read the brief message, her brow furrowed.

The boy rocked in place. "If you wanna reply, I can take it back with me an' get it sent for you."

She'd need to reply but not until she'd had a chance to speak with Letta. She tucked the telegram into her pocket. "No, thank you."

Once again his shoulders drooped. He turned and, head low, began to scuff his way up the hallway.

"Wait a moment," Caroline called. He paused, and she retrieved a nickel from the little coin pouch in her pocket. An extravagant tip, but she didn't regret it when the boy's face lit with joy. He smiled his thanks and bounded up the hallway and around the corner. Caroline waited until his thudding footsteps receded, then reentered the apartment.

The boys still slept, but Letta sat up in the bed, her pale face aimed in Caroline's direction. "Somethin' wrong?"

Instead of answering, Caroline quirked her finger, beckoning Letta to come near. They moved to the opposite side of the room from the bed and perched on the tufted settee—Caroline's only sitting-area furniture.

She removed the telegram from her pocket and pressed it flat against her knee. "Remember the messages we sent to your aunt this morning?" She'd had to send two twenty-word telegrams to include everything she wanted to say—informing the woman of her brother's death, requesting instructions concerning his burial, and asking who should be responsible for the children.

Letta nodded, her expression solemn.

"She's responded already. But I'm not sure what to make of it." Caroline read the brief missive aloud, leaving out the intrusive stop at the end of each phrase. "'Can't come. Pauper's grave fine. How old are youngsters?'"

Letta wrapped her arms across herself as if she were cold and stared at the little scrap of paper. "Don't know as I'm surprised she ain't comin'. Last time she came, she an' Pa had a terrible fallin' out. Can't remember what it was all about, but it was a long time ago. Lesley wasn't far outta diapers. She ain't been to see us since, not even at Christmastime." The girl shrugged, tossing her head. "It don't matter. I didn't much like her anyway."

Caroline crumpled the edge of the telegram between her fingers and thumb, wishing she could give Letta's aunt a good pinch for caring so little. "Are you sure you don't know where your mother is? I could send her a telegram if—"

"Don't know." Letta's voice rose on a note of distress. "Pa said she left to take up with some play company. She'd always wanted to be a stage actress. For all I know she could be clear in England." Her chin began to quiver, but she clenched her teeth for a moment, stilling the movement. "An' I don't rightly care. She don't want us, an' we don't want her. Not anymore."

Such a brave statement from one whose spirit was clearly battered. Caroline pointed to the final, blunt sentence on the telegram. "Why would your aunt ask your ages?"

Letta shrugged, holding her hands outward. "Dunno. Been so long since she's seen us, she probably don't remember. More'n likely she's hintin' I'm big enough to be on my own." Another sigh whooshed out. Letta sagged forward. "She's probably right on that. Heap o' girls my age are takin' care o' their own selves already. Some even gettin' married, like Ma done with Pa. She had me when she was just fifteen." She tipped her head, crunching her lips into a grimace. "So I reckon that's what I'll do. Take care o' myself an' Lank an' Lesley, too."

A girl of Letta's tender age should not carry such responsibility. Caroline placed her hand on Letta's knee. "I'll do whatever I can to help you."

Letta fixed Caroline with a helpless look. "But it ain't right for you to have to help with Pa's burial an' such. You ain't our kin or...or anything to us."

The boys stirred, rolling over and rubbing their eyes. Once they were fully awake, she and Letta wouldn't be able to speak freely. Caroline leaned close to Letta and whispered, "I'll send another telegram to your aunt, asking her to reconsider. Will that make you feel better?"

Letta's blue eyes squinted half-shut, giving her a hard look. "Just let it go, Miss Carrie. Truth is, I don't know that I'll ever feel better again." She crossed to her brothers, her steps slow and labored, and sank down to sit on the floor. She held open her arms, and the boys tumbled against her.

Caroline remained in her chair, observing the children through a sheen of tears.

Such a sad picture they presented. Somehow she had to find a way to prove Letta wrong. The girl would feel better someday. Someday soon. But she couldn't make it happen without help.

"Letta?" She waited until the girl shifted to look at her. "I need to make a telephone call. Will you and the boys be all right here alone for a little while?"

A strange look crept over Letta's face—a cross between amusement and sorrow. She offered a brief nod.

"All right." Caroline moved to the door, tossing a promise over her shoulder. "I won't be long." She caught her skirt, lifted the hem above her shoes, and dashed down the three flights of stairs to the lobby. If anyone would have ideas on how best to assist the Holcomb children, her own personal rescuer, Noble, would.

Chapter 19

Caroline

"Of course I'll come. Annamarie, too. We'll catch the earliest train."

Tears of relief filled Caroline's eyes. She knew Noble wouldn't be able to resist offering assistance. His compassionate heart never failed to astound her. But to bring Annamarie... Caroline cringed. "Are you sure? It's a lengthy journey, and Annamarie..." An image of the dear woman flooded Caroline's mind. So fragile. So beautiful in spite of her infirmities.

Noble's low chuckle rumbled through the line. "You know I won't be able to leave her behind when she learns of these children's situation. I'll check train schedules and send a wire with the details so you'll know when to expect us."

Caroline hugged the little earpiece. She hadn't realized how much she'd missed Noble and Annamarie until faced with the prospect of seeing them again soon. "I'll likely be sleeping when you arrive, but you know the address. Just come to the apartment and wake me." She sucked in a short breath, hardly able to squelch her delight. "Thank you again, Noble. You're always there when I need you."

Another chuckle reached her ears, followed by his distinct tsk, tsk, tsk. "You know full well you always have help at hand, Caroline. God is only a prayer away."

She smiled. He'd make a fine preacher. "I know. And I've been leaning on His strength these past days. Especially since the Holcomb children came into my life."

"Good. I'll let you go now. We'll see you soon, Caroline. Good-bye."

She placed the receiver in its cradle and then rested her cheek in her hand. Perhaps it was selfish to ask Noble to bear this burden with her, but she couldn't very well make burial arrangements, see to the children's needs, and complete her investigation. Noble and Annamarie would take excellent care of the children, allowing her to focus on Bratcher's death.

Her pulse sped. As annoyed as she'd been to find Ollie Moore outside that elevator shaft last night, his arrival had proved to be a boon. And now Noble would be here to view the blueprint of the elevator's inner workings. Could the end of her investigation be near? If she'd be leaving soon, she needed to know Letta and her brothers would be cared for.

Their aunt's telegram lay crumpled in her pocket. She patted it, thinking. She'd told Letta she would contact her aunt again, and even though her tired body yearned for sleep, the children were more important than her rest. She'd left her shawl upstairs, but a brisk walk would pump her blood and keep her warm. Determined to convince the woman to make the trek for the sake of her niece and nephews, Caroline headed for the station.

Oliver

Oliver thanked the minister for taking the time to visit with him and then tugged his coat and hat into place. Before departing the chapel, he crossed to the tin plate used to collect offerings and carefully laid a Liberty half eagle in its smooth bottom. Although lesser-valued coins rattled in his pocket, he wanted to repay the kind minister for rushing through his dinner and returning to the chapel to help Oliver understand prayer.

As he walked in the brisk fall air toward his apartment, he contemplated verses the minister had read from Matthew— Jesus's instruction to His disciples. The minister had said Jesus's prayer provided a structure, so to speak, for addressing God. Oliver reflected on the minister's admonition that one should first praise God and seek forgiveness for any wrongdoings before making requests of Him.

The few prayers from pulpits that Oliver recalled had seemed formal and directed more to the listening audience than to God. Father's simple prayers—asking a blessing for food—seemed almost meaningless in light of the seriousness of Letta's and Caroline's requests. When Oliver voiced his thought, the minister assured him all prayers are of value because all prayers are a means of communicating with God. **"The more we talk to Him," the man had said, his expression fervent, "the closer our relationship with Him grows, just as with any earthly relationship. So don't worry so much about how you speak to Him, son. Just talk to Him."**

Oliver paused on the corner to allow two carriages to pass, then stepped onto the cobblestone street, his thoughts rolling onward. **Just talk to Him.** Desire to follow the simple directive stirred in him. Ahead on the boardwalk a bench huddled between two large pots overflowing with shriveled, browning flowers. The explosion of withered stems provided a makeshift screen. Oliver plopped onto the bench, rested his elbows on his widespread knees, and buried his face in his hands.

Head low, eyes closed, he pushed aside the sounds of the occasional wagon and the wind whistling between buildings and forced his attention on addressing God. **Just talk to Him...** "God..." He pushed the single word past his dry lips in a raspy whisper. "The reverend said You're always listening. I guess that means You're listening now. That You hear me." He crunched his eyelids so tight his forehead hurt. "I don't have anything to ask for myself. My life is good. I have need for nothing more."

Except You.

The thought winged from the back recesses of his mind, startling him with the clarity. Had he ever considered such a thing before? No, never. But in that moment, bent forward on a bench in the middle of the city block, he recognized its truth. He—Oliver Fulton Dinsmore— needed God.

He gulped back a strangled sob. "But I don't want to ask You for anything for me.

There's a girl—her name is Letta." A raw chuckle found its way from his throat. "I suppose You already know all about Letta, her brothers, and her father. The minister said You know everything, so I don't need to tell you Mr. Holcomb is sick. Very sick. Letta asked me to pray for him, so here I am, God, praying."

Had he ever struggled more with a conversation? How awkward—how humbling—to bare one's soul before God. Yet he wouldn't stop now.

Moistening his lips, he continued in the same halting whisper meant only for God's ears. "The prayer Jesus offered said we're to ask for Your will. I hope it's Your will for Mr. Holcomb to recover and live to care for his children. That's what I'm asking of You, God—to make Mr. Holcomb well." He paused, trying to recall what should come next. He couldn't think of anything, so he ended the same way he'd heard the minister close his morning prayer. "In Your Son's name I ask this... Amen."

He remained in his hunkered position,

eyes closed, half expecting a reply. When none came, he released a sigh of disappointment and lifted his head. He gave a jolt of surprise. On the opposite side of the street, her skirts swirling, Carrie Lang strode along the boardwalk.

Oliver stood up and waved his hand. "Carrie! Carrie!"

She stopped but twitched in place, as if ants nibbled at the soles of her feet, but she waited for him to trot across the street. He leaped onto the raised walkway next to her. Despite the apprehension on her face, he couldn't stop a smile from growing. He couldn't wait to tell her he'd done as she'd asked—he'd prayed for Mr. Holcomb.

"I'm surprised you're not sleeping," she said. An odd greeting, almost an accusation.

Oliver drew back slightly, his smile faltering. "I could say the same thing to you. You worked last night, too." He jammed his hands into his jacket pockets and risked a grin. "I was glad to see you in the service this morning. You and the children. I'm sure being out of the hospital for a bit did Letta some good."

Carrie's brow pinched. "Yes."

"I'm also glad I spotted you. I wanted to tell you, I—"

"Ollie, will this take long?" She eased sideways a few inches. "I've been on a lengthy errand and left the children unattended. I need to get back to them." "Oh!" He scratched his cheek, still itchy from its recent shave. Since she'd recognized him beneath all that fur, he'd been able to relieve his face of its uncomfortable growth. "Well, then, may I walk along with you?"

She glanced up the street, blew out a quick breath, then offered a brusque nod. Without a word she took off, her heels clipping a steady rhythm on the walkway.

Oliver walked along beside her. He longed to share his newfound efforts to pray, but her demeanor stilled his tongue. She always moved with determination, displaying confidence and grace, but her stiff posture and firmly set jaw spoke of an inner conflict. The fine hairs on the back of Oliver's neck prickled. Something was surely awry.

"Do you want to talk about it?"

She turned her face in his direction without slowing her pace. "What?"

"Your errand. It must have been a very trying one."

They'd reached a corner, and a trolley's bell warned them of its approach.

Stranded until it passed, Caroline fidgeted in place, clearly eager to continue onward. "The errand itself wasn't trying. Anyone can send a telegram. It's just that I'm—"

The trolley rattled past, its brass bell clanging a cheerful farewell. She snapped her mouth closed and charged off the edge of the boardwalk into the street. A carriage pulled by matching Percherons rounded the corner, the broad chests of the large animals bearing down on her. Oliver leaped forward, caught Caroline's arm, and yanked her to safety. She fell hard against him. Instinctively he wrapped both arms around her, holding her upright.

As soon as the carriage rolled by, she

wriggled loose. Her chest heaved in frightened gasps. She turned a startled look on him. "I...I didn't even see it. Thank you, Ollie."

"You're welcome." He panted, too. "Why don't you stand here for a minute and catch your breath?"

"I can't." She snatched up her skirts, quickly looked back and forth, then set off across the street, calling over her shoulder, "I must return to the children. They shouldn't be alone at a time like this."

He followed on her heels. "Having their father in the hospital is a hardship for them, but you wearing yourself out or getting trampled by horses won't help them much."

She stopped without warning and spun to face him. Still caught in a forward motion, he nearly bumped noses with her. She took a stumbling step in reverse. Her mouth fell open, and she clapped her hand over it. "You don't know..."

Her fingers muffled her words, but he heard them anyway. He frowned. "I don't know what?"

Tears filled her eyes. "Mr. Holcomb died early this morning."

She couldn't have surprised him more if she'd socked him in the stomach. He stammered, "But...but I prayed for him." Such a foolish statement. He wished he could retract it.

Sympathy softened her expression. "We all did. But the infection took him anyway." Her shoulders sagged. "I sent a telegram to the children's aunt when we left the hospital, asking her to come and assist the children. Her reply came early this afternoon. She refused to come and instructed me to put her brother in a pauper's grave."

Oliver swallowed a growl of frustration. He didn't know this aunt, but he didn't like her.

Caroline went on in a tired voice. "So I sent a second telegram, hoping to convince her to change her mind, but now I..." She tipped her head, her forehead puckering. "You wanted to tell me something. Is it about the blueprint?"

He'd forgotten about the blueprint in light of his conversation with the minister. And now he didn't want to admit he'd learned to pray. What good had it done? Mr. Holcomb was already gone by the time Oliver had discovered how to talk to God. He would look like a fool if he told her now.

He took her elbow and began guiding her forward at a slower pace. "It isn't important."

Actually, it was important. The deep longing to truly know God that he'd experienced in the midst of his prayer still ached at the center of his being. But would such a relationship benefit him? He'd prayed too late, but Letta, Kesia, and Caroline had been praying all through the man's illness. And still he'd died. So did talking to God make any difference?

He pushed aside his musings. "You sent a second telegram, you said, but you didn't finish your thought. But now you... what?"

She shivered. Dark clouds had rolled in, hiding the sun, and shadows shrouded them with gray. In his warm jacket he hadn't realized how much the temperature had dropped. He whipped off the jacket and draped it over her shoulders. He supposed he'd broken protocol by giving her a covering still warm from his body, and if she refused it, he wouldn't be indignant, but he couldn't stand idly by and allow her to catch cold.

To his gratification, she clutched the lapels and held the coat closed at her throat. "Thank you, Ollie." She sounded more like herself, and the smile she offered appeared genuine.

He smiled in return, warmed even though the cool air now nipped at him. "You're welcome."

They fell into step, their strides evenly matched, and she finally answered his question. "Now I'm wondering if I shouldn't have sent the second telegram. If she comes, it will be only out of obligation or guilt, not true concern for the children. And they've suffered enough without being made to feel as though they're a burden to their only remaining relative."

Oliver decided to state the obvious. "If she's truly the children's only remaining relative, then she is obligated to them. She really has no choice."

"But don't you see, Ollie?" She turned a look of abject misery on him. "They deserve more than obligation. If she doesn't intend to truly care for them, then she shouldn't come at all."

Oliver admired her convictions. Her concern for the Holcomb children touched him, but she needed to be practical. The children required shelter, food, and clothing. As their aunt, this unknown woman had a legal and moral obligation to provide it. He touched Carrie's arm lightly, hoping to soften the blow his words would deliver. "Obligation is better than nothing. At least their needs will be met. You did the right thing."

She stared at him in silence, the disappointment on her face stinging him worse than the cold drops of rain carried on the brisk breeze. She whipped off his jacket and pressed it into his hands. "My boarding hotel is just around the corner. You can take this now."

"Carrie, I'm only trying to—"

"I know what you're saying." She skittered in reverse, her arms folded over herself. "I just don't happen to agree with you. And I never will." She turned and dashed off.

Oliver considered going after her, trying to make her see his point of view, but she was too emotionally entangled with the children to listen to reason. Truthfully, he ached for the children, too. He'd done his best to help, verifying that their father would receive medical care and paying for meals so they wouldn't go hungry. But what else could he do?

Thunder rumbled, and the scattered drops became a steady downpour. He should return to his apartment rather than stand there getting drenched, worrying over a situation he couldn't change. Pulling the collar of his coat up to protect his neck and tugging his hat low, he turned toward the closest trolley stop. He'd gone only a few steps, though, when a frantic cry sealed him in place.

"Ollie! Ollie!" Carrie ran toward him, coils of soppy hair slapping against her wet cheeks. He met her halfway and caught her arms. Her eyes wide with fear, she gasped out, "Letta and the boys... They aren't in my apartment!"

Chapter 20

Letta

Letta yanked on her little brother's arm. "C'mon, Lesley, hurry up. We're gettin' soaked to the bone."

Lesley let out a wail. "Stop it, Letta! You're hurtin' me!"

She yanked him again. "Well then, stop draggin' your feet. We gotta get out of this rain."

Seemed as though the sky dumped buckets. If she'd known this storm was coming, she wouldn't have taken the boys out. But when Miss Carrie left, it seemed a perfect time to make their escape. Not that she wanted to escape Carrie—she was nice enough. But Carrie was bent on bringing Aunt Gertrude to Sinclair, and

Letta wanted nothing to do with Pa's sister.

"I wanna go b-back to Miss C-C-Carrie." Lesley shivered so bad his teeth chattered and made him sound like Lank. "Can't we g-go back?"

"No." Holding tight to Lesley's sleeve, she dragged him along beside her. Lank trailed behind, coughing into his fist. Their feet splashed up muddy water with every step, and rain doused their heads. She hoped Pa had left a good supply of wood in the wood box so she could get the boys warmed up again quick. If they got sick, she didn't know what she'd do. "Soon as we get to the house, I'll fix you some cocoa like you've been wantin'."

Lesley squinted up at her. "Honest?"

In her pocket she had three pieces of chocolate, snitched from a bowl on Miss Carrie's bedside table. If the rain hadn't ruined them by now, she could melt them in some warm milk. "Honest. But we gotta hurry."

"All right." Crunching his hands into fists, Lesley broke into a run.

Letta and Lank did the same. She wished she'd thought of cocoa earlier.

She wouldn't have had to force Lesley out of Miss Carrie's apartment. Gracious, but that boy was pigheaded. If it hadn't been for Lank grabbing Lesley around the middle and wrestling him down the stairs, they might not have gotten away before Miss Carrie returned.

Guilt nibbled at Letta. Miss Carrie would be plenty worried when she got back and found out they were gone. And of course, leaving meant Letta wouldn't be able to get those four dollars for going to school. Without those four dollars she'd have to find a job. But she'd make the boys go to school. They could share their lessons with her, same as they did the days she stayed at the hospital with Pa. She'd keep learning. Sure she would.

Lesley tripped over something and fell flat. He came up spluttering, both knees of his britches torn. Blood dripped from his chin, the heels of his hands, and his knees. He let out a screech loud enough to wake Pa from the dead.

Letta clamped her hand over his mouth. "Hush that! You want people to think someone's bein' murdered? They'll set the cops on us!"

Lank scuttled forward and gave Lesley's shoulder several pats. He looked at Letta, rain dribbling down his freckled face. "Yuh-yuh-yuh-you gotta cuhcuh-carry him."

Although she wasn't keen on the idea, she knew Lank was right. Lesley wouldn't take one step now that he'd hurt himself. She turned her back on the boys and bent forward. "Heft him on, Lank."

Lesley's weight settled on her back, and his skinny arms wrapped around her neck. She looped her hands under his knees and took off at a clumsy trot. At least they didn't have far to go. Their house waited just on the next block.

Lank dashed ahead and had the door open and waiting when Letta stumbled into the yard. The moment she stepped over the threshold, she tipped sideways and dumped Lesley. Lank caught hold of him and kept him from tumbling onto the floor. She gave the door a slam, sealing them in the dingy room. Pa had kept a lamp on a shelf in the kitchen, and she pawed her way to it, leaving a trail of murky water. Lank and Lesley scuttled behind her, one of them holding tight to her soggy dress. She thought about shaking the hand loose, but it was kind of nice to know they were there.

A little box of matches sat next to the lamp, and after three tries she managed to get one lit. She touched it to the wick, and immediately the glow made her feel warmer even though she continued to shiver.

"Lank, get some wood from the wood box so I can stoke the stove. Lesley, go fetch dry clothes from the bureau. You two can change while I get the stove goin'."

Lesley hovered near, hugging himself and blinking away drops of water that ran into his eyes. "An' you'll make cocoa?"

"I'll make cocoa. Now scoot."

The boys scurried off in opposite directions. While Lank filled the stove's belly with chunks of wood, Letta used Pa's knife to carve one chunk into kindling, the way she'd seen Pa do a hundred times. It took more effort, though, than she'd imagined. By the time she got enough kindling to feed a fire, the boys had changed out of their wet things and stood beside the stove in their bare feet, wet hair straggling across their foreheads.

"Hurry up, Letta."

"Goin' as fast as I can, Lesley. While you're waitin', get me a pot an' that can o' milk. Make yourselves useful." She cringed, hearing Pa in her words. But the boys moved off to obey, letting her focus on starting the fire. If she weren't so wet and cold and shivery, she'd have no trouble. She'd started the stove every day since Ma left. Of course, Pa'd kept the wood box and kindling bucket ready. She reckoned that would be her job now. Worry struck. Had she taken on more than she could handle, running off with the boys?

She poked at the little pieces of splintered wood, pushing them together so they'd work better. Lesley limped over, pan in hand, and Lank followed with the can of milk and the can opener. Lank held out both items to her, and she snorted. If she was going to take on more responsibility, the boys would have to help. "You ain't helpless, Lank. Poke that can your own self."

Lank shot her a startled look. Pa had never let them mess with the opener—the sharp point could do some damage. But after a moment's hesitation, Lank placed the can on the table, hooked the opener on the ridged edge, and gave a push. Frothy milk bubbled up around the hole and trickled down the side of the can. Pa would've been upset about the mess and the waste, but Letta didn't scold.

"Pour it in the pan now. Lesley, step back and give Lank some room."

When Lank carried the pan of milk to the stove, a grin creased his face. Letta'd never seen him look so proud. She rewarded him with a nod, then set the pan in the middle of one of the lids at the back of the stove. She didn't want Lesley poking his nose over it and getting burned.

She dug the pieces of chocolate from her pocket. Their wrappers were sodden, but hopefully the candy inside wasn't ruined. She laid them on the table and then pointed her finger at the boys. "Stay outta these. I won't put 'em in 'til that milk's steamin' good. I'm gonna go change into dry clothes, and I'll finish the cocoa when I get back. You two just sit close to the stove an' get warm. All right?"

The pair nodded in agreement, then settled side by side on the bench closest to the stove's heat. Satisfied they'd be fine, Letta hurried to the bureau. In the shadowy corner out of the boys' sight, she scrambled out of her wet things and into a dry petticoat, camisole, and gingham dress. She started to pull on a pair of Pa's wool socks—her toes felt close to freezing—but she couldn't make herself put them on. So she crossed on bare feet to the stove and sat next to Lesley, slipping her arm around his narrow shoulders to make up for being rough on him during their walk.

"Your knees an' hands feelin' any better?" She used a gentle voice this time.

"They sting some." He touched his chin. "Hurts here, too."

Letta tipped his head up and squinted at the spot. He'd have an ugly scab by morning. "You'll prob'ly be sore for a few days. You hit hard. But you're tough. You'll be all right."

Lesley grinned.

Lank held his hands toward the stove. "Wuh-wuh-we goin' tuh-tuh-to school tuh-tuh-tomorrow?"

Letta chewed the inside of her lip. Much as she wanted to keep up with lessons, school would be the first place Miss Carrie'd come looking for them. They'd have to lay low for a few days, hiding under the bed or even in the neighbor's outhouse if somebody came snooping, until Carrie gave up on finding them. She shook her head. "Not tomorrow. Maybe not for a week or so."

She turned stern. "But then you'll be goin' back. You'll learn all you can, an' you'll share it with me, you hear?"

Lank scowled, and Lesley's lower lip poked out in a pout. Lesley said, "What you gonna do while we're goin' to school?"

"I'll be workin'." Letta turned a sour look on the boys. "Somebody's gotta buy food, ya know."

Lesley nudged Letta's arm. "Miss Kesia'll feed us, don'tcha think?"

Letta shifted and scowled at Lesley. "You two stay away from Miss Kesia, you hear me?"

They both stared at her, wide eyed. Lesley said, "How come?"

"You go to the café, and Carrie'll find out about it. Then she'll take us to her place again, an' she'll give us over to Aunt Gertrude. That what you want?"

Lank shook his head hard, but Lesley shrugged. "Dunno."

"Well, then, lemme tell you. You don't wanna go to Aunt Gertrude's. She's real fat, an' she's mean, an' she'll make you sleep in the barn with rats." Letta had no idea if she was speaking the truth, but she had Lesley's attention. "She hated Pa, and she hates us. We'd be sorry as sorry can be to go to Aunt Gertrude's."

Lesley scrunched up his face. "Then why's Miss Carrie wantin' us to go to Aunt Gertrude's? I thought Miss Carrie liked us."

Letta sighed. "Miss Carrie does like us, Lesley. But she ain't our ma. She ain't our aunt or cousin or nothin'. She's just a lady, an' she can't be takin' care of us. That's why she asked Aunt Gertrude to come. She wanted to find somebody to take care of us. The thing is, she don't know Aunt Gertrude like I do."

Steam rose in curling ribbons above the pan. Letta jumped up and stirred the milk before it scorched. Swirling the spoon through the creamy liquid, she added, "But you two don't need to worry none. I'll take care of you. You just gotta do what I tell you, all right? Long as you do what I say, we'll be fine. All right?"

They bobbed their heads in unison, and Letta let out a breath of relief. Five days. Maybe a week. Even if Aunt Gertrude did come to Sinclair, she wouldn't stick around longer than that. She'd put Pa in the ground and then skedaddle. And Miss Carrie'd give up by then and go on about her own business. If she and the boys could stay out of sight for just five days— maybe a week—everything would be fine.

Caroline

"I'm sure they're just fine."

Ollie's bland statement did nothing to calm Caroline's ire. Lightning flashes split the sky, followed by booms of thunder. The wind blew, sending the heavy rain sideways. She paused in her hundredth trek from one side of the lobby to the other and stared out the window, praying for the storm to pass so she could go track down Letta and the boys. Thinking of them wandering around in the torrential downpour tied her stomach into knots.

Ollie rose from the sofa, where he'd plopped himself an hour ago, and crossed to her. "Carrie, Letta's a resourceful girl. She'd take her brothers to shelter. You don't need to worry so."

Why must he be so calm and rational? Of course Letta was resourceful. Of course she'd take her brothers to shelter. They'd returned to their house—Caroline was certain. But just because they weren't wandering the streets didn't change the fact that they'd run away from her. From her, who'd been nothing but kind to them! Their choice left her heart bruised and aching. She didn't deserve to be treated so thoughtlessly, and the moment the storm cleared—she wasn't foolish enough to go out with lightning bolts sending spikes of fury toward the ground—she intended to pound on the warped door of the Holcombs' shack and demand an explanation.

She aimed a disgruntled look at Ollie. "I'm not worried. I'm mad."

He raised one eyebrow. A grin tweaked his cheek. "Oh, you are, huh?"

"Yes. Good and mad. At the children and at you."

Both of his eyebrows flew high, and he traded his teasing grin for a look of surprise. "At me?"

"Yes, you."

"Why me?"

His genuine confusion sent her frustration up a notch. Folding her arms over her chest, she glowered at him. "Because you're so...so unflustered. Those children did a foolish, thoughtless thing by leaving the way they did. Just because I know where they are doesn't mean I shouldn't be upset with them. And you should be, too!"

He blinked twice. "I should?"

"Of course you should! Here you are, stuck in the lobby of my boarding hotel in damp clothes when you could be snug and warm in your own bed, soundly sleeping."

He burst out laughing.

She balled her hands into fists, battling the urge to punch him on the arm. "What's so funny?"

At her reaction he stilled the raucous laughter, but his eyes continued to twinkle. "I'm sorry. But if you could see yourself." Another chortle escaped, but he turned it into a cough—a feeble attempt to mask his humor. "You might be fierce enough to go to battle, but you're the sorriest looking warrior I've ever seen." He reached out and tugged a loose strand of her hair, which trailed against her cheek. "Why don't you go up to your room, change out of your water-soaked dress, and run a comb through your hair? It would make you feel better."

The fact that he was right only infuriated her more. She turned her back on him, aiming her gaze out the window again. "I'm just fine."

"You're not fine, Carrie." He moved closer—close enough that his breath touched her cheek. "You've been given a tremendous fright, your feelings have been hurt, and you're cold and wet to boot."

So he did understand. Even so, she didn't want him to be calm and reasonable. She wanted him to get angry. To stomp his feet. To rail at the children's insensitivity. His unperturbed behavior only served to make her feel childish and melodramatic. But to tell him so would probably earn another round of laughter.

He went on quietly, "Changing clothes won't fix your trampled feelings, but it'll help some. So why not go?"

The storm wasn't letting up. It might last all night. Did she intend to stand here stewing in a muddy dress with her hair hanging down her face in tangled ribbons, watching lightning decorate the sky? She should do as he suggested. But she didn't move.

Hands descended on her shoulders. She didn't resist when he turned her to face him. Instead of humor, concern glowed in his eyes. "Carrie, by now Letta, Lank, and Lesley are probably sleeping in their own beds. They'll be fine until morning. Go take care of yourself. Please?"

His hands, so broad and strong, gently caressed her shoulders. The caring in his eyes sent warmth spiraling through her. Caroline's resolve to be stalwart, to be independent, to never need anyone slowly faded, and she felt herself leaning toward him, wanting to simply melt into his embrace.

What was she doing? She bolted away from his touch and skittered toward the staircase. "You're right. I...I should change." More than her clothes. "You... you should..." He should what? Leave? Stay? She was an investigator. She was supposed to solve problems. But she hadn't a clue what she wanted him to do. So she turned and ran.

Chapter 21

Oliver

Oliver waited until after midnight for Carrie to return to the lobby. But she stayed up-stairs. Twice he set off for his own apart-ment, but both times lightning chased him back. He finally lay on the couch in her lobby and slept. He awakened early to birdsong. A peek out the window showed clouds hanging like ghostly sheets in the gray sky, but no rain was falling, and fingers of sunlight sneaked through tiny gaps in the clouds, promising the storm had passed.

He stretched and twisted his torso, working out the kinks the lumpy couch had put in his muscles. Then he set off in the damp morning toward the Holcombs' house. After Carrie had gone upstairs last night, he'd had a chance to think through what she'd said, and he'd discovered a niggling hint of irritation. Even in the midst of mourning, Letta should have had enough sense not to go traipsing off in the middle of a thunderstorm. She'd put herself and her brothers in a potentially dangerous situation, and he intended to let her know without any uncertainty how displeased both he and Carrie were with her choices.

After he'd delivered a thorough scolding, he'd haul all three of them to Kesia's for breakfast. He'd missed his dinner last night, thanks to those runaways, and he was half-starved. He might as well fill their stomachs, too, while he was at it.

His feet were soaked—again—by the time he reached the Holcombs' little house. Shaking each boot by turn to remove as much mud as possible before stepping inside, he frowned. The leather was cracked, the shaft peeling away from the sole. He'd probably have to throw them out. Another reason to take those children to task. He gave the door several solid thumps with his fist, then turned his ear to listen. Only silence from the other side. But they had to be in there. Where else would they go?

He knocked again, banging hard enough to rattle the door in its frame. This time a timorous voice called, "Who's there?"

"It's Ollie Moore, Letta. Open up right now."

Muffled whispers, scuffling feet, and a series of thuds and bumps sounded behind the planked door. Oliver grabbed the knob and gave it a violent wrench. The door opened inward on three children scrambling out of nightshirts and into everyday clothes. He stepped into the room and slammed the door behind him. All movement stopped. Three sets of round blue eyes peered at him from beneath mops of tangled red hair.

Oliver balled his fists on his hips and scowled at the trio. "Finish getting dressed. Then we are going to have a talk."

Letta held a tattered dress against the

buttoned front of her cotton chemise. She thrust out her chin, her eyes sparking. "You can't come bargin' in here an' bark orders at us. You ain't our pa."

No, he wasn't. But in the absence of one, he supposed he was the closest thing to a father they had. The thought both scared him and made him feel accountable. He decided offense was better than defense. "No back talk. Just do as I say."

"I ain't changin' my clothes in front of you." Letta inched backward, holding up her dress like a shield. "Gonna change in Pa's bedroom. C'mon, Lank an' Lesley."

Oliver waved his hand at the pair of boys, who hadn't budged. "Go on. Get yourselves changed. But make it quick. Like I said, I want to talk to you. And I'm short on patience."

The boys whirled and clattered after their sister. The door slammed into its frame, and silence fell in the main room. Oliver sank onto a bench next to the stove and rested his elbow on the table. A pan, empty save a scorched ring on its interior, sat on the stove. The table held three mugs and a smear of melted chocolate. Apparently they'd at least had a little something for supper.

Minutes ticked by as he waited for them to emerge. How long did it take kids to pull on a dress or britches and a shirt, anyway? He called out, "You about done in there?" No answer. He raised his voice. "Letta, hurry up now. Do you hear me?" Again, not a sound in reply. Frowning, Oliver stomped across the room and pressed his ear to the bedroom door. Nothing. But cool air crept from the crack under the door.

A sick feeling replaced his hunger. He yanked the door open. The window yawned wide, the simple muslin curtain flapping against the windowsill. And all three children were gone.

But they hadn't been gone long.

Oliver spun and ran to the front door. He reached for the doorknob, but before he could grab it, he heard someone call, "Letta, are you in there?" and the door swung inward. It hit him square in the side of the face. Stars exploded behind his eyes, dizziness assailed him, and he fell backward. On the way down he slammed his head on the bench he'd vacated. He lay on the floor, his head pounding and the room spinning.

Through his blurry vision, he witnessed Carrie bending over him, horror on her face. "Dear Lord in heaven, what did I do? Ollie! Ollie, are you all right?"

His head hurt so badly he wished she'd knocked him unconscious. Unfortunately, he felt every fierce throb. He moaned, "Don't you know how to knock?"

"I'm so sorry. Here, let me help you."

He wasn't entirely sure he wanted her help, but he didn't resist when she took his hands and pulled him into a sitting position. He bent his knees and pressed his palms against the crusty floor to give himself a more secure base. How could his head spin so wildly and remain attached to his shoulders?

She caught his chin between her fingers and angled his face toward the weak band of sunlight flowing through the open door.

She grimaced. "You're going to have a black eye, I'm afraid. It's already swelling and turning colors."

"Dandy." Oliver gingerly fingered the knot forming on the back of his head. No blood, so he hadn't broken the skin, but it stung like fury. At least if that spot bruised, his hair would cover it. Maybe he shouldn't have shaved off his whiskers after all.

Carrie wrung her hands, deep furrows lining her brow. "Do you think you can stand?"

"I'm not even sure I can think." Rolling onto one hip, he caught hold of the bench, and then he slowly pulled himself upright. He wobbled, but he managed to keep his footing. He sucked in several deep breaths, willing the throbbing in his head to abate.

Once he'd proved his ability to stand, Carrie seemed to lose her deep concern for him. She leaned sideways, peering past him first on one side, then the other. She turned a frown on him. "The children aren't here?"

"They were here. But when I showed

up, they went out the window."

Her eyes flew wide, just as the children's had when he'd burst in on them. "You let them go?"

Oliver cupped the side of his head and scowled at her as best he could through his swollen eye. "I might have caught them had you not knocked me flat."

She grabbed his hand and pulled him out the door. "Come on! We have to find them!"

The rapid movement brought a new rush of dizziness. He yanked free of her grasp and caught hold of the porch post. He clung, panting. "I...I can't run. Not yet." Closing his eyes, he waited for the spinning to pass. "Go ahead on your own. They can't have gotten far."

He expected to hear her receding footsteps, but instead the porch boards bounced beneath his soles. An arm slipped around his waist. He popped his eyes open—well, one of them—and looked into her upturned, penitent face.

"I'm truly sorry I hit you with the door. It was an accident."

"I know." He draped his arm over her shoulders and allowed her to lead him off the porch. They moved slowly across the bare, muddy yard toward the road.

"I'll take you to Kesia's and have her see to your injuries. I'm sure some of the regulars there will be willing to form a search party and help me find the children. Then you can rest."

Rest sounded good. He couldn't recall ever experiencing such an intense headache. "Thank you, Carrie."

"It's the least I can do."

"I should say so."

She shot a startled look at him, but she apparently saw the grin twitching his lips, because she released a light, airy laugh. "I suppose if you can tease, it means you're going to live after all."

"Unfortunately, I believe I shall live, although I dare confess, given the incredible discomfort now pervading my skull, a lack of consciousness is much preferred."

She drew him to a stop. "Ollie, are you still teasing?"

He blinked at her, confused. "What?"

She shook her head. "Never mind. Let's get you to Kesia's."

Caroline

He'd done it again—slipped into a mode of speech incompatible with that of a laborer. In fact, he'd just delivered one of the most eloquently phrased statements she'd ever heard. Would a bang on the head cause a tongue to form flowery locution? She'd not encountered such an odd reaction to a head injury in the past, and given her line of work, she'd delivered her fair share of clops to others' heads. But this was her first unintentional one. She only wished Ollie hadn't been the victim of her ill-timed burst through that doorway.

The moment they crossed the threshold of Kesia's café, the owner rushed to them, hands outstretched.

"Oh, just look at your poor face!" Kesia curled her arm around Ollie's waist on the other side and guided him to the closest stool, which happened to be occupied. "Rupert, shift offa there an' let this poor boy sit. Why, he must've been besieged by bandits!"

Caroline cringed. "No bandits, Kesia. Just a door."

"And a bench," Ollie added, dropping onto the stool. He placed his bent elbow on the counter and rested his head in the V.

Kesia looked from Ollie to Caroline, her face registering bafflement. "Have all his senses been knocked loose?"

Caroline quickly explained the circumstances of Ollie's injuries, including their pursuit of the Holcomb children.

Kesia shook her head, clicking her tongue on her teeth. "Such a sad situation all the way around. A father gone, a man wounded, an' children wanderin' around sad an' lost. Gonna be spendin' time on my knees over these situations, I can assure you."

Caroline left Ollie in Kesia's care and turned to the men seated around the counter. "As I just told Kesia, the two little boys who have been taking their meals here and their older sister are missing. They've run away." How it hurt to know they'd run from her. She pushed aside her bruised feelings and used her briskest, most professional tone. "I would very much appreciate assistance in locating them. Would any of you be willing to aid in the search?"

The men muttered, looking at each other or down at their plates.

Kesia smacked her palm on the counter, and the men all jumped. "Listen here, you well-fed bunch o' ne'er-do-wells. If you ever want to taste my peach pie or apple cobbler again, you'll hop down off them stools an' turn this city upside down. 'Cause I'm tellin' you right now, until those youngsters are safe under Miss Carrie's roof, my stove won't be holdin' one pan o' baked goods!"

"Aw, Kesia," one of the men groaned, "you can't mean that. We don't even know those young uns."

She jammed her fists on her hips and

bounced a fierce glare across each face. "That don't matter. The Good Book says, 'Inasmuch as ye have done it unto one of the least of these my brethren, ye have done it unto me.' You wanna try explainin' to the Lord Almighty why you're turnin' your back on some o' His precious children?"

Mutters rolled around the room.

Kesia pointed her finger at the door, her double chin quivering. "Now, every last one o' you, get out there an' find those young uns! The man who hauls 'em here to me'll be rewarded with a triple-layer sour cream cake."

The man who'd previously argued sat up straight. "With chocolate icin'?"

"On top an' between the layers."

With a whoop he leaped off the stool and scrambled for the door. The others swarmed after him.

Kesia turned a triumphant smile on Caroline. "That's how you get things done." Then she placed her hand on Caroline's arm, her expression serious. "Sure am sorry to hear about Mr. Holcomb dyin'. The Lord giveth, and the Lord taketh away. I'd hoped He might answer our prayers on the givin' side this time." She sighed, and tears welled in her eyes. "What'll those poor children do without him?"

"They have an aunt in Baldwin City," Caroline said, hoping to comfort Kesia. "I've contacted her, and I trust she'll come. She's reluctant. According to Letta, she hasn't seen the family in several years. But they are her brother's children. Surely when she meets them and sees what fine children they are, she'll have a change of heart and decide to give them a home."

"I'll surely be prayin' for that." Kesia returned to Ollie, touching his shoulder. "An' as for you, my dear Ollie, I'm thinkin' a cold rag on that bruise'll do you some good."

Ollie didn't lift his head. "Thank you, Kesia. I shall welcome your ministrations."

Kesia's fuzzy eyebrows lowered into a sharp V. "Huh?"

Caroline pursed her lips and shook her

head. She pointed to her own temple, then Ollie's, sending a silent message to the older woman.

Kesia angled an odd look in Ollie's direction, but then she shrugged. "Carrie, you gonna go hunt our missin' youngsters?"

With the men eager to earn their sour-cream-cake reward, Caroline trusted the search to them. "No, ma'am. I need to arrange their father's burial and visit the telegraph office to check for a reply from their aunt." And from Noble as well. She eased her way to the door. "I'll come back later to see how Ollie fares. Hopefully someone will have located the children by then. If so, please keep them here until I return."

"Oh, I'll hang on to them rascals. I'll tie 'em to the stools if I hafta."

Caroline laughed. "I doubt that will be necessary. Ply them with cookies, and they'll stay." Kesia waved her out the door, and Caroline headed for the under-taker's. But halfway there, she changed course and went to the telegraph office instead. If the children's aunt was coming, she should make the funeral arrangements for her brother.

A sense of unease filled her. She couldn't quite determine the reason for her discomfort, but she knew it related to the children's aunt. As Noble and Annamarie had taught her, she turned her concern into a prayer.

Lord, work Your will with the children and their aunt. Letta, Lank, and Lesley need someone to care for them, but if this woman isn't meant to be the one, please make that clear. But please move swiftly. My time here is nearing its end, and I can't leave them unless I know they' ll be all right.

Chapter 22

Caroline

Noble and Annamarie's train was scheduled to arrive Tuesday morning, so Caroline stayed awake to meet them at the station. The past few days she'd caught only snatches of sleep, and one more day of wakefulness couldn't do much more damage.

She walked to the station, her breath forming little clouds of condensation.

The weekend's rain had brought fall temperatures, and even though it was only the end of October, the air held a nip that reminded Caroline of snow. Letta, Lank, and Lesley scuffed along behind her, keeping just out of arm's reach. The children, having been located by one of

Kesia's most loyal customers and brought back in disgrace, hadn't spoken a word to her since their return. She blamed their closed mouths and hunched shoulders on the cold, but inwardly she knew she was being punished for some unknown misdeed.

Caroline prayed that Noble or Annamarie, with their experience in reaching out to troubled children, might work a miracle and heal whatever had been damaged between the trio of red-headed waifs and herself. She also hoped Noble would offer advice on how to respond to the telegram she'd received from Gertrude in Baldwin City. Such a terse message: "Send them on next train." Send them? To a complete stranger? And without a chaperone? Any number of dangers could befall three children traveling alone. Caroline had sent yet another message, politely requesting the woman make her own travel plans to retrieve the children, but as yet no reply had arrived.

She glanced over her shoulder at Letta.

The girl held her head low, her lips set in a grim line. Should she have shared the telegram with Letta? She'd kept it secret, believing the girl had enough worries without fearing she and her brothers would be sent to the aunt they hadn't seen since she was a small girl. Maybe asking Letta's feelings about her aunt's message would allow them to talk freely again, the way they had before.

At least Letta had participated in choosing a location for her father in the paupers' graveyard east of town. She'd selected a spot beneath a towering oak tree. Although now almost barren of leaves, come spring the tree would provide a lovely canopy. There'd be no marker and not even a coffin. Instead, the hospital mortuary had wrapped his body in strips of cloth cut from tattered white sheets. But the chapel minister, Reverend Willoughby, had agreed to meet them that afternoon and speak some words, giving the children at least the semblance of a service.

Kesia promised to attend, Noble and

Annamarie would certainly go, and of course Caroline would be there to offer moral support to the children. But Ollie would be absent. Kesia had been so concerned about Ollie's strange demeanor that she had brought in a doctor. The man determined Ollie had suffered a concussion when his head hit the bench and had ordered three days of bed rest. She was glad the door hadn't caused the greater injury, although had she not conked him with the door, she supposed he wouldn't have fallen at all.

Thinking about standing at the graveside without his strong presence left her unsettled. She gave herself a mental shake for her ridiculous feelings. The night she'd come so close to falling into his embrace haunted her. She'd never behaved so brazenly with anyone before. Yesterday's separation from him had offered her an opportunity to process her strange desire, but she hadn't come to any conclusions. Perhaps a private talk with Annamarie would help her make sense of these unfamiliar feelings for Ollie

Moore.

The Number Fourteen—Noble and Annamarie's train—had already arrived, its gleaming engine belching clouds of steam into the air, when she and the children reached the depot. Her dear friends stood beside the baggage car, Noble's arm wrapped protectively around Annamarie's slight frame. Caroline's heart lurched when she spotted them. No matter how old she got or how short their time apart was, whenever she joined them again, it was a sweet homecoming.

Pointing, she whirled and told the children, "They're here! Come!" Then she dashed ahead, trusting the three to follow. At her approaching footsteps, Noble turned, and the fan of lines beside his eyes spread with his beaming smile. He held his arms wide, and she catapulted against him, as uninhibited as a child.

He laughingly scooped her off the ground, dislodging her knitted scarf so it fell down her back. "You said you'd be sleeping! What a fine surprise to see you here." He set her feet on the boardwalk, tugged the scarf back in place over her hair, then chucked her under the chin with his knuckles—a gesture left over from her childhood.

Caroline flashed him a bright smile, then turned to Annamarie. The hug she bestowed on Noble's wife was gentle, cautious, but no less sincere.

Annamarie hugged back, her thin hands curled over Caroline's shoulders. Tears filled the dear woman's eyes. "Ah, our Caroline. How good to see you again." Then clinging to Caroline's arm with one hand, she turned to the row of silent, staring children. She smiled warmly at each in turn, completely unaffected by their indifference. "And you must be Letta, Lank, and Lesley. No school today?"

Caroline said, her voice low, "Their father's burial is today. I kept them out."

Annamarie nodded, sympathy softening her expression. She extended one hand toward the children. "I'm so glad to meet you. Carrie told us all about you, and I'm so eager to become friends."

After a moment's hesitation Lesley

stepped forward and took Annamarie's hand. She leaned down a bit, her movements stiff, and looked directly into the little boy's eyes. "I'm very sorry to hear about your father, Lesley. My father died when I was just your age—eight— and I remember how sad it made me to know he was gone."

Lesley curled his stubby little fingers over Annamarie's and wrinkled his nose. "You were sad to lose your father?"

"Yes, I was. I loved him very much."

Lesley caught his lower lip between his teeth and ducked his head as if fighting a private war. Then he rose up on tiptoe so his mouth was near Annamarie's ear. "I loved my father, too, even though he was mean sometimes. Letta an' Lank aren't sad, but I am. I wish he didn't hafta die."

Annamarie cupped Lesley's chapped cheek with her arthritic hand. Although Lesley fell silent and Annamarie didn't say a word, the pair seemed to communicate silently. The little ragamuffin boy and the gray-haired, humpbacked woman—so different yet woven together by a ribbon of grief.

Looking on, Caroline battled tears. She risked a glance at Letta and Lank and noted tears swimming in their eyes. Within minutes of arrival, Annamarie and her gentle ways had already begun to melt their hardened hearts just as she'd managed to break through Caroline's carefully built defenses more than a dozen years ago. The woman worked magic with children.

Caroline sent up a quick prayer of gratitude, then issued a soft introduction. "Letta, Lank, these are my dearest friends, Mr. and Mrs. Dempsey."

Neither child spoke, but they shook Noble's and Annamarie's hands by turn, nodding when Noble and Annamarie offered words of greeting. Then Letta curled her hand over Lesley's shoulder, pulling him against her side. Lesley went, but he kept his face aimed toward Annamarie as if fearful of losing sight of her.

Noble stepped near, transferring Annamarie's hand from Caroline's elbow to his own. "I hired a closed carriage so Annamarie needn't breathe in the cold air. There will be room for all of us." He angled an impish grin at the children. "But of course none of you would like to take a carriage ride, am I right?"

Lesley wriggled beneath Letta's restraining arm. "Is it gonna be pulled by reindeer?"

To Noble's credit he didn't laugh. "What makes you think reindeer might pull our carriage?"

The child pointed to Noble's full, white beard. "Ain't you Santa Claus?"

Caroline coughed to cover her amusement. She'd wondered the same thing when she'd first met Noble. And over the years she'd discovered he possessed a heart as giving and open as Saint Nick's.

Noble heaved a mighty sigh, feigning great disappointment. "I wish I could tell you otherwise, but, no, I am not that jolly old elf." Noble shepherded the group toward a line of horse-drawn carriages. "But I can tell you that he and I are very close friends, and he doesn't mind at all that I've borrowed his beard. He will not, however, lend me his red coat and hat."

Lesley stared at Noble in open-mouthed amazement for several seconds, then he burst out laughing. "You're funnin' with me!"

Noble laughed, too, and rubbed his hand over Lesley's head. "Indeed I am. You're very clever to realize it."

Lesley flashed a grin at Letta. "He says I'm clever." Letta merely shrugged in reply.

At the carriage Noble lifted Annamarie inside, then Lesley. The little boy snuggled as close to Annamarie as he could get without sitting on her lap. Caroline climbed in and sat opposite Annamarie and Lesley. Letta and Lank crunched in next to her. They were tight, three abreast, but she wouldn't complain.

Noble said, "I'll fetch our bags, and then we can be on our way." He closed the door, sealing them in the leather interior.

While they waited for Noble to return, Annamarie began a steady flow of questions. At first only Lesley answered, but soon Letta dropped her guard a bit and offered a few stilted replies. Lank remained silent, which didn't surprise Caroline. The boy rarely spoke even to his brother and sister. But his interested gaze bounced back and forth between Annamarie, Letta, and Lesley, and longing to be included clearly shone in his eyes.

Two successive thuds overhead signaled the arrival of their bags, and then the door opened, revealing Noble's smiling face. He climbed in, rocking the carriage. Lifting Lesley from the seat, he slid in next to Annamarie. Then he perched Lesley on his knee. The boy sat as proud as a king on his throne. Noble announced, "To the Troubadour Hotel we'll go. Children, I'd like you to be our lunch guests. Yes?"

Before Letta or Lesley could reply, Caroline intervened. "Instead, Noble, I'd like it very much if you and Annamarie would agree to lunch at a little café downtown." She couldn't wait for her longtime friends to meet her newest friend. And when the three of them began working together, the Holcomb children would soon be laughing and smiling. If only Ollie could join them. Then her circle would be complete.

Her body gave a jolt. She blamed the involuntary start on the carriage's sudden forward movement, but she knew the truth. Her casual inclusion of Ollie in her makeshift family rocked her to the core. That man had somehow managed to weasel his way into the center of her life. Ludicrous. Unwarranted. Even unwise. But did she want to send him packing?

She refused to contemplate the honest answer to that question.

Chapter 23

Letta

A stubborn red leaf broke loose of its branch above Letta's head. She watched it swirl downward and land on Pa's sheet-shrouded chest. She stared at the bold color on the white cloth. Like a splash of blood. Her stomach turned a flip.

Lesley stepped from beneath her arm and flicked the leaf with his finger.

The leaf caught the breeze and whirled into the hole on the other side of Pa's body, out of sight. Lesley returned to her and snuggled close. Letta gave him a squeeze to thank him.

On the far side of the grave, the minister read from a big black Bible—something about mansions. Letta almost snorted.

Miss Carrie'd said the minister would say words about Pa, but instead he talked about mansions. Letta knew what a mansion was. She'd seen them in the nicest part of town. Tall houses of red or brown brick with white spindles on their porches and lots of lacy-looking wood trim, set on lawns of thick green grass. So different from the little unpainted clapboard house where she'd lived with Pa and her brothers. Mansions? What did that have to do with Pa? She wished they'd hurry up and put Pa in the ground so she could take her brothers and go.

Lesley shifted from side to side, his brand-new boots squeaking. Mr. Noble and Mrs. Annamarie, as Miss Carrie's friends told her and the boys to call them, had taken all three of them to the general merchandise store after lunch and let them choose a whole outfit to wear to Pa's burial. Letta didn't understand why they needed new clothes when Pa just wore strips cut from an old sheet, but she wouldn't argue. Lesley'd never owned anything other than Lank's hand-me-downs, which were plenty worn-out by the time he got them.

Lesley's pride in those shiny new boots made her want to smile. But she didn't. A burial wasn't a place for smiling.

Behind her someone wept softly. Either Miss Kesia or Miss Carrie—Letta couldn't be sure. But she wouldn't turn around and look. Neither Lank nor Lesley cried, so she wouldn't, either. But it was harder than she'd imagined to keep her tears inside. Not until they'd arrived at the graveyard and seen Pa's body laid out next to a black hole, like an open mouth waiting to swallow him up, did it all seem real.

Pa was gone. Really, truly gone. Just like Ma. Except not like Ma, because Ma could come back someday. Not that Letta expected her to. Not that Letta wanted her to. But Ma was still alive as far as Letta knew, and Pa was dead. Dead. Dead was forever. A big lump formed in her throat. Tears pushed hard against her eyes. But if she started crying, would it be for Pa or for herself? She didn't know. She only knew if she started, she might not be able to stop.

So she tightened her arms around Lank and Lesley and looked up at the tree branches. At the last waving red leaf with a little bit of gold around its edges. And she didn't cry. Not one tear.

Caroline

Caroline pressed a handkerchief into Kesia's hand. The older woman smiled her thanks and dabbed at the tears rolling down her wrinkled cheeks. Caroline wondered at her own failure to shed tears. Sorrow weighted her chest, heavy as a boulder, but her eyes remained dry even when the children stepped forward at the minister's invitation to toss a handful of dirt on top of their father's body.

Kesia, Noble, Annamarie, and Caroline participated in the sad tradition, each parading past the grave and releasing their own handfuls of dirt atop the sheet-wrapped body stretched out in the hole's depth. Was there a more dismal picture than clods of black dirt scattered over a white sheet? Caroline turned away from the grave and hurried across the soggy brown grass to the other adults, who surrounded the children.

The minister bade them farewell. The gravediggers took up their shovels and began the task of covering Mr. Holcomb's body. Caroline slipped her arm around Annamarie's waist, ready to suggest they board the carriage and return to the hotel.

But before she could offer the suggestion, Noble stepped forward and put his hand on Letta's shoulder. "You were very brave, Letta. I'm proud of you for being strong for your brothers. But remember there's no shame in crying. God gave us tears to help us release our hurts. If you need to cry, no one will think less of you."

His deep voice, tender in its delivery, brought the sting of tears to Caroline's eyes. How many times had he spoken to her in just that way? Even when she resisted him, pretended to ignore him, told him to stay away, he was always kind.

And eventually he'd earned her trust.

Letta sent a brief, unsmiling glance in Noble's direction, then stepped away from his hand. "I don't need to cry. C'mon, boys." She fixed Caroline with a warning look. "We're goin' home now."

"Oh, but—"

Noble held his hand out to Caroline, silencing her protest. "I have an idea." He addressed the boys, wisely recognizing if he won them, Letta would follow. "Mrs. Annamarie and I rented a suite at the hotel. The suite has two large sleeping rooms as well as a lounging room with a fireplace. We would like it very much if you would join us there. You'd have your own room to be alone if you wanted, but we could also have time together in the lounging room." He smiled, his merry eyes warm and inviting. "We'd like the opportunity to become better acquainted with you."

Letta's gaze narrowed. "Why?"

Noble's smile remained intact. "Why not?"

The girl scowled, drawing back slightly.

Annamarie inserted, "Please join us, children. The suite truly is too large for just the two of us. We'd welcome your company."

Lesley tugged at Letta's sleeve. "Ain't never stayed in a hotel before. I wanna go, Letta. So does Lank, don'tcha, Lank?"

Lank's head bobbed once, ever so slightly, but his eyes glowed with longing.

"Can't we go, Letta? Huh? Huh?"

Letta huffed. "You're an awful pest, Lesley."

The little boy hung his head.

Letta gazed down at her bereft brother, and a hint of remorse softened her scowl. "All right, then. If you boys wanna go—"

The boys' freckled faces lit with joy. Lesley let out a whoop and galloped the three short paces needed to reach Annamarie. He caught the woman's hand and beamed at her. "We're comin', missus! We're comin'!"

Annamarie smoothed Lesley's untamed hair into place, but she aimed her smile at Letta. "I'm so glad. Let's go then, shall we?" The boys fell in step on either side of Annamarie, and Kesia commandeered Letta's elbow, guiding her along behind the happy trio.

Noble captured Caroline's hand and slipped it into the bend of his elbow. Maintaining a slow saunter that put them several feet behind the others, he released a long, slow sigh. "So tell me, my dear, are those dark circles under your eyes due to your responsibility at the factory, the burden of taking charge of these three orphaned youngsters, or something else entirely?"

Caroline kept her gaze ahead, afraid if she met Noble's eyes, he'd discover her uncertainty concerning her feelings for Ollie. She forced a light laugh. "I'm tired, Noble. Working nights and not being able to sleep days..." She waved one hand toward the children, a rueful grin tugging at her lips. "Those three have completely disrupted my world."

Noble pressed her hand to his ribs. "But they're worth it?"

A full smile broke effortlessly across her face. "You've taught me well. Yes. They are worth it."

He chuckled. "I suspected as much. But..." His smile turned to a concerned frown. He drew her to a halt several yards from the waiting carriage, where Kesia, Annamarie, and the children stood in a small circle, visiting quietly. "You can't go without sleep, Caroline. I left word with the Labor Commission that I'd be gone at least a week. During this time Annamarie and I will assume responsibility for Letta and the boys. This will enable you to get your rest but also to complete the investigation."

Caroline blew out a relieved breath as a weight seemed to roll from her shoulders.

Noble went on. "I was pleased to know a blueprint of the elevator exists. Have you had an opportunity to view it yet?"

She shook her head. The children's disappearance, Mr. Holcomb's burial, and Ollie's concussion had sent her attention in different directions.

Noble gave her hand a pat and set them in motion once more. "Perhaps you'll be able to do so tonight. But for now"—he raised one snow-white eyebrow and pointed his finger at her—"we shall drop you at your building, and you are to sleep the rest of the day. Don't give a thought to the children. Annamarie and I will take good care of them. You simply rest. Agreed?"

Although she still needed to seek Noble's advice about the children's aunt, the thought of uninterrupted sleep proved too much of a temptation. "Agreed. And thank you."

Caroline punched her timecard and dropped it in her slot. She then retrieved her tools from the metal locker near the break room and hurried toward her station. The hours of sleep and reprieve from worry had revived her, and she couldn't resist giving a little hop-skip as she rounded the corner.

Immediately she plowed into a solid body and bounced backward. "Ooph!" The air whooshed from her lungs, forcing her to double over. The hammer slipped from her hand, bounced off the floor, and clunked her hard on the shin. She let out a yelp of pain.

"Serves you right," came a caustic voice.

She lifted her head to find Gordon Hightower glaring at her. What was he doing here?

"You really need to be more careful, Miss Lang."

His derogatory tone, coupled with the memory of slamming Ollie with the door, raised her defenses. "I couldn't see around the wall."

"I'm not interested in your excuses." He bent over and scooped up her hammer by the handle, then bounced the iron head lightly against his palm. "You're lucky you didn't break anything, or I would have needed to extract payment."

A chill wiggled its way down Caroline's spine. His extracted payment wouldn't be a monetary one. Eager to escape his leering grin, she held out her hand. "I apologize, Mr. Hightower. It won't happen again. Now, if you'll return my hammer, I have work to do."

"Yes, work... Odd that you would mention work." He stepped forward, but instead of placing the hammer in her hand, he caught her wrist and yanked her hard against him. His hot, senna-scented breath washed across her cheek. "We've had this conversation before, Miss Lang. You seem an intelligent woman, yet you can't seem to follow simple instructions. Let me tell you again. You were sent to third shift to do a specific job. Sealing crates. That's all you're to do. You aren't to ask questions. You aren't to snoop in elevators. You are to seal crates. Seal crates. **Seal crates.**" His voice grew harsher, more sinister, with each repetition. "Do you understand?"

Her heart pounded in fear. She tried to answer, but her dry tongue seemed stuck to the roof of her mouth. She might as well have been a mouse caught in a trap, staring into the face of a hungry tomcat. Helplessness weakened her knees.

Hightower curled his hand around the back of her neck and shook her, his lips set in a snarl. "I'm waiting for an answer,

Miss Lang. Do you understand?"

Too frightened to do otherwise, she squeaked, "Yes. I...I understand."

"Good." He released her with a slight shove.

She fell against the wall, grateful for its sturdy support.

Hightower extended the hammer to the side and let it fall. The iron head clanked resoundingly against the concrete floor. "Get to work, Miss Lang. You're wasting time." He tugged the lapels of his jacket into place, smoothed a finger over his mustache, then sauntered off, his head at an arrogant angle.

Caroline pressed her back securely to the wall, her trembling legs unwilling to carry her forward. Hightower knew. Somehow he knew. But how? Until tonight she'd never seen him lurking in the factory during the third shift. Someone must have tattled. And to her knowledge only one person was aware that she'd made a sketch of the elevator's inner workings.

Nausea rolled through her gut. He wouldn't betray her...would he?

Chapter 24

Gordon

Gordon strode around the corner, then stopped and wheeled back to peer from his hiding spot. At his last meeting with Carrie Lang, she'd seemed more annoyed and surprised than truly concerned. But he'd managed to put some fear in her this time. How gratifying to see her cowering against the wall, face as chalky white as the unpainted plaster behind her. Even from this distance he noted the tremble in her hand as she reached to retrieve her hammer. He covered his mouth, muffling his laughter when it took her three tries to hook the tool's handle through the loop on her belt. Then she scurried up the hall toward the crating area as if pursued by a swarm of bees.

He let the laugh roll, unfettered. Finally he'd succeeded in silencing her endless questions about Bratcher. But then he felt a tinge of regret. Such fun he could have had if she'd refused to comply. Up close she smelled sweet, like lilacs. Her womanly form, warm and padded in all the right places, fit neatly against him. He wouldn't have minded stealing a bit of pleasure from her, but there'd been too many workers milling about. Not that any would intervene. They had more sense than to risk their jobs for one foolish woman who didn't know how to keep her curiosity to herself. But he didn't care for voyeurs. When he took his pleasure from Miss Lang—and he would make good on his threat if he received one more report of her putting her pretty little nose where it didn't belong—it would be in private. Where he could enjoy her at his leisure. He tapped his lips with one finger, brow puckered. Should he have held back a bit, given a milder warning so she might be brazen enough to continue gathering information? No. Regardless of the fun he'd sacrificed, he had a greater reward waiting. Once the factory was his— completely his—he'd be free to sample whatever and whomever he liked.

He sauntered up the hallway in search of the night foreman. A quick conversation with Alden, and then he'd head home. His work here was done. For now.

Oliver

Oliver caught a glimpse of his reflection in the small round mirror above his wash basin. He groaned. Over the past couple of days the colors had expanded and brightened. A veritable garden of blues, purples, and greens bloomed along the side of his face. When would the bruises fade? As much as he'd disliked lazing in his bed—even as a child, he'd fought against lying about in a sickbed—he'd cheerfully dive back under the covers if it meant avoiding the inevitable questions and teasing he'd receive from his coworkers at the factory.

He plopped his hat on his head, adjusting the brim low and to the side, an attempt to hide at least a portion of the bruises. The eye was still swollen, but thanks to Kesia's enthusiastic application of cold, damp cloths, he could hold it open enough to see—a vast improvement from two days ago when he viewed the world through a mere slit. A dull ache remained in the back of his skull, but he was thankful the deep, throbbing pain had departed. He moved across his small bedroom, gathering his jacket, gloves, and scarf. His scarf lay on the floor beneath a straight-backed chair, and when he bent to retrieve it, no dizziness attacked. Yes, he was well enough to return to work.

Where Carrie would be waiting to view that blueprint.

Thoughts of Carrie hurried him to the door and onto the street. After delivering him to Kesia, she'd disappeared. Not that he'd expected her to visit him at his apartment—that would be highly improper—but he would have welcomed a note. Kesia could have delivered it when she came to check on him. The dear lady had visited three or four times each day of his forced rest. Didn't Carrie worry at all about his injury? He wouldn't have taken her to be so uncaring. But maybe she was just busy. After all, she had to supervise the Holcomb children, plan a burial, and work nights. She had plenty to do without fussing over him. Still, he wished she'd found time for at least some contact.

Here he was bemoaning her absence again when he should be thankful she'd stayed away. Maybe it would have been better if the door had slammed into his chest rather than his head. It might have knocked Miss Carrie Lang from his heart.

He hailed a passing hansom cab and paid the driver two bits to tote him to the factory. His first night back he didn't want to wear himself out with the walk and be unable to complete his duties. Part of his duty tonight, albeit a personal one, would be retrieving those blueprints for Carrie. He also intended to extract the reason she was so keen on seeing them. If his suspicions were correct and she was hiding something from him, it might help him find the courage to sever his ties with her completely.

He arrived late—more than twenty minutes past clock-in time. Hightower would probably write up a complaint against him, but so be it. According to the rules Father had put into place for all the workers, Hightower would need three write-ups before he could release him. Just this morning Father had said he'd bring Oliver's masquerading to a halt at the end of the year. So he'd leave long before Hightower had compiled enough valid excuses to terminate his employment.

As he gathered his cleaning supplies, he couldn't resist a light chuckle. He wished he could be a fly on the wall when Father told Hightower his own son had been mopping floors and greasing gears. He supposed he shouldn't gloat—it wasn't polite—but he didn't like Hightower, and he didn't mind saying so. As a boy, he'd often envied the unknown lad Father had selected from the Chicago orphanage to work in his factory. Back then his dislike for Hightower had centered around Father's seeming interest in him. But as Oliver had become acquainted with Hightower the adult, his dislike became personal. The man was a cad through and through.

Bucket, rags, and scrub brush in hand, he moved across the wide crating area toward the break room. After his days away he imagined there'd be plenty of scrubbing to do in the room where the workers ate their meals. He passed Carrie, who was bent over a crate, tack pinched between her finger and thumb. He eased up behind her and leaned in so she'd hear him over the factory noises. "Good evening, Carrie."

She jumped, bouncing the hammer off her thumb. With a sharp intake of breath, she dropped the hammer and shook her hand wildly, her lips set in a grimace of pain.

Oliver put down his cleaning items and

stretched his hands toward her. "Let me see."

She yanked her hand away, glaring at him. "Don't bother. It's nothing."

Her thumb was already swelling. Soon it would be as colorful as his face. He cringed. He truly hadn't intended to startle her. Cupping his hand beneath her elbow, he steered her toward the little room used by the staff doctor. "Come on. The night-shift doctor can wrap that up for you."

She tried to wrench free of his grasp. "I told you, I'm fine. Let me go."

He gave her an impatient look. Why was she being so stubborn? "Carrie, your thumb clearly is not fine. Look at it."

She did.

"It'll be as large as a sausage if you don't get it wrapped."

She clamped her jaw tight, but she moved along beside him without any further arguments. When they reached the infirmary, Oliver ushered her through the door. But the doctor wasn't in the room. Oliver crossed to the door leading to the sick bay, opened it, and peeked inside. No one was in there, either. "Where could he be?"

Carrie hovered near the doorway, cradling her thumb against her bodice. "It doesn't matter. I can still hold a tack. I'll go—"

Oliver dashed across the floor, the sudden movement causing a slight ringing in his ears. Would dizziness follow? Catching hold of her elbow again, partly to keep her from leaving, partly to keep himself upright, he pulled her toward the examination table in the center of the room. "Climb up there," he said. "I'll wrap your thumb."

"Ollie, really, you needn't—"

Lowering his brows, he affected a stern frown. "I'm not going to argue with you." He paused, allowing his lips to curl into a teasing grin. "You made sure my wound was tended. The least I can do is return the favor."

"You returned the favor all right." She looked ruefully at her thumb and its blackening nail. "As they say, 'Turnabout is fair play.'"

He helped her onto the edge of the table and then began opening cabinet doors, looking for bandages. "Just be glad the hammer didn't bounce off your head. You can't get a concussion from a whack on the thumb." He located a roll of thin strips and carried it to the table. "Hold out your hand, thumb up, please."

With her lower lip sucked in and her brow furrowed, she watched him unroll the narrow cotton cloth. Her obvious nervousness made him nervous, and he sought the means to put her at ease. Conversation might take her mind off his ministrations. While he wound the strip around her thumb, snug but not too snug, he asked, "What is it about our elevator that stirs your interest?"

She yanked her hand back, unraveling the bandage. "Why?"

He gathered up the strip and reached for her hand again. "Because you were going to tell me. Remember? We had a deal."

Shoving her hand behind her back, well out of his reach, she fixed him with a glare that could curdle milk. "Yes. We had a deal. But if I honor my part and tell you the reason, are you going to run off and report everything I say?"

Her accusation set him back a pace.

She went on, her tone brittle. "Tell me the truth. Have you been tattling on me?"

The word "tattling" almost made him laugh. Such a childish word. But when he thought about it, wasn't that what he'd done? He'd observed her without her knowledge, had gathered information, and had shared it with his father. He preferred to think of his actions as investigative rather than gossipy, but he supposed in this case they were the same. He didn't know what to say, so he stood stupidly before her with his head throbbing and his heart aching.

"You have, haven't you?" She didn't wait for his reply but hopped down from the table and pushed past him. "I can't believe I trusted you. Relied on you. I—" Her voice broke on a strangled moan. She stifled the sound and held her chin high. "Stay away from me, Ollie Moore. I want nothing to do with you." She darted out the door.

Oliver started to run after her, but the room spun. He sagged against the doorjamb, one hand on his head. "Carrie!"

She passed two other craters, who watched her race by and then turned their gazes on Oliver. Their faces twisted into matching, knowing smirks. Oliver inwardly groaned and moved to the examination table. He propped himself against it, willing the lightheadedness to pass. He needed to explain to Carrie the purpose of his reporting. He'd only wanted to prove to his father that they had no reason to distrust her. But how could he do so without divulging the truth of who he was? He'd gotten himself entangled, and there seemed to be no escape.

The look of betrayal on Carrie's sweet face pierced him to the center of his being. Now alone in the quiet infirmary, he experienced a longing to share this burden and find reparation from the One who held all the answers of the universe. But just as his prayers for Mr. Holcomb had been offered too late, he feared these prayers would be useless. She'd never trust him again. Unless...

As quickly as his swimming head would allow, he headed for the janitor's closet and the tin tube that held the blueprints for the elevator.

"Moore!"

The shout brought Oliver to a halt. The night-shift foreman, Alden, jogged toward him. Oliver shifted in place, eager to complete his own errand. "Yes?"

Alden took a look at Oliver's face and barked out a laugh. "Guess the boss wasn't kidding when he said you'd gotten a good knock on the noggin. Reckon that smarts some, huh?"

Oliver grimaced. "Some."

"How'd it happen?"

"Ran into a door." A partial truth, but no way would he admit Carrie'd done it.

The foreman laughed again. "Well, now that you're back, you got some catching up to do. Two nights ago one of the new hires fell asleep and let a boiler get too hot. A vat of raspberry filling bubbled over. Hightower said to leave it for you to handle when you got back on duty since he couldn't trust the newly hired first-shift janitor to do it right."

Oliver nearly rolled his eyes. He knew better than to be flattered.

"It's dried and hard now—it'll probably take a hammer an' chisel to get that vat an' the floor around it clean again."

Oliver edged toward the janitor's closet. "You want me to do that now?"

Alden scowled. "We can't use the vat until it's clean."

Stifling a groan of frustration, Oliver nodded. "All right. I'm on my way."

The blueprints—and Carrie—would have to wait.

Chapter 25

Caroline

If Ollie's head hurt half as much as her thumb, Caroline almost felt sorry for him. Pinching tacks became increasingly painful as the night progressed. By the time the lunch break buzzer blared, her thumb appeared twice its normal size, and the nail wore a purplish-black half moon. The constant throb beneath the nail made her nauseated. She'd been anticipating the apple fritter Kesia had packed for her midnight dinner, but food had lost all appeal. Which was just as well, because she had a more important task to tend to than eating.

As workers filed toward the break room, Caroline sidled up to the other craters. "I'm going to the infirmary—see if the doctor is back so I can get my thumb wrapped." She held up the purple appendage to validate the need. They nodded at her, one grimacing at the sight of her thumb. Satisfied they'd carry the tale to the other workers if anyone— namely, Ollie—happened to notice her absence, she turned and headed in the direction of the doctor's little examination room. But halfway there, with a furtive glance over her shoulder to be sure no one saw her, she changed course and made her way to the janitor's closet.

Ollie had indicated the blueprints were on a shelf. The closet wouldn't be so large she'd need assistance in locating a few drawings. Don't let him catch me, please. The plea, more a demand than a prayer, exploded from her pattering heart. "Him" covered both Hightower and Ollie. One man had frightened her, but the other had shattered her. She didn't have the strength to face either of them at that moment.

She closed the door behind her, sealing herself in darkness. Arms outstretched,

she moved slowly forward, and something tickled her cheek. She stifled a
shriek—a spider web? No, she'd located
the light's pull cord. She gave it a tug,
and a bare bulb sent glaring light through
the small room. Blinking against the
sudden onslaught, she turned a slow
circle, her eyes seeking anything
resembling a stack of drawings.

Buckets, sponges, boxes packed with
hardware, folded towels, and other
assorted items filled the shelves,
everything placed just so. The closet's
meticulous organization raised a wave of
unexpected sadness. How could a man
who took such care with inanimate
objects treat her so callously? The two
halves didn't seem to fit with each other.

Pushing aside thoughts of Ollie, she
began shifting items, peeking behind
every box and crate. She explored the
bottom three shelves, which were at eye
level or below, but the top shelf was above
her head. She grabbed a bucket, turned it
upside down, and climbed on its bottom,
giving herself enough of a boost to view

the contents of the uppermost shelf.

A stack of folded papers held down by a tarnished tin tube caught her eye. She pushed the canister aside and lifted the papers. To her dismay they were only yellowed, mouse-eaten newspapers, apparently forgotten. Frustrated, she tossed them back on the shelf. They slid against the tin tube, rolling it over and revealing a paper label pasted on its side. A minuscule black-and-white drawing of the elevator filled the center of the label.

Caroline's pulse leaped in response. The blueprints! She grabbed the tube and hopped down from the bucket. Oh, how pleased Noble would be! She headed for the door, tube in hand, but before she stepped out, she made herself stop and think. She examined the tube, measuring it with her eyes. Fifteen inches in length and perhaps three inches in diameter, the tube was large enough to garner notice if she carried it in her hand. Should she slide it inside the full sleeve of her dress? There was ample fabric to accommodate the canister, but she wouldn't be able to bend her arm. The shank of her lace-up shoes was too snug to slip the tube in next to her leg, and she had no desire to carry it beneath her skirt. But somehow she had to smuggle it out of the factory.

Break would end soon, and she needed to return to her post, preferably with a wrapped thumb so no one would wonder why she hadn't seen the doctor. Where could she hide the tube? Then she smacked her forehead. The recent lack of sleep had rendered her incapable of thinking clearly. Why take the tube? Blueprints were printed on paper. She could fold the drawings and tuck them inside her clothing without anyone noticing.

The top squeaked as she twisted it loose. Tipping the tube sideways, she tapped it to release the drawings. Nothing fell into her waiting hand. She tapped it harder. When no rolled pages emerged, she turned the tube upright and held the opening toward the light.

Empty.

The tube was **empty**.

Caroline slammed the lid on the tube

and gave it a toss onto the closest shelf, growling in frustration. Now what? She'd promised to bring the drawings to Noble. If they weren't in their protective tube, where were they?

Oliver

The buzzer blared. Oliver trailed the others leaving the break room. Although he'd hoped to see Carrie, perhaps steal a few moments of time to explain his reason for observing her, he was relieved to hear she was getting her thumb treated. He couldn't help cringing, thinking of how much the thump with the hammer must have hurt. He found no pleasure in having caused her pain, either physically or emotionally. And clearly he'd hurt her or she wouldn't run from him like a frightened deer.

Cleaning the burned vat had taken the entire first half of his shift—such a mess! But now that he'd finished scraping the hardened raspberry cream from the sides of the vat and the floor, he could move on to less taxing duties. He'd never cared much for mopping, but pushing the mop would seem like child's play after dealing with the stiff, sticky globs of two-day-old burnt filling. He would remember to heap praise on every cleaning person he encountered from now until his dying day. They deserved it.

As he headed for the closet to gather his mop and bucket, he glimpsed the swirl of a navy-blue skirt darting around the corner ahead. He frowned.

Hadn't Carrie worn a navy-blue dress tonight? Yes, he'd noticed how the tiny white dots in the fabric stood out more when the white bandage fell across her skirt. But what was she doing on the opposite side of the factory from the infirmary?

He started to follow her, but asking questions would only solidify her opinion that he was an informant. Rather than suspecting the worst, he would assume she had valid reasons for wandering the factory floor during her break.

He reached for the door handle of the janitor's closet and discovered the door was unlatched. Hadn't he closed it when he'd left earlier? Of course he had. He'd distinctly heard the click. So someone had been in there. He stepped inside, pulled the string to the light, then swept the shelves with his gaze. His time of serving as janitor had left him very familiar with the room and its contents, and he easily spotted the one thing that was out of place.

Snatching up the tube, he snarled in frustration. He clanked the tube twice on the edge of the shelf, creating a pair of matching dents. He'd tried so hard to convince Father of Carrie's innocence, wanting to place all suspicion on Hightower's shoulders instead. If she'd taken the drawings, Father would be incensed. But no more than Oliver was. He couldn't defend her if she was going to engage in such sneaky shenanigans.

Although on duty, Oliver left the mop and bucket behind and stormed to the crating station. He strode directly behind

Carrie, caught her hand midswing, and turned her to face him. With the hammer raised, she presented a formidable figure. He pushed the hammer-wielding hand downward and glared into her surprised face.

"Where are they?"

Yanking her hand free, she matched his glower with one of her own. "Where are what?"

He gritted his teeth. He was in no mood to play games. "The blueprints, Carrie. What have you done with them?"

"What have I done with them?" Her eyes widened. "You're accusing me of taking them?"

"Yes, I am. You wanted to see them. You obviously didn't visit the infirmary"—he gestured toward her unbandaged thumb—"and everyone else was in the break room. So what other explanation is there?" He leaned in, pinning her with a narrowed gaze. "What did you do with them, Carrie? Tell me now."

She pressed her injured hand to her chest and gawked at him. "I did nothing with them. They weren't even there!" Pink flooded her cheeks, deepening to a bold red as awareness seemed to blossom in her expression. "You... You!" She waved the hammer, her eyes narrowing to slits of fury. "Did you hide them in retaliation for me refusing to answer your questions earlier? I expected better of you, Ollie. You promised to show the blueprints to me. Promised! And I trusted you to be a man of your word. But instead you squirreled them away somewhere. Well, once again I've been proved the fool, but I will never—"

He shook his head, the meaning of her emotional tirade filtering through his veil of anger. "I didn't squirrel away those blueprints. How could I when you took them?"

"I didn't take them!" She nearly shrieked the statement.

The other craters stopped their work to stare. The night foreman, Alden, bustled around the corner and charged over to Oliver and Carrie. Hands on hips, he bounced a furious frown over the two of them. "What's goin' on here?"

Carrie stepped to the far side of the crate, her arms folded tightly over her chest and the hammer clutched tightly in her fist. "Nothing."

Oliver added, "Just a misunderstanding."

Several tense seconds ticked by while Alden stared first at Carrie and then at Oliver. Finally he bobbed his head. "All right. I'll let it go. But from now on save your catfights 'til after quittin' time. Both of you have jobs to do, an' unless you want a write-up, I suggest you get to them."

"Yes, sir."

Oliver and Carrie spoke simultaneously, both through clenched teeth. Alden strode away, barking at the other craters to pay attention to their own work.

Oliver sucked in a mighty breath and expelled it in a huge whoosh. "We aren't finished with this conversation, Carrie."

She dug in her apron pocket and withdrew a tack. "Unless you intend to tell me why you hid those blueprints from

me, I have nothing more to say to you."
She bent forward and added another slat
to the top of her crate, her lips set in a
grim line.

Oliver threw his hands in the air,
fighting the urge to grab her shoulders
and shake some sense into her. Stubborn,
headstrong, infuriating woman! He'd
get no satisfaction from her now, and
Alden was probably lurking around the
corner to see if his orders would be
followed. Oliver had no choice but to
return to work. But he wasn't finished
pursuing the topic of the blueprints. And
Carrie had better be ready to give an
explanation as soon as the shift-change
buzzer sounded. He wouldn't accept
anything less than the truth from her.

Chapter 26

Gordon

"The two of them were goin' at it worse than a pair o' prizefighters. Thought maybe she was going to bounce her hammer off the side of his head."

Gordon pinched his chin, contemplating the meaning behind Alden's statement. The foreman waited, fully expecting payment for divulging another snippet of information. But until Gordon understood the significance of the fight between Ollie Moore and Carrie Lang, he wouldn't give even a penny reward.

He caught Alden by the sleeve and pulled him away from the flow of workers entering for the morning shift. On the lower level the third-shift workers were gathering their belongings to leave, Moore and Lang among them. He wished Alden had stayed downstairs, listening for any further exchange, before hightailing to report to Gordon.

Gordon snorted, being deliberately derisive. "So they had a fight. You've broken up skirmishes between workers before. Why is this one different?"

Alden's brows pulled down. He scratched his head. "It's different 'cause you told me to keep my eye on those two. Before, they'd always seemed to be in cahoots, heads together whisperin'. But this time they were goin' at it—pure, spittin' mad."

Gordon ducked his head to hide his smile. Sounded as though the lovebirds were choosing to fly their separate ways. That suited Gordon fine. He didn't encourage friendships among the workers. Friends tended to confide in each other, to join forces. And if they ganged together, it'd be harder for him to stay in control. So this falling out could only be a good thing.

He lifted his head and forced a nonchalant shrug. "But you don't know what had them all worked up?"

"Somethin' about blueprints."

Gordon sucked in a sharp breath, nearly swallowing his tongue. "Did you say blueprints?" Cold air whisked through the open doors, but sweat broke out on Gordon's forehead.

Alden shrugged. "Sounded like it to me. But I didn't hear the whole argument. Only caught the tail end of it."

The only blueprints of which Gordon was aware were the ones for the elevator. After Bratcher's unfortunate—or fortunate, depending on one's view-point—plunge, he'd hidden the elevator drawings in the secret compartment of his desk. He'd felt the need to hide everything concerning the elevator and Bratcher's fall. Why would Moore or Lang be interested in those blueprints unless his initial suppositions about Lang were correct and she was seeking information about Bratcher?

Beads of sweat dribbled down his

forehead and stung his eyes. He swiped the moisture away with the back of his hand and forced a weak laugh. "You must have heard wrong. Blueprints? Why would a crater and a janitor be fighting over blueprints?" He clapped Alden on the shoulder, his hand trembling. "I think you need some sleep, my friend. So go home. And take a rag to the inside of your ears before coming back to work tonight."

Alden scowled, but he skulked off with his hands in his pockets.

Gordon hurried up to his office and set his typewriter on the desk. He rolled a crisp sheet of paper onto the platen, composing the letter in his mind. He set his fingers on the keys and began to tap.

Dear Mr. Dinsmore,

I believe it would be to your benefit to make a return visit to the factory before the end of the month. Some things have come to light concerning Miss Carrie Lang and the young man you recommended for employment, Ollie Moore, which you should find of great interest...

Oliver

Oliver trailed Carrie. He hadn't called out to her. He suspected she'd only ignore him. And he didn't want to talk to her in the open, where other workers might overhear. They'd caused enough furor during the night, attracting Alden's attention. Rumors would start flying if he wasn't careful. The last thing he needed was the workers watching him more closely.

So instead of heading to his own apartment to sleep—his aching head yearned for sleep—he followed Carrie toward her boarding hotel. He'd catch up just before she stepped inside, and they'd get to the bottom of the mystery surrounding the missing blueprints. He knew he didn't have them. And the more he'd thought about her strong reaction to his accusation, he wanted to believe she didn't have them, either. The residual effects of his concussion made it difficult to think rationally, but if they could set aside their irritation with each other and combine their thinking, surely they'd find a likely reason for the canister in his closet to be empty.

Steam rose from the grates alongside the cobblestone road, swirling around her skirts as she bustled past. Her heels click-clicked against the stones, intrusive in the quiet of early morning. With only a sliver of sunlight hovering on the horizon, the sky wore its morning coat of pinks and yellows, the colors reminiscent of the deep blush in Carrie's cheeks and the gentle highlights in her red-brown hair. Odd how the most unlikely things held connections to Carrie. This woman fascinated him beyond anyone he'd known before. But she also frustrated him. He preferred being fascinated, so he could only hope their conversation would dispel the negative emotions she'd stirred with her belligerence.

She was only yards from the front door of her building. She'd get away if he didn't move now. Oliver broke into a trot, ignoring how much the jarring against the concrete walkway caused his head to throb. She must have heard him coming, because she wheeled around, hands up-raised as if to fend off an attack and terror etched into her features. She quivered from head to toe, and he knew it wasn't the chill air causing her tremors. He'd frightened her. Remorse smote him.

He came to an abrupt stop at least a dozen feet away from her. "It's all right, Carrie." He snatched off his cap. "See? It's just me—Ollie."

Her entire body sagged with a relief. Then she straightened and fixed him with an irritated look. "What are you doing here?"

"I told you we needed to talk."

Her expression turned grim. "And I told you there was nothing left to say."

"But there is." He took one step forward, ready to catch hold of her if need be. "Carrie, I didn't take those blueprints." He spoke softly, fervently, truthfully, looking directly into her wary eyes. "When I discovered they were missing, I could think of only one other person who wanted to see them. You."

Her eyes snapped, but her brow pinched as if being angry took more effort than she could muster. "I didn't take them."

Oliver nodded slowly, his gaze never wavering from hers. "I believe you." He did, too. He didn't know why, but somehow, deep down, he knew she told the truth. If only she would believe him. Trust him. He couldn't explain why, but he wanted her to trust him. "Do you believe me?"

For long seconds she merely stared into his face, seeking, not even seeming to breathe. Then she let out a big sigh, her breath hovering in a cloud around her face. She nodded. "Yes, Ollie. I believe you didn't take them."

He broke into a smile so big his bruised eye hurt. But it didn't matter. She believed him. He dared another step forward.

"But why are you tattling to Hightower about me?"

He froze in place. Hurt and disillusionment colored her tone. He'd rather she was angry than deeply wounded. She might believe him about the blueprints, but she still held some incorrect suppositions. "Carrie, I have not spoken one word about you to Hightower."

Her brow pinched, a myriad of emotions playing across her features. "But when I asked if you've been reporting about me, you didn't deny it."

No, he hadn't. And he wouldn't deny it now. Licking his dry lips, he formed a truthful reply. "Because I have been compiling information for the owner of the factory, Mr. Dinsmore"—how odd to refer to Father so formally—"concerning many happenings at the factory."

"So you're more than a mere janitor?"

Cautiously, Oliver nodded. He waited for her to question his purpose for compiling information, but she stood in silence for several seconds, lips sucked in, brow puckered in thought.

Tipping her head to the side, she mused, "So if you didn't take the blueprints, and I didn't take them, then...where are they?"

"I don't know. But can we go inside? It's cold out here." At her nod of agreement, he held the door open for her, then followed her to the little lobby area. She crossed to the sofa where he'd spent the night only four days ago. He found it hard to believe how much had transpired in such a short time. Where Carrie was concerned, it seemed he constantly rode a seesaw—one minute sailing high and the next plunging low. Yet he didn't begrudge even one second of their wild adventure. What kind of hold did this woman have on him?

She sank onto the sawdust-stuffed cushion, her mouth stretching with a yawn. "Let me think... How long has the elevator been in the factory?"

Oliver shrugged, traveling backward through time in his mind. Father had installed the elevator when Oliver was still a boy. He recalled riding it up and down while still wearing knickers. "I believe it has an 1881 patent. Twenty years ago? Maybe more."

"It's likely been serviced at least once during that time. Perhaps the blueprints were taken out when workers did repairs and they neglected to put them back."

Oliver perched beside her, holding his hands wide. "But wouldn't they take the protective tube, too? Why take only the blueprints unless whoever took them wanted to hide the fact the canister was empty?"

Carrie frowned, her expression more thoughtful than irritated. "You make it seem as though some sort of conspiracy has taken place."

He leaned back, considering her statement. The information he'd uncovered concerning Bratcher being in the factory on a Sunday when no one should have been there seemed to point to a conspiracy. Or at least some shady doings.

Oliver's flesh tingled as disconcerting thoughts flooded his mind. He examined Carrie's tired face. "Carrie, you haven't told me why you're so interested in the elevator. Does your interest have anything to do with Harmon Bratcher?"

She looked sharply away. "Does it matter?"

A man had died—perhaps had been murdered—in his factory. It mattered a great deal. He decided to share a bit of what Father had told him. "Hightower thinks you're related to Bratcher and wish to uncover proof that the factory is somehow accountable for his death so you can sue us."

She kept her gaze angled away, but a slight smile curled her lips. "Hightower has a very active imagination."

Oliver touched her arm—a light touch but a deliberate one. "Is he right?"

"I'm no relation to Harmon Bratcher," she said, "and I have no interest in suing the factory."

Although relieved to know she wasn't out for money, Oliver wasn't completely satisfied with her vague statement. "Then why your interest? You did promise to tell me, remember?"

She released a rueful chuckle. "I'm not sure it matters anymore, to be honest. Without those blueprints I don't know how..." She closed her eyes and lowered her head. For several seconds she sat so still Oliver wondered if she'd fallen asleep. But then she jerked her head up to face him, determination evident in the firm set of her jaw. "Ollie, I'm exhausted, and you must be, too. We should get some sleep. But this evening—at suppertime—could you come to Kesia's? There's...someone I want you to meet. Someone with whom I think you should talk."

Oliver blurted, "Who?"

She gave an impatient shake of her head. "Never mind that now. Will you meet me?"

How could he resist such an intriguing invitation? "Of course I'll meet you."

"Good." She stood, covering another yawn with her injured hand. Then she turned a look on him—a look of intense reflection that froze him in his seat. She spoke, but the words seemed intended for herself. "I hope I'm not making a mistake."

Before he could question her cryptic statement, she rounded the corner and disappeared from sight.

Chapter 27

Caroline

"What were you thinking to involve a factory worker in our investigation?"

Although Noble spoke quietly without a hint of disapproval, his query still stung. Caroline rested her clasped hands on the little table Kesia had set up for them in the corner of the café. Annamarie had stayed behind at the hotel with the three Holcomb children, allowing her to visit undisturbed with Noble. "I'm not trying to bring him in as an official investigator for the commission. But he's been doing some sleuthing on his own—for the factory's owner, he said—and unless I miss my guess, he has uncovered helpful information. It will be beneficial for us to combine his findings with mine." Noble's expression didn't change. Caroline added on a timorous note, "Won't it?"

Noble raised one brow. "I don't know. It depends on his trustworthiness. If he tells the purpose of our investigation of the factory, and the owner tells the managers in the factory, we might very well be sabotaging any hope of discovering the truth about Harmon's death."

"I don't intend to tell him our purpose for being there." Caroline cringed, hearing her own words. She'd accused Ollie of being less than truthful with her, yet she deliberately hid truth from him. As much as she relished her job, ensuring future workers could enjoy safer environments, she would never adjust to the necessity of deception. "He knows I'm concerned about the age of some of the workers. We can let him assume our investigation is related to Bratcher's campaign to change the child labor laws. If we—"

"Carrie?"

The quiet voice behind her took her by surprise. She turned to find Ollie standing just inside the doorway. She leaped up, aware of Noble also rising. Had Ollie overheard her final statement? Her heart fluttering, she gestured him forward.

"Ollie, please meet Mr. Noble Dempsey, a dear friend of mine." Her words came out breathy, as if she'd just run a footrace. She drew in a lungful of air to calm herself. She'd suggested this meeting and didn't need to be apoplectic over it. "Noble, this is Ollie Moore, a janitor at the Dinsmore chocolate factory." She wished she could introduce Ollie as a friend, but that would only inspire speculation in Noble's mind. Yet another thing she must keep hidden. Her stomach twisted in regret.

Ollie moved toward Noble but stopped a couple of feet away. The two men stood in a face-off, which left Caroline battling the urge to giggle. Both tall, one broad chested with a full white beard and one well toned with cleanshaven cheeks, and both wearing expressions of part curiosity, part guardedness. Although they shook hands and murmured greetings in a gentlemanly fashion, they might have been preparing for a duel. Caroline would have given a five-dollar gold piece to know what each was thinking in those brief seconds of assessment.

Noble extracted his hand from Ollie's grasp. He turned to Kesia. "We're ready for supper whenever you'd like to deliver it, Mrs. Durham."

The woman nodded. "Three plates o' chicken an' dumplings on the way!" She smiled and waved at Ollie, who smiled and waved back, then she bustled into the kitchen.

Noble held his hand toward the third chair at the table. "Please join us, Mr. Moore."

Ollie, instead of sitting, held Caroline's chair.

With a self-conscious smile she slid onto the round wooden seat. "Thank you." Aware of Noble's curious gaze, she turned her attention to smoothing her skirt across her knees.

Noble sat, bracing his ankle on his opposite knee, as Ollie sat and stacked his arms on the table. He flashed a smile—a bit lopsided thanks to the swelling on the side of his face. "Sorry if I was late. I thought I heard you talking about Bratcher when I came in."

Caroline looked to Noble, silently giving him permission to divulge as much or as little as he wanted to concerning their investigation.

Noble cleared his throat. "You weren't late, Mr. Moore. Car...rie and I were simply reviewing what we know about the incident that claimed Harmon Bratcher's life. I was well acquainted with the man, and I fully supported his interest in raising the age of child laborers to sixteen. His death came as quite a shock."

Ollie frowned, drumming his fingers on his elbows. "It was a shock for me, too. There'd never been a death at the factory before. Mr. Dinsmore has always insisted on the safest working conditions for his employees. But Mr. Bratcher was more than an inspector, wasn't he? In fact"— Ollie's voice took on a bit of an edge, as if testing Noble—"he was something of a rabble-rouser, trying to incite unrest among workers."

Caroline bit back a gasp. "Are you saying he deserved what he got?"

Ollie shook his head, turning a frown on her. "Of course not. Even rabble-rousers have a right to their say, thanks to freedom of speech. I'm just saying his noisemaking could have made somebody mad enough to want to silence him. Maybe for good."

Kesia plopped aromatic, steaming bowls of thick chicken gravy oozing between mounds of moist dumplings in front of them. She brushed her palms together. "Anything else? Besides coffee, I mean. I've got a fresh pot brewin' an' will bring it over soon as it sings."

"This is fine, Mrs. Durham. Thank you," Noble said.

"Looks good, as always," Ollie added.

Kesia beamed. "All right, then. You enjoy your dinner. Holler if you're wantin' more." She scurried off.

Noble said, "Shall I ask the blessing?"

Caroline and Ollie nodded in unison. They closed their eyes while Noble offered a simple thank-you for the meal. After the "amen" Noble lifted his fork and began cutting the dumplings into smaller pieces. "Mr. Moore, would you have any idea who might have wanted to silence Bratcher?"

Ollie gave a start, as if he'd forgotten what they'd been discussing before the food arrived. He swept his napkin over his mouth. "No, sir. But I imagine anyone who employs younger workers would be motivated to end his crusade."

"Including Dinsmore?" Noble continued eating, seemingly unconcerned. The simple query hung in the air for several tense seconds.

Ollie placed his fork on the table as if his appetite had fled. "You can't think Fulton Dinsmore had anything to do with Bratcher's death." A bald statement, not a question.

Caroline flicked a worried glance at Noble. She'd never heard such defensiveness in Ollie's voice. Had Noble stirred a hornet's nest?

Noble lifted his head, his expression bland. "Didn't you just say anyone who employs younger workers might wish Bratcher ill? Dinsmore certainly falls into that category. He has a substantial number of young employees in his factory."

Ollie's lips formed a grim line. "Yes, he does. And for good reason." Pushing the bowl aside, Ollie leaned toward Noble. "A lot of the children working at the factory come from poor families, families who have trouble putting enough food on the table. The salaries the youngsters earn benefit the entire family. I know Carrie thinks those children ought to be in school, but the truth is they're getting an education by working. They're learning a trade."

He shifted to look at Carrie. "If you want to know how much can be learned by working in a factory, ask Gordon Hightower. He started out as one of Dinsmore's box makers when he was ten or eleven years old. Now he manages the entire operation—second only to Fulton Dinsmore himself. Hightower's success proves what can happen if youngsters start working at an early age."

Shifting his attention to Noble again, he went on in the same passionate tone. "Mr. Dinsmore believes in giving young workers a chance to better themselves, so he and Harmon Bratcher were on opposite sides of the child labor battle. Even so, he'd never deliberately harm someone."

"You seem to know Fulton Dinsmore quite well." Noble said what Caroline was thinking. She sat with her fork poised over her untouched bowl. What would Ollie say next?

Pink splashed Ollie's cheeks. He ducked his head, picking at a bit of loose paint on the edge of the table. "Well enough to know he isn't a violent man. Besides, he lets Hightower run the place." Ollie flinched as if he'd tasted something unpleasant. "Fulton Dinsmore comes once a month for meetings with Hightower. The night Bratcher died, Dinsmore wasn't anywhere near the factory."

Noble took another bite of his dumplings, chewed, swallowed, and then tossed out a casual comment. "But he wouldn't necessarily have to be on the grounds to arrange an...accident."

Ollie leaped up, bumping the edge of the table. Broth sloshed over the edge of Caroline's plate, and she let out a squawk of surprise. Ollie glared at Noble. "Mr. Dempsey, friend of Carrie's or not, I won't let you speak that way about my...my boss. He's a good man. A hardworking, honest man. Do not cast aspersions on his character."

Noble's eyebrows rose. One side of his mouth twitched beneath his mustache. "I meant no offense. I'm merely searching for possibilities. My comment wasn't intended as an accusation."

Caroline held her breath, watching Ollie. Fury pulsated from him. The vexation had exploded from nowhere, taking her by surprise and raising questions in the back of her mind. Why was he so protective of Fulton Dinsmore?

Noble motioned toward Ollie's chair and plate. "Please. Sit back down. Eat your dinner before it grows cold."

Ollie shook his head. "I'm not hungry. I came here at Carrie's invitation. I thought we'd talk about the elevator, try to determine who took the blueprints. But instead"—he offered Caroline a brief, apologetic look, then turned a murderous glare on Noble—"you began a character assassination on someone I admire. And I want no part of it."

Tossing his napkin on the table, he took one sideways step toward the door. "I don't know why Harmon Bratcher was in the factory that Sunday. I don't know how he fell down the elevator shaft. But I do know this: Fulton Dinsmore is innocent of any wrongdoing. And now, since there seems to be nothing more I can do for you, I bid you both good night."

"Ollie, wait!"

Ignoring Caroline's plea, he turned and strode out the door.

Caroline watched him disappear. Aggravation rose from her middle and made her tremble from head to toe. She turned toward Noble. "Why did you goad him so? He'll never help us now."

Noble chuckled. He patted Caroline's hand. "Ah, my dear, you weren't paying attention. He's already been very helpful."

Caroline frowned. "He has?"

"Indeed. I now know on whom to focus our investigation. Oh, we still need evidence to convince a court of law, but I'll be quite surprised if my instincts are proved wrong."

Caroline shook her head hard. "I'm not following you."

"Of course you're not. Because when you're in the presence of that young man, you're suddenly rendered incompetent."

"Wh-what?" Heat seared her face. She lifted her napkin and fanned herself ith it.

Another chuckle, indulgent and fatherly. "There's no harm in mindless flirtation, Caroline. In fact, I find it rather refreshing that you can lower your guard enough to enjoy a bit of coquetry. You're entirely too serious most of the time." He gave her hand a squeeze and then reached fo his fork. "Eat your dinner. While you e' I'll enlighten you on what your so-ca janitor inadvertently divulged. And then, when we've finished our business, I'll take charge of the youngsters and ask Annamarie to sit down with you for a womanly chat." He winked, mischief twinkling in his eyes. "I believe our Caroline might have need of romantic advice."

Chapter 28

Oliver

Oliver set his feet with such force the impact jarred his entire skeleton. By the time he reached his apartment, his jaw ached and his head throbbed. He flopped into the overstuffed chair in front of the cold fireplace. What an insufferable man! And Carrie claimed him as a friend.

He envisioned them in the corner of Kesia's café at that cozy little table—brought in especially for their tête-à-tête, apparently—with Dempsey's snow-white head tipped close to Carrie's cinnamon-colored coils. At first glance he'd recognized that the pair shared a special relationship. The man was old enough to be Carrie's father, but he'd seen enough of what his mother called May-December romances to know that some women preferred older men. He wouldn't have expected it of Carrie, though. He'd hoped—

He jolted to his feet and paced the room. Why had Carrie invited him to meet Noble Dempsey? Noble, indeed. Ignoble was more like it, flinging out such drivel about Father. He'd gone, fully expecting whomever she brought to have knowledge of the elevator. To be subjected to accusation and innuendo had bruised him even more deeply than the door smacking his head. She hadn't deliberately struck him with the door, but this blow—this blow to his heart and ego— seemed calculated. And he'd walked right into the situation as recklessly as he'd plowed into the door.

If Carrie was in league with this Dempsey, who seemed determined to find Father accountable for the death of Harmon Bratcher, then they had a bigger issue to overcome than her desire to see the child labor laws changed. Sinking back into the chair, he held his aching head in his hands and closed his eyes. **God**... But the prayer ended on a single, strangled word. He didn't know what to ask.

Caroline

Laughter spilled from the smaller of the two sleeping rooms in Noble and Annamarie's suite. Caroline looked toward the sound, a smile tugging at her lips despite the heaviness in her chest. How gratifying to know the children at least were happy.

Annamarie settled in the chair facing Caroline, and she shook her head, fondness shining in her eyes. "Noble's getting them all wound up again. He's so good at it. Then, when it's time to sleep, he becomes all bluster, telling them if they don't settle down, they'll have no goodies in their stockings come Christmas."

Caroline released a light laugh. "He did the same thing to me when I was Letta's age, as I recall. And I never believed his bluster, because while he issued his threat, his eyes sparkled."

"Letta, Lank, and Lesley don't believe him, either," Annamarie said. She sighed, gazing toward the doorway. Her brows pinched together. "I worry they're growing too attached to Noble. You know how hard he is to resist."

Caroline felt certain Ollie could resist Noble. Ollie hadn't liked Noble. At all. But she didn't want to think about Ollie. "Has their aunt Gertrude responded to the telegram Noble sent?"

"Not yet. But she might have decided to save her dime and simply do what he requested—come for them herself. He made it clear he won't put them on a train unattended and send them to her."

Caroline hoped the aunt would respond to Noble's telegram more positively than she had to the ones Caroline had sent. Those children needed someone.

Annamarie reached into the basket beside her chair and withdrew a snarl of red yarn and a pair of knitting needles. "Do you mind if I work while we chat? I'd like to finish these scarves for the children before we leave for home."

Tears pricked behind Caroline's eyes. Annamarie's fingers were so bent from arthritis that holding the needles had to cause her much pain. Yet she chose to push past her discomfort to gift the children. Caroline forced a light tone. "Maybe you should teach me to knit so I could make them matching mittens."

Annamarie sent Caroline a teasing look over the top of the needles. "If you prove as adept at knitting as you have at cooking, the poor children will be elderly before they receive their mittens."

Caroline only shrugged, offering a halfhearted grin. Not even for Annamarie would she learn to cook.

Annamarie went on. "If their aunt hasn't come for them by the end of the week, Noble said we'll take the children to Baldwin City ourselves before we go home."

Knowing the children would have supervision—either from their aunt or from the Dempseys—took a great burden from Caroline's mind. She leaned forward and pressed her hand to Annamarie's knee. "You and Noble do so much for children. It's a pity—" She bit down on her tongue, sitting back in her chair.

Annamarie sent a warm smile at Caroline. "No need to look all sorry over there. It's true Noble and I weren't blessed with children of our own. And I admit, for years I resented God for it. But think for a moment, Caroline." Her expression turned pensive, and her hands stilled on the needles. "If I'd had children of my own, do you suppose Noble would have brought you home? Or any of the other children he saved from difficult situations? Of course he wouldn't have. And even if he'd tried, I wouldn't have allowed it! We'd have been too busy with our own. So you see? God had a plan in leaving me barren. My womb has been empty, but my heart?" A smile curved her lips. Tears glittered in her eyes. "My heart overflows."

Caroline slipped from her chair and knelt beside Annamarie. She cupped her hands gently over the older woman's, the partially completed red scarf dangling between them. "I love you, Annamarie. And Noble. I don't know what I would have done without you." Memories of the years before Noble scooped her up and carried her from the Remingtons' house sneaked from the far recesses of her mind, but Caroline resolutely drove the dark recollections back to their hiding places. Those early years no longer mattered. "I hope I can make half as much difference in the lives of children as you've made in mine."

"You're already making a difference." Annamarie gently extracted her hands and put the needles to work again. "But of course Noble and I pray you'll be blessed in ways we weren't."

Caroline rose and crossed to the window. Only darkness greeted her eyes. And her own reflection in the glass. She might have been the only person in the world. Loneliness struck. She said quietly, "If God is wise—and I believe He is—He'll withhold family from me."

"Caroline, such a thing to say." The mild reprimand stung as much as if Annamarie had flayed her with harsh words.

Caroline returned to Annamarie's chair and perched on the arm. "It's true. God knows I'd be a horrible mother and an even worse wife." She couldn't cook, she disliked cleaning, and the thought of being responsible for a baby made her break out in a cold sweat. "Thanks to Noble's training, I'm a decent agent, though, and I find great fulfillment in helping to make factories safer places for people to work. And when I've helped change the laws so children—all children —attend school every day, I'll know I've done what I'm meant to do."

Annamarie paused again in her knitting to place a hand on Caroline's arm. "Are you sure, Caroline, that it will be enough?"

Caroline frowned. "Of course. Think of the good it will do for the current children and all the children to come."

"But I'm not speaking of the current children and the children to come, dear girl. I'm speaking of **you**. Will it be enough?"

Uncertain how to answer, Caroline sat in confused silence.

Annamarie lay her knitting in her lap and took both of Caroline's hands in hers. "Noble thinks you feel something special for the man who works at the factory—Ollie Moore. Is he right?"

She wouldn't lie to Annamarie. Very slowly she nodded.

A smile broke across Annamarie's face. "Oh, that's wonderful!"

"No, it isn't." Caroline stood and paced the room twice. "It's foolhardy. And it's distracting. And I have to stop thinking about him **right now**."

"But why?" Annamarie patted the arm of her chair, inviting Caroline to sit. "Tell me about him. Is he a God-fearing man?"

Caroline sank onto the rolled arm, reflecting on Annamarie's question. Ollie had agreed to pray for Mr. Holcomb, and he'd been in church this past Sunday. She nodded.

"Is he handsome?" Annamarie's dark-brown eyes twinkled teasingly.

Immediately a picture of Ollie filled her mind—tall, with wide shoulders and a trim waist. Even in work dungarees and suspenders, he cut a dashing figure. Heat filled Caroline's face. A self-conscious giggle escaped. "Annamarie, really..."

The woman grinned, arching one brow. "Are you afraid I'll set my sights on him if you tell me? Remember, I've already captured the finest man God placed on the earth, so you needn't worry I'll chase Ollie Moore around the block."

Caroline laughed out loud, then clapped her hand over her mouth. Annamarie looked so demure with her silver hair slicked back in a neat twist and her slender body attired in a dignified suit of sage green. Her teasing always took Caroline by surprise. She sighed, shaking her head in amusement. "Annamarie, you are a scamp, but I love you."

The teasing faded from Annamarie's eyes. "And we love you. So much so we want you to be happy. If this man could make you happy, then—"

Caroline bounced up. "He can't." She

stepped to the fireplace and braced her hand on the mantel.

"Why not?"

"Because our entire relationship"—did they have a relationship?—"is built on half truths. I can't tell him who I really am. And I know he's holding back something from me." Ollie's cultured speech echoed in her mind. And then something else leaped from her memory.

When Ollie had shared Gordon Hightower's worry about Caroline being one of Bratcher's relatives and therefore seeking a reason to bring a wrongful-death suit against the factory, he'd said "sue us." **Us.** Not "him" or "the factory" or even "the owner." At the time her weariness had kept her from fully comprehending the meaning of his statement. But now her heart pounded like a bass drum as questions—and suppositions—raced through her mind.

Annamarie's dear face registered concern. "Caroline, what is it?"

"Nothing." Caroline scurried to the hall tree near the door of the suite and removed her shawl. Seeing the deep furrows in Annamarie's face, she forced a smile and returned to plant a kiss on Annamarie's soft cheek. "Don't worry. I just remembered something, and I...I need to take care of it before I go in to work tonight."

Annamarie caught Caroline's hand, holding her in place. "Are you sure you're all right? Your face is ashen."

With a grin Caroline pinched her cheeks. "Is that better?"

Annamarie's expression didn't change.

Caroline beamed a big smile and tossed her head, making the little coils that always escaped her bun bounce against her cheeks. "You needn't look so distressed. I'm fine. Honestly." She leaned down and embraced her friend. "I'll come when I get off in the morning to walk the children to Kesia's for breakfast and then to school. We can chat then, all right?"

"And you'll tell me what important errand has you dashing out the door?"

Caroline wasn't sure she'd have all the answers she was seeking by tomorrow morning, but she hoped to have uncovered at least one bit of information—the truth of who Ollie Moore was. She said, "We'll talk more tomorrow. Please tell Noble and the children good night for me." She headed for the door.

"Caroline?"

The worry in Annamarie's voice brought Caroline to a halt, but she didn't turn around.

"Please be careful. Don't do anything rash. If you have feelings for this man, God can remove whatever barriers seem to be keeping you apart. Will you trust God and seek His guidance rather than relying on your own instincts?"

Slowly Caroline turned to face Annamarie. She forced her lips to form a smile while inwardly she quivered. "I'll try."

Annamarie nodded, apparently satisfied. "Very well. Good night, Caroline."

She stepped into the hallway and then leaned against the wall, allowing her head to sag. Had she just lied to Annamarie? From the first time she met Ollie Moore, she'd felt a tug toward him. Yet the more time she spent with him, the more confused she became. She started to go back in and ask Annamarie if God would prompt her to engage in such a puzzling, uncertain, frustrating relationship. But, fearful of Annamarie's answer, she crossed the tails of her shawl over her waist and headed for the factory instead.

Chapter 29

Letta

"Luh-Luh-Letta?"

Letta snuffled and rolled over on her cot to face the bed where her brothers lay under a fluffy blanket. Although the cot was more comfortable than anything she'd slept on before, she wondered what it would be like to sleep in the big feather bed. "Hush, Lank. Mr. Noble told us to go to sleep now." She liked the big man well enough to mind him.

"I know, buh-buh-buh-but gotta ask you suh-suh-somethin'."

Lank rarely used words, and over the years Letta had learned to read his gestures. But with the room all dark, she couldn't see well enough to understand.

Listening to him talk hurt her heart and made her impatient, both at the same time. "What'cha want?"

"Cuh–cuh–cuh—"

Lesley sat bolt upright. "We're wantin' to stay here instead o' goin' back to our house. Can we, Letta?"

She tossed aside her covers and hopped out of the bed. The cot let out a mighty squeak, and she cringed. Would Mr. Noble or Mrs. Annamarie hear her moving around? She paused, ear turned toward the door, but when no footsteps approached, she tiptoed across the thickly carpeted floor and sat on the edge of the boys' bed. She scowled at the pair. "That's a stu—" She stopped herself from using the word Pa had thrown at his children. "That idea won't work, Lesley."

Lesley's long eyelashes swept up and down once. "Why? We like it here."

Letta liked it here, too. She liked the big, clean rooms and the nice furniture. She liked the indoor plumbing where all she had to do was turn a couple of knobs, and hot water came right out of the pipes.

And everybody got fresh water for their bath. She liked how a maid came in every day and cleaned up after them. And mostly, she liked Mr. Noble and Mrs. Annamarie. But they still couldn't stay. "Don't matter. This is a hotel. Costs a heap of money to stay in hotels."

"But Mr. Noble's payin' for it."

Lesley had an answer for everything. Letta huffed in aggravation. "Sure he is, but he don't live here. He's just stayin' here for a little while. He an' Mrs. Annamarie'll be goin' back to their own house soon. Don'tcha remember them tellin' us they're leavin' come the end of the week?"

Lesley folded his arms over his skinny chest and poked out his lip. "Then I wanna go with 'em. I like 'em, Letta. I like 'em a lot. An' so does Lank. Mr. Noble, he never tells Lank he's a imbecile. An' Mrs. Annamarie talks real nice an' smells real good. So can we go live with 'em?"

Letta understood why Lesley wanted to live with the Dempseys. She liked them, too. Down deep, she'd started wishing they were her pa and ma. Or maybe her grandpa and grandma since they were white haired already. But she knew it was all pretend. Nice as they were, they'd never said anything about keeping Letta and the boys.

"No, we can't." Her whisper came out on a harsh note, but she did nothing to temper her voice, knowing Lesley wouldn't listen to reason otherwise. "Remember that telegram Mr. Noble sent to Aunt Gertrude? He read it to us first so we'd know what he was doin'. What did it say?"

Lesley lowered his head. "He told Aunt Gertrude to come get us."

"That's right." Letta gave her little brother a push that sent him against his pillow. "So no more talk about wantin' to live with 'em. You neither, Lank. They don't want us." Sadness washed over her. She finished on a sigh. "No sense in wishin' they do." She rose. "Now both o' you go to sleep."

She lay down on her squeaky cot and covered up with the soft blanket. Then she stared, wide awake, at the ceiling.

Neither Lank nor Lesley spoke again, but every now and then she heard one of them sniffle. Probably Lesley. Lank wasn't given to tears any more than Letta was. But she reckoned his heart was aching just as bad as hers.

Ma hadn't wanted them. Pa hadn't wanted them. And now Mr. Noble and Mrs. Annamarie were ready to hand them off to an aunt who didn't want them, either. Letta's lower lip quivered, and she clamped her jaw hard. So nobody wanted them. So what? They didn't need anybody anyway. And come tomorrow, soon as Miss Carrie dropped them off at school, she'd take her brothers by the hands and find someplace for them to live where nobody'd find them or bother them again. They wouldn't stick around where they weren't wanted.

Caroline

Caroline headed for her work station, tool belt dangling from her hand. Her gaze turned in every direction, her pulse thrumming in apprehension. Or was it anticipation? When Ollie Moore was involved, she couldn't be certain of anything anymore. She only knew that when she saw him, the questions lingering on her tongue would spill forth. And she wouldn't relent until he'd given satisfactory answers.

She rounded the corner to her work station and came to such a sudden stop her feet slid on the concrete floor. Ollie was standing beside the low cart of filled boxes awaiting their lids. His unsmiling gaze met hers, and all the questions she'd intended to spew dissipated. In their place a desire rose to see him open his arms in silent invitation, an invitation she would accept without a moment's hesitation.

Apparently she hadn't gotten enough sleep earlier that day.

Giving herself a shake to cast off the odd longing, she set her feet in motion and marched directly to the cart. She hooked the tool belt around her waist, set her feet wide, and gave him what she hoped would be interpreted as an imperious look. "I would have a word with you."

"That suits me." He stepped around the cart, caught her by the elbow, and began propelling her across the floor.

She let out a squawk of dismay and smacked at his hand. "Release me!"

His lips set in a grim line, he kept a grip until he'd guided her inside the janitor's closet and closed the door behind them. The bulb hanging overhead was already on when they entered, letting her know he'd planned this clandestine meeting. She darted to the opposite side of the little room and stood glowering at him. Had Gordon Hightower forced her inside a closet with him, she'd have been frightened out of her mind. But the only emotion coursing through her as she faced Ollie was anger.

"What are you doing? We're on duty— we can't be holed up in here together. What will people think?"

He gave her a snide look. "Odd that you'd be concerned about what people think, considering..."

She pinched her brows together. "Considering what?"

"Never mind. It isn't important." He took a forward step, his expression hard. "I need to get something straight with you. Whatever information you're seeking about Harmon Bratcher's death, you're wasting your time trying to blame Fulton Dinsmore. I will not allow you to sully his good name, and should you choose to persist in this...this **witch hunt**, I shall be forced to act with all due haste and have you removed from employ at this factory." His articulate speech poured out effortlessly as he staunchly defended the owner of the factory.

Us. He'd said us when speaking of the factory. Understanding dawned. She jabbed her finger at him and found her voice. "Ollie Moore? Or is it Dinsmore?"

He lifted his chin. Neither the factory worker attire nor the purplish and yellow marks on his face could hide his proud carriage. He patted his palms together in subdued applause, a sarcastic grin on his face. "Well done, Miss Lang. You've discovered one small truth." Then his expression hardened. "And now that you know who I am, you know I can make good on my promise to send you packing. My father is well respected, his reputation as a fair, philanthropic man reaching far beyond the bounds of Kansas. Your accusations, even though unfounded and unsubstantiated, could cast a permanent shadow on his character. So I must insist they end here and now."

To Caroline's surprise, her indignation melted, and in its stead came an envy unlike any she'd experienced before. Ollie so clearly loved his father. Admired and revered him even. To have a father so deserving of loyalty must have been a delight beyond all others. To her chagrin, tears pooled in her eyes, and she blinked them away, praying Ollie wouldn't notice.

"Carrie?" He took a step toward her, true regret coloring his tone and softening his stern features. "I've wounded you with my harshness."

He hadn't, but she wouldn't correct

him. She had no desire to share the real reason for her emotional reaction.

He went on kindly. "I meant to speak my mind—I **needed** to speak my mind—but I allowed jealousy to overcome chivalry. I assure you I was taught better by both of my parents. Please forgive me."

She sniffed, frowning. "Why would you be jealous?"

He grimaced. "Never mind. Will you accept my apology?"

She wanted to stay angry. To be indignant at having been duped into believing he was only another worker. Even to resent him for his affluent upbringing. But looking into his sincere, remorseful face, she couldn't find it within herself to refuse. She nodded.

A small smile—one holding warmth—curved his lips. "Thank you, Carrie." The smile faltered. "But my apology doesn't erase my expectations. I still insist you cease trying to blame my father for Bratcher's death."

Caroline forced a cavalier shrug. "I've

already eliminated him as a possible suspect. Noble and I—" Had she really intended to divulge Noble's suspicion? She'd told Annamarie she was a good investigator, but she'd become far too lax on this particular job. And the reason for her lack of focus stood before her in tan dungarees, a blue shirt, and brown-and-yellow-striped suspenders, with a flat-billed cap sitting rakishly upon his head.

She started to move past him. "The foreman is going to be looking for me if I don't get to work." She paused, worry making her mouth dry. "You...you won't turn me in as an infiltrator, will you?"

"It's to my advantage to learn the truth. So, no, I'll keep your purpose here a secret."

Heaving a sigh of relief, she moved toward the door.

"Will you keep mine?"

She angled her head, puzzled.

"I must remain Ollie Moore to the others. You see, I joined the ranks as an employee to gather information about the inner workings of the factory from the viewpoint of a common laborer. My findings will enable me to make changes that benefit each person in my employ. But if they know I'm the boss's son..." He held out his palms, offering a shrug.

"I understand." His desire to make things better for the workers touched her more deeply than she cared to admit. "You'll remain Ollie Moore." She turned again to leave.

"Wait. There's something else I want to tell you."

She shifted in place, eager to escape the closet, the man, and the odd feelings he conjured within her.

"I want to know what really happened the night Bratcher died, too. Yes, it was deemed accidental, but I'm not sure all the facts were placed in evidence before the determination was made."

He had her attention. She gazed at him, her breath trapped in her lungs. "We need to fully examine the elevator, and we—"

"We?" Caroline shook her head. "This isn't your investigation, Ollie. It's mine."

"I'll help you."

"No."

"You were willing to accept my help before. Why not now?"

Before he was Ollie Moore, a fellow employee. But now he was Ollie Dinsmore, son of Fulton Dinsmore, owner of Dinsmore's World-Famous Chocolates Factory. But how ridiculous it would sound to speak the reason aloud. She scowled. "Because."

He rolled his eyes.

"And don't roll your eyes at me."

He did it again.

Caroline huffed. "Will you let me pass before I'm given another write-up? One more and Hightower will let me go."

Ollie smirked. "Not without my father's approval, and my father won't approve it without my agreeing. So you see, Carrie,"—he leaned close, his eyes sparkling—"you need me as an ally. But we won't be able to investigate during operation hours. We need to come when everything is closed and there are no watchful eyes."

He was right. Someone had been

reporting to Hightower, or he wouldn't have made threats against her. Even so, she wasn't convinced she should continue joining forces with Ollie. She grabbed the doorknob and turned it, but before she could push the door open, Ollie placed his hand over hers.

"Meet me at the back door at seven o'clock Sunday morning. We can set aside any snooping until then to avoid attracting attention. But on Sunday we'll be able to explore at our leisure without worry." His warm fingers slid across the back of her hand, sending tremors of awareness up her arm. "Yes?"

She'd probably regret the decision for the rest of her life, but she opened her mouth and blurted a simple reply. "Yes."

Chapter 30

Letta

Chill air whisked across the plains and lifted the collar of Letta's coat. She smacked it back into place with a grunt of annoyance. Beside her, Lank tripped on a railroad tie and nearly went down. She reached for him, but he caught himself in time, sent her a sour look as if she'd caused his toe to catch, then hunkered into his jacket and kept moving ahead without a word. She glanced back at Lesley, who plodded along, dragging his heels. For most of the first hour of their journey, he'd walked on the shiny rail, hands extended like a tightrope walker. He and Lank had thrown rocks into the thick grass alongside the tracks, chased rabbits startled by the rocks, and dashed back to her, all smiles from their adventure. They'd even considered it a game to hide in the thick brush when a train came, covering their ears against the clamorous chug, chug and rattle of the passing cars.

But as morning slipped away, the wind picked up, and the novelty of walking the railroad tracks wore off. Both boys had become grouchy. She was feeling grumbly, too. They'd ditched all their books behind the school's outhouse except her Bible—she couldn't bear to leave the only gift she'd ever received. The Bible's weight in her pocket pulled at her shoulder, and the handle of the lunchpail Miss Kesia had packed for them that morning cut into her fingers, making them ache something fierce. Her shoulder hurt, and her fingers hurt, and her feet hurt. She didn't know how much longer she'd be able to keep moving ahead.

She shifted the pail to her opposite hand again and searched the landscape in both directions. The sun wouldn't go down for several hours yet, but she and the boys would need shelter when dark fell. She'd expected to reach another town by now. According to their teacher, Wichita was only fifteen miles south, and the train went right through it. She didn't have a watch to know the time, but the sun was high overhead—past noon, for sure. They'd been walking for more than four hours already. How much farther could Wichita be?

"I'm hungry, Letta." Lesley's whining voice carried over the endless whistle of the wind.

Lank nodded his agreement.

Letta chewed her lip. She'd hoped to hold the boys off 'til midafternoon at least. They wouldn't be getting any supper unless she found a farmer's root cellar she could rob. She started to tell them to wait, but her stomach rumbled, too. She sighed. Might as well have a little something.

She turned and sat on the silver rail, placing the bucket between her feet and rustling through it. Both boys sat opposite her, their eyes on the bucket. She announced, "We got sandwiches, cookies, apples, an' my biscuits from breakfast." She'd deliberately tucked them in with the lunch items, thinking ahead.

Lesley stuck out his hands. "I want a sandwich, my apple, an' a cookie."

Letta shook her head. "Huh-uh. Can't have it all. Only one thing right now."

Lank scowled. "Wuh-wuh-why?"

"Gotta save some for later." Letta turned a stern look on the pair. "You'll thank me when you're hungry again and there's still somethin' in the bucket to eat."

The two fussed, but when Letta didn't give in, Lesley settled for an apple, and Lank took a sandwich. Letta ate her leftover biscuits, which were dry and tasteless but at least helped fill her stomach. As they were finishing, the familiar rumble of an approaching train vibrated the ground beneath them.

"Let's go!" She snatched up the bucket, took Lesley by the hand, and with Lank on her heels, raced to a stand of scrub trees growing alongside the tracks. They crouched behind the sheltering brush and watched the train whoosh by. The ground trembled, making Letta's skin tingle all the way to her scalp. She'd always wanted to ride on a train, but after having her hair tossed and her body rattled by its force, now she wasn't so sure she wanted to climb on board one. They'd probably be louder and rattle even more from the inside.

The locomotive rounded a bend, and Letta led her brothers from their hiding spot. Lesley's mouth stretched into a wide yawn. He grabbed Letta's hand and pulled. "Do we gotta keep goin'? My feet're tired. I wanna rest."

"Muh-muh-me, too," Lank said.

Letta hooked the bucket handle over her arm and scowled as fierce as she could even though she wanted to sit and rest awhile as much as they did. "We gotta get to Wichita."

"What's in Wichita?"

"Our new home, that's what! But we won't ever get there if we keep stoppin' to rest."

Lesley poked out his lips. "We ain't stopped but this one time."

"I know, but like I said, we gotta keep movin'." She dropped her grumpy act and tried another tack. "C'mere, Lank. Let's you an' me play hopscotch on the ties. You find a rock to toss ahead. Betcha we can hop farther'n Lesley."

Lesley folded his arms over his chest. "I don't care if you can hop farther. My feet're tired, an' I wanna rest."

Letta stifled a groan. He was getting too smart to fall for her tricks. She grabbed his arm and yanked him onto the tracks. "Walk or hop—I don't care. But just keep goin'. We gotta get to Wichita so I can find us a place to stay. Out here in the middle of the fields, there ain't no hotels where we can sleep tonight."

Lank turned a curious look in her direction. "Huh-huh-hotels cost muh-muh-money."

"Yeah," Lesley said, wrinkling his nose. "How you gonna pay for a hotel, Letta? You got money?"

She did. Two five-dollar pieces and

some smaller coins. It had stung her something fierce to take that money from Mr. Noble's coin purse when he was busy trimming his beard that morning. But how else would she take care of her brothers until she found a job? Someday, when she'd managed to work enough to set some money aside, she'd pay Mr. Noble back. Thinking of the money as a loan helped ease her conscience. Even so, she wouldn't admit what she'd done.

"Why don't you stop askin' questions an' just walk?" She double-stepped, putting herself several strides ahead of the boys. Flicking a glance over her shoulder, she taunted, "You two're just a couple o' slowpokes. Can't even keep up with a girl."

This time her challenge worked. They galloped past her and kept a brisk pace, occasionally throwing triumphant grins over their shoulders. Letta pretended to be put out with them, but inwardly she smiled. If the boys kept their feet moving that fast, they'd reach Wichita in no time.

Lesley's question echoed in her

mind—"What's in Wichita?" She wished she could have said, "Somebody who wants us." But wishing didn't change anything. Nobody waited for them in Wichita. Because nobody'd ever wanted them, and nobody ever would. But she'd spend her last breath making sure neither Lank nor Lesley ever figured out she was the only one who wanted them around. Somehow she'd make sure she was more than enough.

Caroline

Someone banged on Caroline's door. She awoke with a start and blinked into the sunlit room. Her gaze fell on the alarm clock on the little table beside her bed. Two forty-five. She didn't need to get up for another forty-five minutes in order to collect Letta, Lank, and Lesley from school. She pulled the pillow over her head, determined to ignore whoever stood in the hallway.

Bang, bang, bang! "Carrie? Carrie, are

you in there?"

Caroline groaned. The boarding hotel's manager must need something important to be so persistent. Muttering under her breath, she traipsed to the door and flung it open. The woman offered an apologetic look.

"I tried to tell the fellow you were sleeping, but he insisted he needed to talk to you."

Caroline scowled. "What fellow?"

"The one who's on the telephone. Called himself Mr. Dempsey." Caroline thanked the woman and rushed down the flights of stairs and then ran breathlessly into the little telephone cubby. She pressed the receiver against her head and gasped into the horn, "Noble? Is everything all right?"

"I'm sorry to have awakened you, Caroline, but the children's aunt is here. She arrived on the two o'clock train and came to the hotel. I thought you might want to walk her to the school and introduce her to the children. I'd go, but Annamarie isn't up to an outing, and I don't want to leave her alone."

Noble's consideration toward his wife knew no bounds. Caroline, although still tired, couldn't help but smile at the concern in his voice. "Of course I'll come. Let me run a comb through my hair and wash my face. I'll catch the trolley and should be there in fifteen minutes or so."

"Just come right on in. The door will be unlocked."

Caroline disconnected the call, raced up the stairs to freshen up, then raced back down to meet the trolley. As promised, she was entering the door to Noble and Annamarie's suite in a little more than fifteen minutes, which would allow her a bit of get-acquainted time with the children's aunt before they went to the school.

Noble rose when Caroline entered, gesturing toward a sober-faced woman with graying hair and a gaping patched coat seated next to Annamarie on the sofa. "Caroline, please meet Mrs. Gertrude O'Malley, who's come from Baldwin City."

The woman remained rooted on the sofa, forcing Caroline to bend down and shake her hand. "It's nice to meet you, Mrs. O'Malley. I'm so thankful you've come."

Mrs. O'Malley pursed her lips. "Don't know that I had much choice but to leave my man tendin' the farm by himself an' come, seein' as how you folks wouldn't send the young uns to me any other way."

Noble cleared his throat. "I'm sorry your trip is inconvenient for you, Mrs. O'Malley, but I'm sure you understand the necessity of accompanying the children on such a lengthy journey. Besides, the train ride together will give you a little time to become acquainted with them before you reach your home."

Mrs. O'Malley harrumphed.

Caroline slipped into a chair to keep from towering over the woman. "I believe you'll be happy to meet Letta, Lank, and Lesley. They've just started school, but their teacher says they're making excellent progress. Letta's already reading from the third-year primer, and Lank is able to add two-digit sums in his head. They're fine children—very polite and smart." Pride in their accomplishments squared her shoulders, and she smiled, expecting Mrs. O'Malley to express amazement or approval.

Smoothing her hand over straggly wisps escaping her bun, the children's aunt sniffed. "Don't know how anything spawned by that lazy, no-good brother o' mine could be called polite or smart, but I reckon I can hold my judgment 'til I see 'em." She offered a speculative look. "How old are those youngsters by now?"

Apprehension niggled at Caroline. "Letta is nearly fourteen, Lank is ten, and Lesley is eight."

Mrs. O'Malley snorted. "Eight... That'n won't be much help."

Startled, Caroline glanced at Noble, who gazed at Mrs. O'Malley with a worried frown on his face.

The woman continued as if she'd forgotten anyone else was in the room. "But if the two older ones are willin' to make up for his lack, I suppose I can take all three of them." She heaved a huge sigh and turned to Annamarie. "Wouldn't've come for 'em at all if my man hadn't convinced me of it. Raised my own already. Had no desire to raise another set. Ya see, me an' my brother we was twelve years apart in age. I married young, an' he married late, so our young uns were even more years apart. Now that all o' mine are outta the house, me an' my man been workin' the farm our own selves. Gettin' to be a bit much, seein' as how we're up in years. So my man says, 'Gert, if those kids've got strong arms, get 'em. Better'n payin' for hired help.'" She flipped her hands outward. "So I came."

Annamarie covered her lips with her fingers and stared at Mrs. O'Malley, clearly aghast. Caroline understood Annamarie's reaction. She wanted to leap across the floor and shake the woman until she developed a bit of compassion. Curling her hands over the armrests of the chair, she looked at Noble, beseeching him with her eyes to say something.

Noble cleared his throat. "Mrs. O'Malley,

you do plan to allow the children to attend school, do you not?"

She blinked. "How they gonna work the farm if they're sittin' in a schoolhouse?"

Caroline stood. "Mrs. O'Malley, you—"

Noble stepped forward. "Schooling is important, Mrs. O'Malley. Learning to read, write, and figure sums will benefit the children as they grow into adulthood."

Mrs. O'Malley scowled in reply.

Caroline asked, "Did you attend school?"

"Enough to learn readin', writin', an' such. I get by just fine."

"Did you send your children?"

"My boys weren't interested in goin'." Defensiveness colored the woman's words. "An' my man said they was needed at home. Those seeds don't jump in the ground on their own, ya know." She sent a scathing look at the other three adults in the room. "Why're you all on me about school, anyway? When you sent me that message, you just told me to come get these kids 'cause they was my responsibility. Well, if they're my res-ponsibility, then I'll tend 'em the way I see fit."

Caroline sucked in a sharp breath, and Noble put his arm around her shoulders. She appreciated his comforting presence, but she needed something more. "Mrs. O'Malley, if the children want to attend school, will you allow them to go?" She held her breath.

Mrs. O'Malley struggled to her feet. She balled one fist on her hip and gave Caroline a disgusted look. "Have you got rocks in your ears that keep you from hearin'? My man sent me after those kids so we'll have some help runnin' our farm. The kids can't be workin' the farm if they're in school. But"—she lifted her bony shoulders in a shrug—"durin' the winter months, when things're slow, I reckon they can go."

Caroline's heart gave a hopeful skip.

"If they can get themselves there. Can't imagine my man hitchin' the team durin' the cold months to tote 'em. But if they've a mind to walk to school, I won't tell 'em no."

Caroline's hopes immediately plummeted. Those children wouldn't walk through snow to school—not without encouragement. And clearly this woman and her "man" had no intention of offering encouragement. Mr. and Mrs. O'Malley were no better than her own parents had been, seeing children as workhorses. Why had she been so determined to send Letta, Lank, and Lesley to their only relative? They'd be better off in the county orphanage or on a poor farm. At least then they'd receive an education.

Mrs. O'Malley began buttoning her threadbare coat. "You gonna take me to get the young uns now? Ticket master told me I can leave on the eight o'clock tonight. Figure the sooner I get them kids to Baldwin City, the sooner we can all settle in together." She shook her head, sighing. "Sure hate goin' out in that brisk wind again. Near cuts through me. Would rather have another cup o' tea." She gazed pointedly at the cup sitting on the table at the end of the sofa.

Annamarie, ever gracious, said, "If your

train doesn't leave until eight, there's no need for you to rush off to the school." She sent a look filled with meaning to Caroline. "Why don't you retrieve the children and bring them back here? I'll pour Mrs. O'Malley another cup of tea, and she and I will chat while you're gone."

Noble gave Caroline a few pats on the shoulder, nodding at his wife. "Yes, that's a fine idea. Perhaps I'll go along—stretch my legs a bit."

Mrs. O'Malley tossed her coat aside and sank back on the sofa. "Sure won't argue about another cup o' tea. I'd take extra cream an' sugar in this cup, too."

Chapter 31

Caroline

Caroline nodded her thanks to the doorman for opening the door, then paused while Noble gave the man a penny for his service. The moment they stepped from beneath the hotel's green canopy, Caroline turned to Noble.

"I don't like her. I don't like her at all."

Noble slipped his gloved hand through Caroline's elbow, tempering his strides to match hers. "Nor do I, dear one."

"Then let's put her on the train and send her back to Baldwin City. Alone." They paused at the corner and allowed two wagons and a fine carriage to pass, the horses' hoofs and wooden wheels clattering against the damp cobblestones.

Noble's fingers gently tightened on her arm. "I understand how you feel, but, truthfully, we haven't any choice but to send the children with her. By their own admission, they have no other relatives. She's obligated, both morally and legally, to provide for them."

Helplessness brought a sting of tears. Caroline's chin quivered. "So there's no way to keep them here now that she's come?"

Releasing her elbow, Noble put his arm around her shoulders and tugged her tight against his sturdy side. "I'm afraid not, Caroline."

She slipped away from Noble's arm and hugged herself, her steps slowing as they approached the broad stairway leading to the double doors of the huge brick schoolhouse. "Why can't the laws better protect children, Noble? She openly admitted she only wants them to work her farm. She even dared to complain about little Lesley's age, claiming he's too young to be of any use."

Without warning, her mind whirled

backward in time, and she envisioned herself as an eight-year-old being led by the hand from her parents' house to a waiting carriage. She'd been so excited when Mr. Remington lifted her into the fancy rig pulled by prancing, majestic horses. Shivers of delight had danced through her as she'd wondered, in little-girl whimsy, if she would now live like a princess in a castle.

But no princess tower had awaited her.

She stopped at the base of the stairs and choked back a sob. "We can't send them, Noble. We can't. Isn't there some way to prevent her from taking them?"

"You know the laws as well as I do. We have no legal standing." He paused, his thick white brows crunching together. "If she refused to take them, they could become wards of the state, but..."

"That would be better than being hauled off to serve as her unpaid help. Why, they'll be no better than...than slaves!" Caroline swallowed a lump of bitter regret. "I shouldn't have contacted her. When Letta told me her pa and aunt were in conflict with each other, I should have simply contacted local authorities and had the children placed in the county orphans' home."

He cupped his hands over her shoulders and gave her a gentle shake. "Caroline, Caroline, you're letting your emotions overcome good sense. The orphans' home would offer no more than this aunt is offering. In both places the children would receive food, shelter, rudimentary education...and little else." Noble clicked his tongue on his teeth. "My dear, the children found their way into your affections. They've also won the hearts of Kesia and Ollie Moore. Don't you believe, if given an opportunity, they'll do the same with their aunt and uncle?"

She gazed into his tender face, seeing once again the gallant knight who'd rescued her from her dungeon of despair. She grasped his wrists and clung to them. "Do you think so, Noble?"

A smile crinkled his eyes. "Having had only a few days with them myself, I don't know how their aunt and uncle will be able to resist falling in love with them. They might take the children to serve as workers. But I believe, given time, they will grow to love Letta, Lank, and Lesley."

"Oh, I hope so..."

Noble tugged Caroline into a fatherly embrace. "Do more than hope, dear one. Pray."

Caroline nodded against the scratchy wool coat. "I will, Noble. I promise."

The bell clanged, the doors flew open, and children spilled down the stairs in an excited throng. Caroline and Noble stood to the side, watching the faces flood past. The stream changed from a steady flow to a trickle, and finally silence reigned. But the Holcomb children hadn't emerged.

Caroline flicked a frown at Noble. "I wonder if the teacher is keeping them late for some additional tutoring."

"Let's go find out." Noble escorted her up the stairs and into the building. All three children attended the first-year class, and the door to their classroom stood open in invitation. Noble peeked inside, then pulled back. "No one is in there."

Caroline looked into the room, noting the rows of empty desks. She crossed to the one shared by Lank and Lesley, Noble trailing after her, and touched the scarred top with her fingertips. Where could they be?

Footsteps approached, and the children's teacher, Miss Key, breezed through the door, flipping through a stack of papers in her hands. Noble cleared his throat, and the woman looked up. "Oh! Excuse me, I didn't realize anyone was here." She smiled at Caroline. "Miss Lang, correct?"

Caroline nodded. "Yes."

Miss Key moved toward her desk. "I'm glad to see you. I had written a note to send with Lank, letting you know how much better he is doing now that I allow him to write his responses rather than recite them. Let me get it for you." She began shifting items on the desk's cluttered top. "Ah, here it is." She turned, holding a folded piece of paper aloft.

Caroline stepped past Noble and took the note, an idea floating in the back of her mind. "Miss Key, did Lank know you'd written me a note?"

"No. Why do you ask?"

Sighing, Caroline turned to Noble. "If he knew a note was being sent home, he might surmise it was a criticism."

Noble nodded in understanding. "Which would make him want to sneak away rather than bring the note home. A typical schoolboy reaction. And of course Letta and Lesley would go with him."

Miss Key looked from Caroline to Noble and to Caroline again, confusion on her face. "Sneak away?"

Caroline nodded. "Yes. Is there another way for the children to leave the schoolhouse?" She inched toward the door, eager to pursue them.

"No. The teachers monitor the hall and ensure that all the children leave through the front doors. We don't want to accidentally leave a child behind when the building is locked at night."

Caroline started to ask, "Then where—"

At the same time Miss Key began, "Were the—"

They both stopped. Caroline stifled her impatience and nodded toward the teacher. "Go ahead, please."

"Were the children ill today? I know they missed several days due to their father's death, but I was surprised when none of them came to school today."

Caroline's pulse leaped into double beats. "They did come to school today. I walked them here myself after breakfast." She pictured them standing in a row on the porch with Letta between the boys, hands lifted in farewell. She'd waved good-bye and then hurried to her apartment, eager to sleep.

Miss Key frowned, shaking her head. She opened her attendance book and pointed to the empty boxes where check marks would indicate the children's presence for the day. "They weren't here."

Caroline staggered toward Noble, hands extended. The note about Lank slid from her fingers and floated to the floor. Noble's boot crushed it when he stepped forward and caught hold of her hands. She sought strength from his steady presence.

"Is something wrong?"

Miss Key's voice penetrated the fog surrounding Caroline. She forced a calm reply. "Apparently the children have run away." Then her bravado melted, and she threw herself into Noble's arms.

Letta

"What was that?" Lesley threw himself against Letta, and she wrapped her arms around his trembling frame. The echoing howl came again, haunting against the gray countryside.

Letta gave her brother's shoulders several assuring pats. "It's just a coyote, Lesley." At least she hoped it was a coyote and not a wolf. She didn't think a coyote would eat children. But a wolf? She couldn't be sure.

They'd left the railroad tracks at sunset, seeking a place of shelter. But they'd wandered aimlessly across stubbled ground and thick-grassed plots, and they hadn't found so much as a hollow log to climb into for the night. Now with full dark upon them, she could hardly see ten feet in front of her. If a barn or other building waited out there, she wouldn't know until she ran smack into it.

Lank pressed close on her other side. "Scuh-scuh-scared."

Letta was, too, but she couldn't admit it. She had to be brave. So she huffed out a snort. "No mangy ol' coyote spooks me. Listen." She lifted her face toward the sky, pursed her lips, and let out a wavering howl. The boys giggled, and she smiled in satisfaction. "Now you try."

In unison they imitated her. They dissolved into more giggles, but their laughter stopped when the coyote let loose another howl—this time louder. Closer.

"Take the bucket, Lank." Letta pressed the bucket—empty now but still useful if they came across anything worth gathering—into Lank's hand, then curled her arms over the boys' shoulders. "Come on now. Gotta be a shed or somethin' out here so we can bed down for the night."

Their feet crunched against dried grass, loud in an otherwise quiet surrounding. The wind had finally died down, and it didn't so much as whisper through the wild growth. Letta squinted at the thick shadows, her heart praying, praying, praying for a shed or a barn or even a lean-to where she could curl up with Lank and Lesley and sleep, safe from harm. If only the moon would poke its head out of the clouds. Then maybe she could see.

Ahead, a dark shape shot from the grass. Lesley screeched, and Lank swung his arms around Letta, clunking Lesley on the shoulder with the empty bucket. Lesley set up a wail. The shape rose no higher than Lesley's head, flew a dozen yards, then dropped in the grass again.

Letta shook loose the boys and gasped, "Hush up, Lesley. It was just a prairie chicken." But it took a good three minutes for Lesley to stop bawling and for her chest to stop heaving.

She leaned forward, trying to catch her breath, and when she straightened again, the clouds shifted enough to allow a shaft of moonlight to flow toward earth. The pale glow fell on the shake roof of a dilapidated wooden shed. Lank pointed, and Letta nodded. "I see it. C'mon."

They trudged forward, Letta scanning the dark grounds in both directions. Even though she wanted a place for them to stay, now that they'd found one, she worried about going in. Was this somebody's home? If someone was in there already, would they think she and the boys were intruders and fire a rifle at them?

She stopped, pulling on the boys' jackets to stop them, too. "Wait here," she whispered. The two clung to each other, their eyes wide in their white faces. Letta crept forward, cringing at the crunch beneath her feet. She rose up on tiptoe, rested her fingertips on the window ledge, and looked inside. Black. Pitch black. If somebody was in there, she wouldn't know.

"Letta?" Lesley's wavering whisper reached her ears.

She shot a scowl in his direction and hissed, "Shh!" Then she tipped her ear toward the window, listening. Not a sound came from inside. Just to be sure, she banged her fist on the side of the shed, then ducked down in case somebody fired out the window. Her heart pounded so hard her ears rang, but no guns fired, and nobody yelled. The place was empty.

Collapsing against the rough wall, she waved to the boys. "C'mon over."

They scuttled to her, arms outstretched. She caught their hands, and together they inched their way around the side of the building until they located a door. Someone had nailed two boards in a big X across it, but she and Lank gave the boards a few yanks. The rotted wood gave way, throwing Lank on his bottom. Lesley covered his mouth and giggled, and Lank came up grinning.

Letta rolled her eyes, but she couldn't help laughing at the two of them. Laughing felt good after the tension of the last few minutes. "Get in there," she said, shaking her head in amusement. They stepped over the threshold, and Letta shut the door behind them. Inside was black as pitch and smelled like dust and mold and neglect, but they'd found a shelter. God had heard her prayers.

Moving cautiously—even with her eyes wide open, she couldn't see a thing— Letta pressed her hands to the boys' back and shuffled them to the far side of the small room. Then she tugged their jackets, drawing them to the floor with her. She leaned against the wall and curled her arms around her brothers. They rested their heads on her shoulders, releasing twin sighs.

"Go ahead an' sleep," she prompted, giving their shaggy heads a few pats with her cold fingers. "I'll stay awake in case somebody comes around."

"'Night, Letta," Lesley murmured. Lank snuggled in. Within minutes their deep breathing let her know they'd faded off.

With effort she held her eyes open and kept her gaze aimed at the door. When morning came, she might find out she'd put her brothers to bed on a pile of mouse droppings, but for now they felt safe. That was all that mattered.

Chapter 32

Caroline

"Ungrateful little brats..."

Caroline gritted her teeth. If Gertrude O'Malley referred to Letta, Lank, and Lesley as brats one more time, she might lose her temper. The woman didn't possess even a thimbleful of charity. Where was her concern for the children?

"Can't believe I spent my time an' money comin' here." Mrs. O'Malley paced the raised walkway outside the train station, her thin face set in a fierce scowl. "What am I s'posed to tell my man when I get back? He ain't gonna be too happy about us wastin' money on train tickets." She clomped her way past Caroline again, waving her arms. "An' missin' my train yet! If we hadn't gone searchin' my brother's hovel for them brats, I could be on my way by now. As it is, I'll be gettin' there so late my man'll be thinkin' I ain't comin' home at all. Probably leave me stranded in town for the night."

Caroline forced a reasonable tone. "Does Baldwin City have a hotel? Perhaps you can stay there for the night and contact your husband in the morning."

The woman whirled on her, glaring. "You think I got money for a hotel room, too, young lady? You might have dollars to spare, but we're humble folk. We just barely git by. An' now those little brats o' my brother've cost me plenty. Well, I—"

Caroline charged toward her, ready to deliver a tongue-lashing.

Noble rose from the bench, where he'd sat with Annamarie and silently observed Mrs. O'Malley's tromping back and forth, and stepped between the two women. He withdrew his coin purse and snapped it open. "What do you think this trip has cost you, Mrs. O'Malley?"

She stood with her mouth gaping, her

gaze glued on the little purse. Greed brightened her eyes. "Well, there's the six bits for my train fare—both comin' an' goin', mind you. Then the telegrams— them were ten cents apiece. 'Course if I gotta stay at a hotel when I get home, that'll be another four bits for sure."

Noble reached into his purse.

"An' tomorrow's breakfast. Doubt my man'll come get me 'til well after the sun's up, an' I'm gonna need to eat somethin' in the café."

Caroline stared in amazement. Had she ever met a more shameless person?

Noble drew out a shiny ten-dollar gold piece. "Will this recompense you for your trouble?"

Mrs. O'Malley's hand shot out like a striking snake. She pocketed the coin and then lifted her fuzzy chin and sniffed. "Reckon so." She began her pacing again without a word of thanks to Noble.

He moved back to the bench and helped Annamarie rise. He tucked his wife's hand into the bend of his elbow and turned to Caroline. "I suggest we allow

Mrs. O'Malley to wait for the ten o'clock train without us. If we stay here until the train arrives, you'll be late for work."

Caroline gaped at him. "I'm not going in to work tonight."

Noble raised one eyebrow. He caught her arm and guided her from the walkway. "Of course you are."

"Noble! How can I go to work when Letta, Lank, and Lesley are lost somewhere?"

"You can't do anything more than the police are already doing," he said, his calm demeanor failing to ease her worry, "so go to the factory. Do your job, Caroline."

She didn't miss the gentle emphasis on her reason for being in Sinclair. She knew Noble was right. Running willy-nilly through the night wouldn't solve the mystery of Harmon Bratcher's death. But that didn't mean it was easy for her to leave the search to others.

Tears filled her eyes, making the light from the street lamps waver. "I'm just so worried about them, Noble."

Annamarie reached past Noble to touch Caroline's arm. "We're worried, too, but we must put our faith in the police officers who are diligently searching. Even more than that, we must put our faith in God. He knows where they are right now, and He can keep them safe."

Chastened, Caroline hung her head. Hadn't she learned anything from her years living beneath the Dempseys' roof? They'd steadfastly modeled faith before her, guiding her to her own belief. "I'm sorry, Annamarie. Of course I can trust God to watch over Letta, Lank, and Lesley." She lifted her head, offering Noble an apology with her eyes. "I'll do my job. I won't let you down."

Noble kissed her forehead. "You aren't capable of letting me down. Now go on to the factory. Annamarie and I will stop by the police station on our way to the hotel. If there are updates on the children's whereabouts, I'll send a messenger to the factory. All right?"

Caroline thanked him and received hugs from both Noble and Annamarie, and then they parted ways. She hurried through the streets, guided by the glow of street lamps. As she walked, she prayed that wherever the children were, they were warm, safe, and happy. By the time she reached the factory, her time speaking with her heavenly Father had eased the deep worry and replaced it with a glimmer of peace.

She reached the crating area and looked across the floor at the boxes. Instantly an image of Ollie standing and waiting for her the night before filled her memory. Ollie... He'd want to know the children were missing. Strapping her tool belt into place as she went, she hurried toward the janitor's closet, certain she'd find him gathering whatever items he needed to begin his nighttime duties. As she'd expected, he was inside the closet, filling a basket with cleaning supplies.

For a moment she stood in the doorway, simply observing him. The bruises on his face had faded to a greenish-yellow mottled patch—an unattractive hue. Yet he was still infinitely handsome, and her heart fluttered at the sight of him. If only they'd met under other circumstances. If only she were just a woman instead of an investigator with a personal interest in ending child labor and he were just a man instead of the son of a factory owner who hired children to labor at his machines. There could be no future for them, and she had to put the whimsical imaginings from her mind.

All her inner confusion emerged in a simple, single-word utterance. "Ollie?"

He turned toward her. Apprehension tinged his features. "Carrie." His simple response held a tangle of confused emotions as well.

Caroline swallowed. "May I speak with you for a moment?"

He hesitated briefly, then gave a brusque nod. "Of course." He stepped to the doorway and stood, feet widespread, as if bracing himself. "What is it?"

"The Holcomb children..." She gulped, tears threatening. Hadn't she placed them in God's keeping? She must dispel this worry. She sniffed, squared her shoulders, and stated flatly, "They've run away."

Ollie sagged against the doorframe, his stiff bearing dissolving in an instant. "Not again."

She nodded.

"I guess that's why you weren't at Kesia's for supper tonight, hmm? I looked for you."

He had? She pushed aside the bubble of joy that rose with his words. "Yes. First we checked their house. Since that's where they'd gone last time, we were hopeful. But we saw no sign they'd been there. So after searching on our own, we went to the police station and alerted the authorities."

"We." Ollie's expression changed. Hardened. "Meaning you and Dempsey?"

"Noble, Annamarie, Mrs. O'Malley, and me."

Ollie frowned. "Who are Annamarie and Mrs. O'Malley?"

"Noble's wife and the children's aunt." Caroline blew out a frustrated breath. "You should have heard their aunt, Ollie. She—"

Ollie stood upright. "Wait. Noble's wife?"

"Yes, Annamarie is one of the finest people I've ever known. She's been like a mother to me."

Ollie gawked at her for several seconds with his mouth hanging open, reminding her of a fish tossed onto a bank. Then he threw back his head and laughed uproariously. He caught her shoulders. "Noble's wife?" He laughed again, bouncing her with his merriment. "And she's like a mother to you, which would mean Noble..." He gasped, laughter stealing his ability to speak. "Noble is like a father?"

Caroline extracted herself from his grip. Had he lost touch with reality? She found nothing amusing in their conversation. "Of course he is. They took me in when I was eleven years old. They raised me. I couldn't love them more if they were my real parents." She loved them much more than the ones who'd birthed her.

Ollie brought himself under control, and he reached for her again. "Forgive me,

Carrie. It's just that I thought—" He placed his hand over his face, his shoulders shaking in a silent chuckle. When he removed his hand, all humor had fled. "Never mind what I thought. I'm so glad you have them. They obviously mean a great deal to you."

"Yes, they do." She observed him for a few seconds to be certain he wouldn't break into another fit of unbridled, unwarranted mirth. "They came to Sinclair specifically to help me locate a suitable temporary placement for Letta, Lank, and Lesley while their father was so ill. Then they chose to stay and help find a permanent home for them. I don't know what I would have done today if they hadn't been here. When I went to school and discovered the children were gone, I—" A sob cut off her words.

Compassion flooded his face. His hands curled around her shoulders, and she found herself drawn into a snug, comforting embrace. Noble had held her just this way on many occasions, but the feelings that exploded through her were far different from any she'd known before. Within the circle of Ollie's strong arms, her cheek pressed to his firm chest while his heart thrummed beneath her ear, she experienced a sense of being cherished. As if she belonged totally and completely to someone.

She coiled her arms around his torso and clung, eyes closed, reveling. She allowed herself the glorious escape for the span of a dozen heartbeats. And then reality crashed around her. What was she doing hugging Ollie Dinsmore? What must he think of the brazen way she'd melted against him?

Jolting free of his arms, she skittered backward several steps.

He looked at her in confusion. "Have I done something wrong?"

No, he'd done nothing wrong. He'd merely offered comfort—something she'd desperately needed. But in her heart she'd taken the embrace to levels where it shouldn't have been. She slapped at her skirt, feigning great interest in removing a few specks of sawdust that had transferred from his trousers. "No. No, of course not." She spoke briskly. Even tartly. Holding her head high, she went on. "Now that you know about Letta, Lank, and Lesley, I..." She swallowed. Must he look at her that way— as if she'd somehow pierced him? "I have work to do."

She turned to flee, but his hand caught her arm, sealing her in place. She looked away, her pulse pounding with such ferocity she feared he would feel it beneath his grasp.

"Carrie." His voice rumbled near her ear, low and full of compassion. "I care about those children, too. I have connections. Father's money opens doors to which some don't have access. If I can help find them, you know I will. All you have to do is ask."

Slowly she shifted her face until she met his gaze. She read concern in his eyes. He cared. Yes, he cared. But his statement about his father's wealth had just solidified the vast differences between them. **Why, God, did You allow these**

feelings for Ollie to grow when there's no hope for us?

Still caught in his grasp, she bobbed her head in a shaky nod. "If you want to engage your...your contacts in searching for the children, I would be indebted to you."

A sweet smile tipped the corners of his lips. "Consider it done. Is there anything else I can do?"

Very gently she twisted her arm and stepped from his touch. "Yes. Yes, there is." She drew a deep breath. "You can pray that they're found quickly and returned safely."

Oliver

Dismay flooded Oliver, making his knees feel weak. Two opposite desires warred within him—to refuse or to receive her challenge to pray. The strange longing that gripped him whenever someone mentioned God took hold with such pressure that he found it difficult to draw a breath.

Carrie stood expectantly before him, waiting for his reply.

"Carrie, I'll—" He started to say of course he'd pray. The words had stumbled from his tongue in the past even though he hadn't known how to honor them. But this time they wouldn't come forth. He took a deep breath and opened his mouth, determined to speak. To his surprise, instead of a confirmation, a question spilled out. "Are you sure prayer does any good?"

She gawked at him. "Of course it does. Prayer does much good."

He couldn't deny the conviction in her voice and in her expression, but he still held doubts. "I prayed for Mr. Holcomb. I prayed for him to recover. So did you and Kesia and Letta. But he died. If prayer does any good, why didn't the man live?"

"Oh, Ollie..." The sorrow in her tone cut Oliver as deeply as if she'd picked up a knife and plunged it into his stomach. "Mr. Holcomb was very, very ill. The Bible says, 'To every thing there is a season...

A time to be born, and a time to die.' Perhaps it was Mr. Holcomb's time."

An unsatisfactory answer. "Then why pray at all? If the outcome is already decided, what difference does it make if we pray?"

Tears winked in her eyes. Regret smote him. He was distressing her. She was already worried about the children, and he'd made things worse with his questions. Lifting one hand, he shook his head. "Never mind. It isn't important. I'll be sure to have Father contact our friends in law enforcement to—"

She reached toward him, capturing his hand. She held it between both of hers, looking up at him with such deep affection that whatever he'd intended to say fled. "Ollie, it is important. Prayer is very important, because it's part of developing a personal relationship with God. Do you know God?"

Of course he knew of God. Who didn't? He started to say so, but something in her expression held his tongue. He sensed her question went much deeper than simple head knowledge. The longing attacked again, stronger than ever. Unable to speak, he shook his head.

A slow smile grew on her face. She squeezed his hands, her eyes slipping closed, and she murmured, "Yes, now I know. Now I know." He sensed she wasn't speaking to him, so he remained silent.

Giving his hands one more squeeze, she released him and stepped back.

She wriggled in place, almost giddy. "Ollie, when our shift ends, I'm to meet Noble and Annamarie at Kesia's for breakfast. Will you join us?"

He tipped his head to the side, examining her eager face. "Does your invitation have anything to do with prayer...and God?"

She nodded, her eyes shining with unshed tears. "Then I'll be there."

Chapter 33

Letta

Icy shivers crawled up and down Letta's spine, awakening her. Her eyes slid open. A dim band of sunlight flowed at an angle through a wide-open door across from her spot on the floor. She blinked several times, confusion striking as hard as a stout wind. This wasn't the hotel room she'd been sharing with her brothers. She glanced left and right. Panic sent her pulse galloping. Where were Lank and Lesley?

She bolted upright and staggered toward the open door, cobwebs and grit and whatever else cluttered the floor falling from her clothing as she went. She scanned the area in all directions. Not a sign of the boys. Where could they have gone? Her body quivered in eagerness to pursue them, but uncertainty about which direction to search left her rooted in place. Fear turned her mouth to cotton.

Cupping her hands beside her mouth, she hollered, "Lank! Lesley! You'd better come here right now!"

In reply she heard giggles, then Lesley's cheerful crow. "He got 'im, Letta! He got 'im!"

The call came from somewhere ahead. Letta inched forward and finally noticed a trampled path in the grass leading over a nearby rise. She took off at a clumsy trot and met the boys coming from the opposite direction. Fear gave way to anger in one rush. She planted her fists on her hips. "What're you doin' out here? You want somebody to see you?"

Lesley shrugged, his smile undimmed. "Nobody around to see us. We was careful. But look what Lank caught!"

Lank held up a stick with a plump catfish speared on its end.

Letta forgot about being angry. She

stepped past Lesley and stared in amazement at Lank. "How'd you do that?"

Lank grinned, shrugging. Lesley piped
up, "There's a creek just over yonder.
Lotsa fish in it. Lank hopped out on a rock
an' waited for one to swim by. He missed
the first couple of times, but he sure got
this one!"

Letta examined the stick, noting its
sharpened point. "Did you make this?"

Lank nodded. He reached into his
pocket and withdrew his penknife, one of
the few gifts Pa had bestowed on him.
Lank always carried it. She'd never seen
him do anything more than whittle with it,
though. She hadn't known he could be so
clever.

Her mind whirling, Letta put her hand
on Lank's shoulder. "Do you think you
could catch another fish?"

"Shuh-shuh-sure!" Lank pulled the fish
from the stick, plopped it in Letta's hands,
then trotted off with Lesley scampering
along beside him. Letta followed, holding
the dead fish by its limp tail at arm's
length. She watched Lank give a nimble

leap onto the flat surface of a rock a few feet from the creek's edge. He crouched and scanned the water, his face serious and his arm holding the stick like a spear. Then, quick as a cat, he jammed the stick into the rippling stream. He held it aloft, a grin lighting his face and a wriggling fish flopping on the end of the stick.

Lesley jumped up and down. "You done it! You done it!"

Letta wanted to jump in excitement, too, but instead she called, "Toss that one over here, Lank, an' then stab some more. Many as you can. All right?"

Lank bobbed his head, making his thick hair bounce.

Letta dropped the fish Lank had given her onto the creek bank by Lesley's feet. "Lesley, you stay here with Lank. I'm gonna go get the lunch bucket. We can use it for water." It was small, but it was better than no bucket at all. "I'll scrounge around that shack, see if there's anything in it we can use."

Lesley rocked in place, his bright face tipped upward. "We gonna stay here for a while?"

Letta scurried off and didn't answer. She needed to prowl the area a little more—make sure others weren't living close enough to notice them coming and going. But if things worked out the way she hoped, they might not have to go on to Wichita after all. Food and shelter— that's all they needed. And it looked like they just might have found it.

Caroline

All through the night shift, Caroline had wavered between walking to the café with Ollie and leaving ahead of him to catch a few words with Noble and Annamarie before breakfast. In the end she decided she needed the time with her dear friends more than she needed the time with Ollie. Being alone with the man made it difficult to think clearly. This morning she needed to have full control of her faculties, so when the shift buzzer blared, she tossed her tool belt into her cubby and took off at a trot for Kesia's, trusting that Ollie would soon follow.

Panting with exertion from her run through the morning chill, she dashed into the café, already crowded with early-morning diners. Kesia greeted her with a broad smile and held a pot and tin cup high. "C'mon in here, honey, an' set yourself at the counter there next to Noble an' Annamarie. I'll pour you a cup."

Caroline glanced down the length of the counter. Kesia had apparently saved three stools in a row for her and the Dempseys, but the next three stools were already occupied by other patrons. Ollie wouldn't have a place to sit with them. Removing her scarf, she crossed to Kesia and whispered, "Ollie's joining us. Do you think..."

Kesia's head bounced in one quick nod. Turning to the men seated at the counter, she bellowed, "All right, fellas, I need one more seat there at the end, so everybody shift one stool to your right."

"Aw, Kesia," the one closest to the Dempseys griped. "I'm in the middle o' eatin'."

Kesia shook her head in mock exasperation. "Did I tell you to leave your plate behind, Luther? Take it with you, you chowderhead. C'mon, now, everybody shift."

The men muttered, but they followed Kesia's directions, and within a few seconds they'd all gathered at the opposite end of the counter. Kesia beamed her approval. "Thank ya, fellas. God'll reward you for your kindness."

"Rather have a bowl o' your peach cobbler free o' charge, Miz Kesia," one of them joked, and she laughed. She clunked the cup on the counter in front of Caroline and sloshed aromatic brew to the brim.

"Thank you, Kesia," Caroline said, grateful for the coffee and for Kesia moving everyone to accommodate Ollie. "He and I need to have an important discussion, and I hope Noble and Annamarie will help." She smiled at the pair, who raised their eyebrows in silent queries. Caroline reached across the counter and captured Kesia's hand before the woman could scurry away. "I'd like your involvement, too."

Kesia nodded somberly. "You know I'll do whatever I can for you an' Ollie." She leaned in, her eyes glinting. "Are you wantin' some advice on romance? Been a few years, but I reckon I can recall enough to help you some."

"No!"

Annamarie chuckled, and Noble coughed into his hand. They both grinned at Caroline.

Her face became an inferno. She pulled her brows into a scowl. "This has nothing to do with romance."

Kesia's face fell. "Oh... Well, I just figured, seein' how the sparks fly every time you two—"

"Sparks do not fly between us, Kesia," Caroline said firmly.

Kesia raised one eyebrow and pursed her lips. She couldn't have voiced her disagreement more eloquently.

Eager for a distraction, Caroline snatched up her cup and took a gulp. The hot liquid scalded her tongue. Slapping the cup back on the counter, she stated, "Ollie and I have only one thing in common—the Holcomb children."

Kesia chuckled and swished her hand across the counter, sending a flurry of leftover crumbs to the floor. "I've seen romances start between folks with less in common than that." Then she turned serious again. "Any word on them youngsters yet? Spent so much time prayin' for them I almost didn't sleep last night."

Noble said, "Nothing as of early this morning. As soon as we've finished breakfast and Carrie goes to her apartment to sleep, Annamarie and I intend to park ourselves at the police station and remain there until we're given a complete report of all the areas searched thus far." He cupped his hand over Caroline's. "We won't quit until we locate them."

"Neither will I."

Ollie's voice, from right behind her shoulder, gave Caroline a jolt. She spun on the stool and found him so close her toes brushed his pant leg. The heat that had flooded her face earlier returned.

"You took off without me." Not an accusation, only curiosity.

"Yes. I...I wanted to tell..." With Kesia's chatter about romance, she hadn't had a chance to prepare her friends about the subject she wished to address. But why worry? Noble and Annamarie, and even Kesia, were so comfortable with their faith they'd have no difficulty sharing with Ollie. She hopped off her stool and flapped her hand at it. "Here. Sit. Between Noble and me. It'll make it easier for all of us to...talk."

Ollie, his hands twisting his little hat into a pretzel, didn't move. He looked pointedly at the stool she intended to claim. Understanding dawned. Releasing a nervous titter, she clambered onto the stool. Did he have to be such a gentleman? With each encounter he became harder to resist. But at least now she understood why God had allowed their paths to cross. He needed what she had—faith. Part of her regretted it couldn't be more, but she recognized the selfishness of the thought. Nothing—including any human relationship, no matter how close and loving—could carry more value than knowing God on a personal level.

Ollie slipped onto the stool and placed his hat over his knee. He glanced first at Noble and then Caroline, a boyish grin twitching at his cheek. He shrugged. "So...who's going to start?"

Letta

"You gonna be able to get a fire started, Letta?"

She glanced at Lesley, who hunkered on the opposite side of the rock circle she'd formed in a bare spot near the creek. While Lank had cleaned the fish— a repulsive chore—Lesley had gathered small twigs and dried leaves, as well as a pair of small rocks, which Letta now banged together in the hopes of igniting a spark. "Pa started our fire in the stove this way. So it oughta work."

Lank peered over Letta's shoulder. "Puh-Puh-Pa's rock was fuh-fuh-fuh—"

"Flint," Lesley said.

"Flint," Lank repeated. He tapped Letta's shoulder and held out his hands. She set the rocks in his hands and watched him turn them between his fingers, face all scrunched up in thought. Finally he nudged her aside, placed the rocks together just so, and snapped his hands as if tearing a piece of paper in half. A tiny spark flared.

Lesley whooped. "Do it again, Lank!"

Lank did it again, and again, and again, and finally on the fifth try one of the brittle leaves caught fire. Letta watched, amazed, as Lank gently blew and layered more leaves and eventually little twigs over the tiny flame until it multiplied into several dancing tongues. He grinned. "Guh-guh-got firewuhwuh-wuh-wood?"

Lesley scrambled for the sizable branch Letta had dragged over earlier, and he and Letta began snapping it into pieces. It took some doing to break apart the bigger sections, but one by one they fed

Lank the lengths of wood. Soon a good-sized fire blazed in the middle of the rock circle.

They each poked chunks of pink flesh with sticks and held the meat over the flames. As the fish cooked, the smell nearly turned Letta's stomach inside out with hunger. When the flesh was white and starting to fall from the sticks, they sat back on their bottoms and feasted on fresh-cooked fish—the best-tasting meal Letta could ever remember eating.

"This's good," Lesley said around a huge bite. "You're a good cook, Lank."

Lank hunched his shoulders, grinning as his face blazed red. Tears stung Letta's eyes. Lank looked so proud. And she was proud of him. So she told him so. He went into a deeper crouch, almost disappearing inside his jacket, but he peeked at her from the corner of his eye, and she read the gratitude shining there.

When they'd finished eating, Lank tossed handfuls of dirt over the fire until not even one ember remained. Then they headed toward the little shack, their tummies full. Lesley caught Letta's hand and swung it, humming as they walked.

Lank sidled up next to Letta, the handmade spears bobbing on his shoulder. "Wuh-wuh-we goin' to Wuh-Wuh-Wuh-Wichita now?"

Letta slowed to an amble. Despite the chill breeze pushing at her back, peacefulness settled over her. Even though she missed Miss Carrie, Mr. Noble, Mrs. Annamarie, and Miss Kesia, she liked it out here away from everyone, with only Lank and Lesley for company. She glanced at Lesley, who went on humming as if he hadn't a care in the world. Then she looked at Lank. His eyes seemed to beg her for...something.

All at once she understood. This morning she'd seen him do things she didn't even know he could do. Maybe he hadn't known he could do them, either. She'd never seen such pride in her brother's face. Usually he hung his head in shame, afraid to talk. For as long as she could remember, folks—including Pa—had called him names. Dummy. Imbecile.

Village idiot. Mushmouth. Mean, hurtful names. But out here he wasn't any of those things. He was Lank the fisherman. Lank the fire maker. Lank the able.

She stopped, drawing the boys to a halt with her. Lesley's tuneless hum ceased. Letta clung to Lesley's hand and looked Lank straight in the face. "Do you wanna go to Wichita?"

Lank shook his head, his lips pressed into a firm line.

Letta turned to Lesley. "How 'bout you? You wanna go or stay?"

Lesley jerked her hand as he danced in place. "Stay!"

Letta blew out a happy breath. "All right, then. But it'll take work." She sent a warning frown across to both grinning boys. "That shack's a wreck. We're gonna have to do a heap o' cleanin'—all of us workin' together."

"We can do it," Lesley claimed.

Lank bobbed his head with enthusiasm. "Wuh-wuh-we can."

She looked full in Lank's face. "I believe you could do it all by yourself, Lank. But you won't have to. 'Cause you got me an' Lesley, too." She slung her arm around Lank's shoulders and aimed the boys toward their new home.

Chapter 34

Oliver

Oliver leaned both arms on the counter and gave Noble Dempsey his full attention. At their first meeting he hadn't cared much for Noble, but over the past hour he'd developed a grudging respect for the man. Even-tempered, wise, patient. Maybe a little dogmatic but balanced with tact. He had many of the same characteristics Oliver admired in his father. But Noble also seemed to possess something more—a deep, peaceful assurance that stirred a longing in the center of Oliver's soul. "So you're telling me all prayers are answered but some are answered no?"

Noble nodded, his thick white beard bobbing against the V neck of his black-and-white-checked vest. "That's exactly right."

Oliver frowned. "But that doesn't make sense. According to what the chapel minister told me awhile back and what Carrie said earlier..." He sent a quick glance in her direction and found her gazing at him with unwavering focus. She looked so sweet he had to quickly turn away before he gave in to temptation and placed a kiss on the end of her freckle-dotted nose. "God wants us to talk to Him because it draws us closer to Him. But wouldn't a no answer drive us away?" He'd ceased any attempts to pray following Mr. Holcomb's death, feeling as though he'd been ignored.

"Why should a no drive us away?"

Oliver blinked twice, confused by the man's seeming ignorance. He gave a brief laugh. "Who wants to share their deepest wants and then hear no from someone who supposedly cares for them?"

Kesia plunked a plate of eggs, grits, and bacon in front of the lone remaining breakfast eater at the other end of the counter, then bustled over and gave the back of Oliver's hand a sharp smack. "Stop an' think about what you're askin'. Ain't been so long ago you were a youngster livin' under your pa's roof."

Oliver still resided under his father's roof. He frowned. "What does—" She pointed at him, silencing him. "Did your pa love you?"

"Sure he did. He still does. My father and I have always had a close relationship."

"Didn't he ever tell you no when you was growin' up?"

Oliver's lips twitched, seeing where she was going. "Certainly he told me no when he deemed my request frivolous or unwise." He fixed Kesia with a smile. "But my father isn't God. You can't compare the two."

Kesia nodded so hard her double chin tripled. "Oh yes I can, 'cause God is your Father. Only thing is, He loves you even more'n your earthly father could. An' He knows all about your life, even how the decisions you make today'll affect your tomorrow. That's why He has to say no sometimes. He knows that some o' the things we want just ain't gonna be good for us further down the road."

"You see, Ollie," Noble added, drawing Oliver's attention, "as humans we're very shortsighted. We can only see what's happening now. But God, with His omniscience, views our lives from beginning to end. He always wants the very best for His children, so when He denies one of our prayers, it isn't out of a sense of power or judgment or indifference. He knows tomorrow, and His answers— whether yes or no or wait until later—are in keeping with what is best for us."

Oliver still didn't understand. "Was it better for Mr. Holcomb and his children for him to die?"

Beside him, Carrie let out a long sigh. She'd been largely quiet during their discussion about prayer, allowing Noble and Kesia to do most of the talking. But now she drew in a breath and placed her hand over his wrist. Her gentle touch, combined with the fervent look in her eyes, held him captive.

"Ollie, I don't think any of us here can answer that question. If Mr. Holcomb had gone to a doctor when he began suffering the pain in his stomach, he might be alive today. But he ignored the pain, allowing it to progress to a place where doctors couldn't cure it. Even then, God could have answered our prayers to heal Mr. Holcomb despite the doctors' inabilities. Why He didn't is beyond my understanding. Letta, Lank, and Lesley have now lost their father in addition to their mother. Such a hard, painful, senseless loss for them to suffer. I can't know how this will create anything good for them, although I do trust that in time God will reveal the answer to our questions. But I can tell you this..."

Tears glistened in her eyes. Oliver held his breath, eager to hear whatever she had to say, eager to find some element of truth to which he could cling. He wanted to believe so badly a sweet flavor of longing flooded his mouth.

"The worst thing to befall me as a child

became my deliverance. My parents handed me over to a wealthy family when I was eight years old so I could be trained as a house servant. The Remingtons paid handsomely for me, and I was told I had to remain with them until my eighteenth year to earn back what they'd given my parents."

Oliver's mouth fell open. In this enlightened time she'd been given out as a bond servant? "You worked for them for ten years?"

A sad smile toyed on the corners of her lips. "No. My sentence was shortened significantly on a winter day when Noble visited their home as part of an investigation into ongoing abuse, reported by former servants in their household. He demanded to inspect the entire home, and although he met with resistance, they eventually allowed him to enter. He found me in my little room beneath the kitchen, burning with fever and nearly dead. He carried me out, took me to his home, and, along with Annamarie, nursed me back to health. I suffered a lengthy illness, but they didn't give up."

Her eyes slipped closed. "I was unconscious much of that time, but I remember hearing their voices lifted in prayer to God, begging Him to spare my life." She opened her eyes. One tear slipped over her thick lashes and rolled down her cheek. "And He answered. Their prayers, Ollie, brought me back from the brink of death."

Oliver zipped his attention to Noble and Annamarie, who held hands and gazed at Carrie through tear-filled eyes. He turned back to her, eager to hear the rest of her story. "Why didn't you return to your parents when you were well again?"

She grimaced. "I did. Oh, I begged Noble and Annamarie not to take me, but they said they had to. The law wouldn't allow them to keep me. So they took me home, and my parents were furious that I wasn't with the Remingtons any longer. When Noble told them I couldn't go back to the Remingtons, my father claimed they'd just find someone else willing to pay for my services. I was eleven by then.

He knew I could fetch a good price." She looked past Oliver to the Dempseys, and her face took on a glow of admiration. "So Noble offered to purchase me. My father accepted without a moment's thought." She looked at Oliver again. "But Noble and Annamarie didn't treat me as a servant. I was their daughter—loved, educated, disciplined."

Her face pinched, as if she was recalling something unpleasant. "During my years with the Remingtons, I begged God to let me go home. And God left me in that awful house with people who didn't care at all about me." Her lower lip trembled, and Oliver turned his hand upside down, linking fingers with her. She gazed at their joined hands for a moment, and when she raised her face again, she'd gained control of her emotions.

"I understand why now. Had I not been in their house at that time, Noble wouldn't have found me. And I wouldn't have found my true home." She drew a deep breath as if sharing her story had exhausted her. She finished in such a quiet voice Oliver had to tip toward her to catch the words. "If I'd not spent those first years laboring for the Remingtons, I wouldn't understand the pain and hardship of spending one's childhood years working. I wouldn't care about making things better for today's children. So, Ollie, when God said no to my pleas to go home, He had a reason."

Oliver's heart twisted within his chest. Such an amazing woman... She'd suffered greatly, yet instead of carrying bitterness, she'd chosen to use her experiences to better the lives of others. He wanted to tell her how much he admired her, but she went on in a stronger voice.

"Knowing He had a reason for the no answers in my past allows me to trust Him for the no answers today." She squeezed his hand. "Do you understand what I'm saying?"

Oliver quietly absorbed all he'd heard. He couldn't deny Carrie's story had touched him deeply. To find the good in the midst of such heartache took courage, fortitude...and a touch from Someone much bigger and stronger than any human could be. He offered a slow nod. "I understand, Carrie. Thank you for telling me about your childhood." He turned to include the others. "All of you, thank you for taking the time to explain why you pray. You've given me much to consider."

Carrie's fingers tightened on his, drawing his attention again. Her face, lifted to him, held an expression of hopeful expectation. "And you...believe?" She appeared to hold her breath, her shining eyes fixed on his.

Oliver sought his own heart. The Dempseys, Kesia, and Carrie were all sincere and had given valid reasons for their belief in prayer's purpose. Something deep inside of him yearned to possess what they had. His life was full of the extras most people lacked, yet their peacefulness and inner joy in spite of sorrow made him feel as though he was the one left lacking. He wanted to grab hold with both hands and simply believe, but a niggle of doubt held him back.

He'd prayed. He'd prayed with his full heart, but he'd waited too late. He was already twenty-nine years old. Had he waited too long to seek a relationship with God? Kesia had called God his Father and him God's child, but he wasn't a child any longer. Could a man who'd gone his entire life unmindful of God's presence suddenly become a child again?

A lump of sorrow filled his throat, and he swallowed. "I...I'm not sure."

His regret multiplied when Carrie lowered her head, her shoulders slumping in defeat. But even to put a smile on her face, he couldn't confess to believing. Not yet. To hear how God worked through someone else's prayers wasn't enough. He needed to experience it for himself.

Carrie released his fingers, clasped her hands together, and held them beneath her quivering chin. Her gaze boring into his, she whispered, "I'll be praying, Ollie, for God to make Himself known to you. I won't stop until you've accepted Him for yourself."

"I'll be prayin' the same thing," Kesia stated.

Noble and Annamarie added their

intentions to lift Ollie to their Father. Hope ignited in Ollie's chest. God had answered their prayers in the past.

Which meant He could very well answer their prayers concerning him. But... A chill sent a tremor from his head to his toes. They'd said God had replied no when He knew a refusal would prove more beneficial for the asker later. What if God decided it wouldn't be beneficial to know Oliver Dinsmore on a more intimate level?

Chapter 35

Gordon

Gordon scanned the faces of travelers disembarking from the passenger car. Dinsmore would have purchased a ticket in one of the finer cars, where they sat upon tufted velvet cushions, sipped brandy, and watched the passing landscape through windows draped with tasseled curtains. Gordon had never traveled in one of those cars, but he would. Someday.

He adjusted the knot of his tie so it rested directly below his Adam's apple. Fulton Dinsmore always dressed impeccably. Gordon chose to do no less. For this meeting he'd donned his newest suit, pinstriped white on darkest charcoal gray, tailored to fit his frame. The suit's dignified color and style provided a perfect background for his crisp white shirt and bold scarlet tie.

Although the other men milling on the boardwalk sported hats—mostly homburgs, given the time of day—he preferred a bare head. No hat could compete with the splendor of his thick black waves. Even the matron at the orphanage—a dour, rigid woman who would have done well as an army general had she been born a man—had allowed him to avoid the biweekly shearing because she deemed his hair far too fine to crop into quarter-inch tufts. He spotted Mr. Dinsmore's stately black top hat, and he stepped forward, waving his hand to capture the man's attention. Dinsmore wove between the other travelers and approached Gordon, one gloved hand holding the carved ivory head of an ebony cane, the other extended in greeting. His gray coat was unbuttoned, revealing a pinstriped charcoal suit and ivory waistcoat. A gloating smile formed on

Gordon's face when he realized he'd dressed comparably to his soon-to-be-former boss. The attire seemed further confirmation he was destined to take control of the factory.

"Thank you for responding so promptly to my letter." Gordon employed his most respectful tone. "If the situation wasn't of the utmost importance, I wouldn't have troubled you."

Dinsmore clapped Gordon's shoulder —a solid whack that jerked his neck. "If it concerns you, Gordon, it will concern me as well. I was happy to oblige."

"Do you have luggage?"

"No. I intend to return home on the nine o'clock. I assumed we would be able to complete our business in one day."

Gordon nearly preened. Obviously Dinsmore had faith in Gordon's ability to handle the situation without the boss's assistance, or he would have come prepared for a lengthy stay. Smiling broadly, he gestured to the decade-old barouche carriage he'd rented from the local wainwright early that morning.

Although its brass trim had tarnished a bit over the years and the canopy's fringed trim appeared frayed in some places, the conveyance was the finest available and allowed him to hire a driver to transport Dinsmore and him to the factory. Sitting on the leather seat, protected by a canopy, with a liveried driver on the high front seat, he always experienced a rush of importance. A heady feeling.

The men settled onto the squeaky, cushioned bench. Gordon had already directed the driver to travel the main streets rather than following the shorter, more direct route to the factory. Busy streets were noisy streets, making it difficult to engage in conversation. Gordon wanted to be in his own chair, looking across his desk at Fulton Dinsmore, when they had their talk. His chair was his throne, and in his office Dinsmore was the lackey.

Besides, he liked the way people turned to watch the barouche, pulled by the pair of steel-gray horses with bouncing black manes. When Gordon made the chocolate factory his own, he'd purchase a carriage and matching steeds. Or perhaps he'd choose one of the newfangled horseless carriages appearing on the streets in the most prestigious cities. Such a vehicle would certainly garner attention. He almost laughed, imagining it.

"Here we are, sir."

The driver's droll voice pulled Gordon from his daydreams. He clambered out of the carriage, placed a fifty-cent piece in the driver's hand with a grand flourish, and then turned to Dinsmore. "Shall we go in?" Dinsmore trailed Gordon, one step behind, his hat held in the crook of his arm and the tip of his cane tapping the floor as he went. Gordon enjoyed his lead position. He allowed his gaze to rove across the various workers, inwardly beaming at their industriousness while maintaining a stern facade. He led Dinsmore to the stairs and, when they reached the landing, gestured for him to precede him up the hallway.

Dinsmore strode through the open doorway of Gordon's office and seated himself, resting his cane against the edge of his chair. He laid his hat, brim up, on the corner of Gordon's desk, then removed his kidskin gloves and slipped them into his pocket. Crossing his legs, he sent Gordon an attentive look. "Now, what seems to be the trouble?"

Gordon frowned at the man's take-charge attitude. To gain control again, he took his time closing the door, crossing to his observation window to latch the sound-muffling solid shutters, and then settling himself in his desk chair. Finally he angled his head and aimed what he hoped would be interpreted as a deeply concerned look at his boss.

"As you know, I've insisted on no fraternization between male and female workers." Gordon linked his hands and rested them on the edge of the desk. "Trifling behavior leads to a lack of concentration on one's task, which is detrimental to the overall operation of the factory. I have always presumed you agreed with my opinion concerning male-female associations. Was I incorrect?"

Dinsmore frowned. "No. I've supported your reasoning."

"I apologize for questioning you, but I needed confirmation of your agreement before I addressed the deeply troubling issue brewing within the factory walls." Gordon injected as much gloom as possible without sounding histrionic.

"What is this 'deeply troubling issue'?"

Gordon paused to pull in a long, slow breath, as if gathering his thoughts. "I've received word from the night foreman that Carrie Lang, the young woman you commended on your previous visit, and Ollie Moore, the man you recommended for employ, have begun meeting clandestinely on a regular basis."

Dinsmore's brows descended.

Gordon waited for the man to say something—to ask for clarification or details—but he merely sat in silence with a stern frown on his face. Satisfied he'd captured Dinsmore's full attention, Gordon cleared his throat and continued. "They've been seen entering the infirmary together, talking privately during breaks, and having a rather heated discussion in the middle of the crating station—a veritable series of tête-à-têtes. All during working hours."

"Was Bratcher the topic of these exchanges?"

A delighted cackle built in Gordon's chest. So Dinsmore recalled their previous conversation about Carrie Lang's apparent interest in Bratcher's demise. He sat forward a bit, eager to share all he knew.

"Yes. The two are in league, it appears, and I'm fearful they'll stir up other workers, given time. At the very least they're wasting work hours on topics unrelated to their assigned tasks." Gordon straightened his shoulders and looked imperiously down his nose at Dinsmore. "I believe it is in the factory's best interest to remove these two workers from the employ list immediately."

Dinsmore held one palm upward. "Slow down now, Gordon. I agree, from what you've said, one could surmise Lang and Moore are combining efforts to create some sort of skirmish. But we could also surmise they're simply discussing work and disagree about how certain things should be accomplished."

He'd hoped for instant approval. Dinsmore's failure to offer it left Gordon wordless.

Dinsmore went on. "After all, a man died. Isn't it realistic to presume workers will hold some concern? Perhaps Lang and Moore, being diligent workers, are merely discussing ways to prevent another casualty. These tête-à-têtes, as you called them, could be completely harmless."

Gordon snapped out, "If these discussions are so harmless, would they need to take place behind closed doors? They've been seen leaving the janitor closet after having sealed themselves inside for indeterminate lengths of time." He curled his lip in a sneer. "Call me suspicious, Mr. Dinsmore, but when a man and a woman shut themselves in an enclosed space, they're rarely engaging in something innocent."

The man pinched his chin and stared outward. Gordon almost chuckled.

He'd finally gotten through. While Dinsmore was off balance, Gordon went in for the kill.

"I want to give them both immediate notice for discharge." He yanked the prepared papers from his desk drawer and shoved them across the desk. "Will you sign?"

Dinsmore's gaze dropped to the papers. For long seconds he sat motionless, staring. Then with an abrupt motion he rose, grabbing his hat and cane in one smooth sweep of his hand. "I need some time to contemplate the best course of action. Releasing workers without just cause goes against my conscience. Before I sign the discharge papers, I need to have a word with my... Moore." He peered down at Gordon through narrowed eyes.

Gordon squirmed, feeling like a bug beneath a child's magnifying glass. "I'll return before the end of the first shift. You'll be waiting?"

Gordon nodded. What other choice did he have?

"Very well." Dinsmore frowned. "I'll gain an understanding of this situation, I can assure you." He turned and strode from the room.

Gordon flopped into his chair. Just who was this Ollie Moore? And why did Dinsmore hold him in such high regard? There was something fishy about the boss's interest in that cocky janitor. Could there be a triangle of troublemakers infiltrating Gordon's domain? He thumped his desk twice and then cradled his aching fist. Perhaps Moore and Lang weren't his only worries.

Oliver

Rubbing his eyes, Oliver tried to bring himself to full wakefulness. He'd been asleep maybe an hour—probably less— and had it not been Father at the door, he would have demanded to be left alone. But he couldn't send his own father away.

So he sat on the edge of his lumpy sofa in his nightshirt, bare feet planted wide on the faded carpet, and stifled a mighty yawn.

"I'm sorry to disturb your slumber." Father's voice held regret, but he sat ramrod straight on the single chair in the room rather than offering to leave so Oliver could sleep.

"It's all right. I don't imagine you'd visit unexpectedly if it weren't important." Now that Oliver was coming awake, worry nibbled at the back of his mind. "Is something wrong at home? Mother?"

"No, no, nothing like that." He rose and paced the circumference of the room, seeming to examine every detail from the cracked plaster walls to the stained lace curtains hanging limp from their rods. He stopped and released a short huff. "How do you live here?"

Oliver coughed a short laugh. The apartment was quite different from his third-floor suite in his family's yellow-brick home in Wichita. But how could he maintain his facade as a mere factory worker if he chose anything other than a simple abode? Although at first he'd found the dwelling dismal and unsatisfactory, he'd adjusted to it. Especially after seeing how the Holcomb children lived. "It isn't so bad."

Father shot him an odd look but didn't argue. He crossed back to the chair and sat stiffly on its edge. "I was summoned to town by Hightower. His concerns about Miss Lang have not diminished. Instead, they've intensified."

Oliver blew out a breath. "Father, haven't my reports offered you any assurance that Miss Lang isn't interested in filing a suit against us?" He'd deliberately painted Carrie in a favorable light. Why would Father believe Hightower over him?

"Your reports seemed to withhold certain details."

Oliver leaned into the lumpy sofa back. My, but he was tired. "What details?"

"Your trysts with her in the janitor's closet, for one."

Oliver leaped to his feet. "I've had no trysts with Carrie!"

Father raised one eyebrow. "You deny meeting alone with her?"

He couldn't deny meeting her alone. But he could deny the purpose. Their consultations were never of a personal nature. Heat exploded in his chest and expanded outward, setting his entire frame on fire as he faced a secret truth. When he'd been alone with Carrie in the private, quiet room, he'd desired to steal a kiss. The day he'd held her—to offer comfort—he'd relished the feel of her soft form resting lightly against him. She'd fit so neatly in his arms, as if she was meant to be there.

"Oliver?"

Oliver ran his hand over his disheveled hair. He sank back onto the sofa. "We did meet. Alone. But it wasn't what Hightower thinks. Carrie isn't that kind of girl." He met his father's steadfast gaze. "Carrie suspects—and I'm prone to agree, given some information I've uncovered— that Harmon Bratcher may have met with foul play. She's only interested in either proving or disproving her theory.

Nothing more."

"Is she a relative of Bratcher's?"

"No."

"Then why her interest?"

Oliver swallowed. He'd made a promise to Carrie. Although he'd never kept anything from his father, he'd honor it. "I can't tell you."

"Why not?"

"I gave my word."

Father paused, his brow furrowing. "But you're certain she isn't seeking to bring a suit against the factory?"

"Yes, sir."

Father leaned back in the chair, pinched his chin between his thumb and fingers, and peered for several long minutes at Oliver. He remained still beneath his father's intense perusal, although sitting there in his nightshirt with his hairy legs sticking out left him feeling much less than confident.

Finally Father gave a firm nod. "Very well, Oliver. If you believe this young woman's intentions are honorable, I will trust your instincts."

Oliver hadn't realized he'd been holding his breath until his lungs emptied in a whoosh. "Thank you, Father."

"But I do have another question."

Oliver tipped his head, waiting.

"What are your intentions concerning Carrie Lang?"

Chapter 36

Oliver

"In—" Oliver gulped. "Intentions?"

Father removed his jacket, tossed it over the arm of the chair, then propped his elbows on his knees. The sternness in his eyes faded, but his gently furrowed brow gave evidence of concern. Concern for his son. Oliver didn't want to displease this man.

"You seem quite determined to defend the woman. Even protect her. You're an honorable man, Oliver. I know this because I raised you to be an honorable man, and you've never once in all your growing-up years given me reason to hang my head in disgrace. But I'll be honest with you. Right now I'm questioning whether I should sign the papers Gordon laid out for your discharge and take you back to Wichita with me."

Oliver's mouth dropped open. "He wishes to dismiss me?"

"You and Miss Lang." Father shook his head as if puzzling over something. "Gordon's a driven man and also a dependable man. I've watched him grow up, taking on more and more responsibility, eventually proving himself capable of handling the operation of the factory. He's always done exactly as I've asked, and because I trust his judgment, I've never denied his requests. Maybe I shouldn't deny this one."

"But why? Carrie's an excellent worker." Even though she was there under false pretenses, she never shirked her duties. She performed as well as and perhaps even better than her coworkers. "And I complete my tasks as I've been instructed, always to the best of my ability." Although, admittedly, his best efforts were often lacking.

"But you both broke one of Gordon's

most stringent rules by consorting with each other." Father jabbed his finger at Oliver. "By your own admission you and Miss Lang have spent time together during work hours. He has grounds to discharge both of you."

"But not without your signature." Oliver stared at his father, hardly able to believe they were having this conversation.

Father fell into another long, thoughtful silence, during which Oliver wanted to crawl out of his skin. If he was released, he wouldn't be able to assist Carrie in her investigation, and he wouldn't be able to gather his own ideas for improvements once he took over. If he was let go, he'd have to slink home with his tail between his legs. And he wouldn't see Carrie again.

He couldn't stay silent another second. "Father, you aren't going to sign my discharge papers, are you?"

Slowly his father shifted his gaze until it met Oliver's. "Give me one good reason why I shouldn't."

"I can give you several!" But then Oliver couldn't form a coherent sentence. The thought of never seeing Carrie again rendered him unable to think, let alone speak.

Father nodded, his expression knowing. "You've fallen for the girl."

Oliver sat, silent, unmoving. He couldn't—he **wouldn't**—deny it. Carrie's selflessness, her compassion, and her simple beauty had spun a web around him. He was caught, and he had no desire to free himself. But Father would never approve a relationship with her. Father and Mother had plans for him—plans that didn't include a woman whose parents had sold her into servitude. As pointless as it was to have fallen in love with her, he still wouldn't deny his feelings. He owed Carrie at least that much.

"Yes. Yes, Father, I have grown to care deeply for Carrie Lang."

"That's reason enough to take you out of Sinclair and back to Wichita, where you belong."

Oliver gathered his courage. "And if I choose not to go?" His words were said with the same respect he'd always shown his father. But even so, Father's frown grew fierce.

"You would defy me?"

He'd never gone against his father's instructions. Not even as a rowdy youth. To consider doing so now left him trembling inside. He wished he'd donned his shirt and trousers before having this talk. A man shouldn't confront his father for the first time while dressed in a red-and-white-striped nightshirt. He sat up straight, hoping a formal bearing would detract from his very informal attire. "I don't want to defy you, Father. But I came to Sinclair to complete a task. To ready myself for leadership in the factory. If I leave now, before I've finished what I set out to do, how can I have any respect for myself?"

He stood and crossed the short distance between the sofa and the chair. The carpet felt scratchy against his soles, and he fought the desire to fidget. He looked into his father's mustached, lined face, and a feeling of love swept over him. If Father insisted, he'd return to Wichita.

He couldn't break his father's heart by defying him. But how he hoped his father loved him enough to trust him.

"I'll not do anything to bring disgrace on the Dinsmore name. I know who I am." And he knew what his station required. He swallowed the lump of regret that threatened to choke him and continued. "Allow me to complete my purpose here. And allow me to assist Carrie in determining the truth about Bratcher's death. The truth will only benefit us—all of us." His voice dropped to a raspy whisper. "Allow me to stay."

Caroline

Caroline's alarm clock jangled. She rolled over and slapped at it, then blinked, surprised. Had she actually slept? For hours she'd tossed and turned in her bed, fighting the desire to go search for Letta, Lank, and Lesley. Only Noble's firm, yet kind, instruction to leave the search to the authorities and take care of herself—**"What good will you be to the children if you exhaust yourself to the point of illness?"**—kept her from surrendering to temptation. Yet she'd been certain she'd never relax enough to fall asleep. To have slept soundly gave evidence of how badly she'd needed the rest.

She rolled out of bed, her stiff joints protesting, and visited the bathroom at the end of the hallway. In the midafternoon she never had to wait since the other boarding hotel residents were still at their jobs. Then she dressed and combed her hair into a simple twist. She didn't need to be at the factory for several hours, which would allow time for her to walk around the city in the hope of catching sight of one of the Holcomb children.

Father, please let them be found! The prayer, offered so many times over the past two days, formed without effort and winged from her heart to the heavens.

She clattered down all three sets of stairs to the ground level and stepped, breathless, onto the sidewalk. A light drizzle fell—barely a mist—shrouding the city in a cloak of gray. Such a gloomy color. She preferred sunshine yellow. Especially when applied to the flecks in Ollie's eyes. She gave a little start. She needed to think about the Holcomb children, not Ollie. Determinedly setting her feet in motion, she began moving toward the center of town.

Policemen regularly checked the Holcomb house, hoping to find that the children had returned home. But thus far they'd not witnessed anyone either coming or going. The children would be hungry, and Lank had successfully pilfered food in the past, so Caroline intended to visit each of the general stores selling food items and ask if a red-headed boy, or a pair of them, had been seen in the store.

The first two stores were crowded with Saturday shoppers, and the frazzled clerks couldn't recall a red-headed boy coming in but wouldn't swear there hadn't been one. Caroline moved on to the third mercantile, a smaller store with fewer people filling the aisles. The woman proprietor took several minutes to talk with Caroline, asking and answering questions, but it soon became clear that neither Lank nor Lesley had been in the store.

Frustrated, Caroline stepped back outside to discover the gentle mist had turned into a light rain. With a sigh she pulled her shawl over her head and moved to the edge of the boardwalk, preparing to cross to the opposite side of the street. A fancy carriage approached from the left, and she paused, impatiently waiting for its beautiful pair of steel-gray horses to pass by so she could continue her errand.

From within the carriage's covered section, a deep voice suddenly commanded, "Driver, stop!"

The driver pulled back on the reins, and the carriage came to a halt directly in Caroline's pathway. Shaking her head in vexation, she started to pass behind it, but the voice came again, freezing her in place.

"Miss Lang?"

She edged to the carriage and looked over the side of the protective box. Mr. Fulton Dinsmore was perched on the leather seat. A silk top hat covered his hair, and a gleaming black cane stretched from his gloved hands to the toes of his polished boots. He looked every bit the aristocrat, and immediately she felt dowdy in her simple frock and woven shawl draped over her head like a little old woman.

She flipped back the shawl, settling it around her shoulders, and formed a polite reply. "Good afternoon, Mr. Dinsmore. How nice to see you again." The first time she'd seen the man, something about him had seemed familiar, and now she understood why. His silver goatee and curled mustache had detracted from his eyes, but now she saw from whom Ollie had inherited his unique eye color. Gazing at Mr. Dinsmore's face, she received a glimpse of how Ollie might look in another thirty years. Handsome. Distinguished. Unapproachable. The realization set her back a few inches.

Mr. Dinsmore leaned forward and peeked from beneath the fringed canopy. "The rain is increasingly strong. You'll soon be soaked with no umbrella to block the moisture. Climb inside here. My driver will deliver you wherever you need to go."

Caroline only needed to cross the street and travel the length of a block to reach the next store. She started to say so, but then she realized what a rare opportunity she was being offered. Would she ever again have a few minutes of uninterrupted time with the man whose employment log held a greater percentage of young workers than any other factory in Kansas? With a smile of appreciation, she said, "Thank you, sir. That's very kind."

He held out his hand, she took hold, and he hoisted her aboard. She settled onto the seat, smoothing her damp skirts as best she could. He gave her an imperious glance and said, "To where should I direct the driver?"

To lengthen her time with the man, she said, "The Troubadour Hotel on Third

Street, please."

His eyebrows rose momentarily. He tapped the driver and repeated her directions. The driver flicked the reins, and the carriage rolled forward. Mr. Dinsmore shifted into the corner of the seat and pinned her with an interested look. "Are you staying at the Troubadour?"

Caroline stifled a laugh. He would be appalled if he saw her temporary dwelling. "No, sir. Some friends are staying there, and I plan to dine with them this evening." Thanks to Noble and Annamarie's teaching, she could communicate with grace. She sent up a silent prayer of gratitude for all they'd done for her as she waited for Mr. Dinsmore to reply.

"I see." He tweaked one tip of his mustache with his kidskin-covered fingers. "On my last visit you expressed concern for some children whose father was ill. Mr. Hightower informed me the children are no longer spending their nights in the infirmary. May I presume their father has recovered and therefore you've been relieved of the burden of their care?"

Caroline's heart twisted. She hardly viewed caring for the Holcomb children a burden. "I'm sad to report their father passed away." She started to tell him the children were missing, but something held her tongue.

"Unfortunate..." Mr. Dinsmore pursed his lips briefly—a slight show of sympathy. "Have they been placed in an orphanage?"

"Not yet."

"Well, if they need a means of providing for themselves, I'm sure Hightower can create openings for them at the factory. I'll alert him to—"

Caroline's chest grew tight. "That won't be necessary, sir." She added, belatedly, "But thank you."

He gazed at her for several seconds. Then he cleared his throat. "How are you getting along at the factory? If I understand correctly, you'd not engaged in factory work prior to your arrival in Sinclair. Are you finding the work satisfactory?"

She wondered if he truly cared or if he was merely making small talk. But she decided to answer honestly. "I'm able to complete my tasks, as assigned, and the compensation is adequate."

His lips twitched, and his eyes began to twinkle. She'd seen Ollie's eyes spark in just that way, and she fought a smile, anticipating a teasing comment.

"Quite diplomatic, my dear, but I sense an undercurrent of disquietude."

The man was astute.

"What about your employment fails to meet your expectation?"

He'd opened the door. She would walk through it. Pulling in a breath of fortification, she met his intense gaze and spoke honestly. "I'm disquieted by the number of children I see working the factory floor. Children, in my opinion, should spend their daytime hours beneath a schoolhouse roof and their nighttime hours sleeping."

Mr. Dinsmore had the audacity to chuckle. "You are opinionated."

Caroline didn't smile. "I have reasons for my opinion, sir."

"And I have reasons for hiring children."

Although she didn't mean to, she snorted—a short, derisive grunt. "Yes.

It's to your financial advantage." Aware she was treading on dangerous ground—the man could terminate her employment and thereby end her investigation with one word—she couldn't seem to hold back once she'd started. The captive audience proved too convenient. "With children drawing a quarter of the wages of a man, anyone can see how crowding your employment log with youngsters results in greater profits for the factory. But at what cost, Mr. Dinsmore? I'll tell you—the cost of these young people's childhoods. And a childhood is not something that can ever be regained."

He gazed at her, his expression as bland as a sated cat holding the tail of a mouse for the sake of frightening it. "You're mistaken, Miss Lang. In my factory every worker is treated equally in regard to compensation. Men, women, children... Their wage is dependent upon the job performed and their years of service."

Caroline stared in disbelief. Such bald

lies he'd delivered with a straight face and glib tongue. Did he think she possessed no sense? "My co-craters, all men, find double the pay of my earnings at the end of the week. The children receive only half of what I draw." She pursed her lips disdainfully. "Unless you count the bag of imperfect candies sent with them each Saturday as a bonus."

His eyebrows descended. His fingers tightened on the head of the cane, seeming to strangle the poor horse. "You speak untruths, Miss Lang." His voice turned hard, his gentility slipping. "Dinsmore's has welcomed workers of all ages and genders, treating them equally in every fashion, including compensation. Many of my adult employees began as children, learned to perform a task with precision, and advanced to more skilled—and therefore higher-paying—positions over time. My factory has been a school in and of itself, meeting the needs of countless young people and their families over the years." His green-gold eyes narrowed into slits. "I advise you to silence your offensive surmising lest you meet with unpleasant consequences."

A chill attacked Caroline, completely unrelated to the brisk breeze flowing through the carriage. Had he just threatened her?

The carriage stopped, and the driver glanced over his shoulder. "We've reached the Troubadour, sir."

Mr. Dinsmore turned a regal smile on the man. "Thank you." Then he faced Caroline, and the steely glare returned. "Employment at Dinsmore's is a privilege, young woman. Do not abuse it. Now"— he sat back in the seat and smiled as though there'd never been a cross word between them—"enjoy your dinner with your friends, Miss Lang. It was a delight to have this brief time to become acquainted."

Caroline clutched her shawl closed with one fist and pulled herself to the edge of the seat with the other. "Yes. It has been... enlightening. Good day, sir, and thank you again for the ride."

The driver assisted Caroline from the

carriage. She remained at the edge of the street until the conveyance rolled away, then she darted for the hotel's front doors as quickly as the rain-slick cobblestones allowed. She could hardly wait to tell Noble what she'd learned.

Chapter 37

Letta

Two plump raindrops landed on Letta's head, and she looked skyward with a scowl. The clouds had started rolling in midday, bringing a chill air with them. But she'd hoped no rain would come.

She pocketed Lank's knife and began tossing the fillets of catfish she'd stripped from their bones into the lunch bucket. She'd learned to clean fish—something she wouldn't have thought possible a few days ago—but she hoped she wouldn't have to learn to eat the fish raw. She shuddered at the idea. But they had no stove in their shack, and not even Lank, who'd proved to be amazingly skillful, could keep a fire going in the rain.

Hopefully, the rain wouldn't last long. They'd collected a good supply of sticks and would have dry fuel ready when they could move outside to build a fire.

Lank and Lesley came running from the rise beyond the shack, dragging something that looked like a large blanket. She snatched up the bucket and trotted to meet them. "What'cha got there?"

Lesley beamed, showing off the gap where he'd lost a tooth yesterday. "Found an old busted-up wagon down yonder in a gully. We was hopin' there'd be somethin' good in it, but there was only mouse nests. But this cover was still there. It's chewed up some, but we peeled it off an' brung it home anyway. Lank says we can use it for...somethin'."

The wet plops from overhead came faster. Letta ducked inside the shack, gesturing for her brothers to follow. "Well, leave it out there for now, an' get in here before you get soaked." Maybe the rain would wash away some of the mouse droppings clinging to the rough fabric. After all the cleaning she'd done—as best she could with a broom of stiff reeds gathered from the creek— she didn't want to bring that filthy thing inside.

She closed the door behind them and crossed to the corner they'd deemed the kitchen even though it didn't have a stove, a table, or even shelves. She put the bucket of fish next to the cluster of rusty tin cans holding wild onions, watercress, and a few walnut meats. When Lank had found the battered cans in the weeds behind the shack, Lesley had wanted to line them up and throw rocks at them. But Letta had taken them to the creek, rubbed them as clean as possible with sand, and used them as her cupboard. The cans might not be much, but they were better than nothing, and it made her feel warm inside to know she was taking care of her brothers.

Turning from the corner, she spotted the boys hunkered in the middle of the floor tracing a tick-tack-toe game in the dirt with a stick. They looked so happy, relaxed. A smile threatened, but she couldn't smile at them. They'd disobeyed her by wandering so far from the shack. Even though they'd found something useful, she had to make it clear to them to stay close. If somebody spotted them, they'd have to leave.

Balling her hands into fists, Letta gathered her indignation and stomped over and planted her foot in the middle of their game.

They both looked up, eyes wide. Lank exclaimed, "Huh-hey!"

Letta put her fists on her hips and glowered at the pair. "Listen, you two. I told you to stay close, an' you didn't do it."

They lowered their heads like a pair of whipped pups. Pa had made them cower that way. Letta's heart turned over. She crouched down beside them and gentled her voice. "I'm glad you're tryin' to find things we can use here. I know you're just tryin' to help. But it ain't safe to go traipsin' off that way. We're far from town. There's critters out here—wild ones that might see the two o' you as a mighty good dinner. Then again, you might come across some folks who don't take kindly to us makin' use o' this shack. They could run us off, right back to Sinclair, where the sheriff'll put us on a train an' send us to Aunt Gertrude."

To her relief, they listened instead of arguing. She cupped their shoulders with her hands. "From now on you gotta do what I say an' not go by yourselves any farther'n the creek behind us or the scrub brush at the top o' the rise. An' never, never go toward the railroad tracks." Somebody would spot them for sure if they went in that direction. She tightened her grip on their skinny shoulders. "Do you promise?"

The two exchanged a look. A guilty look.

Letta gave them a little shake. "What'samatter?"

Lank chewed his lower lip, ducking his head. Lesley squirmed beneath her hand. He bobbed his head at Lank. "Tell her."

Lank slipped his hand into his jacket pocket and pulled out a fistful of wrinkled, marble-sized, pinkish-yellow lumps. He held them out to Letta, a sheepish look on his freckled face. "Wuh-we was guh-guh-gonna get a bunch muh-more o' these an' suh-suh-s'prise you."

Letta plucked one of the lumps from Lank's hand. It felt squishy between her fingers. She pinched it hard and discovered a large seed—a pit—taking up most of the space underneath the wrinkly skin. Juice dribbled across her hand, and she licked it. Sour! She made a face and wiped her hand on her skirt. Plopping the smashed lump back with the others in Lank's dirty palm, she coughed a short laugh. "Glad you was thinkin' of me, but that's not the nicest surprise I ever had."

"That's only part o' the surprise." Lesley bounded upright, nearly dancing in excitement. "Them little things don't taste all that sweet, but we know how to sweeten 'em up."

Letta looked at Lank. He grinned at her. She bumped him with her elbow, teasing a little. "You got a bag o' sugar hid somewhere, Lank? It's gonna take a whole lot to make them things taste good."

Lank giggled.

Lesley shook his head. His hair fell over his forehead, and he pushed it aside with a thrust of his hand. "No, but he found honey!"

They'd been messing around with a beehive? Letta jumped up, her heart firing into her throat. She got angry all over again. "You better not've been pokin' at some bees' hive! Those things'll sting you somethin' fierce!"

Lesley waved both hands at her, and Lank rose, his wide eyes expressing innocence. Lesley said, "We just found it. Didn't bother it. Not even a bit. Lank wouldn't let me."

Letta could imagine Lank holding Lesley back.

Lesley chattered on, his voice shrill. "But Lank knows how to get the honey without us gettin' stung. That's why we brought that cover with us. Lank wants to throw it over the hive, then light a fire inside it. Smoke the bees out. Then we can get at the honey."

Letta gazed at Lank in amazement. A slow smile pulled on her lips. She let it grow. "Lank, you know how people wanna call you dummy an' such?"

Lank hung his head. Plump tears quivered on his lower lashes.

Letta grabbed his chin and made him look at her. "You ain't a dummy, Lank. Not even close. An' don't you ever let nobody call you that again. You're the smartest person I know."

The tears spilled down Lank's cheeks, but he smiled so big his whole face lit. "Thuh-thuh-thank you, Letta."

"An' ya know what?"

The boys chorused, "What?"

Letta grinned. Her mouth watered, thinking of mixing the fruit, walnuts, and honey together. "Soon as this rain stops, we'll go honey gatherin'."

Caroline

"At the least," Caroline said, cradling a steaming cup between her palms in lieu of sipping the tea Annamarie had poured for her, "there is a large gap in communication between Gordon Hightower and Fulton Dinsmore. At the most, someone is a liar. But at this point I can't figure out who deserves the title—Hightower or Dinsmore."

It pained her to speak ill of Ollie's father, yet the man had chilled her with his veiled threat. Had Dinsmore played a role in Harmon Bratcher's accident? And, even more difficult to consider, did Ollie know of his father's participation, and had he misled her regarding his reason for being at the factory? What if, instead of gathering information to build his leadership abilities, he was actually there to make sure his father's deeds remained hidden?

She needed to share all these concerns with Noble, yet to do so meant breaking her promise to Ollie to keep his identity a secret. So she hugged the warm cup and kept her deepest worries inside.

Noble stroked his chin whiskers, apparently deep in thought. In the ensuing quiet, the patter of raindrops on the windowpane became a lullaby, soothing some of the disenchanting thoughts rolling through Caroline's brain.

"There's really only one way I know to uncover the truth, and that's to look at the financial records." Noble spoke softly, as if in deference to the sweet melody of the rainfall. "Hightower, as the book-keeper, will have detailed reports of incoming and outgoing funds. Although the compensation issue is unrelated to Harmon's death, as far as we can tell, discovering who is being untruthful about the payment workers receive at the factory might lead us to another clue. So we need to find a way to look at the records."

His serious tone reactivated the uneasy feelings Caroline had briefly set aside. Her hands began to tremble. She set the teacup on the table next to her chair before she spilled the liquid. "I might have an opportunity to do that tomorrow."

Noble raised a brow. "Oh?"

Her mouth felt dry. How odd to plan to sneak into the factory with a man who could be working against her rather than with her. She quickly informed Noble of

Ollie's invitation to meet her at the factory's back doors after all the night-shift employees had vacated the building so they could examine the elevator's workings without fear of someone seeing them and reporting them to Hightower.

Noble frowned. "How is he able to enter the factory when it's closed?"

Caroline experienced a twinge of conscience as she answered, knowing it was only a partial truth, given Ollie's identity. "He's a janitor."

"Ah, yes, of course." Noble sat forward. "Caroline, you've been an agent for six years now—sufficient time to hone your skills and develop your instincts. I trust you to know your job, so please don't misunderstand what I'm about to say." He fit his hands together, gripping so tightly his knuckles turned white, offering mute evidence of his inner turmoil. "This case is different. Your investigations have always involved possible breaches of safety issues, never the possibility of a murder. If someone in that factory deliberately ended Harmon Bratcher's life to protect himself and his illicit dealings, he won't be averse to taking a second life, especially when he believes it's only a nosy factory worker."

Caroline nodded slowly while a thousand spiders raced up and down her spine, sending chills of trepidation through her extremities.

"If you'd rather I continue in your stead, no one in the commission, including me, would look askance at you or lose respect for you. You can walk away right now, Caroline. It's your choice."

Noble's offer proved how much he cared about her well-being. But she couldn't accept. She wanted to complete the investigation, and, even more, she wanted to discover if she'd erred in trusting Ollie. Her own self-worth depended upon her findings. With a smile she reached across to Noble and placed her hand over his fists. "I love you for being willing to replace me. I understand your concerns, and I assure you I'll be very cautious in proceeding. But I started this investigation, and I want to finish it.

With your blessing, of course."

Noble turned one hand and gripped hers. Hard. Assuringly. Confidently. "You have my blessing. And more than that, my dear, you have my prayers."

Caroline nodded gravely. If some of her worries proved valid, she might very well need those prayers before tomorrow came to a close.

Chapter 38

Oliver

Oliver checked his timepiece, frowned, then made another pacing journey back and forth behind the row of garbage cans near the factory's service doors. Hadn't he and Carrie decided on seven o'clock? It was already ten minutes past seven, and no sign of her.

He'd watched her clock out, just as they'd planned, and leave with the other workers a little more than an hour ago. When she'd scurried up the sidewalk in the direction of her boarding hotel, he'd expected her to take a detour, work her way around the block, and return. But instead she'd completely disappeared in the early-morning mists. Had she changed her mind about meeting him?

Yesterday's rain had created more puddles in the graveled patch where wagons pulled in to receive the crates of chocolate. Oliver eased around them, mindful of the difficulty of washing muddy spatters from the bottom few inches of his pant legs. Odd how being forced to perform the rudimentary chores himself had awakened a sense of diligence. When he returned home, he would express frequent appreciation to those who saw to his laundry.

He reached the loading-dock doors and perched on the damp edge of the hip-high dock, sending another glance up the alley. Still no Carrie. He'd give her twenty more minutes, and then he'd go in alone. Even if she'd lost interest in investigating whether or not Bratcher could have accidentally fallen to his death, he wanted to know. He wanted to be able to tell Father. Because if his suspicions were correct, and Gordon Hightower had orchestrated the man's death, his first act as the new owner of Dinsmore's

World-Famous Chocolates Factory would
be to search for a new manager.

Or maybe he'd just fill the position
himself.

He paused, considering the feasibility
of such a plan. Father had always remained
president of the company while allowing
others to oversee the actual operation.
Oliver wouldn't criticize Father for the
choice. His philanthropic endeavors,
made possible by his freedom from the
duties of management, had benefited
many over the years. But Oliver toyed
with the idea of being a more hands-on
owner, so to speak. He'd enjoyed mingling
with the workers, learning their names,
and becoming acquainted with their
concerns, both work related and personal.

His ideas went against the societal
separation that he'd been trained to
follow, yet the thought of working
alongside his employees rather than
keeping a distance gained in appeal the
longer he remained among their ranks.
Perhaps he could continue Father's
tradition of philanthropy but focus it more

on his own employees. The mantle of leadership began to feel more comfortable on his shoulders as he considered the option.

The patter of footsteps on cobblestones captured his attention. He darted to the edge of the building and hid himself in the shadows, squinting through the rays of dawn. A woman approached, her skirts held above the ankles of her boots and her head down, revealing an explosion of auburn corkscrew curls. A smile burst across his face. She'd come.

He remained rooted in his hiding place and greeted her in a muffled whisper. "Carrie, over here."

Her steps slowed, and she searched the area until her heart-shaped face aimed in his direction. He waved his hand, alerting her to his location, and after a moment's pause she slipped behind the cans.

"I thought you'd decided not to come," he said with a hint of chiding.

"I was hungry, so I walked uptown and located a vendor cart. Here." She held out a paper-wrapped bundle. "I purchased an extra sweet roll for you."

He appreciated her kindness, but he was much too tense to eat. Armed with information about the elevator shared by Father after he'd grudgingly agreed not to sign Oliver's discharge papers, he wanted to complete their task. He tucked the packet into his jacket pocket and took her arm. "Thank you, but I'll eat it later. Right now we have a job to do." He guided her to the double doorway, then retrieved the ring of keys from his belt. With a surreptitious glance right and left, he inserted the proper key in the lock and twisted it. The door creaked open. Oliver gestured for her to enter.

Carrie shivered and hung back. "It's dark in there with the clouds hiding the sun and all the lights off."

Oliver peered through the gray shadows. He'd always loved the sound and smell of the factory, but empty of its workers and its machines silenced, the factory floor seemed a gloomy place despite the aroma of chocolate filling the air. He gave her a gentle nudge on the lower back, ushering her over the threshold. "I know. But the dark is really to our benefit. If it were light in here, someone might see us moving around and alert authorities. Everyone in town knows the factory is closed on Sundays."

He pulled the door shut behind them and secured the lock. Then he stood for a moment, listening to her deep breaths and waiting for his eyes to adjust to the dim surroundings. When he felt secure to move, he touched her elbow. "Come. We'll get an oil lantern from my closet and use it when we're away from the windows. Will that help?"

She nodded, and when he pressed her forward, she didn't resist. They moved along together, their wet soles squeaking against the concrete floor and her skirts swishing in rhythm with the whish, whish of his trouser legs. The farther they ventured into the factory, the richer the aroma of chocolate became, filling his senses. Or perhaps it was the aroma of the woman beside him stirring his chest to beat in double thrums. His pulse had increased its tempo the moment she appeared, and it showed no signs of returning to normal. Simply being in her presence gave him pleasure. He truly was smitten.

And oh, how hard it would be to end their fledgling relationship before it even had a chance to bloom.

Pushing aside those gloomy thoughts, he stepped inside the closet and located a small tin of matches and the coal-oil lantern placed there in case of emergencies. Still inside the room, he lit the wick, settled the globe into place, then held the lantern aloft by its curved handle. The glow fell on Carrie's still form just outside the door, illuminating the serious expression on her face. The desire to protect her and put her at ease rose.

"We'll be all right," he said, speaking quietly even though they couldn't disturb anyone. "Are you ready?"

She hugged herself, but she nodded. "Let's go."

The elevator lurked at the end of a wide

hallway, its gaping mouth seeming to wait to swallow them up. To dispel his childish imaginings, he shared with Carrie the things he'd learned from Father about the elevator. "Our freight elevator has the design patented by Elisha Otis. The inventor himself displayed the elevator at the New York Crystal Palace Exhibition back in 1854, so it's hardly a new design, but its proven safety measures have become very popular over the years. Father insisted on an elevator safe enough for passengers even though it was meant to haul crates up and down."

When they reached the elevator, Oliver handed Carrie the lantern. "Hold that up here, and let me show you something."

She angled the light toward the iron gate, and Oliver pointed to a sprung latch.

"See? The bed releases this catch by brushing against it. So if the bed isn't in position for entry, the gate won't open." He gave the gate a tug, and it groaned as the crisscross of iron bars crunched together, creating an opening for them to enter the bed. He stepped inside, gesturing for her to follow. She did so, and the wooden platform swayed gently on its cables. He took the lantern from her and aimed the light toward the side, where an iron bar carved with zigzagging teeth ran up and down. "But this is what makes the Otis elevator truly unique. See those teeth?"

She stretched out her hand and touched one tooth. "Yes. I observed those when I was in here last and wondered about their purpose. They look vicious—like a crocodile's mouth."

He chuckled at her picturesque speech. "They're meant to be as strong as a croc's jaw. Should the cable be severed, the elevator box is equipped with safety brakes that catch on the teeth, keeping the box from falling to the bottom of the shaft. Want me to show you?"

"No!"

He couldn't resist laughing at her horrified expression. "I was only teasing, Carrie. Apparently when Otis showed his elevator at the exhibition, he did just that—had someone cut the cables while he stood inside the box. People were amazed. And the elevator always saved itself, thanks to those teeth." He furrowed his brow, examining the sides again. "That's why I find Bratcher's accident so puzzling. Father chose this elevator because it's known to be the safest one. Obviously the bed didn't fall, so somehow Bratcher entered the shaft when the bed wasn't settled at one of the floors. But how, when the doors are designed not to open unless the bed is at floor level?"

Carrie made a slow circle in the elevator, seeming to examine every inch of the walls on all sides. When she completed her survey, she shrugged. "I don't know. But given the safe construction of the elevator, it does seem unlikely that he would accidentally fall. Unless..."

Oliver leaned close, his curiosity aroused. "What?"

"You can't open the door unless the bed is pressed against the catch. But will the elevator rise or descend to another level if the gate is left open?"

"I'm not sure. But there's one way to

find out." He grinned, eager to test her theory. "Let's give it a try."

Caroline

Caroline heaved her weight against the gate on the upper-level landing, grunting along with the groan of the hinges. She stepped into the hallway, and Ollie trailed her, a look of joy on his face. "Carrie, you solved the mystery! If someone neglected to close the door after entering the elevator and rode from the upper to a lower level, then it's possible for someone to come along and fall into the shaft."

"It's true we've discovered it's **possible** for someone to accidentally fall down the shaft. But"—she grimaced, taking no pleasure in dampening his delight—"we still haven't proved it wasn't deliberate." She trailed her finger over the crossbars of the iron gate. "Wouldn't anyone who used the elevator have been warned about the importance of closing the gate before sending the elevator to another level? An open shaft is an invitation for danger." She glanced at him, noting his euphoric grin had disappeared. Her heart ached at the change in his demeanor, yet she had to be honest. "Would any of the workers in the freight area be careless enough to leave the gate open?"

Ollie leaned his shoulder on the wall, releasing a heavy sigh. "Unless they were overly tired or rushed, no. They all seem to be very dedicated, responsible men. So the likelihood of it being an accident diminishes."

Unable to bear his slumped shoulders and somber tone, she brushed his arm with her fingertips. "We don't know for sure yet. We need to explore further."

He caught her hand, clinging as if in need of encouragement. "How?"

She swallowed, aware that her next words could cause Ollie much pain. Yet he needed to know what his father had said to her. "Can we sit? I—I need to tell you something, and I think it would be better if you were sitting down."

His scowl deepened, but he nodded

and guided her away from the elevator to a stack of empty crates. After choosing two of them, he settled them in the middle of the hall. He placed the lantern on the floor between them, then held his hands out in invitation. She sat, and he plopped onto the second crate, facing her and resting his hands on his widespread knees.

"All right, Carrie. What is it?"

Calmly, without even a hint of malice, she shared the details of her conversation with Fulton Dinsmore. She watched Ollie's expression change from concern to disbelief and finally to anger. She asked, very gently, "Is it possible your father might have left the door open, knowing Bratcher would be unaware of the missing elevator box when he—"

Ollie leaped up and exploded. "No!" He ran his hand over his hair, stomping back and forth between the walls. "Of course not! My father isn't capable of...of planning a murder."

"But, Ollie, he specifically warned me about 'unpleasant consequences.' What could be more unpleasant than falling down a dark elevator shaft?"

"He wouldn't do such a thing!" Ollie roared the words, his cheeks mottled red with anger. He stormed over and leaned close, his face only inches from hers. "You're wrong, Carrie. I know you're wrong. If anyone is to blame, it's Hightower—not my father!"

She understood his fury. If someone made allegations against Noble, she'd react in the exact same way. And she ached at having caused him pain. She adopted a calm, even a placating, tone. "Then explain the discrepancy in him telling me all workers are compensated equally and the differences I've seen in pay envelopes. Surely you've observed some of the workers taking out their pay and placing it in their pockets or purses. Haven't you noticed that the women's and children's envelopes always contain significantly less than the men's? Something doesn't make sense, Ollie."

He remained bent forward, his narrowed gaze spitting daggers at her, and she braced herself for a verbal attack. But then he swept his hand over his face, and when his fingers trailed away, the intense rage was gone. He sank onto the crate and propped his elbows on his knees, his head hanging low.

"You're right. Something...is amiss. Something...requires explanation." Raising his gaze, he looked at her with such agony that tears spurted into her eyes. "When Father and I talked, he told me..." He paused, swallowing. "He told me Hightower has always followed his directions. If he told Hightower something had to be done about Bratcher—that Bratcher was causing trouble that could interfere with the factory's successful continuation—then maybe... Maybe..." He covered his face with his hands. A groan poured out, a tormented release.

Caroline couldn't bear watching him suffer. She longed to wrap him in her arms and offer comfort. During the course of their conversation, she'd become convinced that whatever had befallen Bratcher, Ollie had possessed no prior knowledge of it. His innocence thrilled her, yet she couldn't celebrate, seeing how their inspection of the elevator and her sharing about the conversation with his father had wounded him.

"Ollie?" She spoke tenderly and waited for him to lower his hands. "What we need to do now is discover the truth concerning wages. We need to see the books. The truth will be found there."

He nodded slowly and swallowed again, the sound loud in the silent hallway. "You're right. As hard as it is for me to question my own father's behavior, I have no choice." Slowly, as if his joints had stiffened during the past minutes, he pushed to his feet.

Bending down, he caught the handle on the lantern. "The books will be in Hightower's office, I'm sure. He serves as bookkeeper as well as manager and hiring agent." A rueful chuckle rolled from his chest. "Such power Father has bestowed on the man." He held his hand out to her. "Come."

She rose and caught hold. His fingers

were icy—a sure sign of his turmoil. She'd save him the distress of branding his beloved father a liar if he'd allow it. "Are you sure you want to do this? I can go alone."

A sad smile quavered on his lips. "I have to know the truth."

She nodded, and she clung hard to his hand, hoping her grip might offer a touch of comfort. "All right."

Ollie kicked the crates from the middle of the hallway and then turned toward the corner leading to Hightower's office. "I'm sure one of my keys will open Hightower's door." His face was grim, his fingers clamping painfully around hers. "Let's get this over with."

Chapter 39

Oliver

The first three keys on Oliver's ring proved ineffectual in opening Hightower's door. Three remained, and he found himself offering an unexpected prayer—**Please, Lord, let this work**—as he inserted the fourth one in the lock. He let out a gasp of surprise when it turned and the door swung inward.

He gestured Carrie over the threshold, his body abuzz with nervous excitement. Even though the factory belonged to his family, he couldn't deny feeling like a burglar as he entered the room. He paused for a moment just inside the door, then impulsively snapped the door closed behind them and twisted the lock. He turned to find Carrie staring at him with a wary look on her face. He stepped toward her, concerned. "Are you all right?"

"Why did you lock the door?"

Oliver glanced behind him at the turned lock, then shrugged. "I don't know for certain. It just seemed the right thing to do."

Her wariness remained. "I'm not fond of being closed in this office." White walls barren of photographs or paintings surrounded them. A large desk, its top cleared of everything except an ornate oil lamp, and three leather chairs were precisely arranged in the center of the bare wood floor. Two tall oak cabinets, each with four file drawers, stood sentry in a corner. Oliver shuddered. The room was cold, impersonal. Much like its occupant. Being closed up in the room felt like being closed in a tomb. Yet he didn't move to open the door.

He held his hand toward Hightower's desk. "Let's just get busy, hmm? The sooner we find those books, the sooner we can get out of here." Cold sweat was beading across his body, making him fidgety. He'd make a lousy agent.

Carrie crunched her lips together into a scowl, but she crossed behind the desk and began opening drawers. Oliver stood beside her, peeking at the drawers' contents. Hightower apparently had a taste for spirits, as the large drawer on the bottom right held three half-empty bottles of liquor and a small glass cup. Office items—envelopes, pens and ink, notepads, rubber stamps—were neatly organized in other drawers.

Oliver frowned. "He has to have the books here somewhere." He moved to the file cabinet and began rummaging through drawers. He discovered file after file of employee records, some dating back fifteen years. Oliver whistled through his teeth. Hightower might be cold, but he was meticulous. As Father had said, the man knew his job.

Behind him, Carrie released a little grunt. He looked over his shoulder and saw her yank on the bottom left-hand drawer. She shot him a disgruntled look.

"This one's locked."

Oliver crossed to her and crouched down, angling the lantern to illuminate the brass-plated lock. "I don't have any keys small enough to fit this, but..." He looked at her hair. "Do you have a hairpin?"

She pawed around in the heavy bun weighting the back of her head and pulled one loose. A coil of hair came with it and fell along her neck, inviting Oliver to travel its length. She caught him looking, and his face heated. He plucked the pin from her hand and set to work on the lock. After a few deft flicks, the catch clicked.

"Aha!" The exclamation left his throat without conscious effort. He pulled the drawer open and withdrew a black bound book. He placed it on the desk, settled the lantern beside it, and opened the cover. Carrie leaned in, and together they examined page after page of entries. As he looked, his elation began to build. He tapped a page, angling a grin at Carrie. "See? It's just as Father said. Salaries are contingent upon the position and the number of years on the job. He told you the truth."

Carrie's brow puckered. "That's what this says, but..." She stood upright, gazing into the gaping drawer for a moment. Then without warning she dropped to all fours.

Unnerved by her action, Oliver immediately ducked down beside her. He whispered, "What is it?"

She began pawing the drawer—one hand inside, one hand outside. "Something isn't right. Look at the big drawer with the liquor bottles. It's twice this deep, yet when viewed from the outside, the drawers appear to be the same size." Her hands stilled and her face lit. "I knew it!"

"What?"

She tapped the bottom of the drawer with her knuckles, grinning at him. "It has a false bottom."

He gawked at her. "For what purpose?"

She let out a little huff and punched him lightly on the shoulder. "Ollie, think! The books don't match what I've witnessed on payday. If Hightower is recording one amount but paying a different amount, some money is unaccounted for. Where do you suppose that money is?"

Excitement built in Oliver's chest. "In the secret compartment?"

"At least some sort of records are probably there." She bent over the drawer again. "Help me find a means of opening the compartment."

Oliver lowered the lantern, and after searching for a few minutes, he discovered a metal catch. He pressed it, and what had appeared to be the bottom of the drawer folded upward on a hidden springed hinge, revealing a compartment beneath. The lantern's glow fell on a second leather-bound book resting atop a flattened curl of papers. Oliver handed the book to Carrie, then reached for the papers. He unrolled them and stared in open-mouthed amazement. He'd found the elevator blueprints.

Lifting his gaze to Carrie, he shook his head. "What all has Hightower been doing?"

Carrie had opened both books and was examining them side by side. She gave him a brief, grim look. "He's been stealing from the factory. Apparently for several years. I need to show these records to Noble. He'll be able to determine the extent of the financial damage." She tore out several pages from the middle of each book, folded them together, and jammed them into her pocket. After flipping the record books closed, she shoved them toward Ollie. "Put everything back like we found it, and let's go."

Oliver rose and picked up the lantern. The light bobbed around the room like a bouncing moonbeam. "You're leaving the evidence?"

She patted her pocket. "I have all the evidence I need right here. But if Hightower finds the books missing, he'll know we're on to him. We can't take them with us."

Oliver nodded, acknowledging the sense of her statement. Even so, it infuriated him. He wanted to confront Hightower immediately.

Carrie must have guessed his thoughts, because she touched his hand. "Justice will be served, Ollie, but we need to do this correctly. Allow the authorities to deal with Hightower."

Oliver sighed. "Very well. Let's—"

Footsteps intruded. Someone was climbing the stairs.

Oliver and Carrie froze in place, their gazes colliding in wide-eyed looks of shock. Carrie clawed at his hand and mouthed the words, "We have to hide." He quickly extinguished the wick on the lantern, then searched the room—a foolish expenditure of time. There weren't any hiding places in the stark space. But his gaze found the square observation window that gave Hightower a view of the factory floor. He tiptoed to the window, opened the shutters, and looked out. A narrow ledge—perhaps ten inches wide—ran the length of the loft and overlooked a fourteen-foot drop. He broke into a cold sweat just thinking of stepping out on that ledge, but where else could they go? Someone fumbled with the door lock, and he frantically motioned to Carrie. His brain screamed, **Help, help!** As she scurried to his side, a soft clatter, followed by a muffled curse, told him whoever was trying to get in had dropped the key ring. They'd been gifted with a few extra seconds to escape. Panic making him clumsy, Oliver lifted Carrie onto the window ledge and helped her swing her legs to the other side. She stepped out, pressed her back to the wall, and inched sideways. Oliver placed the lantern on the ledge, then scrambled out. He pulled the shutters into position as the lock squeaked and the door hinges whispered.

He braced himself against the wall on the opposite side of the window, his head turned so he could look at Carrie. She stared back, her eyes wide and her lips set in a taut line. Hightower's cheerful whistle drifted from behind the shutters. What was the man doing here on a Sunday? And when did he plan to leave? Dizziness assailed Oliver as he glanced at the dangerous drop at the end of his toes. They couldn't stay here all day.

Another prayer formed in his mind— **Lord, help us, please**—and on its tail came an idea. Moving slowly and cautiously, he hooked the lantern's handle in his fingers, then gestured to Carrie to move as far from the window as possible. He began inching the other way, gritting his teeth at the soft skritch sound of his clothing catching on the rough wood wall behind him.

Carrie nodded in understanding and eased in the opposite direction. When he'd gone as far as the ledge would allow, Oliver realized the shadows had completely swallowed Carrie. Unease gripped him, but he reassured himself with the knowledge that if he couldn't see her, Hightower wouldn't easily spot her, either.

With sweat dripping from his forehead to his chin, he pressed one damp palm to the wall behind him and angled himself to give his other arm room to swing. The lantern's handle squeaked as it swayed, and he cringed, expecting to hear Hightower walking to the window. But the man's whistling apparently hid the soft squeak. The tune continued as if nothing was amiss.

For a moment Oliver hesitated. Would the shrill, discordant tune also cover the sound of the lantern hitting the floor? If so, the plan would fail. He'd have to make sure the noise was loud enough to capture Hightower's attention. Gritting his teeth, he braced himself and swung his arm as hard as he could without losing his balance. The lantern flew from his hand and sailed toward the floor, where it landed with a crash.

Hightower's whistling ceased. Steps thundered, and a beam of light spilled outward as the shutters were peeled back. Hightower's face poked through the window opening. He bellowed, "Who's out there?"

Oliver held his breath, his pulse beating out a frantic message—**Don't let him find us. Don't let him find us.** After only a few seconds, which felt like hours, Hightower ducked back in. Moments later the office door banged against the wall, and then his feet clattered on the stairs.

Oliver eased his way toward the window,

and Carrie approached from the other side. He assisted her through and then fell in behind her. He risked a glance through the window in time to see Hightower pause on the floor below and look up. Oliver instinctively ducked. Uncertain whether they'd been spotted, he caught Carrie's hand and scrambled for the door.

Hand in hand, they dashed to the elevator hallway, but when he started to pull Carrie inside, she shook her head. She mouthed, "Too loud." She pulled him, instead, to the stack of crates along the wall and squirmed in behind them. They crouched behind the barrier, Oliver folding Carrie within his arms to make themselves as small as possible. Their breath released in matching soft bursts. Did she regularly do these kinds of things while on assignment? How did her heart survive it? He felt as though his would burst from his chest while he huddled, listening for Hightower's approaching footfalls.

They came, pounding toward them and

then thumping past. Oliver peeked between slats, catching a glimpse of Hightower's stiff form in front of the elevator. The man turned a slow circle, his face crunched in displeasure. Oliver tightened his grip around Carrie, and she pressed the bulky coil of her bun against his neck, their bodies fitted as snugly together as two spoons in a drawer. They remained as still as a garden statue while Oliver willed Hightower to give up his search and return to his office. Seconds ticked by so slowly it seemed as though time had ceased to pass at all. Finally Hightower blew out a blast of air. He charged past them and wheeled around the corner, his arms swinging. His feet thumped down the stairs once more, his indistinguishable mutters rising over the echoing thuds.

When the footsteps faded, Oliver crept from behind the crates, drawing Carrie with him. "Let's get out of here."

She nodded, her face white.

Although he knew it would be noisy, Oliver chose to take the elevator rather than risk encountering Hightower on the stairs. If the man had gone to the opposite side of the factory, he might miss hearing its groaning gears. Oliver kept the prayer rolling in the back of his mind as he and Carrie rode the elevator downward. The bed jerked into place on the lowest floor. He gave the gate a shove, then grabbed Carrie's hand, and they dashed for the door. Once outside, they raced around the corner and continued running.

Oliver pulled Carrie through an alley and behind a shed, then collapsed against the rough wood wall, his lungs heaving, his hand still holding tight to hers. He listened for sounds of pursuit, but to his relief Hightower didn't come after them. They'd escaped.

Thank You, Lord...

Carrie shook her head. "Oh my. That was close."

Oliver squeezed her cold fingers. "Too close." He pulled in a long breath and then released it slowly, willing the tension of the last minutes to fade. "I hope I never have to do something like that again."

A slow grin climbed her cheeks, which were starting to show a bit of pink now that they were safe. "You aren't going to enroll in a Pinkerton course?"

He released a low, wry chuckle. "Never."

Her grin broadened, and she let go of his hand. "Fortunately you won't have to, because—" Her eyes flew wide, her fingers groping at her pocket.

Oliver's pulse scampered back to frantic beats. "What is it?"

Her face paled. "The pages I tore from the records books. I...I must have dropped them."

Chapter 40

Gordon

Gordon checked the last entry door to the factory, then turned and frowned across the empty work floor. All the doors were locked, just as they should be. None of the windows were open. He'd checked the break room, the infirmary, even the closets... Not a soul anywhere. Yet someone had to have been in the building for that lantern to end up in the middle of the floor. With the installation of electric lights two years ago, lanterns were no longer needed. Unless someone was sneaking around where he shouldn't be. He shook his head, clearing the ridiculous thought. He was letting his imagination run wild. Who would be here on Sunday?

Besides him, that is. They'd kept a supply of coal-oil lanterns secured on hooks around the work floors in case the factory lost electricity. Given the vibration from the machinery, one of the hooks had probably come loose. A simple explanation. Satisfied all was well, Gordon headed across the floor again. He approached the shattered lantern, and he paused to tap his toe against one shard of broken glass swimming in a pool of coal oil. Should he clean this up? Some of the younger workers came in barefoot. But then he shrugged and moved on. The first-shift janitor could see to it Monday morning.

Thoughts of janitors led him to Ollie Moore, and he gritted his teeth.

Why hadn't Dinsmore approved Moore's discharge? He'd signed off on Carrie Lang. Gordon's lips twitched, anticipating the pleasure of sending the woman out the door. He'd not been able to snag a moment of enjoyment from her, but he wouldn't complain. At least he wouldn't have to worry about her and Moore plotting against him. But he couldn't help wishing Dinsmore hadn't insisted on keeping Moore.

Gordon ambled slowly up the hallway, chewing the inside of his mouth.

Not once in the six years he had managed the factory had Dinsmore denied a request for discharge. So why keep Moore? Had Dinsmore planted him here as a spy? Did he owe the man a debt and the job repaid it? Why approve one but not both? He pondered forging Dinsmore's signature on the paperwork. He'd done it on other papers and had never been caught. Only the apparent relationship between Dinsmore and Moore kept him from following through on the desire. Moore would tattle, and then Dinsmore would find reason to distrust Gordon. He couldn't risk that. Not this close to his plans coming to pass.

Up ahead the elevator waited. Gordon strode toward it at an easy pace, but then he froze in place. The gate was open. Gordon's entire body began to quiver. On trembling legs he forced himself to inch forward, his unblinking eyes aimed at the floor. If a gaping shaft greeted his eyes, as it had the night Harmon Bratcher took his tumble, would he be able to keep himself upright?

The elevator bed swung at an even level with the factory floor. The relief was so intense he buckled forward and braced his hands on his knees. He took several seconds to collect himself. Then he reached to close the gate. But he froze with his hands on the cool iron as realization dawned. When he'd been upstairs at the loft level, the elevator was waiting. How had it gotten down here? Unless...

His mouth went dry. He wasn't imagining things after all. Someone had been in the factory. Someone had ridden the elevator from the loft to the main level and then escaped. But the locked doors... Gordon slapped his forehead, silently cursing himself. The only other people with keys were the janitors. That included Ollie Moore. Gordon would bet his last penny he knew the name of the factory's intruder.

Although he hadn't ridden the elevator since Bratcher's demise, Gordon stepped onto the bed. The platform swayed slightly, making his stomach roll, but he resolutely pressed his finger on the button. The elevator jerked into motion, and he kept his gaze angled away from the sliver of dark shaft exposed between the walls and the elevator's square bed. On the top level the elevator jolted to a stop with a loud creak. Gordon pushed the gate aside and nearly fell into the hallway.

He must have been holding his breath the entire ride, because his chest heaved with gasps of air. Leaning against the wall, he filled his lungs again and again with sweet oxygen. Then, revived, he pushed himself upright. As he did, his gaze drifted across a clump of folded papers lying near a stack of crates in the hallway. Curious, he picked them up. The hallway was shadowy, only a slight shaft of light sneaking around the corner from where he'd left his office lamp burning, but he didn't need much light to recognize his neatly penned numbers filling columns and rows.

Gordon slapped his leg with the pages

and barked a curse. Moore had been in here, and he'd discovered Gordon's secret. Just as Bratcher had. Gordon wadded the pages in his hand and charged to his office. He slammed the door, then leaned against it, panting, stewing, seething.

Moore knew. Which meant Dinsmore would know soon. They had to be in cahoots. There was no other logical explanation. And they'd left Gordon with no choice. Bratcher had been silenced before he could share his findings. Not deliberately, but certainly fortuitously. Moore would have to be silenced, too, before he could get to Dinsmore. Gordon stumbled across the floor and dropped into his desk chair, propping up his head with his hand.

Nausea flooded his gut. He didn't like Moore. He didn't even like Dinsmore, although he grudgingly appreciated the confidence the man had placed in him all those years ago. But disliking them didn't make it any easier to think about killing them. He drooped lower in his chair. Should he take the money he'd already squirreled away and leave? Start over somewhere else?

He slapped the desk top, groaning, "Noooo." He'd worked too long and too hard to get this far. This factory was meant to be **his**. He'd poured more of his sweat into it than Dinsmore had. He'd earned ownership. He'd have to arrange things so he could stay. And that meant Moore—and possibly Dinsmore—had to go. Bile filled his throat. Stealing from Dinsmore was easy. Impersonal. But murder... Could he really do it—kill two men? He gagged at the very thought. But if he didn't, he'd lose everything.

Sitting bolt upright, he gulped air to rid himself of the queasy feeling. He hadn't worked this long, fought this hard, just to give up. The men had to go. There was no other way.

Caroline

Caroline scurried toward her boarding hotel, Ollie moving briskly alongside her.

He touched her elbow, his fingers brushing as gently as a butterfly's wing.

"Even though we don't have the pages, we know what they showed."

Dear Ollie... He'd done nothing but offer assurances their entire walk. As much as she appreciated his desire to relieve her guilt, it didn't help. A court of law wouldn't accept her words. She needed evidence. So she'd have to go back and retrieve the proof. There was no other choice. But she wouldn't tell Ollie. He'd insist on coming, too, and she'd be placing him in danger.

As they approached her boardinghouse, her safe haven, she slowed her pace. Ollie automatically tempered his stride as well, and she swallowed a smile at how well they read one another. As if they were meant to be together. But such a ridiculous thought. She sighed, her breath forming a little cloud. "Thank you, Ollie. I'm relieved our findings confirmed your belief in your father's innocence. Apparently Hightower has been fooling him for a long time."

Ollie's brow pinched. He lowered his gaze and scuffed the ground with his toe. "I don't know if I'm more angry or sad. Before I was born, Father handpicked Gordon from the boys at a Chicago orphanage for training in the factory. He's treated him more like a son than an employee all these years. Father trusts Gordon. This betrayal will devastate him."

"Will you call him?"

Ollie shook his head. "No. I can't tell him something like this over the telephone. I need to see him face to face." He yawned behind his hand, then offered a sheepish grin. "Excuse me. All the excitement is catching up with me. Although I'd like to sleep, I'm going to pack a bag, head to the train station, and go to Wichita. I can be back before shift time tomorrow. Father might return with me, too." His expression turned forbidding. "Although I know how hard this will be for Father, I confess I will take great joy in catching Gordon Hightower by the collar and tossing him to the curb."

Caroline curled her hand over his forearm. Beneath her palm his muscles were taut, tense. She pressed gently. "Don't confront Hightower. If he knows you're aware that he's changing the books, he'll run. He has money hidden away somewhere, and if he collects it, we might not be able to bring him to justice. Tell your father, but don't let Hightower know you're aware of his duplicity. Not yet."

He looked at her for a moment, but then he sighed and relaxed. "All right, Carrie. You're the investigator. I'll trust your wisdom in the matter."

His faith in her pleased her more than she could say. She smiled her thanks, and he responded with a weak grin of his own. She dropped her hand from his arm. "Go now. I'll catch a quick nap and then visit the police department to see if there's an update on Letta, Lank, and Lesley before I report to Noble. He'll be very interested in what we discovered." She turned to leave, but he captured her hand, holding her in place.

"Carrie?"

She looked into his gold-flecked eyes of palest green, and something at her very center melted. Oh, how she loved gazing into his eyes. "Yes?"

For long seconds he simply smiled down at her, his expression warm and admiring. Finally he spoke, his words drifting forth on a sigh. "Thank you."

"For what?"

"For helping prove my father's innocence. After the way he spoke to you—even seeming to threaten you."

She held up a hand to silence him. She'd only been doing her job. But he went on.

"Thank you for trusting me enough to go out on that ledge." Teasing put a sparkle in his eyes, and she laughed softly, briefly ducking her head. He caught her chin and lifted her face to his again. "But mostly, thank you for telling me about God and prayer."

Her heart caught.

"I prayed today. I prayed, and each time God answered. He kept us from being discovered." Awareness bloomed across his face, his eyes glowing with some inner joy that defied description. "He listened, and He answered. He rescued us."

Although later she might regret it, she couldn't stop herself. She threw her arms around his neck and hugged him hard. His arms closed around her, and for several seconds they clung to each other, sharing a moment of discovery.

Then she pulled loose, catching his hands to remain connected with him. "He answered because He cares, Ollie. He loves you. And, yes, He is our Rescuer. He rescued us from sin and eternal separation from Him when He sent Jesus into the world to bear the penalty for our wrongdoings. The Bible says, 'Believe on the Lord Jesus Christ, and thou shalt be saved.' Saved, Ollie. Rescued. Saved to do His will and to walk with Him eternally."

Tears stung, and she sniffed. Her eyes shut as she poured her secret thoughts to her Father. **Lord, if You brought me to this man to help him find his way to You, then I accept Your will. But**

please comfort my selfish heart. I want to be so much more than the one who introduces him to his Savior.

Ollie's fingers tightened on her hands, and she gazed at him. His sweet face was distorted by her veil of tears, but she still glimpsed his smile. "Thank you. I'm saved, Carrie—for all eternity."

She fell into his embrace again, tears of joy flowing down her cheeks. Even if she'd failed in the mission Noble had sent her to do, she'd witnessed a beautiful rebirth in Ollie's spirit. No mission, no matter how successful or satisfying, could ever be better than knowing Ollie's soul was redeemed.

With a self-conscious giggle, she tugged free of his arms. "You'd better go if you intend to get to Wichita and back before tomorrow evening."

He nodded, a hint of regret on his face. "You're right." Tenderness crept across his features. He took one step backward but kept his hand extended toward her. "I'll be praying for the Holcomb children to be found."

She planted her feet firmly to prevent them from dashing after him. Oh, how appealing she found this man. But her missions here—her Noble-given mission and her God-given mission—were nearing completion, and she'd soon have to tell him good-bye. She'd only make it harder for herself if she gave in to these desires. She forced a smile. "Safe travels, Ollie."

"Thank you. Enjoy your rest, Carrie."

She remained on the hotel stoop, watching him until he reached the corner.

He paused, turned back, and waved again. Lifting her hand, she returned the farewell, her heart doing cartwheels. He rounded the corner, and with his departure she was free to see to her own errands.

With a determined stride, she retraced the path they'd taken to escape. She'd rest, but first she needed to regain the proof of Hightower's fraudulence. She would either find those dropped pages, or she'd discover a way to take the entire books. Either way, she'd bring the truth to light.

Letta

Letta hunched over her Bible, underlining the words with her fingers as she painstakingly read aloud to Lank and Lesley. Mrs. Annamarie had read the story of Daniel in the lions' den to them one night in the hotel, and Letta had decided to share it again in the hope the thoughts of lions would frighten the boys enough to keep them close at hand. But some of the words were harder than she'd realized. They'd nearly nodded off during her slow reciting of the tale.

She finished, "'He delivereth and rescueth, and he worketh signs and wonders in heaven and in earth, who hath delivered Daniel from the power of the lions.'" She closed the Bible and found Lesley staring at her.

"Who's 'He'?"

Letta blinked twice. Hadn't he been listening at all? "'He' is God."

"What's 'deliveruff'?"

Letta sighed. "That's just a fancy way of sayin' **delivered**—means the same as rescued."

"Ohhh." Lesley nodded. He sat upright, perky as a prairie dog hopping out of its hole. "Can we go bee huntin' now?"

"We're not bee huntin'," Letta said, shaking her finger at her brother. "We're honey gatherin'. It's not the same thing."

Lesley shrugged, grinning. "But can we go?"

"Soon as Lank gets together everything we need."

Lank unfolded his legs and rose, his smile bright. "Aw-aw-already got it. Luh-let's go."

Letta, her arms loaded with the empty tin cans and lunch bucket, trailed behind Lank and Lesley as they led her along the creek. Lank bent forward, burdened by the bundle of sticks on his back and the lumpy wad of cloth in his arms. But he didn't voice a word of complaint. He talked, though—jabbering away with Lesley as if they were all going on some merry journey. Letta marveled at the changes she'd seen in Lank over the past days. He held his head high instead of cowering. His confidence grew hour by hour, and she was so glad she'd brought the boys out here away from town and everybody else. This was where they belonged.

Lesley pointed ahead. "See up there, Letta? See that old busted-up wagon and the plum bushes growing around it? The bee nest is just beyond it."

Letta shook her head, battling the urge to scold. They'd sure ventured off too far for good sense. But she was with them this time, so they'd be all right.

As they neared the hive, the bees' drone drifted to their ears. A few plump insects swirled outside the opening to their hive, which they'd built in the belly of an overturned piece of rusty farm equipment. The sight of that machine—either some-thing meant to spread seeds or manure—brought Letta up short. If there was equipment lying around, then farmers had to be nearby. The reminder hacked away at the feeling of safety she'd built over the past couple of days.

She grabbed the sleeve of Lank's jacket, making him stop. "You sure there's no people around here?"

"Wuh-wuh-we looked," Lank said, his eyes wide. "Nuh-nuh-nobody around."

"It's all right, Letta," Lesley chimed in, shifting from foot to foot. "Don't be scared. Lank an' me'll take care of ya."

Letta swallowed a chuckle. Lesley wasn't big enough to fight off a bee, but she wouldn't tell him so. "You come on over here with me," she said. "Lank can get that fire started on his own. He don't need us in the way."

Lesley made a sour face, but he followed her toward the creek. Letta called over her shoulder, "We're gonna go to the other side, Lank. Soon as you get that fire goin', you come, too, you hear?"

"I huh-hear."

Letta caught Lesley's hand. "C'mon."

"I'm comin', I'm comin'." Lesley splashed alongside Letta, his lower lip poked out in a pout. Halfway across the creek, he suddenly stopped, and his body arched as if somebody had speared him.

He screamed.

Letta clapped her hand over his mouth. "Lesley, what ails you? You wanna let the whole county know we're here?"

He knocked her hand loose and screeched again, the piercing sound filled with both fear and pain. He bent over and tugged at his leg. And finally Letta saw what was wrong. A steel trap lay beneath the surface of the water. And Lesley's ankle was clamped in its jaws.

Chapter 41

Letta

Letta crouched in the cold water and clawed at the jagged steel jaws holding Lesley's foot. His wails pierced her ears. Blood painted a line of red in the stream. She cried out, "God, God, please help me..."

Lank splashed into the creek, splattering her arms and Lesley's pants.

"Wuh-wuh-what happened?"

"Trap." Her heart beat so hard it hurt. Her lungs lost their ability to hold air. Her chest pumped with the effort of breathing.

"Luh-let's guh-guh-get him out!"

Letta's shaking hands refused to cooperate, but Lank scooped Lesley into his arms. His face red, grunting with exertion, he lifted Lesley a few inches. A chain rattled. Lesley threw back his head and screamed again—the most agonizing cry yet.

Letta grabbed at him. "Let 'im go, Lank! You're hurtin' him worse!" Lank released his hold, and Lesley fell against Letta, sobbing.

"Chain's holdin' the trap down somehow. We gotta get it off his foot."

Letta wrenched Lesley's hands loose and crouched down again. The icy water lapped at her, sending shivers across her body and making her tremble. But she ignored the cold and closed her fingers around the trap's jaws arching away from the front of Lesley's foot.

Lank dropped to his knees and took hold of the inches of steel behind Lesley's heel. He met Letta's gaze, his eyes fierce with determination, and nodded. Together, they yanked on the trap. Again and again they repeated the jerky motion, their muscles straining against the powerful clamp. But the metal didn't budge.

With every movement Lesley's screams

become more piercing. He clutched at their shoulders, their heads, his icy fingers frantically seeking rescue. Letta rose and left Lank prying at the trap on his own. She wrapped Lesley in her arms. He sobbed harshly, bucking against her grip. She nudged Lank with her foot and snapped, "Hurry up!"

"Tuh-too tuh-tuh-tight. Cuh-cuh-can't get it." Lank leaped up and splashed his way to the bundle of sticks he'd dropped. He lifted one, then another, seeming to examine them by turn. Letta'd seen that same look of concentration on his face while trying to start a fire and holding a handmade spear in his hands. He had a plan.

Rubbing Lesley's shuddering back, she said, "Hold on, Lesley. Lank'll get you loose."

Lank returned, holding one stick in his hands. He dropped into the water and jammed the stick in behind Lesley's heel. Lesley screamed, and Letta muffled the sound by pressing his face to her chest. Lank, his lips crunched tightly together, pressed the stick sideways. The twig snapped, throwing Lank into the water. He came up spluttering, the shattered stick in his fist.

Hopelessness swept through Letta, making her legs weak. She trembled from head to toe as she held tight to her sobbing little brother and stared into Lank's pale face. She was the oldest. She was supposed to take care of them all. But she couldn't do anything for Lesley.

Water dripped from Lank's clothes and hair. He shivered so hard his body went into spasms. "Guh-guh-gotta get huh-huh-help."

Panic chased away the feeling of hopelessness. "We can't! Nobody can know where we are!"

Lank shook his head, his expression turning stubborn. "Guh-guh-gotta!" He struggled toward the bank, his feet slogging through the water. He staggered free of the creek and shot a look of apology at Letta. "Uh-uh-I'll be buhback soon as uh-uh-I cuh-cuh-can!" And then he took off running across the uneven ground.

"Lank!" Letta screamed his name over Lesley's harsh sobs. "Lank, you come back here!"

He didn't even pause.

Caroline

The mournful blast of a train's whistle reached Caroline's ears as she crept along the back wall of Dinsmore's World-Famous Chocolates Factory. Was Ollie on the departing train? Loneliness smote her. She'd always worked alone and had never longed for anyone's assistance. But in that moment she would have given anything to have Ollie at her side.

She shoved the wistful desire aside and focused on the task at hand. Her eyes skimming the ground, she searched the pathway they'd taken earlier when escaping the factory. Knowing how the wind could carry things away, she also peeked behind the trash cans, along the foundation of the building, and in the curb. But the pages were nowhere to be found.

Chances were she'd dropped them inside. And on Monday, when everyone returned to work, one of the employees was bound to discover them lying on the floor. If whoever found them looked at them, they'd surely turn the pages over to Hightower. She stamped her foot, frustration rising in her chest.

If only she were still on the day shift, she'd be able to arrive early and explore without garnering notice. She leaned against the damp bricks and chewed her lip. The first shift was the largest of the three rotations. Could she sneak in with the other workers? New employees joined the ranks virtually each day. Perhaps no one would question her moving through the hallways early tomorrow morning. She'd take the chance.

The decision made, she pushed off from the wall and started toward the street. But she'd taken two steps when a drawling voice drew her to a halt.

"Well, well, well. Miss Lang."

Caroline turned slowly.

Gordon Hightower stood only a scant

two yards behind her, a knowing grin on his face. "What brings you to the factory on a fine Sunday?"

She'd hardly call the day fine. Overcast with a chilly breeze, absent of Ollie's companionship, and now faced with Hightower's less-than-sunny appearance, the day became more dreary by the minute. She formed a smile and lifted her shoulders in a weak shrug. "Just taking a walk."

His gaze narrowed. "You were taking something all right. But it wasn't a walk, was it?"

Her heart hammered against her ribs. He knew! She forced a nervous laugh. "Is it so surprising that I'd be stretching my legs? Crating is a tedious job—not much opportunity to move around. So—"

In one great stride he reached her and curled his hand around her elbow. His fingers bit into her flesh. His snarling face hovered mere inches from hers. "Don't lie to me. You were sneaking around here. Just like you have been since I hired you." He shook her viciously, making her teeth rattle. Holding tight to her with one hand, he slipped his other hand into his pocket and withdrew a familiar wad of folded pages. He waved them beneath her nose. "Is this what you're after?"

Unwilling to lie, yet unable to tell the truth, Caroline stood in silence.

He shook her again and plunged the pages back into his pocket. "How'd you get in earlier? Who gave you a key?"

Caroline's mouth turned to cotton. Although fear roared through her, she refused to give it sway. Looking directly into Hightower's snapping eyes, she spoke honestly. "No one gave me a key." She then angled her head and furrowed her brow. "What are you doing here? The factory's closed on Sunday."

"I'm asking the questions!" He pushed her forward and began dragging her toward the building.

She clawed at his hand, but his grip proved amazingly strong. So she went limp, a tactic she'd learned from Noble. For a few seconds he lost his hold. She swung her arm, striking him hard on the side of the head, then scrambled for freedom. Curses exploded from his lips as he charged after her. This time he grabbed her around the middle. She struggled against him, clawing at his hands and stomping at his toes. He captured her wrists and twisted them painfully behind her, ending the fierce battle.

He laughed, the rollicking sound evil in its delivery. "Well, aren't you the feisty one. That was fun." Keeping his bruising grip on her wrists, he shoved her toward the factory. "We might have to try that wrestling again. But know you won't best me. I'm well practiced at fighting, and I always win."

He kicked the door closed behind them and released her. She scampered several feet away, then spun to face him, panting and rubbing her aching wrists. He set the lock, his leering gaze pinned to her face.

Snatches from Caroline's years of training tripped through her mind, and she grabbed hold of a ploy to bide time —**Keep him talking.** "All right, Mr. Hightower, I confess I was here earlier.

Ollie Moore let me in."

Hightower snorted. "Big surprise."

She blathered on. "He helped me examine the elevator. We didn't want to get in anyone's way, so we needed to do it while no one was working."

Folding his arms over his chest, he nodded at her. "Continue."

"You see, I wanted to verify that Harmon Bratcher's death was an accident. So I needed to see how the elevator functioned. To see if it was possible for someone to accidentally fall down the shaft."

His eyes narrowed. "And what did you determine?"

She swallowed, then spoke in what she prayed was a convincing tone. "If someone, in a lapse of judgment, left the gate open, and no lights were burning, then a person could step into the shaft without realizing the elevator bed wasn't there."

He didn't move. Not even a twitch of an eyelid. "So you're satisfied Bratcher's death was indeed an accident?"

Would he let her go if she agreed? Heart

pattering with hope, she nodded.

A slow smile crept up his cheeks. "I'm so glad you see the possibility. Because, Miss Lang, there will be another accident in the factory."

Cold sweat broke out over her entire body. "You'd be foolish to do away with me, Mr. Hightower. I'll be missed come Monday. Ollie Moore will miss me."

Hightower laughed. "Come Monday, Ollie Moore will be shown your discharge papers. He'll presume you left on your own."

She gaped at him. "Discharge papers?"

"Yes. Fulton Dinsmore agreed with my decision that you should be released from duty here. He signed the papers Saturday afternoon before departing for Wichita."

So Dinsmore's talk about "unpleasant consequences" referred to her losing her job, not being physically harmed. Dinsmore might be indifferent and calcu-lating, but the man truly was innocent of wrongdoing in Bratcher's death. Despite the harrowing position in which she'd found herself, she couldn't withhold a sigh of relief for Ollie's sake.

"You don't seem disappointed by the news." Hightower's words brought her back to the present.

She gave a stiff shrug. "I'm not. Now that I know Bratcher died from an accident, I don't need to stay any longer. So I'll just—" She headed for the door. "You aren't going anywhere." He waylaid her with a firm grip on her arm. He leaned close, his voice turning to a snarl. "There's still the issue of you snooping through my personal records. It was you, wasn't it?"

Denying it would only prolong the inevitable, and confirming it might convince him to surrender. Caroline lifted her chin and fixed him with a steady look. "Yes. I saw the records. I tore out the pages. I showed them to Ollie Moore. He intends to tell Mr. Dinsmore about the discrepancies." Hightower's face mottled with red. His fingers curled so tightly on her arm, Caroline's fingers began to tingle.

Wincing against the pain, she continued. "So you see, Mr. Hightower, your secrets are exposed. Authorities will be notified.

It's over."

"It's not over." He spoke through gritted teeth. "I won't lose this factory. It's mine." With a savage jerk he aimed her for the stairway. Her skirts tangled around her ankles, threatening to trip her, but he hauled her to the lowest level and then into the doctor's office. With a mighty shove he pushed her through the infirmary door and flung her onto a cot.

The pleasing aroma of sweet chocolate mingled with the bitter essence of fear. Caroline's stomach whirled, nausea making perspiration break out across her body. She scrambled to stand, but he rolled her onto her stomach and planted his knee in the small of her back. As his weight settled against her spine, pain exploded through her hips. She stilled, and he captured her wrists. Something—his belt?—tangled around her wrists and pulled tight. She bit back a sharp cry of pain.

His knee lifted. Gathering her gumption, she strained to roll free of the cot, but before she could move, he straddled her back. Out of the corner of her eye, she observed him yank the sheet from the next cot. Then he lifted her skirts out of the way. She kicked wildly, but he managed to tie her ankles together with one end of the sheet and then tied the other end through the crossbar at the foot of the metal frame, creating a short tether.

At last he stood and moved to the head of the cot, where he gazed down at her. "Thank you for alerting me to Moore's involvement. As much as I'd love to deal with you right now, I don't have time. I have to stop him."

Facedown on the cot, her limbs ineffective, Caroline could do little but speak, but she spoke boldly. "You're too late." How she prayed she'd spoken the truth! "He's already left for Wichita to tell Mr. Dinsmore you've been stealing from him."

Hightower's grin turned smug. "How convenient. Because you see, my naive little Nosy Parker, with both of them under the same roof, I can, as the saying goes, 'Kill two birds with one stone.'" He whipped a handkerchief from his pocket. "Let's make sure you can't holler for help before I return, hmm?"

She flopped about on the mattress, twisting her head, but he grabbed a handful of her hair. Her scalp ignited with pain, and once again she stilled her frantic movements. The stiff fabric cut into her mouth as he ruthlessly tightened the cloth, catching several hairs in the knot. Tears pricked her eyes—tears of pain but also of fear.

Hightower shook his head, a rueful grin creasing his face. "Oh, such a shame to leave you. You're so much more appealing than that snoopy Bratcher. Idiot man, nosing through my records to see how many underage workers were on the books. It was none of his business! But you and I...oh, we could have great fun if I didn't need to take care of Moore." He stretched out his hand and traced the line of her jaw with one finger. "But don't worry. I'll be back. We'll enjoy ourselves... later."

She jerked away from his touch. His

laughter rang, and she squeezed her eyes shut against his amused face. Moments later the door slammed shut, muffling the continued sound of his merriment. And, blessedly, Caroline was left alone, unscathed.

Strapped to the cot, silenced by the cloth in her mouth, she could do only one thing.

Dear heavenly Father...

Oliver

The passing landscape blurred, and Oliver blinked several times, clearing his vision. As tired as he was, he couldn't sleep now. He needed to plan how to inform Father of Hightower's deceit while inflicting the least amount of emotional pain. Father's relationship with Hightower had been decades in the making. How often had Father held up Hightower as a prime example of apprenticeship? Gordon Hightower was Father's success story... and Father's downfall.

As a boy Oliver had been jealous of this youth named Hightower, who resided in a town fifteen miles away. He'd wondered why Father took such interest in an orphaned lad, handpicking him from a group of boys living in the children's home, giving him a job, training him. When he'd expressed his jealousy, Father had sat him down and delivered a stern lecture about the responsibility of wealth and leadership. Father's voice rang in Oliver's memory. **"You would begrudge him a place in our factory when he has nothing else to call his own? This boy has no family, no home. But if he learns a skill, his future can be secure."** Oliver had hung his head in shame and assured his father he would never complain about Gordon Hightower again.

He'd broken that promise since taking a lowly position at the factory, pointing out Hightower's penchant for bullying, for pushing his way to the front, for seeming to trample others without concern for their feelings. Each time Father had defended his protégé, reminding Oliver of the man's dismal beginning as an orphan, which surely had left him with feelings of inadequacy and insecurity. Father had said they should practice understanding rather than condemnation. But not even his deep compassion would excuse Hightower's deliberate and methodical theft from the factory over the past years.

Oliver gazed out the window, his body swaying with the car's gentle rocking on the rails, and pondered what had built such selfishness in Hightower. According to Father, giving him the job at a young age paved the way to a successful future. Yet one could hardly consider his involvement in underhanded dealings as success. Somewhere in life Hightower had missed very important lessons. Lessons on fairness, on honesty, on self-control.

A smile twitched at Oliver's cheek. Although he had been raised in opulence, his parents had instilled all those qualities and more in their only child. He'd been given much in the area of material possessions, but he'd also been taught right from wrong and given a strong base of honor on which to build his life.

With a start Oliver recognized what Hightower had lacked during his childhood years—a family. Parents to teach him. He'd learned a job—learned it well—but it hadn't been enough to mold him into an honorable citizen. He and Father needed to give some serious thought about the number of children employed at the factory. Were they contributing to an entire generation of morally lost young people by taking them from school and family to spend their days at machines?

"Oh my goodness!" A woman a few seats ahead of Oliver gasped out the words. "That child will be struck if he doesn't get back!"

A murmur wove through the car. People pointed out the windows, alarm on their faces. Oliver pressed his face to the glass. Ahead, the silver rails curved into a bend. Standing in the middle of the tracks, a young boy waved his hands over his head. He jumped up and down, his thick red hair bouncing with the motions.

Oliver gasped, pressing both palms to the glass. Lank! He charged out of his seat just as the brakes squealed and the car skidded on the tracks. The sudden jolt tossed him to the floor. He scrambled up, and using the seat backs to keep himself upright, he staggered for the landing at the front of the car. He leaped from the little platform and hit the ground flatfooted. A shock traveled up his legs. His knees gave way, and he rolled, but he came up running.

"Lank! Lank!"

The boy turned toward Oliver. His face lit, and he dashed toward Oliver with his arms reaching. Sobbing, he plowed against Oliver.

Oliver hugged the boy, elated. Their prayers had been answered. How thrilled Carrie would be to reunite with this red-haired scalawag. "Lank, I'm so glad to find you. Where are Letta and Lesley?"

Lank's skinny shoulders rose and fell in mighty heaves. He grabbed Oliver's hand and tugged on him, his eyes wide. "Cuh-come! Luh-Luh-Lesley—he's huh-hurt! Fuh-foot in a truh-truh-trap!"

Oliver gripped Lank's shoulders, holding him in place. "What kind of trap?"

"Buh-big one." Lank held his hands about eight inches apart. "Juh-juh-jagged!"

Meant to snare something as large as a panther. Oliver had seen the cruel traps on display in stores. The jaws were designed to remain clamped.

"What's goin' on here?" The engineer stomped over, his face twisted into a scowl. He grabbed Lank's arm. "What were you thinkin', boy? You could've been killed, an' you just gave umpteen passengers the scare of their lives."

Lank wriggled free of the man, reaching for Oliver.

The engineer glanced right and left, his expression wary. "What are you doin' out here anyway? You alone?" He aimed his worried scowl at Oliver and lowered his voice. "This kid could be a decoy for train robbers. We'd better get goin'."

"Nuh-no!" Lank danced in place, tears rolling down his face. "I nuh-need help!

Fuh-fuh-for my bruh-brother!"

The engineer stepped away from Lank. "I don't have time for games, boy."

Oliver flung his arm around Lank's shoulders. "I know this boy, and he isn't playing games. If he says his brother is in trouble, then he needs help. Do you have any tools I could borrow?"

The engineer grunted in aggravation. "Sure we got tools, but I'm not lending them out. What if we need them further down the line?"

Oliver grabbed the man's shirt front with both fists. "Mister, this boy's brother has his foot caught in a trap. What could be more important than freeing him?"

The engineer shook loose. "All right, all right. I'll have the brakeman fetch the toolbox." His face turned hard. "But I'm not holdin' the train. I got a schedule to keep." He stormed off.

Oliver crouched down and cupped Lank's shoulders. "Hang on, Lank. We'll go to Lesley in just a minute."

Lank smiled through his tears. "I buh-been prayin' an' prayin' fuh-fuh-for someone to cuh-come. Shuh-sure am gluh-gluh-glad yuh-you're here."

Oliver hugged the boy, his chest expanding with wonder at the miraculous timing that allowed him to be on the very train Lank waved down. "Me, too, Lank. Me, too."

"Here you go, mister." The brakeman approached, a slatted wooden box with a doweled handle dangling from his hand. "Engineer says drop it off at the next station, an' we'll retrieve it on our return trip."

Oliver snatched the box from the man. "Notify the railroad there'll likely be some people needing to catch a ride on the next passing train."

"Will do."

Oliver nudged Lank forward. "All right, Lank, lead the way."

The boy took off at a trot, and Oliver followed, the tools clanking noisily within the box. The brakeman's voice trailed after them. "Good luck!" Oliver waved a hand in reply, but they didn't need luck. They had God.

Gordon

Gordon fidgeted on the bench. Such a luxurious seat—deeply padded and covered in rich velvet. A seat fit for a king. Yet he couldn't get comfortable.

Emerald tassels swung from the heavy draperies framing the window. One brushed his cheek. He shoved the decorative string aside. It came at him again, and with a grunt he tore it loose and tossed it on the floor. The conductor would probably charge him for the damage, but he didn't care. He wasn't in a mood to be trifled with. Not even by a fuzzy green tassel.

Couldn't the train go any faster? Moore was probably already at Dinsmore's place, spilling what he'd seen. A band wrapped itself around Gordon's chest, squeezing tighter and tighter until drawing a breath became agony. Why did Moore and Lang have to stick their noses where they didn't belong? First Bratcher stumbled upon Gordon's secret while trying to collect information about the number of young workers in the factory. When the man died, Gordon had thought his concerns were over. But Bratcher's death had brought another meddler to the factory—Carrie Lang. And she'd dragged Moore into the middle of it.

When he'd disposed of Lang, Moore, and Dinsmore, would somebody else show up to nose around? He didn't want to spend the rest of his life dodging snoopers. And he didn't want to have to keep eliminating people. He still had nightmares about Bratcher's plunge. Thinking of doing away with the two factory workers and his boss—even if it meant saving his own hide—turned his stomach. He'd do it. He had to do it. But no matter how he'd taunted Miss Lang, drawing on the false bravado he'd carried like a shield during his orphanage days, he didn't relish the task.

A regret-filled groan sneaked from his lips, catching him by surprise. He slapped the seat and sat upright, reminding himself of the truth he'd carried from his earliest years. It was him...or them. If he

chose them, he'd lose everything.
Dinsmore wouldn't ignore the fact that
Gordon had stolen from him—not even if
he returned every penny. But he'd
offer the man one chance to save himself. He could choose to believe Gordon
over that troublemaker Ollie Moore. If he
took Moore's word, then Gordon would
dispose of both men. And the factory
would be his even earlier than he'd
anticipated.

Closing his eyes, Gordon settled into
the seat and folded his arms over his tight
chest. He wouldn't turn back now.

Letta

Letta couldn't stop shivering. Even though
she cradled Lesley in her arms, his body
did nothing to warm her against the chilly
water flowing around her hips.

She'd finally sat down in the creek and
pulled him into her lap. Her legs were
numb from the cold, and her clothes were
soaked all the way to her armpits, but she

had it easy compared to her brother.

The trickle of blood worming its way from his foot had stopped, but his leg was bent at an odd angle, the trap preventing him from straightening it. To her relief he'd cried himself out a little while ago. His head now lolled against her shoulder. Her arms ached from supporting his weight, but she hoped he slept for a long, long time. She didn't even care if her backside froze solid and fell off. She'd pulled him into the creek. Pulled him right into the trap. She deserved whatever discomfort she now suffered. Deserved even worse.

She smoothed Lesley's damp, tangled hair, then pressed a kiss on his temple. When Lank got back with help, she'd tell both boys how sorry she was for failing them. She only hoped they'd forgive her. She didn't think she'd ever forgive herself. At least Lesley could depend on Lank. Lank... Hadn't he surprised her?

Where had he learned to fish, to build a fire, to smoke out bees? Much as she hated to admit the truth, there'd been times she'd shrunk away from him, embarrassed by his stammer. When Pa'd called him an imbecile, she'd seethed, but underneath she'd thought the same. Somebody who couldn't even talk couldn't be bright. But she'd been wrong. Dead wrong. Lank was smarter than her and Pa put together.

That's why she knew he'd bring help. She didn't know how, she didn't know who, but she trusted with every bit of herself—Lank wouldn't fail them. Tears burned, and her lower lip quivered. She rested her cheek against Lesley's tousled hair and whispered, "I'm so sorry, Lesley. I didn't take care of you like I was s'posed to. But don't you worry. Help's comin'. It'll be here soon. Hang on."

She glanced again across the horizon, seeking a glimpse of Lank's wild red hair or torn blue jacket. Nothing yet. She tightened her hold on Lesley and wiggled her legs a little bit, trying to put some feeling back in them. "Don't worry," she said again, this time to herself.

"Everything's gonna be fine. Lank's comin'. Lank's comin' soon." **Please, God, send him soon.**

Chapter 43

Caroline

What time was it? Caroline blinked into the dark room. No windows. No band of light creeping beneath the door. Her eyes had adjusted enough to make out the dark shapes of cots, and she heard the tick, tick of a pendulum clock, but it was behind her, and she couldn't twist her head around enough to see it. What difference did it make anyway? She wasn't going anywhere.

She couldn't wiggle her fingers any longer. They ached, so she knew they were there, but they were useless to her. Her dry, aching throat had probably lost its ability to make noise, too. She hadn't tried to scream in quite a while. Why expend her energy fruitlessly? No one would hear her until the first shift Monday morning, when the factory opened again. And even then, the noise of the machines would cover any sound she managed to push past the gag binding her mouth.

From all appearances the situation was hopeless.

As she lay there in the dark room, bound, unable to speak, memories from her childhood crept from the shadows. She snapped her eyes shut, unwilling to relive those unpleasant days, but images rolled one after another behind her closed eyelids.

A dark basement room. A cot stinking of her own vomit. A rope chafing her ankle. Harsh voices. **"Do it again, and this time do it right! If I find one speck of food on another plate, I'll flay the flesh from your back!" "There'll be no sleep for you until you've learned to break those eggs without crushing the shells. You'll be useless as a cook's helper if you can't perform such a simple task."** Stinging slaps, angry scowls, an empty stomach, an aching soul, and always a weariness so heavy she feared it was etched into her bones.

Those years in the Remington household, she'd been hopeless, believing there was no escape. But God had saved her from a childhood of sadness and abuse and had granted her the opportunity to redeem the ugliness for something good. Would He save her from this mess as well? And what of Ollie, traveling to his father's home, unaware of Hightower's evil intentions? She longed to warn him, but she couldn't even lift her arms.

Dear Lord, please intervene. Prevent evil from having the victory. Be the Rescuer we need, Father, please... Please...

She drifted into a restless sleep, her dreams woven with darks and lights—ugly pictures from her early childhood and flashes of warmth from her years with Noble and Annamarie. Faces—Letta, Lank, Lesley, Kesia, Ollie, Hightower—paraded through her dreams, making her either groan or smile in response.

Suddenly all the dream people gathered into a circle, each carrying a pot or a pan and a wooden spoon. No, not the kitchen. Don't make me go to the kitchen... Caroline's heart pounded as they formed a band of sorts, using the spoons to thump and clang.

Thump! Thump! Thump! "Caroline? Caroline, are you here?"

She huddled in the corner, hiding from the strange parade, hands protectively over her head. **No, don't find me. I don't wanna go in the kitchen!**

"Caroline?"

She jolted awake, her pulse beating as hard as the clanking pots in her dream. The voice... Had it come from inside her head?

"Caroline? Where are you?"

Hope ignited. Real! The voice was real! And she recognized the caller—Noble. She tried to cry out in reply, but the gag muffled her voice. She flopped from side to side as Noble continued to call her name. The mattress squawked in protest, but the soft noise wouldn't carry beyond the door. She needed to make a loud noise—quickly, before he moved to another floor or left altogether.

Taking a deep breath, Caroline rolled sideways and hit the floor. Unable to block her fall, she landed on the side of her head and her shoulder, sending a shaft of pain from her neck to her elbow. But she gritted her teeth and ignored the throbbing. She wriggled her way around to the end of the cot. Then, with a prayer for God's strength winging from her heart, she hooked her heels beneath the crossbar and lifted the cot several inches. She let it fall, her ears ringing with the clank of the iron legs against the concrete floor.

She repeated the action—**clank! ker-clank! clank, clank!**—her face angled toward the door and her heart beating with hope. Would he hear? Would he come?

Thudding footsteps. Noble's voice calling, "Caroline? Is that you? Are you in there?"

She clanked the cot's legs against the

floor once more. Then with a final vicious thrust, she hefted the frame onto its side. The movement flipped her onto her belly again, but the cot crashed against the next one, the clatter of iron against iron deafening in the closed room.

The door burst open, and Noble stepped through. Light flowed into the room, attacking her eyes. She snapped them shut against the onslaught. Seconds later she felt Noble's hands on her head.

"Caroline. Oh, Caroline..." The tenderness in his voice matched the gentle removal of her gag. She gulped great drafts of air, her dry throat burning with each intake. Whatever bound her wrists pulled tighter. She gasped as the band cut into her flesh, but then it was yanked away. Her hands went cold, then hot, tingles attacking with such ferocity she bit down on her lip to keep from crying out.

Noble rolled her over and pulled her into a seated position. Bent on one knee before her, he cradled her against his chest. The comforting beat of his heart pounded in her ear. She closed her eyes as his fingers explored her face, her head. Finally she opened her eyes and blinked. The tears of concern and worry swimming in his eyes stung her even worse than the stabbing prickles in her hands and the throbbing in her head.

"I'm sorry I scared you." Only a hoarse whisper emerged. "But I'm so glad you came."

"When you didn't show up at the hotel this afternoon as you'd intended, Annamarie knew something was wrong." He released her and began to untangle the knotted sheet from her ankles. "I told her you'd probably gotten caught up in exploring the elevator and lost track of time. I only came to assuage her fears. I didn't become concerned until I realized the factory was locked up tight and you weren't in your apartment." He tossed the mangled sheet aside and embraced her again. "Did Ollie do this to you?"

"No. Gordon Hightower." She remembered again his sneering promise, and she struggled to her feet. Forcing the words past her parched throat, she grated, "We have to warn Ollie and Fulton Dinsmore!" She tugged at Noble's hand, explaining the two record books and Hightower's intention to eliminate Ollie and Mr. Dinsmore so he couldn't be prosecuted for theft. Noble's eyes widened in shock as he listened. She finished, "I'm still not sure if Bratcher's death was intentional, but I think he discovered Hightower's scheme to steal money from the factory. So if he was murdered, it wasn't because of his stance on child labor."

Noble slipped his arm around her waist and assisted her out the door and across the factory floor. "We can't do anything more for Harmon, God rest his soul, but hopefully we can prevent anyone else from losing his life because of Gordon Hightower's selfishness. We'll make a telephone call to Fulton Dinsmore and then check train schedules. We'll take the first one available to Wichita."

They stepped from the factory into the long shadows of late afternoon. Although the back alley of the factory smelled musty and hinted of rotting vegetables, Caroline drank in the air. The scent of freedom.

She caught Noble's arm and turned a grateful look on him.

"Thank you again for being my rescuer," she whispered. "You're always there when I need you."

Noble chuckled, although his wan skin still held the remembrance of the worry he'd experienced. "Silly girl... Isn't that what a father is for?"

Caroline smiled and nodded. Yes, that was exactly what a Father was for. She'd have to trust that their heavenly Father, who knew all and saw all, would rescue Ollie and Mr. Dinsmore from whatever vile scheme Hightower had planned.

Letta

The sky slowly faded to a purplish pink in the west. The wind had eased, but the air was colder as darkness crept across the landscape. Letta shivered uncontrollably, but she kept her hold on her brother. No matter how long it took for help to come—because it would come!—she wouldn't let Lesley fall.

He moaned in her arms, twisting his face back and forth against her shoulder. "C-c-cold, Letta. An' m-my leg h-h-h-hurts."

"Shh, I know." She rubbed his back. Her hands were so numb she barely felt the scratchy wool of his coat. "Won't be much longer now. Lank'll get here soon."

"S-s-scared..."

Letta was too, but she wouldn't admit it. The longer she sat there staring at the ugly trap, the more worried she became. Whoever had put that thing in the water intended to catch something big. Would the animal come around tonight while she and Lesley were stuck tight? Resolve stiffened her spine. If some big, ferocious critter attacked, it'd have to get past her to get to Lesley. A shudder rattled through her. **Please, God, don't let some big critter come...**

An odd **clank, clank**—sharp yet muffled—reached Letta's ears. She clutched Lesley close and looked right and left. Was it teeth grinding together? Claws banging against the ground? Her heart pounded hard, and her breath came in little puffs of fear.

Lesley pawed at her shoulder with his bluish fingers, his head hanging back. "W-what was that, L-L-Letta?"

"Dunno." She lowered her voice to a rasping whisper. "But hush!"

Lesley pressed his face to her neck and clung hard, soft sobs shaking his shoulders. She tried to hold her breath so she could hear better. The rattle-clank continued in an odd offbeat, growing louder with each passing second. A terror-filled scream built in her throat, and it took every ounce of strength to hold it inside. She squeezed Lesley, crunched her eyes closed, and listened to the ominous rattle-clank draw closer, closer.

And then a voice. "Luh-Letta! I guh-guh-got help! Me an' Mr. MuhMoore—we're cuh-cuh-comin'!"

The scream she'd held back released in a shuddering cry of joy, relief, and long-held fear. She cried against Lesley's hair. "Help's here, Lesley. You're gonna be fine. Help's here."

Gordon

Gordon moved in his typical stealthy gait along the bricked pathway leading to the Dinsmores' stately home. In the gentle glow of oil-fueled street lamps, the house's pale-yellow bricks took on the appearance of blocks of gold. He paused midway up the walk and allowed his gaze to follow the lines of the white fluted columns supporting the milled portico and all the way to the brass finial topping the three-story-high round turret. How would it feel to look out from the highest windows of that turret?

He allowed himself a moment of uncharacteristic whimsy, imagining look-ing down at the less fortunate passing along the street. When the factory became his, he'd be able to buy a house just like this one. Maybe even bigger. He pulled in a deep breath and released it on a sigh. The dream tingled in his fingertips. Soon, very soon, it would all be his.

But first...the necessary business.

Swallowing the gorge that rose from his belly, he pushed himself into motion and strode up the six wide steps leading to the portico. A large brass door knocker in the shape of a gargoyle's face waited in the center of the carved door. Gordon brought the knocker down hard three times, then stepped back, his pulse roaring in his ears.

Within moments he was rewarded by the door swinging wide open, and none other than Fulton Dinsmore himself stood in the light of a brass-and-crystal chandelier. Attired in a rust-colored, silk dressing jacket tied at the waist and brown leather slippers, he appeared relaxed, even regal. He held a pipe—so highly polished it gleamed in the chandelier's glow—in his mouth.

Jealousy wrapped icy tentacles around

Gordon's heart. He wanted this life for himself. He pushed aside the raw emotion and forced a smile. "Mr. Dinsmore, good evening."

Dinsmore's brow furrowed briefly. "Gordon..." He removed the pipe from his mouth and gestured Gordon into the foyer, then with a click shut the door behind them. The aroma of the cherry-scented tobacco was nearly intoxicating in the small space. "I presume you're here to clear up the misunderstanding."

Gordon gave a little jolt of surprise. So the man hadn't believed Moore! Perhaps he would be spared the repugnant task of disposing of the pair after all. Relief wound itself around his conscience. He nodded. "Yes, sir." He glanced through the wide doorway into a beautifully decorated parlor. "Is Moore here?"

"Moore? No." Dinsmore led him into the parlor, where a fire crackled behind the grate, cozy and inviting. "Have a seat. Is Moore coming, too?"

Confused, Gordon sank into one of the chairs facing the ornate fireplace. Had

Carrie Lang lied to him? If Moore wasn't here, where was he? He loosened his dry tongue and spoke calmly. "I thought he might have carried the tale of the... misunderstanding."

Dinsmore settled into the chair opposite Gordon's, a puzzled frown on his face. "No, I haven't seen Moore. However, I had a rather unsettling telephone call late this afternoon from a man named Noble Dempsey, apparently an agent with the Kansas-Nebraska Labor Commission. He claimed you'd"—Dinsmore chuckled— "kidnapped Carrie Lang."

Gordon's jaw dropped in genuine shock. "Wh-what?" Who was Dempsey? How had this unknown man become entangled in Gordon's activities?

Dinsmore nodded. "I was quite surprised myself." He paused and drew a few puffs on his pipe, sending up delicate wisps of richly scented smoke. "Additionally, he accused you of stealing funds from the factory." Dinsmore waved the pipe, a dismissive gesture. "Of course I told him he must be mistaken. Why would you do such a thing? You receive a substantial salary. Besides, I've seen the books. There's no evidence of misallocation of funds."

Gordon relaxed into the wing chair, a slow breath easing from his lungs. "Yes. Yes, he—" He concocted a tale, spewing it as easily as he might recite a grocery list. "He made the same false accusations to me, and Carrie Lang threatened to doctor the books to convince you I'd been involved in wrongdoing. We were right to discharge her. The woman is a trouble-maker. She's likely brought this man Dempsey into her game as a means of hiding her own duplicitous actions."

Dinsmore puffed on his pipe, his brow furrowing. "But for what purpose?"

Gordon leaned forward. "Revenge, of course. From the time she arrived in the factory, she's relentlessly pursued the cause of Bratcher's death, refusing to accept it was an unfortunate accident. Although she's made claims to the contrary, I still think she may be related to the man and seeking retribution for his demise."

He sat back, smug in his ability to fool the man seated before him. "I allowed her the privilege of thoroughly examining the elevator, and she finally admitted the probability of an accidental fall. With her means of filing a wrongful-death suit removed, she likely turned her attention to making false allegations against me and creating turmoil between us in the hope she'd be paid for her silence."

"You may be right." Dinsmore set the pipe in a tray on the table beside his chair and rose. "Regardless, I'm glad you came, as it saved me the trouble of traveling to Sinclair to resolve the confusion. Now..." He smiled, stretching. "It's getting late. Let me show you to a guest room. You can return to Sinclair after a good night's rest."

Gordon rose but moved toward the front door rather than the winding staircase. "Thank you, sir, but now that we've cleared the air between us, I think it best if I go to the train station. I'll take the earliest return to Sinclair." He chuckled, lifting his shoulders in a shrug.

"After all, I have responsibilities at the factory." Namely determining how this Dempsey fellow had discovered what he'd done with Carrie Lang.

Dinsmore smiled broadly and clapped Gordon on the shoulder. "Always dependable—that's what I like best about you, Gordon." His hand closed over Gordon's shoulder, the pressure firm, fatherly. He looked directly into Gordon's face. "Thank you for your dedication to Dinsmore's. I'm glad we had this talk."

Such a fool! But Dinsmore's ignorance was his—and Gordon's—bliss. "Thank you for trusting me, sir. I'm...glad, too." Relief at having been released from the ugly task of disposing of Dinsmore nearly buckled his knees. He eased down the steps, determination stiffening his spine. Dinsmore was spared, but he still needed to silence Moore and Carrie Lang for good.

As his foot met the lowest riser, two men stepped from the shadows near the house and blocked Gordon's pathway. "Gordon Hightower?"

He blinked at them, irritation mingling with apprehension. He resorted to bluster. "That's correct. And I'm in a hurry. I'll thank you to move aside."

One man came forward and took hold of Gordon's arm.

"Here now!" Dinsmore stepped onto the portico, his frown stern aimed at the pair of intruders. "Why are you accosting this man?"

"Police business," the man holding Gordon's arm said. Only then did Gordon notice the silver badge pinned to the chest of the man's dark coat. His mouth went dry.

The second officer caught hold of Gordon's other arm. "Please go inside, Mr. Dinsmore."

Instead, Dinsmore hurried down the steps. "What do you want with Gordon?"

The officers propelled Gordon toward a wagon waiting at the edge of the street. The first one called over his shoulder, "We have a few questions for him concerning accusations leveled by Mr. Noble Dempsey. He has to come with us."

Chapter 44

Caroline

"My dear, you're going to wear out the soles of your shoes if you don't stop your endless pacing."

Caroline paused in her trek across the station floor and sent a sheepish look in Noble's direction. Parading back and forth wouldn't make the minutes pass faster. Yet she couldn't sit. Not until she'd reached Wichita and had seen for herself that both Ollie and his father were fine. After being tied up and threatened by Hightower, she believed him capable of anything.

Noble patted the seat beside him. "Come. Sit."

She checked the round clock suspended on a bracket from the station wall.

Twenty more minutes until their train departed. She supposed she could manage to sit still for that amount of time. With a sigh she lowered herself onto the wooden bench and leaned back.

Noble patted her knee. "Stewing won't help, Caroline. Haven't we prayed and asked for God's protection over your friend Ollie and his father?"

Of course they had. Just as she'd prayed for Letta, Lank, and Lesley to be found. The faith she'd learned from Noble and Annamarie's patient tutelage fought against the fear and doubt nibbling at her heart. She blew out an aggravated breath and sat forward, planting her hands on her knees and holding her spine stiff. "I'd feel better if Mr. Dinsmore hadn't been so...lackadaisical. Why can't he see the truth?"

Noble chuckled, placing his arm around Caroline's shoulders and drawing her against the bench's high back. "He placed his confidence in Gordon Hightower. To believe the apprentice to whom he dedicated such time and trust has tricked him makes him question himself. So he sees what he wants to see."

Caroline frowned at Noble. "He's stubborn and foolish."

Noble's chuckle rumbled again. "He's human. But the police believed us. They'll be on alert, so you needn't worry." He gave her shoulder a light squeeze. "Dear one, in this life we will encounter people like Hightower and Dinsmore, who follow their own pathway instead of the one deigned by God. They spend their entire lives scrabbling for something to satisfy them and always come up empty. Instead of being angry with these men, we should pity them. They're lost. They need our prayers."

Caroline peered at her beloved mentor through a sheen of tears. "I know you're right, Noble. And I want to trust God to work instead of worrying, the way you and Annamarie have taught me. But it's so hard. How do you do it?"

With a gentle smile Noble placed his thick palm over Caroline's fists, which lay tightly balled in her lap. "Very simply,

Caroline, you open your fists"—he peeled her fingers free of their curl and turned her hands palms upward—"and you give the worry over to the One who is capable of carrying it." The warmth of his smile eased a bit of the tension in Caroline's stiff frame. "Jesus tells us in the eleventh chapter of Matthew, verse twenty-eight, 'Come unto me, all ye that labour and are heavy laden, and I will give you rest.' He'll honor the promise, but you must do your part in laying down the burden."

Caroline fell silent, thinking of Noble's kind instruction. Hadn't she been weary since she was a child? She'd fought so hard to overcome the scars inflicted by the labor of her childhood. Thanks to Noble and Annamarie, she'd discovered an element of healing, yet she knew she still clung to some burdens.

Lowering her head, she spoke to the One who beckoned her to trust. **Father, open me completely to You so I might walk free of the weariness plaguing me. Ignite in me a trust so pure and true that nothing can shake it.** Just as

Noble's tender smile had warmed her from within, the Presence of God fell around Caroline like a sweet covering of fresh-scented dew. Her hands relaxed, her fingers opening not only to release her burden but to accept the gift of peace being bestowed from above. A smile formed on her face—a face moistened by the tears slipping from beneath her closed lids and running in warm rivulets down her cheeks. **Thank You, my dear Lord and Savior. You've rescued me again...**

The floorboards beneath her feet vibrated, and a train whistle cut through the air. She opened her eyes and swept the tears from her cheeks, rising with Noble to watch the locomotive approach.

Noble touched her elbow. "It's the Number Sixty-Three, our train." As the engine belched to a shuddering stop at the station, he guided her forward to join a spattering of others who waited to board.

A conductor hopped down from the nearest passenger car and held up both hands to the passengers. "Back off, folks!

Got a medical emergency on board. We need to get these folks to a doctor soon as possible, so move aside and let them pass. Step back, step back."

Mumbling with curiosity the passengers complied. Caroline, in the middle of a small throng, automatically winged up a prayer for the ill person, whoever it was. A man with a child cradled in his arms stepped onto the little platform. Shadows shrouded them, but clearly the child wasn't moving. Two more children followed on the man's heels. The conductor assisted them onto the boardwalk, and the lanterns hanging from the station's porch roof illuminated their faces.

Caroline gasped and grabbed Noble's arm. "It's Ollie! And he's got Lesley!"

Oliver

Oliver kept his arms snug around Letta and Lank. Lank drowsed against his shoulder, but Letta remained alert, her body stiff and her gaze aimed at the door behind which a doctor tended Lesley's wounds. He fought a shudder, recalling the vicious tears in the boy's flesh. He'd caused more pain as he'd cut the trap loose from its chain and then released its catch. Lesley's tormented cries still rang in his ears. How he prayed the doctor would be able to save Lesley's leg.

At the end of the hallway, Carrie and her friends, Noble and Annamarie Dempsey, talked with the hospital bookkeeper, presumedly arranging for payment. He released a disgusted sigh. Money... Everyone wanted their money. Hospital administrators, Gordon Hightower, even Father. Oliver didn't begrudge the hospital being paid for its services or Hightower being compensated for his labor, but he wished dollars and cents didn't carry more importance than people. In the past few days, he'd witnessed too much harm committed in the pursuit of money. **Lord, don't ever let me fall in that trap...**

Carrie and the Dempseys moved up the hallway as the door opened, and the doctor stepped out. Oliver gently shifted Lank to the bench and rose to meet him.

Letta rushed at the man, wringing her hands beneath her chin. "How's my brother? Is he gonna be all right?"

The doctor offered a kind look and put his hand on Letta's shoulder. "He suffered some deep cuts—through the muscle tissue all the way to the bone, which was snapped. I've stitched him up as best I can and set his leg. He'll wear some nasty scars for the rest of his life, but I'm confident the leg will heal and he'll be back to running and jumping in, oh, perhaps three months' time. Keeping him as still as you did and in the cold water was the right thing to do, young lady."

Tears welled in Letta's eyes. She lowered her head. "I didn't do right, mister. I took my brothers away to keep 'em safe, but I let Lesley get hurt. He wouldn't've stepped in that trap at all if it wasn't for me."

Oliver stepped forward and curled his hand lightly around Letta's neck. "Don't blame yourself, Letta. This was an accident. No one's to blame."

The doctor nodded. "Listen to Mr. Moore." He turned to Oliver and lowered his voice. "I'm thankful you came along when you did. Much longer, and Lesley might have gone into shock. He's a very lucky boy."

Letta sniffled. "Can I go see him now?"

"Yes, he's asking for you. Just don't bump his leg or let him wiggle around too much." The doctor laughed lightly, giving Oliver a knowing look. "Keeping that one down may prove to be a challenge."

Carrie moved up beside Oliver. "We'll meet the challenge, doctor. Don't worry. Thank you for seeing to him."

The doctor strode up the hallway, and Letta dashed through the door. Both Noble and Annamarie followed her into the room. Oliver started to go in after them, but Carrie held out her hand and stopped him.

"Ollie, can we talk?"

Her serious tone and somber expression raised a prickle of trepidation, but he nodded and guided her to the bench where Lank was curled in a ball, snoring. She sat and lifted the boy's head onto her lap, opening a few inches of space for Oliver. He wriggled in between her and the armrest. The fit was tight, but he didn't mind. He rested his arm across the back of the bench, enjoying the feel of her soft form pressed against his side.

She lifted her face to him, and tears twinkled in the corners of her eyes. "I'm so grateful you're all right. When Gordon Hightower threatened to harm you and your father, I feared—"

Oliver jolted. "Wait... What?"

Her eyes widened. "Weren't you there when the police arrested him?"

"Wasn't I where?" Oliver shook his head in confusion. "Carrie, you aren't making sense. I was on the train to Wichita when Lank jumped on the tracks and forced the engineer to stop. I left the train to help Lesley. Then we flagged down another train and rode back to Sinclair. I never made it to Wichita, and I never saw Hightower. When did you see him?"

Carrie's mouth dropped open, and she

raised a trembling hand to cover her lips. Sobs—soft yet harsh—shook her shoulders. Oliver dropped his arm around her and let the weeping run its course. Then in broken words she told him about Hightower tying her up inside the factory and threatening to harm her, him, and his father to prevent them from exposing his thievery.

Oliver listened in amazement, his heart beating in fear. His legs felt weak, but he started to rise. "I have to warn Father."

"Ollie, it isn't necessary." Carrie smiled. "Noble called the police in Wichita. They sent two officers to your home, who took Hightower into custody when they found him in the yard. He hadn't hurt your father. All is well."

Oliver collapsed against the bench, so relieved he felt weightless.

Lank stirred, and Carrie stroked his tangled hair until he drifted off again. She gazed down at his peaceful face, and a smile played at the corners of her lips. "Ollie, do you realize Lank may have saved your life?"

Oliver pinched his brows. "How?"

"By stopping the train, he kept you from reaching Wichita, where Hightower planned to ambush you and your father. If you had made it and had convinced your father of Hightower's wrongdoings, both of you might be..." She stopped, as if unable to form the words.

Oliver's skin went cold. "I knew Hightower was a bully, but I hadn't suspected the extent to which he'd go." He searched her sweet face, noticing for the first time a purplish mark on her forehead, nearly hidden by the curling mass of her bangs. Anger rolled through him. He brushed the bruise with his fingertips. "Did Hightower do that to you?"

"I bumped my head on the floor when I knocked over the cot, trying to alert Noble to my presence. Oh..." A sheepish look crept across her face. "Noble broke a window to get in. We'll replace the glass."

"I'll take care of the damage myself." He leaned forward and placed a kiss on the purple mark. "A window is a small price to pay for your rescue."

A pleasant flutter winged through her chest at his tender gesture. She quickly shifted her attention back to Lank. "I can hardly believe Lank is the one who stopped the train. I wouldn't have thought him capable of being so bold."

Oliver smiled down at the exhausted boy and chuckled softly. "Apparently Lank has discovered many abilities in the past few days. According to Letta, he single-handedly kept them stocked with fish, built fires, and even snared a prairie chicken. Of course, the children couldn't find the courage to kill the poor bird, so they just let it go, but even so...he caught it."

Carrie lifted her startled gaze to him. "Lank did all that?"

Oliver nodded, recalling the pride glowing on the boy's face as he'd shared their adventures. "Apparently our Lank here has been a keen observer and learned a great deal by watching others. And now that he's found the courage to speak, hopefully people will begin to recognize just how intelligent he really is."

Oliver put his hand on Lank's hair. "He's a special boy. And he deserves a bright future."

Eyes wide, mouth open slightly in astonishment, Carrie glanced quickly at Lank and back at Oliver. "Lank...is speaking?"

Oliver couldn't stop a laugh. "You should have heard him convincing me to help Lesley. And then on the train, coming here, he never stopped talking. Oh, yes, he is speaking."

"But...but his stammer...?"

"He still stammers. Chances are, he always will. But he doesn't seem to be bothered by it as much now. Maybe those days alone on the prairie, with his brother and sister depending on him, helped him set aside his worry about being called a dummy. He knows he isn't one, so"— Oliver shrugged again— "he's discovering the courage to overcome his fear."

Carrie finally shook her head, looking down at Lank with an expression of tenderness. "Lank is very brave. Much braver than I am..."

Oliver started to question her strange statement, but the door to Lesley's room opened. Noble, Annamarie, and Letta stepped into the hallway, the adults flanking the girl.

Noble crossed to the bench. "Lesley is sound asleep, and an orderly assures us he'll stay with him. We're going to take Letta and Lank to our hotel and let them sleep as late as they like. You two should do the same."

As much as he wanted to continue their conversation, Oliver glimpsed the dark circles under Carrie's eyes. She'd had a harrowing day and needed rest. "That's a good idea, Carrie."

She gently shook Lank to wakefulness and helped him stand. The boy swayed a bit, and Carrie put her arm around him. But even while supporting Lank, she kept her gaze on Oliver. "You need your rest, too. Are you going to your apartment?"

"Yes. But I'm going to walk you to your boarding hotel first."

To his delight she didn't argue. Outside the hospital, waiting for a coach to transport Noble, Annamarie, and the children to the hotel, Carrie suggested, "Shall we meet for supper tomorrow evening at Kesia's? She'll be happy to see Letta and Lank since she's prayed so hard for them to come home. And"—her gaze drifted to Lank, who leaned sleepily on Letta's shoulder—"we have some decisions to make concerning where the children will go next."

Letta sighed. "Well, I ain't gonna run off with the boys again. Seein' Lesley get hurt like he did pretty much cured me of goin' off on our own."

"I'm very happy to hear that." Carrie smiled warmly at the girl, and Oliver was struck again by her kindness. She could have scolded—she had every right, considering the fright they'd all suffered, wondering where the children had gone—but she chose to forgive. How he admired her tender spirit.

The coach arrived, and Annamarie turned to Carrie and Oliver. "Are you sure you don't want a ride?"

Oliver deferred to Carrie. If she chose to

ride, he'd be disappointed, but he wouldn't blame her. He knew she was exhausted. His heart skipped a beat when she thanked Annamarie but declined the offer. After hugging both Noble and Annamarie, Carrie placed a kiss on Letta's then Lank's cheek and bade them good-bye.

The horses clopped away, and Oliver offered his elbow. With a smile Carrie slipped her hand through the bend of his arm, and they set off, their matching strides carrying them down lamp-lit boardwalks. The night was quiet, the city asleep beneath a blanket of stars. The clouds had finally cleared, giving them a glimpse of the heavens above. Although hesitant to disrupt the peacefulness, Oliver cleared his throat and raised a question. "Am I invited to supper at Kesia's, too?"

She wrinkled her nose at him. "Of course. You're the children's rescuer. Why wouldn't we include you in a welcome-home supper?"

"Good, because I want in on the discussion of where the children should go. And it isn't to their grouchy aunt."

Her laughter trickled out, making him smile. "I couldn't agree more about the aunt." Then she turned serious, releasing a soft sigh. "If I had a house, I'd take them myself. But I'm not sure it would be in their best interest. I'm gone so much with my job. They need better supervision than I could give." She aimed a curious gaze at him. "What are your thoughts?"

Oliver shook his head, grinning at her. "Oh no. Not tonight. Not as tired as we are. This conversation needs to take place when we're all well rested and our stomachs are aching from Kesia's good cooking. We'll discuss my idea tomorrow."

She affected a pout, but he only laughed at her, and a smile chased the pucker away. He deposited her safely inside her foyer and raised her hand to his lips to deliver a lingering kiss on her middle knuckle. Her eyes widened, but she didn't pull away. He said very softly, "Good night, Carrie. Sweet dreams."

She hugged her hand to her breast. "I...

I will."

He left smiling. But as he strode away through the night, his smile faltered. He knew Carrie's stance on child labor. She'd fight him. He might very well destroy the sweet friendship they'd developed as well as any hope for something more. But the Holcomb children needed a way to provide for themselves. He'd plead his case, and he prayed she'd be sensible enough to listen.

Chapter 45

Caroline

"Kesia, this is the best catfish I've ever eaten." Caroline forked up another bite of the flaky white fillet coated with cornmeal crumbs.

"That's only 'cause you haven't tried Lank's catfish," Letta claimed, beaming at Caroline from her stool at the end of the counter. Beside her, Lank blushed crimson. She nudged him with her elbow and added, "You gonna teach Miz Kesia how to cook catfish, Lank?"

Lank hunched his shoulders and grinned. Crumbs clung to his chin, and he batted them away before answering. "Guh-guess I cuh-could teach her if she's guh-guh-got a mind to learn."

The adults laughed, Caroline included. How marvelous to hear Lank speaking with such freedom! And how marvelous to be able to laugh rather than cringe when someone mentioned cooking. Might God be bringing her a deeper healing from her past?

Kesia reached over the counter to bop Lank lightly on the top of the head. "Don'tcha be setting up a café an' givin' me competition now, young man, you hear?"

Lank giggled. "Duh-don't worry, Muh-Miz Kesia. I'd rather cuh-cuhcatch 'em than cuh-cook 'em."

She winked. "Then we'll just hafta go into partnership, hmm?"

Lank nodded and turned his attention back to his plate.

Caroline popped her last bite of catfish into her mouth and pushed her plate aside. Noble and Annamarie had already finished, but Ollie still had several hush puppies. Propping her chin on her hand, she observed him finishing his meal while chatting with Lank and Letta, at ease in their midst. Knowing his background, she marveled at his ability to fit so comfortably with common folk. He'd make an excellent leader for the factory's workers.

She had so many reasons to celebrate. The children were back, and Lesley would recover from his injuries. Hightower's plan had been squashed, and he now sat in a jail cell in Wichita. Noble was pleased with her report about Harmon Bratcher, especially since Hightower had grudgingly admitted leaving the elevator gate open in his haste, thereby creating a danger into which Bratcher unknowingly walked.

Yet sadness tried to weave itself into her soul. Her time in Sinclair neared its end. Once the children were settled somewhere, she, Noble, and Annamarie would return to their home in Lincoln. She'd likely never see Ollie, Kesia, or the children again. She touched the spot on her hand where Ollie had pressed his lips last night, and the emotions that had burst through her chest at the tender gesture attacked again. **My heavenly**

Father, I don't want to tell these dear people good-bye... Tears stung, and she lowered her head lest someone see and ask the reason for them.

"Caroline?"

At Noble's soft query Caroline sniffed hard and raised her face. "Yes?" He gestured to the table Kesia and Ollie had dragged out for their use.

"Let's gather over here and let the children enjoy their dessert while we visit." She'd fallen asleep last night praying for God to help them make the best decisions for the children's placement, and she sent up another quick petition. Pave the way, Father. She followed Noble and Annamarie to the round table, aware of Ollie close behind her. He held her chair for her, and she offered a quavery smile in appreciation.

Noble, ever the advocate for needy youngsters, took control. "I believe we all agree the children's aunt is not an ideal caretaker for them. However, according to the laws of the state, as their only living relative—"

Caroline opened her mouth to protest, but Noble held up his hand, silencing her.

"...she has to make the choice not to assume the responsibility. I took it upon myself to send her a wire early this morning, informing her of the children's situation. I received a reply midafternoon, and just as I suspected, she has no desire to bring them to her home, given Lesley's injury."

Caroline sighed with relief, and Noble squeezed her hand in understanding.

"But that does leave us with a dilemma." Noble linked his hands on the edge of the table. "If Letta were the only one, Annamarie and I would consider taking her in."

Tears appeared in Annamarie's eyes as she gazed across the floor at Letta and Lank. "I've fallen in love with all three of them. But at our ages, and with my failing health, we simply aren't capable of assuming responsibility for two young, active boys."

Noble offered his wife a handkerchief and then continued softly. "The children must have supervision. I realize residing in an orphanage isn't the same as being with a family, but I inquired about space at the children's home in Wichita. They said they could accommodate all three children—the boys in the boys' home, and Letta in the home for young women. But I wanted to confer with you, Caroline, and with Mr. Moore—or should I begin calling you Mr. Dinsmore?"

A crooked smile tipped Ollie's lips. "Just call me Oliver."

Oliver... Caroline swallowed a smile. He'd always be Ollie to her. "Oliver, then." Noble gave a brief nod. "You've both been involved with the children, so I wanted you to share your thoughts before final decisions are made." Caroline hung her head. Despite her prayers God hadn't whispered in her ear. She sent a sad look across the table. "I honestly don't know what's best, Noble. As I told Ollie last night, if I had a different position, if I could be available to them, I'd take them in myself."

Kesia scuttled over with a pot of coffee

and several mugs. She clanked the mugs onto the table while saucily arching one brow at Caroline. "An' they'd starve with you, who refuses even to learn to boil water for an egg."

Caroline gathered her courage and placed her hand over Kesia's wrist. "I was wrong to refuse your kind offers, Kesia." The older woman's jaw dropped. Caroline looked at Annamarie. "And yours, too. I hope you'll forgive me for my stubbornness. God and I had to remove the final vestiges of a burden before I could make myself place a pan on a stove again. But"—she drew in a deep breath, savoring the sense of heaviness falling away—"I'm ready now."

Annamarie held her hands high, a smile breaking across her face. "Thank the Lord!"

Caroline grinned, but then she sobered. "Since I can't provide for Letta, Lank, and Lesley, perhaps Noble should make the arrangements to have them taken to Wichita."

"Now just hold up there." Ollie leaned

in, his brow furrowed in a scowl. "I haven't had my say yet."

Kesia plunked a fist on her hip. "An' just what's your say, Ollie?"

"I say...let Letta and Lank earn a wage that will allow them to stay right here in Sinclair, where they've always lived, and that will meet their need for food, clothing, and shelter." He raised his chin and shot Caroline a challenging look. "Let me put them on the employee roster at the chocolate factory."

Fury fired through Caroline's chest. She leaped up and glowered at Ollie. "Absolutely not! Those children will attend school!"

Ollie rose, too, holding his hand out to her. "If you'd let me finish—"

She pushed his hand aside, so angry her entire body trembled. How could he suggest such a thing after she'd shared her own childhood hardships with him? How could a man who so tenderly kissed her hand be hardhearted enough to subject Letta and Lank to a childhood of labor? She whirled on Noble. "Noble, call the children's home. I'll take them there myself."

"Carrie..." Ollie's voice, full of gentle concern, tempered her rage. "Let me finish, please? Then if you still want to take the children to Wichita, I won't stop you. I'll let you do what you deem best."

She stared into his face for several seconds while a battle took place within her heart. Slowly, deliberately, she unballed her fists and laid her concerns at the feet of her Rescuer. With a slow nod she slipped back into her chair.

Ollie sat, too, and folded his hands on the table. His pose reminded her so much of Noble she almost smiled. He cleared his throat. "As you already know, Carrie, my father has long chosen to employ younger workers with the intention of instilling skills that will benefit them throughout adulthood. I've always agreed with his reasoning. We're both far too aware there are parents who will send their children to work—whether for selfish reasons, such as your parents did, Carrie, or simply for the extra income the family needs to survive. Either way, we can't change the fact that children will be entering workplaces."

Caroline huffed. "You make it sound so hopeless! Harmon Bratcher's voice has been silenced, but others have taken up the cause to end child labor. Eventually the laws will be changed."

Ollie nodded, completely calm in the face of her vexed complaint. "Eventually, yes, but in the meantime how do we best meet the educational needs of children who are in a factory or other workplace instead of a classroom?"

An impish smile grew on Noble's face. He tipped his head toward Ollie. "You have an answer for the question, don't you?"

Ollie pulled in a breath, his expression turning wary. "Well, sir, I believe I might. But I'd like your opinion on its feasibility." He rested his elbows on the table and leaned in. Kesia, still holding the coffeepot in her hand, pressed in between Caroline and Noble. Ollie went on. "Last night after I dropped Carrie at her boarding hotel, I started thinking about how Lank and Lesley spent a few nights in the factory's infirmary. The infirmary is rarely used, because when people are ill, they go home. So the room sits there, empty. I started thinking..."

Kesia leaned in even closer, nearly squashing Caroline's ribs against the table edge. "What? What?"

Ollie angled his face toward Caroline, a hint of pleading in his eyes. "What if we were to use the infirmary as a classroom? Anyone under the age of sixteen who works at Dinsmore's would be required to spend half of his or her shift in school."

Caroline gasped, hardly able to believe what she'd heard.

"I'm certainly not opposed to your plan," Noble said before Caroline could speak, "but don't you think parents will choose to send their children elsewhere if they're only drawing half wages?"

Ollie shook his head. "You don't understand. They'd be paid a full wage, but part of their job would be to"—he looked at Caroline again—"learn."

She stared at him in amazement. How she'd misjudged him. Shame flooded her, and she touched his arm. "Ollie, that's a marvelous idea. Earning a wage, learning a skill, and gaining an education." She frowned. "But can the factory absorb the cost? You have a significant number of young workers employed. If they change to half-time work, you'll have to hire more workers to replace them, which means paying more wages. And do you intend to hire a full-time teacher?"

Ollie shrugged, a grin giving him a boyish appearance she found irresistible. "Well, I won't be paying Hightower's ridiculously extravagant salary anymore. And the factory's done very well." He lost the teasing look and put his hand over hers. "It's time I honor my father's example of philanthropy and give back a portion of what we receive. Providing an education to youngsters who might not otherwise receive one seems a good start."

Annamarie patted her palms together, her smile bright. "Oliver, I think it's a fine idea. And who knows? Perhaps other factory owners will learn of your on-site classroom and choose to emulate the idea. You might start a trend to benefit future generations."

Ollie chuckled and ducked his head in apparent embarrassment. "I don't know about future generations, ma'am. I just asked God to find a way to help Letta, Lank, and Lesley. If anything else comes of it, it will be His doing—not mine." His fingers closed on Caroline's, sending warmth all the way through her.

Kesia smacked the coffeepot onto the table. "Well, this is all fine an' good for keepin' those youngsters out of mischief durin' the day, but what about at night? Who's gonna make 'em do their homework, tuck 'em into bed, an' listen to 'em recite their nighttime prayers?"

Caroline had gotten so caught up in Ollie's plans for a schoolroom within the factory, she'd forgotten that the children still needed a home. She gave Ollie a helpless look, which he returned. Noble and Annamarie also sat in silence, exchanging looks of worry.

Kesia let loose with a joyous chortle. "I'll tell you who's gonna." She jabbed her thumb against the ruffled front of her apron. "I am."

Caroline's jaw dropped open, and Ollie squawked, "You?"

Kesia scowled. "Well, of course me. An' why not? I missed them red-haired scalawags like nobody's business the whole time they was gone. I kept prayin' and prayin' for God to bring 'em back to me. An' He did, so why shouldn't I plan on keepin' 'em? Besides"—a girlish giggle spilled out—"I can use their help takin' care o' that batch o' kittens livin' on my back stoop. Seven of 'em, for gracious sakes!"

Caroline curled her hand over Kesia's arm and spoke gently. "It's a fine thing you want to do, Kesia, but you don't have room for seven small kittens, let alone three active children. Why, there's barely space for your little cot and a rocking chair in the living portion of your café."

Kesia shook her head, releasing a huff.

"Well, silly girl, I'm not gonna keep 'em here. We'd have to stack up like cordwood at night. Their papa left 'em a little house, didn't he? My café can be an eatin' place from now on, and for the first time since my dear husband went to glory, I'll have a real house an' a family again. An' maybe when Letta's a little older, she'll want to work alongside me here." Tears filled her eyes. She curled her hand over Caroline's shoulder. "Lemme have 'em, Miss Carrie. Don't haul 'em off to some orphanage where they won't get the love an' attention they need. I'll take good care of 'em. You can count on me."

Caroline rose and hugged the woman, her heart overflowing. Although she supposed she should seek Noble's counsel first, she said, "You have my blessing, Kesia. I couldn't have chosen a better mother for them."

Kesia's sturdy arms tightened, and she sniffed loudly in Caroline's ear. Then she pulled back and shook a finger under Caroline's nose. "But that don't mean I'm lettin' you off in learnin' how to cook. Even if you aren't gonna be cookin' for those rascals, you need to be seein' to your own dinners. So first thing tomorrow mornin', we'll start your cookin' lessons."

Sorrow descended like an anvil on Caroline's chest. She swallowed tears and clutched Kesia's warm hands. "But my job in Sinclair is done now, Kesia. I'll be...leaving."

The sound of a clearing throat reached her ears. She turned slowly to find Ollie pinning her with a fervent look.

"Carrie, about your leaving..." He tipped his head, the little tweed cap angling over one ear. "I'd like to talk to you about that."

Chapter 46

Caroline

Caroline walked the periphery of the infirmary-turned-classroom, notepad and pen in hand. Twenty-eight heads bent over arithmetic papers, industriously adding and subtracting. Over the past two months, word had spread about the full-time wage for part-time work and part-time schooling, and Ollie's list of hopeful hires was longer than they could accommodate. As Caroline observed the fortunate ones who filled the desks, she sent up a prayer for those waiting to find the means to be satisfied, both financially and educationally. There were so many needs...

Her inspection complete, Caroline

waved to the teacher. Mr. Voegel, a retired schoolmaster whose love for learning trickled onto every student who crossed the infirmary's threshold, nodded in reply, and she headed across the factory floor toward the loft for her end-of-the-week meeting with Ollie.

As always, when preparing for a few moments of time with him, her heart began its dance of eagerness. Although she'd managed to maintain a professional front in keeping with her position of employee to boss, she'd never been able to squelch the joyous reaction she felt. She loved him. Foolish? Yes. Even pointless, given their current status as employer and employee. Still, with everything she had, she loved him. For his strength, his kindness, his well-founded sense of right and wrong, and—admittedly—his pleasing appearance. No man possessed greater attractiveness than Oliver Fulton Dinsmore attired in a three-piece suit. Although she did miss the rakish cap and striped suspenders from time to time.

She tapped lightly on his door, and his familiar voice called, "Come in, Carrie!" Smiling, she stepped through, leaving the door open behind her.

"How did you know it was me?"

He looked up from an open ledger. His pale eyes crinkled with amusement. "For one, you're always timely. We set our meeting for three-fifteen, and it is now precisely fifteen minutes past three."

She glanced at the lovely pendulum clock hanging between two landscape paintings and confirmed his statement.

"For another, I would never mistake your delicate yet determined rap on my door. The sound is as distinct as the delightful curl in your hair."

Caroline slowly lowered herself onto one of the spindle-backed chairs facing his desk. Her pulse stuttered. During her three months as Dinsmore's environmental safety manager—a position he'd developed to make the best use of her investigative skills—he'd never stepped beyond the bounds of professionalism. But commenting on her hair, which she likened to rusty corkscrews, could hardly be considered businesslike. She didn't know how to respond, so she toyed with one loose curl and sat in silence beneath his smile.

He set aside the ledger and folded his hands on the desk top. "I'm ready for your report. Any concerns to discuss?"

His change in demeanor from teasing to practical put her at ease, and she shared the notes she'd gathered since their last meeting. After discussing the possibility of replacing the current rolling carts with mechanized conveyor belts, Ollie sat back in his chair and rested his linked hands on the taut front of his vest.

"You've done well, Carrie. I'm very pleased with the suggestions for improvement."

Warmed by his praise, she ducked her head. "Thank you."

"Have you been as successful with Kesia?"

She lifted her face, startled. "Pardon me?"

His lips quirked into a grin. "The cooking

lessons."

"Oh!" A giggle rose in her throat. She'd changed apartments, moving into one equipped with a small kitchen so she could practice in her own home rather than at the café, lest her concoctions frighten away Kesia's customers. Some of her attempts had proved more successful than others. She admitted, "My biscuits are still as hard as rocks, but she pronounced my dumplings delectable."

"Are you baking biscuits or making dumplings for your supper tonight?"

Where was this leading? She answered slowly, choosing her words with care. "I intend to purchase a trout on my way home and fry it in cornmeal batter."

His eyebrows rose. "I'm quite fond of trout."

"Would you like to join me?" Why had she asked him to dinner? Forward! Foolhardy! And dangerous. She still hadn't mastered the art of frying. The trout might turn out as dry and stiff as old boot leather. Please let him decline!

"I would like nothing better." He rounded the desk, took her elbow, and escorted her to the door. "Six-thirty?"

Something in his gaze stole her ability to form words. Mute, she bobbed her head in agreement.

"Wonderful! I'll be there. And I'll bring a bottle of apple cider." He winked. "Unfermented, of course."

She scurried off before she embarrassed herself with another uncontrolled giggle.

Just as Caroline removed the frying pan from the stove, a **tap! tap, tap, tap** followed by a softer **tap, tap** came from the door. Nervously wiping her hands on the full apron covering her dress, she scurried around the tiny table filling the center of her kitchen area and twisted the doorknob. Her gaze collided with Ollie's, who stood in the hallway with a jug in one hand and the most bedraggled-looking cluster of flowers she'd ever seen in the other. She clapped her hand over her mouth to keep from laughing.

"That's not very polite," he said, his brow crunched into a mock scowl. "It's December. This is the best I could do."

She took the dried, drooping mess. Two leaves broke loose and fell to the floor. She stifled another giggle. "Thank you. I think." She tipped her head and examined the brown stems. "Where did you get these things?"

"From a long-forgotten vase in the corner of the lobby downstairs."

"Hi, Carrie!"

The second voice startled her so badly she squished the dried stems in her hand, severing three of them. A freckle-faced boy wearing Ollie's old tweed cap and beaming a gap-toothed smile swung the tip of a wooden crutch over the threshold and came in.

Caroline gasped, "Lesley!"

Ollie shrugged sheepishly. "He's my chaperone. Is it all right?"

"Of course it is!" She leaned down and hugged the little boy. She saw Letta daily at the factory, where she took part in the new half-work, half-school program, but both Lank and Lesley attended the city school during the day, preventing her from having much time with them. Her worries about being alone with Ollie faded in light of Lesley's cheerful presence. She straightened and gestured to Ollie. "Well, come on in and join Lesley and me."

He stepped through the doorway, removing his top hat as he came. She gazed at his neatly cropped hair, her fingers itching to smooth a few tousled strands into place. Realizing where her thoughts had drifted, she motioned toward the table. "Dinner's ready. Have a seat, and I'll serve the trout."

She'd set the table for two. Lesley leaned his crutch on the wall and plopped into one chair. Caroline stood for a moment, flustered, but then Ollie went to the corner, pulled out the crate she used to store canned goods, and perched on it. She offered him a grateful smile, then quickly collected another plate and some silverware from her small cupboard and clanked them on the table before bustling over for a platter and wooden spoon to dish up the trout. Her hands shook so uncontrollably she broke the fillet into pieces. A nervous laugh tittered out. "I'll be just a minute."

Ollie rose and lifted the jug. "May I pour the cider?" His calm, steady presence juxtaposed with her flightiness made her feel addlepated. Tears threatened. Ollie said, "Carrie?"

She turned slowly. She glanced at Lesley, who gazed up at her in curiosity, then turned to Ollie. "I'm sorry I'm being such a ninny. I haven't cooked for anyone before. Not ever. And I'm terribly afraid it will taste awful. Or even make you sick."

Ollie placed the jug on the table. She stood frozen in place as he moved slowly toward her. He stopped within arm's reach and smiled—a sweet smile as tender as a caress. "Then maybe I should take your mind off supper for a few minutes. Give you a chance to collect yourself. Hmm?"

"Y-yes. Perhaps."

"Very well. Let me tell you my purpose

in coming here this evening." Her mouth felt dry. She wished she could take a sip of the cider.

"I wanted to tell you you've done an exemplary job at the factory."

She forced a weak smile. "Thank you."

"As difficult as it was for you to leave the bureau, I believe you've enjoyed the opportunities your new position has afforded you."

He was right. She loved seeing the young people blossom as they gained knowledge, and she held no regrets about trading her investigator job for the one at the factory.

"I feel as though we've become a team, working together to improve the conditions for the workers."

She felt the same way. She offered a nod.

"I can't imagine losing you as a partner."

She lowered her head, longing sweeping through her. Hadn't she told God if her purpose in crossing paths with Ollie was to help him establish a relationship with his Father, it was enough? But hadn't she also admitted a desire for more? That desire now created an ache in the center of her breast. How much longer would she be able to continue working for him, serving as a manager in his factory, when their employee-to-employer relationship wasn't enough? "Ollie, I—"

"You're fired."

She jerked her gaze to meet his. "Wh-what?"

Ollie squared his shoulders. "That's right. Your job at the factory is finished, so...you're fired."

"Ollie!" She stamped her foot. Only Lesley's presence prevented her from planting her heel on his toes. "You just said you couldn't imagine losing me as a partner! But now you're letting me go?"

"As the environmental safety manager, yes. But"—he stepped forward and captured her in his arms—"I have another position I'd like you to fill."

Stiff within the circle of his arms, she gave a derisive humph. "And what is that?"

"My wife."

Her eyes flew wide open. Her muscles wilted. She eased into his embrace. "Your...your wife?"

"That is, if you'll have me." He drew her even closer, the pressure of his strong hands on her spine sending tingles of awareness to her scalp. "I know we don't always see eye to eye, Carrie, but I love you. My happiest moments have been with you. I want you by my side from now until our final breaths. Will you marry me?"

She drew in a slow breath, savoring the sweet moment of acceptance. He loved her. He wanted her in his life. His proclamations were a gift beyond description. Her hands curved over his shoulders, and her lips parted, eager to accept his proposal.

But he stepped away, lifting one finger. "One moment, please." Under Caroline's and Lesley's puzzled gazes, he stepped to the platter holding the broken chunks of fried trout. Realizing what he was about to do, Caroline held her breath. He pinched a piece and poked it into his mouth, chewed thoughtfully, and swallowed.

He turned to her with a satisfied smile on his face. "Now that I've determined I won't starve, feel free to answer."

Caroline's breath released on a note of laughter. Lesley covered his mouth and giggled. Caroline winked at the boy, then moved toward Ollie, shaking her head. He opened his arms, his eyes shining with love and mischief. Life with Ollie would certainly never be dull. "Yes, Ollie. My answer is yes."

He let out a whoop and scooped her from the floor. She clung to his neck, her laughter spilling as freely as the happy tears coursing down her face.

He lowered her until her soles met the floor. His hands cupped her cheeks and tilted her face to him, and then his lips descended in a kiss salty from the trout. She licked her lips and murmured, "Mm, I am a good cook."

And Ollie's laughter filled the room.

Dear Reader,

Thank you for taking this fictitious journey with Carrie, Ollie, and the other residents of Sinclair, Kansas. Although this story is a product of my active imagination, some elements of truth are hidden amid the pages.

During the Industrial Age, many children were sent to work to help support their families. The workday was long, and jobs were often unsafe and unhealthy for young workers. By 1900 more than 10 percent of Kansas children between the ages of ten and fifteen were employed in agriculture, manufacturing, and domestic service. Kansas law required that all children between the ages of eight and fourteen had to go to school for at least twelve weeks a year, but often work prevented children from attending school.

Investigators, sent by the Bureau of Labor, either openly or secretly collected data concerning safety practices within different industries. These investigators were rarely welcomed since employers found it financially beneficial to keep children, who earned lower wages than adults, on their employment rosters.

Thanks to the diligence of some of these investigators as well as other citizens who believed children needed to obtain an education, changes came. In 1905, Kansas passed a law that prohibited children under the age of fourteen from working in factories, meat-packing houses, or mines. This law affected nearly two thousand Kansas children, who were released from employment to attend school. Not until 1917 were national child labor laws passed.

Ollie's school in Dinsmore's World-Famous Chocolates Factory wasn't far from the truth. On-site training for workers was once common. In the early and mid-1900s, factories offered a variety of apprenticeships and training programs targeting students as young as fourteen. In some factories, in addition to learning the skills necessary for specific jobs within the factory, attendees also learned to read, write, and perform basic math skills to help them to be more effective workers. Of course, this learning also benefited the students outside of the factory.

Child labor laws and the types of jobs available to young people have changed, but one very important thing remains the same—each person's need for fulfillment. Just as Ollie admitted to possessing an empty place in the center of his soul that nothing of the world seemed to satisfy, we all carry a deep need for a Savior. If you haven't yet discovered the joy and eternal fulfillment a relationship with God through Jesus Christ can bring, I pray you'll reach out for the Savior's hand. He's already reaching for you. When you take hold, you'll discover a peace beyond description, and every longing will be filled.

May God bless you muchly as you journey with Him!

In His love,

Kim

Acknowledgments

Don, Mom and Daddy, my sweet girls, and my quiverful of grandjoys—Thank you for walking this writing pathway with me! Your support, encouragement, and love keeps me moving forward. I love you all muchly!

My awesome critique group—Thanks for churning through the chapters with me! You bless me more than you know.

Choir members from FSBC—How I appreciate your prayers! Thank you for your steadfast support.

Steve Conard—Thanks for your presentation on Hutchinson history and mentioning the "chocolate factory mystery." You planted the seed for this story, and I am grateful!

Pat and Joan Conner—Our "chance" meeting and your willingness to share your Otis elevator with me added such a delightful touch to the Dinsmore factory. Thank you for your kindness to a couple of strangers in town.

Shannon and the team at Water-Brook—What a joy to work with you in bringing these imaginary friends and cities to life. Thank you for your diligent efforts to make the stories shine.

Finally, and most importantly, **God**—You take our dark times, give them a buff and polish, and make them a part of our brightest accomplishments. Thank You for filling me with Your strength, wisdom, and love. I'm never without hope because of You. May any praise or glory be reflected directly back to You.

Discussion Questions

1. As an investigator, Caroline is sometimes put into a position of needing to hide the truth, but as a Christian, she found this necessity difficult. Have you ever been faced with an ethical dilemma in your workplace? How did you handle it?

2. Caroline stubbornly refused to enter the place that she viewed as the source of her childhood trauma. How did holding on to the pain of her past prevent her from truly living in freedom as an adult? How do we overcome the scars that hinder us?

3. Oliver didn't believe God listened to prayer because his prayer for healing for Mr. Holcomb was denied. Kesia likened God's "no" answer to the wise decision of a parent refusing a child something he shouldn't have. Do you believe God knows best? Do you trust Him even when He denies you something you want deeply? How do we maintain our faith in the face of "no" answers?

4. Letta chose to run away rather than trust someone to help her, with disastrous results. Yet one good came of it—Lank discovered his abilities and a source of courage. Have you ever uncovered a positive result in the midst of an unwise decision? Have you seen it as happenstance or as God's means of crafting something good from the ashes of our lives?

5. Both Gordon Hightower and Caroline had experienced difficult childhoods. Gordon chose to become a bully rather than be bullied; Caroline chose to help those who were hurting. Why did one strike out at others and one reach out to others? How are you using the painful parts of your past to weave something positive today?

6. When Caroline was frustrated by Dinsmore's refusal to believe her story about Hightower, Noble advised her with these words: "Dear one, in this life we will encounter people...who follow their own pathway instead of the one deigned by God.... Instead of being angry with these men, we should pity them. They're lost. They need our prayers." Are there people in

your circle of acquaintanceship who have chosen a pathway other than the one God would approve? Do you respond to them in anger or frustration, or do you lift them up in prayer? How can we find the compassion to pray for those who frustrate us?

7. Matthew 11:28 says, "Come unto me, all ye that labour and are heavy laden, and I will give you rest." What burdens are you carrying? What steps will you take to release them into the arms of the One waiting to give you rest?